THE ROAD, AND NOTHING MORE

J. L. Bautista

ANDREA YOUNG ARTS/EL LEÓN LITERARY ARTS

The Road, and Nothing More is published by
Andrea Young Arts and El León Literary Arts
www.andreayoungarts.com
www.elleonliteraryarts.org

Denny Abrams' generous support is gratefully acknowledged.

Publishers: Andrea Young and
Thomas Farber, El León Literary Arts
Editor: Kit Duane
Berkeley, CA

Cover and book design: Andrea Young

Distributor:
Small Press Distribution
1341 Seventh Street
Berkeley, CA 94710
www.spdbooks.org

El León Literary Arts is a private foundation established to extend
the array of voices essential to a democracy's arts and education.

ISBN 978-0-9833919-5-1
LIBRARY OF CONGRESS CATALOG NUMBER: 2012940880
PRINTED IN USA

For Francesca and Billy

PROVERBIOS Y CANTARES XXIX

Caminante, son tus huellas
el camino, y nada mas;
caminante, no hay camino,
se hace camino al andar.
Al andar se hace camino,
y al volver la vista atrás
se ve la senda que nunca
se ha de volver a pisar.
Caminante, no hay camino,
sino estelas en la mar.

Antonio Machado

PROVERBS AND SONGS XXIX

Traveler, your footsteps
Are the road, and nothing more;
Traveler, there is no road,
You make the road by walking.
By walking you make the road,
And turning to look back,
You see the path you never
Will walk again.
Traveler, there is no road,
Just the wake of a ship in the sea.

Translation by J. L. Bautista

PART ONE · THE WAR YEARS

[1937]

As summer ignited in late August, Rosa-Laura caught a nasty cold, probably from so much running outside into the street and down the metro at night when the sirens howled. She lay in bed for three days, feverish and shivery, thrashing through swamps of bad dreams. Her mother soaked rags in chamomile and witch hazel to bathe her forehead, but by 5 a.m. of the day Rosa-Laura disappeared, she was still awake and her mother exhausted. No choices existed for them: this was a day Señora Rosa normally cleaned Señorita Guillermina's house and go she must or lose the only job she still had, the only rail left between them and the plunge of starvation.

Sra. Rosa told her little girl what to do, then checked in with the porter's wife and at her sister's house before heading for work. Anxious and angry, she was halfway across her neighborhood's plaza before she paid attention to the planes droning above her. At almost the same moment, the sirens began their keen, a sound Sra. Rosa hated profoundly. She ran like a spooked goat to the entrance of the metro station and lunged down the stairs, behind dozens of neighbors, all in such a hurry half of them fell to the bottom and risked being trampled by the rest. Sra. Rosa clung to the cold tiled walls and gripped the banister, as bodies whipped past her tiny form.

The bombs hit, the ground shook, then shook again. Sra. Rosa and the others managed to get to the tunnel where the trains used to be boarded. All service had been stopped so that people could shelter in the tunnels and even camp on the tracks during the bombings. Sra. Rosa realized with a sickening sense that these bombs were close, very close, closer than before. More bombs hit, the whole station seemed to shudder, and dirt and dust fell from the arched ceiling. People were crying and moaning. Another bomb. And another. *What the hell are the bastards doing? Don't they know there are people down here? Women, and old men, and children. This is no military installation. There are no army barracks in this neighborhood. It isn't even a "Little Russia," like they say Vallecas neighborhood is.* Sra. Rosa shoved her handkerchief into her mouth and bit down on it hard. Her fists were clenched. In the panic she must have dropped the cloth bag she carried in case she found anything to bring home, and as another bomb hit she concentrated on that frantically: *If there's wood or coal or something in the street, how am I going to carry it?*

Another bomb hit, right above them. A woman next to her screamed, but not much, the sort of scream ejected like a little pill of fright upon seeing a bug or a rat in the kitchen. The sound of the bombs seemed strange, distant, muffled by the huge depth of the station, then Sra. Rosa realized her ears were ringing, probably from the first blast when she was still on the stairs. Her head hurt too, yet nothing had fallen on it except some dust and bits of grouty tile.

She thought the bombing raid went on for hours, but it lasted less than fifteen minutes. The all-clear siren released a long howl, and people began to stand up and climb the stairs of the metro. Sra. Rosa's ears were still ringing, but she went upstairs with the others, everyone talking at once now, chattering, angry, disgusted, swearing, "We-have-had-it-Yes-we-have-Shameless-sons-of-whores," and so forth. Sra. Rosa's ears popped ferociously halfway up, but she still didn't hear well for a few days after that.

Two buildings in the plaza had been sliced in half like loaves of bread. Walls surrounding rooms had been cut away and the private interiors split open to the world. Roofs had shattered into salons, walls had cracked away from bedrooms. To one side of where Sra. Rosa stood, a huge pile of rubble rested, its mass still smoking white dust. Near it, she saw the neighbor boy who lived across the patio from her sister Emilia. He was holding the hand of his big brother. The brother lay on the ground, mouth open to receive one last sacrament from the sky, half the top of his head mashed into black hair and blood. Sra. Rosa stared at the boys for a moment, trying to fit this picture into her mind in such a way that it made some sense. A neighbor woman rushed over, forcibly disengaged the little boy's hand from his dead brother's, and shouted for help. Sra. Rosa felt something cold and hideous rise inside her, and she turned and ran down her street to home.

The building just up the street nearest the plaza from Sra. Rosa's was over 300 years old and often people had said it should be torn down because the rooms were so small, ugly, drafty, and uncomfortable. Had Sra. Rosa been in a mood to appreciate irony that morning, she might have observed that it stood without a chip knocked off it. She didn't pay any attention to that building, however, because she was staring at her own building, which had received a direct hit and was now an eerie carnage of white mortar, yellow stone, beams sticking up like bones, and as far as she knew, her daughter somewhere inside.

[Six years earlier]

The day her daughter was born was one of those summer days that Sra. Rosa always hated. The air lay so thick you could cut it like a tuna pie. It proved the truth of the old saw, *Madrid, nueve meses de invierno y tres de infierno,* Madrid, nine months of winter and three of hell. It was undeniably August, high noon, siesta time, yet Sra. Rosa was marching through her neighborhood and the vicious sunlight in defiance of sane behavior.

She lost her breath as she entered Tribulete Street from the plaza and stopped to clutch at a chalky stone wall. She coughed to clear her dry throat, then began walking again, because she was needed, and she was not the kind of woman to reject such a gift.

She turned the corner at the alley just past the shop that sold fried pig intestines and scattered a couple of pigeons attacking a crust of bread someone had crumbled for them, some starving neighbor no doubt, a sentimental imbecile in Sra. Rosa's estimation. One pigeon putted along ahead of her, the other one limped with a damaged foot behind the first, dirty little city chickens, one a bit gimpy, both trying to avoid getting stepped on, yet unable to give up the feast. Sra. Rosa glanced at the birdies with practical intent. Pigeon stew was not such a bad meal now and then, if one was hungry enough and the teeth strong enough. Sra. Rosa was forty, old by the standards of the day, dressed in relentless black from head scarf to shoes, and *castiza* to the core. Though she was less than five feet tall and weighed only eighty-five pounds, no one in the neighborhood dared bully her. She had been known to insist to anyone she cared to converse with that sentiment was trash—though she was about to find out that total, blind, heart-breaking sentiment was in fact an entity more powerful than a king.

She was heading to a basement apartment with a thin, long bar of windows right at ankle height of passersby. Arriving there, she hurried down five steep, stone steps and entered without knocking. Inside, a single room stretched long, narrow, dingy, a place suffocating in summer and lung-cracking frigid in winter. There wasn't much furniture: a bed scarce bigger than a cot, a chair, a stool, a freestanding coal stove with a pipe pitching crazily up and out into the building's main chimney. A bucket held the water its occupants obtained from a public faucet up the street, and a covered pot sat in a corner for "minor and major waters," to be emptied every day in the building's latrine.

A young woman named Laura lay on the bed, moaning in great anguish, without the strength to move or fight or otherwise hurry up the birth of her child. She had been in labor more than two days now. Sra. Erlinda, the ironmonger's wife, and Sra. Lourdes, who lived across the patio from Sra. Rosa's sister, were already there and grunted both in welcome and relief at Sra. Rosa's arrival. Neither woman looked optimistic about the situation. Sra. Rosa said, "Um," by way of greeting and joined in her neighbors' work without another word.

It did not go well. The girl finally managed to push just enough to allow them to pull the baby out, but as she expelled her baby she also expelled her life and soul along with an obscene amount of blood. Sra. Rosa started to pull out the placenta by hand, but most of it tore and stayed behind. The other two women stopped her needless efforts.

"Ah, Mother of God, have mercy on us poor sinners—she's gone, girls. She's gone," Sra. Erlinda said.

Sra. Rosa felt a hard stone in her throat. She wished she'd come sooner, though what good she could have done was unclear. She'd been able to get off work today only because the kindest of her six employers had let her leave early.

Laura was her brother-in-law's wife, a sweet girl, only nineteen, and with her death, life had once again proved to Sra. Rosa that most times things on this damned earth were foul and mean. She looked at the infant now in her arms, filthy with blood and mucous. It refused to breathe, and she despaired of making it live. She dragged out the mucous from its mouth, but that was not the problem. The creature was quite tired, that's all. Sra. Rosa blew breath into its mouth and prayed silently, urgently, though her whole life she would insist she was not at all a religious woman. The baby coughed out a kind of gasping cry and took a breath, enough to insure a moment of life.

"It's a girl," Sra. Rosa said.

Alive. Sra. Rosa held the baby upright against her chest and then bathed her from a pan of water warmed over the coal stove. The baby mewled again. Since that exchange of life breath, Sra. Rosa felt happy, despite the sad death on the bed behind her, so happy she could barely draw any more breath for herself, suffused as she was with joy, an emotion so novel to her that she could not name it. She fussed over the infant and left the other two midwives to clean up the mess and the body, which they finally covered with a blanket and a few prayers.

The man of the house was not present, because the hard-pressed midwives had unceremoniously sent him outside hours ago. He was a blind man and worked as a bookbinder. He'd sent word that morning to his boss that he would stay home and attend his wife, but men were little more than pests in such a situation, and a cripple double the problem; hence, the midwives had banished him.

The baby whimpered a bit more then took a nap, but not before Sra. Rosa put her index finger in the baby's mouth. The baby took the finger, but did not suck. Still, it was a beginning, an affirmation of the will to survive a while longer, and besides, ceremonies had to be observed. Sra. Rosa with the baby mouthing her finger felt as thrilled as any woman giving her child her breast.

The other women glanced at Sra. Rosa, neutrally. Each of them had children, far too many, and though they didn't share Rosa's evident delight with this orphan, it was fine with them.

"These blankets will never be clean again," Sra. Lourdes said. There was a catch in her voice.

At that point, Rogelio, the dead woman's husband, pushed open the door and like a cricket with one drooping antenna, tapped a step or two into his home. "I want to be with my woman," he said to the air in front of him. "Don't send me out again."

The first time he had ever made love to Laura, he began with one finger hesitating on her face, very lightly running it up her chin, over her mouth, over her nose. The finger was slightly callused, like the rest of his hand, and he was ashamed of this and ashamed of his great need.

"Don't be afraid, love. I'll go slow. But if you got no heart for it now, we can wait," Rogelio had said.

She had said nothing. Her breathing was somewhat fast, then it slowed, and he put all the fingers of his right hand on her cheek, then both hands, very, very carefully felt their way up to her forehead, a high forehead. She had what they called an oval face, and her skin felt like the best vellum. That and her wonderful smell he would always remember. With skin that fine, and that light, perfect smell, something floral and full of the smell of sunshine too, oh, surely she was beautiful. Her head was small and the skull without bumps, which surprised him so much that he nudged his hands once again through her scalp to feel the smoothness of it. Her hair, he had been told, was reddish brown. It felt thick, heavy, long, of a varying texture sometimes silk, sometimes linen, and full of curl and wave. It felt brown this way, not blonde or black, and he could tell colors, most of the time. His friends said that he could feel a person's hair and tell them what color the hair was. It was a subject of much bet-making in the tavern he frequented.

She had long soft lashes and very fine brows. She had a long neck. She had bony shoulders and full apple-round breasts. Rogelio knew—he had been told by other men, men with eyes to see but not much else—that her breasts and slender indented waist were indications of great beauty. Her skin fit well and smoothly over the slight points of bones. He shyly licked her ear, moving his tongue into each crevice and wondering at the bitter yet pleasing taste, then sucked very lightly at the lobe, a small lozenge of firm flesh with a ball of gold embedded in it. Her breathing became deeper, and he sensed that she was not so frightened anymore. At the moment his fingers touched a nipple he felt her hand touch his chest, her breath quickened, and his joy struck him so thrillingly he almost lost himself in sexual frenzy, he almost cried.

∽₰∾

Rogelio had not been born blind. Cushioned within all the memories bounded and categorized by smell, touch, sound, taste, rested a vague and ill-understood memory of color and shapes. He remembered his mother, who smiled at him, and he remembered the village apothecary, who had a ferocious frown, and he remembered a hill behind his house full of things that he now knew were dew, grass, insects, a slug longer than his child's hand, a bird which flew back and forth in front of him and sparkled with a bluish black sheen brighter than the flashy green tree leaves. It squawked and chittered loudly, warning him not to approach a certain thick growth of gooseberry bush, where it probably had a nest.

Sometime after that an illness ravaged the village. He got sick and almost died. His mother did die, and that was the hardest thing that had ever happened to him, much harder than losing his sight. His blindness eventually became an amalgamation of senses as natural to him as sight to others, but to the sighted, blindness defines. He would always be the blind man.

He had a vocation, thanks to a cousin in Madrid who partnered a bookbinding shop. He apprenticed when he was fourteen, like any ordinary working class youth, and set himself to mastering the craft. In those days employees were generally loyal, entering a trade to stay until they retired or died, usually the latter. A blind man had double the loyalty of a sighted man. Rogelio's boss liked him and liked the way he worked long and hard to learn the trade and do it well. Most pleasing was how he could emboss a soft leather cover with gold lettering; he was extra careful with spelling of course, because no one expected him to be any good at it at all. The tips of his fingers gave him a better command of the mysteries of orthography than most university students.

On his way to work each morning he gloried in the sounds and smells of the neighborhood and felt he had a place there, he belonged. The purr and silken female cough of a rare Mercedes taxi always taking a short cut through his poor neighborhood but never stopping, the groan of a milk truck, the near anguish of the motor on a delivery truck, the elegant whirr of a bicycle or the gutteral putt of a motoscooter—these sounds accompanied him to work, along with the smell and the clop-clomp of a cart pulled by a beast, the heaving sound of an old horse, the near silence of a donkey straining along. The sounds of the neighborhood women going to market or gossiping with each other (he heard more than they ever imagined) fine-tuned the day for him. He absorbed the thrill of the knife-sharpener's pan-pipe, the cries of children on their way to school or work, the smells of the marketplace—vegetables fresh and rotted, plums in spring, apples in fall, the sweet, cloying death smells of meat. These fenced and outlined his domain, the things any urban citizen might encounter on his way to work but never noticed, as if sight canceled out every other sense.

꩜

But Laura, not his sightlessness or his occupation, was his definition. He could not believe his luck, for she loved him and told him so. As she was fatherless and her mother ill, there was no one to stop their marriage. He had met her while he was on a short holiday in Soria and wrote to her for months after that, dictating to a priest who was glad to help out in this matter of discreet and modest letters of love. She traveled to Madrid eventually, and they had celebrated the nuptials very quietly one morning about six months after her mother died, in the Church of San Lorenzo. He had two pals from the tavern, his sister-in-law Sra. Rosa, the neighbors from upstairs, and the three men who worked with him at the bookbinding shop. She had no one, no one but him. He bought her orange blossoms, which smelled wonderful and felt like candle wax. By winter, Laura was pregnant. He would have a son who could see him.

꩜

It was not the best time, because what with the political winds blowing and all, fewer and fewer people were buying well-bound books or asking that their old books be rebound. There was an air of optimism and nervousness about that inspired people to read posters and pamphlets instead of books and attend street corner speeches instead of sitting at home using up electricity or kerosene and reading religious prophets or poets or storytellers or philosophers. It was a strange time.

∞

Despite his intimate acquaintance of the neighborhood, his knowing not only every neighbor and every narrow street but every cobblestone as well, he'd wasted the morning of his child's birth wandering around and bumping into things, lost in the caring about his woman.

He stopped at a bar in the plaza and asked for *mosto*, figuring it would help his empty stomach and not derange his head as something more potent might.

"You're here at an odd hour, Sr. Rogelio," the barman said, as if hesitant to probe bad news. Many of the neighborhood men came in at odd hours when they'd lost work, and he was giving the blind man a chance to come clean and air it all out.

"My woman's birthing," Rogelio said.

"Ah, then let's toast it with something better than grape juice," the bartender said smiling.

Rogelio felt the smile in the bartender's voice and smiled himself, but said, "No, I want to be sharp when the women let me back in."

He raised the glass, hesitated, then without sipping, put it down hard enough to scatter drops of the rusted amber liquid. He threw a *céntimo* on the bar, and said, "To hell with the midwives. I'm not waiting outside while my girl suffers. I'm going back."

He tapped his way out. The barman shook his head and drank Rogelio's *mosto* so as not to waste it. *Sometimes men went crazy over love, downright crazy. What man in his right mind, blind or not, wanted to see that? If you needed blood, you could go to a bullfight.*

∞

At the doorway to his home, Rogelio paused and waited for someone to acknowledge his entry. But then he noted the heavy breathing of three women and the slight breath of a fourth being but did not hear his wife. Not daring to interpret this, he tapped his way to the bed, moving his head from side to side as if gathering all the events inside himself.

He held out his left hand down toward the bed and upon feeling her inert body beneath the mucky wet blanket, he dropped his cane, moaned, and sat on the floor. He rocked back and forth for a while, until Sra. Erlinda put her hand on his shoulder and said, "Rogelio, that's enough, get up, you'll get piles sitting on this cement floor."

At that, he began weeping and howling, like a dog that's been locked out in the dark.

Sra. Rosa turned away, but Sra. Lourdes began to pat his back, clumsily, as if he were choking on food rather than grief, and murmured, "There, there, that's life, that's what it's all about, poor girl, she's at peace now, she's suffered enough, you have the baby to think about, you must think about yourself as well, Rogelio," and all the other meaningless, useless words dredged up from drawers of platitudes to express what Lourdes herself knew was inexpressible.

He refused to get up off the floor and gave over to a kind of coughing, masculine weeping. Sra. Erlinda left to find a priest and a gravedigger.

The blind man continued to weep, becoming quieter and quieter, until finally Sra. Rosa approached him as delicately as possible and said, "Um, it's a girl, Rogelio. Very pretty. Tiny. But I think she'll live. It's, um, not her fault. Not her fault. Here, feel her face. It's what Laura would have wanted. She wanted this child, Rogelio. Touch the baby."

He was not a bitter or mean person, and he did not really blame the baby, though the trade of a sweet young wife for a tiny creature that needed so much caring for was a poor bargain indeed. He got to his knees, shakily, stretched out his hand and let Sra. Rosa guide it to the baby's face, her head with its soft spot and downy hair, her long eyelashes, her squished bit of nose, the curlicues of ear on each side of her head. He ran his hand down her tummy, passing over the bumpy tie of the severed cord, then felt for the hand, which took his finger in its grasp. He nodded at the direction of Rosa, sighed, and crumpled back to the floor to weep some more.

"Rogelio, I would like to call the baby Rosa-Laura. If you agree. Rosa-Laura," Sra. Rosa said.

The blind man evinced no shock at this strange proposal. The name should have been Laura: Maria Laura or Laura Maria, or possibly, with a stretch of the conventions, Laura-Rosa. Not Rosa-Laura. Sra. Lourdes, getting ready to empty the pan of bloody water, shook her head in astonishment.

"Call her whatever you want," Rogelio said. "And keep her if it pleases you. I cannot care for a baby."

So, that is how Sra. Rosa came to be the mother of Rosa-Laura, on that obscenely hot, dry day in August, 1931. As for her birth mother, Rosa-Laura never had any pictures of her nor any idea of who her family was, though Rogelio once told his daughter that her mother had come from the province of Soria. Antonio Machado, though born an *andalúz*, also lived in Soria and also found the love of his life there. "Cold Soria, pure Soria," a land of ruined castles, winter snowfalls, impoverished towns, and endless migrations of northern birds, worthy to be the love nest of a grand poet and the birth place of a girl who died too young in a very poor neighborhood far away from her land and without even a photograph for anyone to remember her by.

Hours later, Lourdes and Erlinda the ironmonger's wife left Rogelio's house carrying the bloody clothes from Laura's death bed. Lourdes fought not to weep publicly, twisting her face as hard as she could, clenching her teeth. Some idiot walking past her called out, "Hey blondie, drop that load and come join me for a drink. I know how to help a pretty woman forget her troubles!" She paid him no mind, which was what he had expected anyway. Sra. Erlinda was oblivious to the little event. Unlike Lourdes she didn't get compliments every time she walked on the street. She judged that a blessing.

They washed the blankets at the well in Lourdes's patio, soaking them in the trough with cold water and scrubbing with strong lye soap.

"Poor old Rogelio, only he isn't really that old, is he?" Lourdes said.

"He's in his late twenties, maybe early thirties," Erlinda replied.

Lourdes nodded. Blind people just seemed old or something. Wiser perhaps. Or indefinite, ghostlike. The sad part of all that was that he wasn't too bad looking. Average height, which made him a head shorter than herself, pale clear skin, dark brown curly hair, a good high forehead. He had a nice profile, straight as a statue's, and he stood straight too, and held his ruined head high. His eyes were sunken, of course, his cheeks sunk too. He didn't get much to eat, Lourdes figured.

Poor Rogelio. That girl was all he had had, and now he has a baby—and can you imagine, she muttered to Erlinda, "Rosa is going to *keep* it?"

"Ah," said Sra. Erlinda, "What else, Lourdes? She can't go on being her sister's keeper, especially since that one won't last much longer and the niece might get it too." She did not name the "it," as that would have been courting bad luck and contagion, and she spoke in a low voice because Emilia's—Sra. Rosa's sister's—doorway was just across from where they stood at the pump rinsing out the blankets.

They finished up. Sra. Erlinda took the bed clothing home to dry, as she had a balcony, whereas Lourdes did not. Lourdes lived in one of the oldest buildings in the neighborhood, a two-story *corrala*, where the inner patio had once been a corral for horses and mules. She and her husband and their three boys had two rooms off the lower gallery, one room a kitchen with a hearth that kept them all warm in winter when there was coal to burn, and the other a combination back bedroom and storage space. Their home opened out onto a stone patio with a well in the middle and the latrine at the back end directly opposite the short tunnel entrance leading from the huge double doors that were locked to the street at night. The gallery above protected the lower rooms from rain, but the patio itself was open air. Their building had been modernized in the twenties with a faucet near the entrance so the inhabitants would not have to depend on the cloudy well water to drink. Madrileños drank the melted snow of the Sierra, famous for its purity, sweetness, and softness. Many a traveler staying a night in Madrid would swish up his soap dish in the morning for shaving and find himself foamier than a rabid dog.

Lourdes's sons were out somewhere playing, and she was relieved for the momentary quiet. She sat down, too tired even to boil a cup of chicory, and thought about the fact that she could have offered to take the baby and care for it. Her house was crowded though, food was scarce, the baby would probably die, and thus, the deal did not tempt her to foolishly try and make up for what she had lost.

Her husband had enlisted in the militia and left Madrid several months ago. She hadn't cried when he left and hadn't heard from him since. Everyone said she was brave, as brave as he had been to be one of the first volunteers in the new People's Army. They had told her three boys, "Your mama is a heroine of the revolution." Truth be told, she was as glad to see him go as he was to escape their noisy, burdened, haunted household.

After the death of their last child, their only daughter, everyone had also said, "There now, courage! You'll make another."

She didn't want another—not because pregnancy made her notice foul smells everywhere. Trying to keep food down and never succeeding.

Listening to everyone in *his* family explain yet again how every woman among them emptied her womb in the fields while working and hardly a clue she'd been pregnant at all. Lourdes's belly hung low in pregnancy, she turned white as an aristocrat, and barely gained any weight. No, it wasn't that. It wasn't even that it might be another boy. That her husband would insist on naming it himself again, as he had done for their first two, Abelardo and Anacleto, after his own grandfathers: he had cursed his first-born sons to years of laughter, snickering, ridicule in the schoolyards and workplace with such ugly, old-fashioned names, names you'd give only to village idiots. At the birth of the third boy she had wept and carried on until he reluctantly agreed to let her name it. She chose Augustín, a pretty compromise. Next time around, he might chose something truly hideous, like the name of his father, Gumersindo. God help us all.

No, it wasn't any of that.

She wanted Blanca Maria, the fourth child, the one who had died, not counting a couple of miscarriages. Lourdes was loyal to her daughter, utterly loyal. If she could not have her daughter, she would have no more. She was not loyal to God or the new government or the family or her man or even her boisterous, sturdy sons. Lourdes had loved Blanca more than anyone else in the world, and the truth of that terrified her, because now her joy had all blown away with a summer cough, a slight fever, so fast, so fast. Clearly Lourdes had been punished because she loved the child to the exclusion of all else. Blanca Maria had just reached three. How could it be that a human being could live such a short life?

Lourdes never complained to her friends and neighbors, of course, nor said much at all about it. Her story meant little in this neighborhood where a third of the babies born full-term didn't make it to their first birthday, and another third died before they were five.

Her baby. Sra. Rosa had become a mother in less than a day and quite immaculately. Not that she was a virgin. She was a widow, and her deceased husband had been Rogelio's older brother. So, Sra. Rosa was related to Rosa-Laura, her only child, by marriage alone. Of course, none of that relationship, or lack of it, mattered in the long run. Nor did it matter that Sra. Rosa at forty was an old woman and just as barren as she had always been, because despite all those ridiculous complications, she was a mother. She had her first child. The baby was hers, hers, completely hers. She was bewitched by this strange occurrence, or better put, bewitched by the infant she now carried in her arms, so bewitched that it was hard to remember that a sweet girl had died to make Sra. Rosa's motherhood possible. Later on, when Rosa-Laura was older, Sra. Rosa would describe her birth mother to her, and make it clear the woman was pretty, full breasted, auburn-haired, blue-eyed. Sra. Rosa never wanted the girl from Soria to lose out in this matter of motherhood, though of course she had, spectacularly.

Now Sra. Rosa had to feed her child. Obviously she could not nurse, but whatever else it took to keep this baby alive, she would do it. She rushed along the streets, which refused to cool down even though the sun was very low in the sky, heading toward the Plaza Glorieta de Embajadores and then up La Ronda de Atocha, then she turned at Paseo de las Delicias, a broad street in a decent neighborhood that was bordered by tall London plane trees. Rosa-Laura nestled in a rayon slip of Laura's, now and then emitting a squeak or a kitteny cough. This indication of life overjoyed Sra. Rosa and also terrified her with its faintness.

A woman lived on Delicias whose house Sra. Rosa had cleaned once. This woman had been pregnant at the time and could only afford to give Sra. Rosa fifty *céntimos*—half her usual price. The baby would be about a year old by now and the woman herself bursting with milk. Sra. Rosa intended to call in her debt.

The woman lived up four flights of steep stairs, but Sra. Rosa was used to stairs and used to hauling loads up stairs. This baby was no load at all, so light, so tiny. She cried again with that squeaky kitten mewl. Sra. Rosa, though she certainly would not dwell on bad thoughts consciously as that was bad luck, was frightened for her daughter, her Rosita, and frightened for herself. Surely her daughter would live. Surely all that she had suffered in this life wouldn't reach some kind of miserable depth on the hot streets of Madrid with the death of her daughter, her child, her baby, her laurel-led rose. She was thus learning right on that first day that the world and its minions now had a new and particularly horrifying power over her, holding her child hostage, and that was worse than any hold they held on her own life.

She arrived at the building, entered without saluting the porter, and began to climb the stairs, which were lined with green and caramel-brown tiles stenciled with an acanthus design. This wasn't the kind of place that had hand-painted tiles. The walls were brown and tan, and the banister cast iron, shiny and rickety with use and age, though still strong after two centuries and the passage of a hundred families. Sra. Rosa took all ninety-eight steps and four landings with barely a harsh breath. She came to the door that she remembered and pounded on it with her bony fist.

"Sra. Remedios," she shouted, "Please open the door. It's me, Sra. Rosa, the cleaning lady."

The door opened and a broad sugar cookie of a face peered around it. "Ay, Sra. Rosa, what are you doing here? I have no work for you..."

"It's not work I want, it's milk," Sra. Rosa said. "From you, for this bit here, um, my daughter, the child of my brother-in-law. The birth mother died just a few hours ago, God bless her soul and have the decency to take her into heaven. You are the only one I could think of. I figured you don't need all that milk. Might be happy to give up some of it."

Sra. Remedios looked at Sra. Rosa, who was at least twenty domineering years her elder, in shock. After all, Sra. Remedios was no farm girl, no wet nurse from the village, she was *madrileña* born and bred, she'd lived in the Delicias neighborhood all her life, she was married and a mother of two. And this woman was now demanding she nurse a child other than her own? It might even have been slightly repugnant, the notion of giving her breast to a stranger, even such a lovely stranger as this baby, that Sra. Rosa was now unwrapping from a rayon slip of all things.

Just a tiny girl baby. Barely hours old. Face pale, eyes blue as glass, and look, the sweetheart, it had tiny, tiny eyebrows, two faintly sketched-in lines no more than a hair wide, think of that, a newborn with eyebrows already. And a fine cap of dark reddish brown silken hair. Satiny curled snails of fist, sequins of pink fingernails. The baby blinked its remarkable eyes quite innocently at Sra. Remedios, who was only human after all, so she reached out and took the creature from Sra. Rosa.

Upon giving over her daughter, Sra. Rosa suddenly felt jealous of Sra. Remedios's milky embrace. The feeling was unpleasant, but she bore it. Motherhood means sacrifice too, sharing what one loves most.

"Look," said Sra. Remedios, struggling to regain the upper hand as she led the way to her kitchen, where a robust, dark blonde, pink-cheeked baby was seated in a chair on a fat cushion, and tied to the chair back with a worn bit of blanket so he wouldn't topple onto the floor tiles, "I can help you out right now, but I'm not a wet nurse—Sebastián! Stop that howling, Mama's here. Roberto! Come and play with your baby brother. A girl, how lucky, how lucky, I would love to have a girl, just not right now, Sra. Rosa, understand, I'm too tired for another newborn. Roberto," as a second boy, a chubby ruffian of about three or four, waddled into the kitchen and stared at the women for a moment before addressing the much more interesting project of harassing his baby brother, "don't you poke Sebastián. I am surely going to spank you, and when your Papa comes home..."

Sra. Remedios grunted softly with all this effort and then sat down, pulled out a pale loaf of breast easily from her bodice and began to maneuver a nipple into Rosita's puckered mouth, then stroked the baby's cheeks to get her to suck. Her oldest boy watched this operation with some interest for a moment, then returned to the difficult but necessary job of enraging his baby brother.

"Um, what can I do?" Sra. Rosa said, quietly, not argumentative at all, because now she had to negotiate, and diplomacy (not one of her greatest talents) was certainly required. "Sra. Remedios, um, she must be fed. I can't do it myself."

"This is what you must do," Sra. Remedios said, replete with the experience that would propel her into old-age before her time, "You go to the pharmacy and you ask for a *tetina*. It's a kind of rubber nipple that you fit over a little glass. And you buy cow's milk or better yet, goat's milk, and you boil it, then you skim off the scum and some of the cream, because babies can't take that strong milk, you know, mother's milk is sweeter and thinner. You understand me, don't you? I can't be a wet nurse—besides, look, she can barely suck. Not like my boys, let me tell you. They had pull from the first minute, little brutes." This last was said most proudly, though Rosa-Laura's puny efforts had so stimulated her massive breasts they were just about pouring out the milk like a faucet, so that Sra. Remedios was now enjoying the tranquil yet erotic pleasure of the flow.

Behind her, Sebastián was howling. Sra. Rosa wanted to strangle him, because she was afraid the fat bastard would distract his mother, who then would certainly leave Rosa-Laura in the lurch, half hungry. But Sra. Remedios was a calm young woman. Her sons had drained what little resistance she had ever had, and she was prone to day-dreaming through their screams. She gave herself over to Rosa-Laura, the other unsuckled breast wetting her dress in a wider and wider circle, and smiled at the baby. Rosa-Laura stopped suckling for a moment—it was hard work and newborns are not that hungry—and her button-sized pout of a mouth broadened upward slightly around the huge nipple, the nub of which filled her mouth.

"Oh, Mother Mine," Sra. Remedios said, "She's smiling! Look, Sra. Rosa, she's smiling already! What a prodigy!"

Sra. Rosa choked down her envy and gave herself over to motherly pride, even if Rosa-Laura hadn't smiled at her first. Besides, truth be told, a one day old baby cannot smile. It grimaces, that's all, and Sra. Rosa considered Remedios a fool to give over to such drama for a grimace.

Sebastián had now set up a howl that must have resounded throughout the entire neighborhood and left the family upstairs saying, "What is that lazy cow *doing* to that child!?" Rosa-Laura gave a slight sigh, as if to indicate that she was just too tired to go on, and closed her eyes, Sra. Remedios's ample nipple still in her mouth.

"It's all right, Sra. Rosa, she's too young to take more than a spoonful. She just needed to get the idea, that's all. Here, you take her now, and I'll take Sebastián, you bad, bad boy, you big bad boy, now there, see, there's some pull for you!" And Sebastián lustily set to work showing Rosa-Laura how it's done, but she had fallen asleep in Sra. Rosa's arms. This left only Roberto with no one to cuddle him, and he wandered into the next room to see if there was something he could destroy with appropriate noise.

"There's something else too," Sra. Remedios said. Her voice was low and soft. "There's a place called *La Gota de Leche,* and they have milk for babies, and in six months, there's mush you can make from cornstarch or toasted flour. I think Artica makes it."

"Artica? The cracker makers?" Sra. Rosa said.

"Just that. There's ways, Sra. Rosa, there's ways. She won't starve and you won't need a wet nurse. Just ask at a pharmacy, they'll know."

"Well, thank you. Um, I'll just let myself out now. You continue with that."

"She's a beautiful girl, Sra. Rosa. You must be very happy. I hope my next one is a girl. These boys are killing me," Sra. Remedios said, smiling dreamily.

Just that. *Así es.* For a moment the enormity of the whole thing hit Sra. Rosa hard, those less-than-wonderful aspects of having a child. Like any happy new mother, she had at first treaded blindly down the path she was led, knowing that's what she was here on earth for (so everyone had always told her). She'd said to herself, *¡Alegría! ¡Alegría!*, not imagining for a minute what a mess she'd gotten herself into, this business of taking responsibility for the life of another being. Now, she had a moment of doubt. But not for long. The advent of Rosa-Laura meant that she would now collect her reward of love, affection, companionship, and a life with some meaning, what any human ought to have.

Downstairs in the street, the heat was retreating somewhat and the moon rising in a golden bloom. It was past six and all the gas streetlights were lit. People strolled together or alone down the long avenue, enjoying the night air. Now and then a car would pass—a Mercedes taxi or a small delivery truck, rarely a privately-owned car. There were bicycles, more of those than cars, and every now and then the klop-klop of a cart hauled by a donkey or a ruined horse.

Tomorrow Rosa-Laura would be one day old. What were all the things that could happen to a one day old baby? What tremendous, earthshaking, mountain-moving, sky-falling things? So many dangers to protect Rosa-Laura from. She had to have clothes, another blanket even in this miserable heat, she had to be bathed in warm water, the stove that would warm the water needed coal, and she had to be fed every three hours, at least. The smaller the stomach, the more often the feedings, a teaspoon or two at a time. To suckle her daughter in a few hours, Sra. Rosa would try to find this *tetina* thing; or, make a rag nipple and soak it with milk from the half-liter bottle Sra. Remedios had found and filled for her.

All right then, she'd do it. In order to assure Rosa-Laura a decent amount of time on this tired earth, Sra. Rosa would crawl on her knees up the Cerro de los Angeles, a big old hill outside of Madrid and on top of it a church where it was said God kept his promises.

Sra. Rosa made her living cleaning houses. She was a powerfully good house cleaner. She often said that a woman who cleaned her kitchen floor with a mop and standing up instead of with a scrub brush and on her hands and knees was a *guarra*, and when she said "sow" like that, she stared rudely at the women she was talking to, letting them know she knew that was how they cleaned floors.

She had not begun life as a housecleaner, but it was how she ended up, and she made the best of it. Sra. Rosa's mother was a sly young woman who never had a husband and loaned out money to her neighbors. She got it back doubled, but she died in her thirties despite all her wealth. Sra. Rosa was only thirteen when she and her eleven year old sister, Emilia, lost their mother. Between scandal, harsh laws, inexperience, and innocence, as well as some shameless relatives, Sra. Rosa and Emilia found themselves disinherited and penniless after their mother's death. They lost their house, the good food, the pretty clothes, and Sra. Rosa had to go out and earn a living *de prisa*, and mighty fast she did.

Sra. Rosa became grim and untrusting after that, but she did not complain of lost riches or entertain regrets about the life she might have led. It wasn't her money to begin with anyway, it was her mother's, and her mother had been cheated out of it with early death. When Rosa set to work doing the only thing she knew how to do, she did it with her head held high.

Emilia was not plain and tight-lipped like her older sister. True, she was thin, but her smile was strong and dimpled and her brown eyes large and gently nearsighted. She was accepted into an orphans' convent school on Rosa's housecleaning earnings, despite the shameful secret of their lineage, which had obstructed entrance into better schools. Emilia learned how to sew well enough to help out with the finances of their meager lives. At first she had shown a taste for the vocation; then, something difficult happened, another betrayal of innocence, to Rosa's way of thinking. It could have been utter disaster, but Emilia managed to find a safe shore by getting herself married at sixteen. Her husband was a good man and perhaps never even suspected that he'd saved Emilia's reputation.

Sra. Rosa herself married at the ripe old age of twenty-four (thus becoming a real Señora) and the couple moved to the neighborhood of Vallecas. She felt lonely there. In less than a decade after the ceremony, he returned to his native province without her. Sra. Rosa moved back to the old neighborhood to be near her sister and niece and never talked about the marriage to anyone, even Emilia, because of the shame of barrenness and the strife it had caused.

"He expected water from the well he bought," she said. "but the damned thing was dry." That was all. He died in an accident in his province and was buried there. Sra. Rosa left it alone and never showed up to bring flowers to his grave on All Saints Day. There was some story in all this that her husband was handsome, and also "not right in the head," but that was just neighborhood gossip, never verified or explained by Sra. Rosa.

Emilia had a baby girl, seven months into her marriage, then a boy, and each died. She finally had a baby that thrived, but by then, Emilia's husband was on his last gasp. He died of a harsh and lingering tuberculosis in 1930, leaving her with their daughter barely two years old. To Emilia's and Sra. Rosa's immense relief, this child, Maria-Emilia (everyone called her Mili), was healthy and rambunctious, and both women spoiled her as best they could under their impoverished circumstances. One other thing her husband left Emilia was a grayish spangle spotting the left lobe of her lungs.

Sra. Rosa attended Emilia during each delivery and suffered at each death. She adored Mili. The girl was such a charmer that old desires in her heart to have a child cracked open—desires that were of course, impossible, or so she had come to think. She watched Emilia nurse this last baby and watched her play with the child, her own arms empty, her own heart as barren as her womb. She was happy for her sister, the only person in the world she loved after her mother died, and now she had Mili to love as well.

So, that was a good thing, and Emilia, being a generous and loving person herself, shared her daughter with her sister as much as possible. Still, it was not the same, and both women knew that.

Now, Sra. Rosa at forty, withered, widowed, staring at life through the cracks in the shutters, was a new mother. Miracles occur, more or less.

Sra. Rosa never had the need to return to Sra. Remedios. She was determined to do it all on her own, without any more help. Thus, she figured a favor had been called in and debt resolved, a very tidy outcome.

Yet in those first days of her motherhood she was quickly disabused of the pretty notion that she was now, as she had always been, independent of anyone. For example, on the way home that night, she tried to resolve this issue of feeding and providing for her daughter and ended up indebted.

She stopped by the neighborhood pharmacy, just before it closed at 8 p.m.

She went into the dark, high-ceilinged store, with its display of apothecary jars and dust covered scales, and looked carefully around at the dingy cabinets and drawers. The pharmacist, Don Horacio, sat behind the high oak counter, fiddling with a delicate brass-colored scale, and stared at her over his reading glasses as if she were a peculiar kind of bloodwort or ginger root, then coughed up a mountain of sodden phlegm that he spat into a spittoon.

"Um, Don Horacio, good evening to you, and these cabinets and shelves here, they need dusting. I'm a cleaning woman, best around. I don't cheat or steal. I got a newborn here, my daughter," and she attempted a smile, really a monumental event for her, but the horrible old man just kept peering at her over his glasses so she hurriedly finished her speech, "anyway, she needs things. Um, a *tetina,* a rubber nipple I can put over a glass. You're supposed to have such a peculiar thing I'm told. Um, cod liver oil, and such, do you see? Only, I don't have much money, as you can surmise, Sir, and so…" She had to pause and take a breath. Discourse was not her strength.

Don Horacio looked her over in an antiseptic way. Then, with a froggy blast of voice he said, "I do not bargain, Señora. I am no village apothecary. I am a graduate of the University of Valladolid. Do you see these diplomas?" With a finger encrusted with some phosphorescent chemical and a slight smear of ink, he pointed to the gold and red-sealed certificates festooned with letters that were hanging on the wall. Sra. Rosa could not have read them even if she had cared to do so.

She ended up paying him sixty-five *céntimos* for one *tetina*. Of course, she was ten *céntimos* short and had to promise him she'd be back tomorrow, which angered her, because she never incurred debts and owed nothing to anyone. If she could not afford it, she did not buy it, because *Más vale acostarse sin cena que levantarse con deudas,* Better to go to bed without dinner than get up with debts. Which is easy to say when it's your own dinner you're foregoing, and not the dinner of your darling baby.

⚶

She walked home muttering about Don Horacio's stinginess but soon forgot the son of a whore, because the baby in her arms was so much warmer and closer and cleaner. At the door of her house, she met Doña Pepa, the porter's wife, and showed her Rosa-Laura.

Doña Pepa regarded the child more as a new disturbance to her sleep than a blessed addition to the life of the building, but she cooed over the precious pretty and congratulated Sra. Rosa. She also suggested they both keep this their secret for as long as possible, as Sr. Oswaldo, the porter, being devoted to the owner of the building, might feel it morally imperative to advise him of the new tenant and the owner might, in turn, advise Sr. Oswaldo to raise Sra. Rosa's rent. Sra. Rosa nodded at this wise advice and wondered privately if having a baby made women usually so high-handed with you suddenly kind and considerate, and snotty men like the pharmacist—and hey, why didn't he work in a better neighborhood if he was so grand and *certificated*?—all the more disrespectful.

Since she seemed to be having good luck with Doña Pepa, Sra. Rosa asked the porter's wife if she had some cloth she didn't want that Sra. Rosa could make into a blanket or a sheet or a tiny shift. Doña Pepa considered this some request, because every inch of cloth could be used or traded to the rag man, but for the sake of human kindness and to lessen her days in purgatory she pulled a few pieces of cloth not big enough for much out of her sewing box and gave them to Sra. Rosa. The new mother nodded her head but suddenly couldn't look Doña Pepa in the face, thanked her with a mumbled "Um," and went upstairs. She had now incurred two new debts in less than two hours.

Doña Pepa, still in the glow of the pretty baby, watched Sra. Rosa begin her climb up the stairs to her room. The porter's wife hoped the child would survive, but it was awfully little, and after all, Sra. Rosa didn't seem the motherly type.

Upstairs in her home, Sra. Rosa carefully lay Rosita on her cot, piling up a blanket and a small, smashed, sausage-shaped pillow as walls to surround the baby, who was quietly sleeping, her head turned toward her mother, her pursed lips slightly open. Sra. Rosa hauled out her laundry basket from under the bed and lined it with an old shawl, black of course, because that was the color of everything she wore, then padded it with a piece of blanket that used to be her niece's, and finally put in her pillow-case for a sheet. One had to have sheeting in hot weather. She placed the baby very carefully in the basket, then rearranged and lay down on the cot, her basket of baby right at her head, with no more effort required than to reach out should she need to touch the child. She did so frequently, softly, and the feeling of the touch filled her throat with tenderness.

The one room was all the house she had. Her bed, an iron cot with a corn husk mattress that crinkled and crackled when the sleeper moved on it, was flush against the northern wall. The afternoon sun came in through the window on the west wall. In summer it entered like a pyromaniac and fired up half the tiled floor, burning all the way to the small table in front of the fireplace in the eastern wall and licking at the bed itself. The wall on each side of the fireplace held most of the hooks for hanging clothes, pots, and such. The door was in the south wall where a small propane gas burner sat on a tiled block. Using this stove cost money, more than the coal stove built into the fireplace. In summer there was no helping it, however, and cooler propane fuel had to be purchased for cooking or they'd die from the heat. A clothes trunk sat at the foot of the bed, a shelf hung above the fireplace stove, and for sitting she had a cane bottomed chair and a pine stool. A calendar hung on the wall over the bed, for its picture of the Virgin of Atocha, not its useless numbers. The whole room was tiny, neat, and scrubbed clean. A chamber pot of enameled tin stored under the bed was emptied when necessary down the hallway in the water closet. Downstairs next to the porter's home, tenants had zinc sinks and a faucet for water and laundry. Thus, as buildings in this neighborhood went, it was quite modern and comfortable, and Sra. Rosa had to pay two *pesetas* and fifty *céntimos* rent a month, whereas her sister, in her shabby *corrala*, paid only one *peseta*.

People like Sra. Rosa and her neighbors could not afford to waste things. The streets of the neighborhoods were clean because garbage was picked over and reused and women like Sra. Pepa got up early each to morning to sweep the sidewalks in front of their building and wash them down, vying with the neighbor women or the shopkeepers to see who'd got the cleanest sidewalks that day. Sra. Rosa often joined in to help the porter's wife if she wasn't too much in a rush to get to work. The narrow sidewalks were clean enough to sleep on at that time in the morning, and few dogs were around to soil them. When a man with no shame pulled out the staff of life and pissed against a wall, the neighbors—especially the women—discouraged him with shouts and vile insults about the size and utility of his pole.

Sra. Rosa could buy empty used bottles at shops set up just for that, bottles useful for purchasing liquid soap from the gallon at the drug store or vinegar from the barrel at the tavern or half a pint of raw milk from the local creamery to take home and boil. If she could afford such purchases. She saved emptied cans, rags, and even stale bread if she didn't eat it cooked to mush with milk and sugar. The rag and bone man came by Thursday to trade cheap crockery for this stuff, which he sold to the paper makers.

Paper was saved for wrapping food or selling to the rag man or wiping a dirty ass, though usually not newspaper, as few people in Sra. Rosa's neighborhood bought newspapers. They cost only a *céntimo*, but even if you could read, when a person could survive on two *reales*—half a peseta—a day it was hard to spend a fiftieth of it on some high-faluting polemics that informed you of what you already knew, that the government was made up of a pack of criminals and what Spain really needed was the king/another-dictator/anarchy/ communism/socialism/a-democracy-just-like-America's/etc. What the modesty and morality of the time did not prevent from getting into print, the ever-diligent government censor's office did. Moreover, why should people spend money on a newspaper when any tavern would have one or two newspapers for its customers to read? Madrid prided itself on its cosmopolitan and sophisticated inhabitants, even though half its population might be illiterate refugees from the provinces and villages.

Sra. Rosa took the baby with her to the houses she cleaned every day, and no one complained, because the woman was a treasure, sour face and all. She showed up early, she cleaned as if her life depended on it (it did), and she left every room immaculate. She never talked. She never stole. She might filch a rag or two or purloin a chipped glass, or even eat a day-old hunk of bread that no one wanted anyway except for the rag and bone man, but the ladies who employed her knew that their vases and porcelain, their embroidered napkins and silver spoons, their bracelets and brooches, all, would be safe with Sra. Rosa. If they began to notice after the birth of the housecleaner's daughter that some milk went missing—well, it wasn't much and milk was cheap, for them.

She walked to work every morning, a day for each client and Sunday for rest or a special one-time job, at first carrying her baby, then allowing her toddler to stumble beside for a while until she returned to her mother's arms, then walking hand in hand with her perfect, well-behaved daughter and *um-uming* to Rosa-Laura when the child pointed out marvels like a bird perched on a gateway or a leaf falling from a tall plane tree. Sra. Rosa also observed much movement on the street that smacked of politics, but just as the government, the military, the church, and even the left paid no attention at all to her, she paid little attention to this uproar, the intense cafe discussions, the newspaper stories, the billboards on every corner with huge black or red headlines, the demonstrations that seemed to be happening every five minutes. The marching and the placards she ignored entirely, because they so clearly pertained to men and their closed, powerful world. When Rosa-Laura was old enough to ask about a passing parade, "What's that, Mama?" Sra. Rosa told her that men pretty much held the concession for shameless behavior, and the lot of them marching around in the streets shouting slogans meant nothing to decent people.

The headlines and placards she wasn't able to read. She was ashamed of her near illiteracy, but what could you do? Emilia had gotten good schooling while at the convent, and Sra. Rosa had learned a few words on her own with Emilia tutoring her. *Chamberí*, for instance, the tall moony curve beginning it, the nubbin tipping off the letter at the end. To that pretty neighborhood she headed once weekly to clean a big house, a full second story flat with a wide art-deco balcony almost alive in its organic curvature. The house belonged to Sra. de Madriago.

As for neighborhood gossip about the politics and the times, she did listen to that as the years passed, because she had a daughter to take care of. In other words, she listened with a maternal egotism: What did this story about miners in Asturias mean for her baby's future? What did this demand for new laws and agrarian reform have to do with childcare? The assassination of a left wing braggart, then a right wing blowhard, did this change anything in their lives? And the cars, the ones full of armed men that drove up to certain houses in the night, dragged out the man of the house, and took him away so that he never came back, even in a poor neighborhood like theirs where you would think people had enough problems and not much to do with the government, even this new shiny Second Spanish Republic that promised so much for poor people, what about the cars?

Sra. de Madriago was a monarchist and a strong Catholic. The Republic was anathema to her. Well, of course. She had money and a husband with an important job in a ministry. A husband who wore a good hat, a collar, and white, starched cuffs every day. Sra. Rosa certainly knew about cuffs, as it was she who washed, starched, and carefully ironed the damned things. *"Veté hacer puñetas,"* people said as a way of telling you to go to hell: "Go and make cuffs." They were a nuisance and an annoyance to the woman, but they made the man look fine.

Sra. de Madriago was no younger than Sra. Rosa, but where Sra. Rosa was tiny, skinny, and sallow, with not a curve anywhere on her, her hair straight and gray with only a few strands left of dull black, Sra. de Madriago was comfortably fat, rosy cheeked, and her glossy black hair curled and held neat with tortoise shell combs. Elaborate coral-drop earrings, set in eighteen karat gold and shiny as tin in the sun, hung from her ears. She treated Sra. Rosa neither well nor badly and paid her on time.

Of all her six regular clients, Sra. Rosa preferred Srta. Guillermina, who was very kind and very demented. She could be demanding too, but overall, she was easygoing, generous, voluble, and sympathetic. Her home, a huge flat, was in the Salamanca neighborhood, a high class place and so new it was less than a century old. Srta. Guillermina lived with her mother and her brother, who was a doctor. Sra. Rosa had been with that family since she was sixteen.

At Christmas, the clients gave Sra. Rosa an *aguinaldo*, a bonus, of a few pesetas, or even a *duro*, five pesetas, and a basket of fruit. Srta. Guillermina always gave the most money and always decorated her baskets by hand and made them as beribboned and fancy as she was herself. Sra. de Madriago, on the other hand, was tightlipped and serious when she handed her basket over, often the *pesetas* were missing, and Sra. Rosa came away angry in her own heart. Whatever the basket held, Sra. Rosa usually sold it all, but after her daughter was born, she'd pick out the best banana and the best orange, remove and iron a ribbon or two, and give these things to Rosa-Laura as gifts on the day of the Three Wise Men. The *pesetas* she saved for the baby's education. For many years when she was a child Rosa-Laura thought the word "education" meant a jingly cloth sack hidden away under a loose floor tile.

When all the glorious achievements of the brand-new Second Spanish Republic and its beautiful, idealistic constitution began to be aired by this hero of the people or that one, Sra. Rosa shrugged, but deep down, she hoped that it might mean that her daughter would stand a better chance at a bountiful life than she had had. But, new government or not, she kept on saving those hard won coins because as the Moor said to his son, "Trust in Allah, but tie your camel."

Arturo Contreras del Valle's sister, Guillermina, was as gaudy as a flamenco dancer and lived back in another time and another century where she was young, still beautiful, and surrounded by admirers. She painted her face with white makeup then applied bright round pink clown spots on her cheeks with rouge, used a lurid red lipstick to outline thick, cupid-bow shaped lips, brushed spoonfuls of cakey mascara onto her lashes, then painted more on her thin, arched eyebrows. She wore flounces, ruffles, sweeping fringed shawls, and full skirts, as well as high heels that threatened to topple her like a rotted tree. Their mother wasn't much saner.

It broke the Doctor's heart, their situation, especially since he could not help loving them any more than he could help having to stop in at a certain bar on the Castellana now and then, just to torment himself by imagining the possibilities of another life. Sometimes he thought he was just a stupid slave to uncontrollable desires. But then, so was the rest of the world. Look at this business of the uprising. Was it to be believed?

As for his odd family, its decline had begun with his mother, who was a great beauty in her day and had many admirers. She married two rich men who died very happy with her, and then, as beautiful women do sometimes, she married a third, Montero, a man not rich but quite handsome. Guillermina had been born during the tenure of the first husband. Dr. Contreras knew the dirty stories: his sister looked just like his mother's second husband, his own father. Well, so be it. It made him love Guillermina more. His sister, though a beauty in her youth, had not been as lucky in love as his mother. She had had suitors galore. Her jewelry chest was full of bracelets inscribed with "to my lovely this" and "to my darling that" but no wedding rings. Women were fickle it was true. What could you do? It was woman's nature as surely as it was the nature of the liver and kidneys to strain poisons from the blood. But, it had driven his sad, delicate sister mad. Well, that plus their accursed stepfather, Montero. Nothing had worked out for her.

There were at least fifteen full-sized cabinets throughout their house, made of the finest cherry and ebony woods, ivory inlay and beveled glass, full of magnificent china and expensive dolls and the best books bound in blue, red, and green leathers. His sister also collected porcelain shepherds and shepherdesses, which adorned every undersized Italian marquetry table, console, and corner hutch. His housekeeper, Sra. Rosa, a ferocious woman despite her dwarfish size, told him once they were the devil to dust and keep clean. At the time of this comment from the woman, Dr. Contreras had said that he had seen shepherds and shepherdesses in real life, and they had not dressed in ribbons, lace, and petticoats like the figurines. He wasn't sure the housekeeper had understood his little joke.

Sometimes late at night, when his mother and sister were sleepinwg and he had just returned home after walking the streets at late hours, suffering from an attack of merciless loneliness, he would sit in his magnificent dining room and play with one of the statuettes, running his fingers over its delicate, intricate hands, its bonnet, the shepherd's crook. He was lucky to be alive, lucky no one suspected, lucky he hadn't met a gang of toughs who could have set upon him or worse yet, a bored cop or a civil guard ready to beat him to death for entertainment. Thinking over all of that, listening to the clock strike three or four, he sighed but did not weep or do anything else so melodramatic.

His dining room had massive gilt candelabra atop a table of palisander covered with a huge hand-made Spanish lace tablecloth. The chandelier above it was a glorious upside-down forest of Austrian crystal. When the heavy curtains draping the balcony doors were open, the prism'd light grew leaves of every color imaginable over the walls and ceiling of the room. Sometimes his housekeeper would bring her daughter along with her, a sweet and docile child with marvelous blue eyes—an adopted child. The mother certainly was not capable of producing such a pretty creature. As a baby this child was mesmerized by the chandelier, and even as she got older, she'd still sit in the dining room for hours, quietly watching it perform its dance of colors. If the doctor saw her in the morning before he left for work, he would pat her cheek and give her a chocolate. He knew her mother would not allow her to eat it until they left, so she wouldn't dirty anything in the house.

He remembered the first time the housekeeper had presented herself to his family, on the day of his stepfather's funeral. Evidently she'd come looking for work, although it had appeared at first as if she wanted something else. She was put off by the black reality of the funeral and overwhelmed by all the people at their home. She was very young, though of an age indeterminate, small-figured, unimposing, shorter than he was by two heads, child-sized really. She'd asked for his stepfather. It was strange, and perhaps not an appropriate visit, but Guillermina, always kind and considerate to stray animals, beggars, and the poor, had taken charge and insisted she come to work for them. A few years later, the little maid married. His sister and mother were sorry because the girl had worked out very well. Then, more years passed; she showed up just like that one day and wanted work again. They never asked her what had happened. Affairs of the working class, that. She was all in all an excellent housekeeper.

Mother and daughter survived Rosa-Laura's first five years with the usual close calls, tumbles, a childish fever or two that nearly killed not Rosita but her mother, and reliance on a diet with a lot of vegetables and bread. Sra. Rosa added to her collection of the crazy joy of that first day of Rosa-Laura's life the crazy joy of seeing her take her first step, of hearing her first word—"*Mamá*," of course—and of waking up just before dawn each day and feeling the tiny body curled into hers in the cot they shared when Rosa-Laura outgrew the woven rush laundry basket. Rosa-Laura survived, though she would never grow up a tall woman, much less a fat woman. She would be taller and fatter than Sra. Rosa though, and what more could a mother ask?

As it turned out, there was a lot more for which she could have asked. Peace, for example. Not the peace of sleeping children or neighbors who have finally decided to bury the hatchet after some dispute or another, but the peace of men ceasing to kill each other and anyone else who got in the way of their all-important occupations and self-serving beliefs.

In July of the year Rosa-Laura turned five, General Francisco Franco y Bahamonde left the Canary Islands, where he had been exiled for fomenting the overthrow of the Second Spanish Republic, in a plane thoughtfully provided by an Englishman through the auspices of an editor at Madrid's chief monarchist newspaper. Franco was flown to Morocco where he met up with his own troops of African mercenaries, then invaded Spain to connect with the troops of his cronies, and proceeded once again with his determined attempt to overthrow the government and set up a system to his liking. The insurgents struck hard in eight strategic places, Franco's gun sights on Madrid. It was said Franco expected to take the city without a fight, if not before then after the rest of Spain fell. Even Sra. Rosa, with her mind on other things those days, would have laughed at that notion.

For days and days everyone in her neighborhood talked about the advance of the troops and the formation of emergency workers' committees to run things and get people ready for the war hurtling toward Madrid. A huge anger pervaded because the government would not arm the workers and common citizens. Sra. Rosa was appalled. A war. Shooting and bombs. A blockade of supplies, as if life weren't hard enough. What right did those military bastards have to threaten everyone's livelihood, pursuit of survival? All those years of disappointment, death, hard work, and loneliness, all gone with a smile from her daughter, with another centimeter of growth, with each haircut, each carefully made and endlessly repaired dress—what right did those military bastards have to sully that, to threaten her and her child?

For a short while though, in the midst of these preoccupations, an event happened that allowed Sra. Rosa to think less about the terror advancing on her city and more about how rosy her child's future might possibly be. It began one agreeable September morning about a month after Rosa-Laura's fifth birthday, and two months before the insurgent troops would reach the portals of Madrid. That day was Sra. de Madriago's, and housekeeper and child were in her huge kitchen.

Rosa-Laura sat playing with some empty wooden thread spools, whisking them back and forth across the clean floor tiles of Sra. de Madriago's kitchen and noting with warm pleasure how if she lined them up five by five and then removed two, for example, from each set of five, three were left. This happy game turned out the same every time, no matter how she rearranged the configuration, and it gave Rosa-Laura a deep sense of things being just right and very comfortable.

The kitchen had a massive wood-burning stove, green and cream enamel on black iron, with six burners, an oven large enough to roast a spring lamb, and big lion-paw feet that Sra. Rosa would polish to a glossy black once a week. On the wall hung exactly twenty-four copper pots of all sizes and shapes. Rosa-Laura counted them every time she visited the kitchen. These were, Sra. Rosa had told her daughter, no good for anything except decoration. The long oak table where Sra. Rosa worked was ribbed and ridged with chop marks, the tiled walls glimmered slightly in the early morning light in all shades of glossy green bordered with tiles painted with rabbits and deer and hunting dogs. Rosa-Laura had counted those marvelous animals many times as well.

Sra. Rosa wasn't paying much attention to her daughter that morning, or she might have warned the child about the consequences of sitting on cold tile floors (hemorrhoids, cough, pneumonia). She was laboriously mending piles of stockings. She had washed them the week before, piled them up stiff and dry pair by pair, and today filled the big iron with hot coals and then ironed them to soften them for mending and storing.

This was how they spent mornings at work, Mama at her chores, and Rosa-Laura watching her and playing. Rosa was a good child and did not root around in employers' things or make voices or get lost in the huge houses or disturb people. She was a diminutive ghost, with shiny, reddish-brown hair soft as feathers, big blue eyes as bright as a mouse's, a faint spray of freckles across the bridge of her nose, pale skin, and slightly protuberant upper lip and teeth. More than once a scary employer-lady had given her a pinch or a wink or a cookie, with much smiling and commentary: "What a lovely girl, Sra. Rosa, how lucky you are, what a quiet, sweet child!"

Now she observed her mother thread the needle, pop a wooden sock egg into the toe of a sock, and begin mending. Rosa-Laura climbed up on the bench beside her mother, reached over and took a piece of black thread laying on the table, then got a needle from the sewing box. The needle had a large eye. Rosa-Laura looked at the needle a while, then began to do what she had seen her mother do time and time again.

"Ouch! Oh—oh!"

Sra. Rosa looked over at her and caught her breath: the child had drawn blood trying to manipulate the needle, pushing it in and out of her apron.

"What are you doing, Rosa-Laura?" her mother said. That is, she could see what the child was doing but she could not believe it.

"I hurt my finger, Mama," Rosa-Laura said. She could barely get the words out between a breath and a sob.

Sra. Rosa dropped her work on the table and picked up her daughter. She inspected her then sucked the wounded finger to ease the pain. But, she couldn't help laughing. "What were you trying to do, *hijita?*"

"Sewing," Rosa-Laura said. "Like you."

Then it did hit Sra. Rosa: her child was a prodigy, like one of those you hear about that play the violin around the time they're learning to pee into a chamber pot. Still, it was a pretty big needle, more for basting than sewing.

"Thread the needle again, daughter," Sra. Rosa said.

Rosa-Laura reached over to the table from her mother's lap and took a piece of brown thread then picked up the needle that had hurt her—very carefully—and licked the end of the thread. Sra. Rosa held her breath. The girl held up the thread to the light of the window and then tried several times to poke it through the eye; eventually, she succeeded. Sra. Rosa thought she would faint from excitement.

"We're going to visit Auntie Emilia after work today, *hijita*" she said. "She's going to show you some more things to do."

Auntie Emilia was a seamstress. So for that matter had been Rosa-Laura's birth mother. It was a sign from heaven.

Instead of staying to eat lunch and nap the siesta at Sra. de Madriago's house, thus avoiding a lengthy return to finsih her job in the afternoon hours, Sra. Rosa left at noon hurridly and headed for her sister's home. She dragged Laura Rosa across the city at a fast pace, past fine apartment buildings to the back of the Telefónica on the Gran Vía, glancing now and then at the many huge posters on the walls with the likeness of Gil Robles, the young leader and candidate of the CEDA. It was a party known for its extreme, right-wing, clerical politics. She didn't know the bold lettering proclaimed, "All Power To The Leader," and "The Leaders Are Never Wrong," but it would not have surprised her, as she had judged the subject of the poster-portrait self-satisfied and smug to the extreme. His smugness hadn't saved him from the rage of the city's citizens, who in honor of the uprising of the traitorous generals had ripped most of his posters in half, painted them over with foul words and drawn horns and moustaches on his face, arrows in his forehead, and in one instance, a fat and carefully portrayed object in his mouth that even Sra. Rosa could remember, though certainly never in that way.

Every now and then a truck full of youths passed by, yelling "¡*Abajo!*" this or that. Sra. Rosa held on to Rosa-Laura for dear life and ran down Montera Street toward the Puerta del Sol.

In the Puerta del Sol, Madrid and Spain's absolute center, a contingent of women and youngsters were drilling, carrying sticks over their shoulders like rifles. They wore workers' blue coveralls—*monos*—and followed an old man who shouted marching orders. People in the upscale plaza stood around, laughing and enjoying the scandal of the spectacle, though now and then a shop girl would come out and shout encouragement or a young man passing by would yell, "That's right, comrades, women too! We will all defend Madrid!"

Sra. Rosa crossed Sol and kept on going. Life was getting stranger and stranger, and she did not like it.

She finally entered her neighborhood, passing the site of the Church of San Lorenzo, which had just been burned to the ground. Churches everywhere were being burned, and Sra. Rosa was not surprised. Churches and priests had never done much for her kind. A long time ago at a particularly low point in her short, bitter marriage, she had asked for advice from the priest about what to do with her crazy husband. The priest had shouted and insulted her. The next time she'd entered San Lorenzo, the last time, it had been to get her baby baptized, because children had to be baptized no matter how you felt about the priest. Not to do so condemned an infant's soul.

Everyone in the neighborhood called San Lorenzo "*las chinches*," "the bedbugs," because of the huge number of babies baptized there, in this neighborhood where poverty brought forth more mouths than means to feed them. The church had been built in the 1600s, or so people said, was burned down in the mid-1800s during the short tenure of the First

Spanish Republic, then rebuilt after the overthrow of that fine notion. As she passed the newly burned-out ruins, Sra. Rosa didn't doubt the bedbug church would rise again from its rubble.

The neighborhood as always was covered with a sheen of age and sad secrets over its yellow-brown walls, buildings of old flats, windows shuttered with rotted frames, small balconies of ordinary iron work. The narrow alleyways could barely contain a car, being meant for horsemen, pedestrians, and hand-carts. It was quiet and empty, as everyone was now finishing lunch or sleeping the siesta. Sra. Rosa, with Rosa-Laura now hefted into her arms and the little girl's face pressed to her mother's bony clavicle, passed through the central plaza of the neighborhood by the old water spout and the bonneted metro entrance. Like the neighborhood itself, the plaza had nothing of beauty to commend it beyond its age and air of serene resignation.

She finally made it to Emilia's street, with chest and legs sore from the hourlong march. She ached in every joint and bone, and her feet in their thin hemp slippers had been brutalized by running over the cobblestones. With gasping breath, she leaned against a wall covered with posters that winged out from each side of her tired figure in a long perspective. The prevailing colors of the posters were black and red, and had stylized drawings of workers in heroic poses. The face of Gil Robles was nowhere to be seen. She shifted Rosita slightly, and hobbled toward the entrance of her sister's building.

Emilia and her daughter Mili lived in a single room in the old *corrala*, across the patio from Sra. Lourdes's family.

Entering the patio, Sra. Rosa passed the well and called out, "¡*Buenos*!" to her niece, who was sitting outside the door of her home, playing *el juego de los bonis* with a large, heart-shaped pincushion made of patches of velvet and porcupined with brightly colored glass-headed pins.

"Hey, girl, that your mother's *acerico*?" Sra. Rosa said. She knew the answer, as she had helped Emilia make the pincushion when they were girls; she just wanted Mili to know she knew that the girl was playing with something she shouldn't.

"Auntie! Hello, are you coming to lunch? We have nice things! Mama made an omelet!" Mili was a lovely eight year old, all curls, big dark-brown eyes and long lashes. She managed to be plump, because not only did her mother sacrifice every bite of food to make sure her daughter was well fed, the little girl was so adorable all the neighbors fed her tidbits too. She had caramel colored skin, dimples on her cheeks, a pouty rosebud mouth just like the girls in the posters advertising English cookies, and dimples on her knees as well.

Sra. Rosa managed a slight smile and opened the door to her sister's one-room home without ado. Her sister was at the tiny coal stove preparing lunch, and she turned, as Sra. Rosa carefully put Rosa-Laura down on the narrow bed, which besides the folded table against the wall, the two folded chairs tucked in a corner, and a small, hand-cranked sewing machine that rested on the floor near the curtain, was all the furniture the room held (or could hold).

"Um, tired, that's all," she said to her sister, as if she'd asked a question. "Just come running from Chamberí. They're drilling in Sol. Marching with sticks. Women too. How we going to defend Madrid with women and sticks?"

Emilia nodded seriously and sighed, then coughed for a while. "Mili, *hija*, put out plates for everyone." Her daughter peeked inside the room, then came in and opened the folded table and placed chairs at it. At that point, no one could have moved around the room, they just reached across the table and each other. "Rosi," Emilia said, "do you work this afternoon too?" Her sister nodded. "Let the little one stay with us. I have a jacket to finish. Mili can watch her."

"Good," Sra. Rosa said. "Because I got something important to tell you. Um, Rosa-Laura's going to be a seamstress, like you. Maybe better. She's a genius, Emilia. One of those prodigies."

She described the events of that morning at Sra. de Madriago's house to her sister, and over lunch—a *tortilla española* thick with potatoes and eggs, and a salad of lettuce and tomato—they discussed the implications of the discovery.

"I can take her most days and teach her. Best we do it in the mornings, Rosi, because in the afternoons I try to get out to clients' houses and do fittings and stuff. Maybe she can come with me to a few of those too, to see how it's done, but I have to take Mili, you know, and keeping track of both of them might be a problem," Emilia said.

"But Mama! I'm a very good girl! Everyone says!" Mili said. Her mouth was full of the cakey potato omelet, but her ears were clean and she'd heard every word, even though she was teasing Rosita at that moment, tickling her legs under the table with her toes. Mili had surreptitiously shucked her shoes. Rosa-Laura could hardly keep from screaming out with laughter at her big cousin, the funniest kid.

Emilia said. "OK, good girl, put your shoes back on and stop bothering your cousin." She smiled at her daughter. Sra. Rosa watched her sister and her niece exchange glances and smiles and felt a very, very warm glow in her chest. There might be war at the city gates, but there were also these moments. She dug in to the omelet then speared a tomato slice off the salad plate. She'd better fill up now while she could, because some food had begun to be scarce, and the market vendors had told her she might not see eggs for much longer. It was unsettling, this scarcity. It was one thing to go to a marketplace and have no money, but another thing for there to be no food there at all, whether you had money or not.

"Guess we won't be seeing an orange again for a while," Emilia said to Sra. Rosa, as if reading her thoughts. "Rosi, remember when we were girls, and the orange man came to the neighborhood?" The two girls looked up, expectantly.

Sra. Rosa pondered a moment. "Funny old guy, had a hand cart, and junky little scales. But he never weighed stuff, just counted it."

Emilia chuckled, her thin, lined face breaking into a reprise of her youthful prettiness with her smile. "You see, girls, he'd come often, sometimes twice a week during orange season, with a handcart full of oranges. He'd call out, 'Oranges, I got oranges, eighteen for one *real*,' and all the housewives would come downstairs to buy. And Mama would send one of us, and he was so funny, just a small man with a red scarf around his neck and a cap on his head, and sometimes he'd take the cap off and wipe himself with the scarf, because he sweated, because the load was heavy. I'd wait for the other ladies, but he always noticed me. He would laugh and say, 'Here she is, little Miss Pretty, what do you want, Miss Pretty?' and I'd say, 'If you please, Mister, eighteen oranges,' and he'd count out eighteen, and then he'd say, 'And you're so cute, here's another one. And you're so smart, here's another one. And you're such a good girl helping out your Mama, here's another one,' and he'd just keep on going!"

"Until he got to two dozen," Sra. Rosa said. She was smiling too at the memory. The orange man didn't discriminate between shiny young girls with shy smiles and big eyes, and serious, plain girls who were all business-like. He'd given Rosa a list of compliments and twenty-four oranges for the *real* too.

"You know what a *real* is?" Mili said to her cousin.

Rosa-Laura nodded indignantly. "Course I know. I'm not a baby."

Sra. Rosa smiled even more. "She can count, Mili. She knows a *real* is twenty-five *céntimos*, she can count them."

Mili didn't say anything to that. Rosa-Laura had learned to count when she was only three, and she could count higher than her cousin could, not to mention her ability to add numbers together and come up with correct sums, all of which was embarrassing to Mili as she went to school and Rosa-Laura didn't yet. Neither Sra. Rosa or Emilia ever considered Rosa-Laura's capacity in arithmetic much use. She was no farmer's daughter selling goods in a market stall, after all. A city woman could make money and survive if she knew how to sew, but beyond collecting a salary or a fee for a garment, what use to her was an ability to understand numbers? It wasn't as if she were a rich boy with money and connections to become a mathematician or an engineer or an architect. It wasn't as if they wanted her to become a money lender like their mother either.

Emilia said, "The neighbors told me supply lines have been cut. The trucks aren't coming from the south. We're relying on the market gardens in the suburbs."

"Damn generals," Sra. Rosa said. "Extreme, those southerners. Either señoritos on their haciendas, all dressed up like there's a fair every day, or else there's the poor ones picking up the olives from the ground, and they've got a pair of pants between two of them and no house to put it in."

"Anarchists there," Emilia said. "But one of the four generals, the young one, the one who invaded, he's a *gallego*, and lots say he's the one to watch."

Sra. Rosa grunted. "Well, the saying is true: 'You see a *gallego* on a staircase and you never know if he's going up or coming down.' Sneaky. Clever." She forked in another big gob of moist, salty omelet. As for the other word, she didn't really know what an anarchist was, but there were plenty of them in this neighborhood. She didn't trust them any more than she trusted any politician or for that matter, any *gallego*. Still, there was Madrid and there was the army marching on it. The anarchists and she were on the same side now, against this army headed up by a mysterious northerner, and she hoped the anarchists would make good on all the promises and speeches.

"They say there's Moors with the invaders coming here," Emilia said.

Her voice was low and she had stopped eating, the fork halfway up from the plate to her mouth, but forgotten in the moment. "They say they get into a village and just round up people who don't know the salute, and put them in the bull ring and shoot them all, women too. The navy was supposed to join the generals, but the sailors mutinied and took over the ships and stayed with the Republic. And the army's split in two, half with us, half with them."

"Mama, what's 'Moors'?" Mili said. "The neighbors talk about Moors too."

"Black men," Sra. Rosa said. "Big scary black men."

"Rosi, please," Emilia said. "Mili, darling, it's just a story. They're men from Africa. Hundreds and hundreds of years ago they owned Spain. We kicked them out a long time ago. They're gone. Don't worry about things like that."

"They'll come and take you away in the middle of the night if you've been bad," Sra. Rosa said. She grinned at her niece and nodded her head as if to emphasize the horror of the punishment.

"Rosi!" Emilia said.

Sra. Rosa grinned even more and tore off a piece of bread from the half loaf on the table. Then she poured Rosa-Laura water from the pitcher. Best water in the world, Madrid's.

The first years of Rosa-Laura's life, Rogelio had not come over too often, but once she had begun to speak, and Sra. Rosa taught her the magic word *"Papá,"* he visited regularly. He always brought penny candies and sat on the chair and spoke about his work or related neighborhood gossip. Once he told his daughter that she had a voice like a lovely birdie, and she replied, "And you, Papa, you sound all nice and rumbly, like the trams on the Castellana."

He laughed and laughed over that one, especially since "rumbly" had come out "rumly" and "Castellana," "Casarana." She was growing into a marvelous girl, clearly her mother's child, and as much as he credited Sra. Rosa with the raising of his daughter, he could not help but credit the child's beauty and delicacy to his wife.

He smoked small cigarettes rolled in brown paper with tobacco sticking out both ends so that he often had to lick it from his lips. Rosa-Laura was very interested in how he rolled them with only one hand. Of course, that business brought about the question of his blindness.

"Mama says you can't see and that's why your eyes look like glassy gray marbles and have that cloud thing over them."

Sra. Rosa made a huffing sound from her corner of the room and said, "Apologize to your Papa right now, Rosa-Laura. That wasn't nice!"

Rosa-Laura started to cry at the criticism, and Rogelio said, "Ah, Sra. Rosa, she meant no harm. She's trying to understand what blindness is about. And Papas, too."

"Papas operate by punishing bad children. And she has to learn not to say everything that pops into her head, it's not nice."

Sra. Rosa was strict, that was for sure. She'd even told Rogelio not to give Rosa-Laura candy just because the child had been especially good.

"We did that too much for her cousin, and now Mili thinks that being good is just a trick to get some gift from the big folks. I want Rosa-Laura to be better than that, I do. She has to be respectful."

∽∾

Rogelio was grateful for Sra. Rosa's mothering, but the whole affair of family had not worked out as he had wanted. *Papá* didn't mean a whole lot in Rosa-Laura's world, not even a quarter as much as *Mamá*. He always came to visit them, not vice versa. Sra. Rosa seemed to be uneasy about the place where Rosa-Laura's birth mother had died.

He was thinking about that and not at all about politics early one morning, a month or so before Franco had invaded Spain and began the war. He was on his way to work and moving quickly, as the weather was brisk early at the beginning of that momentous summer, but as he crossed the plaza he stopped to buy penny candies from the lady with the table near the metro entrance.

"Make them coconut, my little girl likes them best," he said, "and a few strawberry ones and maybe a hazelnut or two as well."

"Ah, Sir, such a nice father you are. You may be sightless, but clearly you got what it takes in that department, where lovely children are made, no missing the target there!"

Rogelio paid her his *céntimo* and got away fast. The woman had recently been widowed and though she might have been interested in the abilities of a blind man, he was not interested in courting a woman whose voice was as compelling and as sonorous as a drum roll and whose body smelled like sugar, tobacco, and a lifetime without bathing.

So, when he arrived at the bookbinding shop, somewhat late, he still wasn't thinking of much else beyond his close call with the candy widow and whether or not there were enough coconut sweets to make Rosa-Laura happy. To his surprise, both of the men who worked with him, one an older guy and the other with six months still to go on his apprenticeship, were standing outside smoking and debating—debating whether or not to go home, of all things.

"What's this about?" Rogelio said to them.

"The boss has company," the older man said. His voice was very low, and Rogelio could hear the fear in it.

"A customer?"

"Naw, some *fachas*, three of 'em," the apprentice said.

"Shut up! You want to get us all beat up?" the older man said.

"For God's sake, tell me what's happened," Rogelio said. Now he was angry and afraid. *Falangistas*, members of the Fascist Party, the *Falange*, sometimes entered a work place where the owner was a known red, for example, or a Jew or a socialist, and beat up the people there. Then, to compensate by greasing the wheel of justice with oily blood, the communists or the anarchists or someone on the left would go out looking for blue-shirts to beat up. Those were the colors early that summer, red for the Left, blue for the Right. The thing was, the owner of the shop where Rogelio worked was no red or blue-shirt. He was just a guy who bound books, beautifully. True, he did read a distressingly suspicious wide variety of books, but so did many priests.

Suddenly, the thugs came out the door of the shop pushing aside his two co-workers and nearly knocking over Rogelio.

"Get out of my way, you useless bastard, go beg on a corner," one said. The voice came from above Rogelio's head, well above, and the shove had come from someone equally big. The voice continued, "And you two cuckolds, what are you staring at? Fixing our mugs on your memories are you? Cretins. Go find a real job, whore-sons, do something honorable for your country!"

Rogelio's comrades must have found some courage somewhere in their fear and hesitation, because all of a sudden someone took a swing at someone else, and Rogelio moved hard into the next portal, pressed against the door behind him, and raised his cane so as to use it as a weapon. He would hate to crack it or break it, but he had some honor too, even if he was a cripple. In front of him, a wind of action and the grunting, popping sounds of punches landing, foul name calling. And then it was over. He heard one, then two, then three men running off.

"What's happened? *Chicos*, are you there?" he called out.

"Aw, yeah, my ma's going to kill me when I come home like this. My jacket's tore," the apprentice said. He slurred his words, as if swallowing blood through a split lip.

"She's going to kill you when she sees that face. Your mouth's a mess. Maybe your jaw is cracked or something," the other man said.

The boss came out and said, "I don't have enough trouble with those bullies that you guys have to fight with them and wreck your hands?"

"*Joder*, Sir, they insulted our mothers," the apprentice said.

They all went inside, heated with the fight and pleased with themselves. As it turned out, the fascists had come to warn the owner to inform on any customers that put in orders for any disreputable books to be bound, and they also wanted to know where certain neighborhood presses were located and if they were printing leaflets these days. The boss didn't know where the owner was, swore ignorance about everything else as well, and nearly got a beating himself, but as he was seventy years old, they just slapped him, insulted his parentage and lineage, and demanded he drop his pants to prove he was not a Jew. The old man told the thugs they could beat him senseless but he wasn't about to surrender his dignity in front of strangers at his age. They reconsidered their demand, then threatened him that if it turned out some faggot kike liberal was having his pervert books bound there, they'd find out, come back, and burn down the shop.

"It's a disgrace and a shame," the boss said. "Our best customers are the homosexuals and the Jews and the professors. What are we to do?"

The incident disturbed Rogelio deeply for days, but then the invasion occurred, and the city turned loyalist one hundred percent, the *fachas* all disappeared from public view, hidden and waiting for their comrades marching toward Madrid.

The winter of 1936 was a brutal affair, and not just because of the miserable, foggy weather and the thunderstorms, which usually came only in spring and summer. The invaders brought in a storm of their own. They massed right on the northern perimeter of Madrid on November 7, and suddenly, they were inside the city itself, on the university grounds. The defense was ferocious, and evidently, unexpected. At one point, the invaders got past the palace and into the Plaza de Oriente, but were beaten back, man by man, cobblestone by cobblestone. The insurgent forces settled on the outskirts of the city, mostly to the north and southwest, and began a hard siege, lobbing mortars like stone pinecones into the city daily. Whenever the pounding would begin somewhere, sirens keened. The University of Madrid continued to be a battleground, as did the southern and western peripheral neighborhoods. In the valleys surrounding Madrid, battles grew like outbursts of virulent disease.

Sra. Rosa and her neighbors began to notice strangers and foreigners even in their own neighborhood. Right after the first tremendous assault, refugees poured in from occupied and often bombed-out villages, and volunteers from all over the world arrived in Madrid to form the International Brigades. The people of the city couldn't leave, and as the outsiders flooded in, things began to get crowded and volatile. Some people in the better neighborhoods did abandon their homes, fleeing to other cities: Valencia if they were for the Republic, Seville or Valladolid if they sided with the insurgents. It didn't take long for their houses to be confiscated, either formally or quite informally.

There was debate about sending all children out of Madrid after that, and Sra. Rosa listened carefully to the women gossiping in clusters on every corner, disseminating what news they had from their husbands, the newspapers, the market-vendors. There was food, but soon it was rationed, so people had to wait for hours in lines to get it. All night long, people tried to sleep and dream to the sound of mortars, cannon fire, the occasional gunshot. They woke up in the morning to find bullet holes in their portals and another man gone. A person could catch a tram to the front, and people did, to see if it was really true, to join, to watch, to bring some food or drink to a husband, a lover, a brother.

People did their best. Neighborhood committees were formed, headed up with the usual altruists, idealists, loudmouths, and opportunists, but leadership or no, everyone was determined to "rise to the occasion," to meet this challenge, and to be helpful and share supplies and courage with each other. "Who does the difficult things in this world? Those who can!" At the same time, there were also many denunciations and settling of old scores. Soon, all the men in Sra. Rosa's neighborhood between the ages of fifteen and sixty were in militias patrolling the city, at the front fighting, dead, in jail, or fled.

Sra. Rosa got up before five just as before, but now instead of six houses to clean, she had only three, and the trek again passed through lines of men and sometimes women drilling with rifles, not sticks, though some of the arms held were fifty years old, real blunderbusses. She had to be sharp and listen for the sound of bombs, gunfire, and buildings collapsing under mortar fire. She began to worry about Rosa-Laura and wondered if it were best to leave her with Emilia, or, on the days her sister could not take her, at home alone, or somewhere else, like the bowels of the metro, where no trains ran anymore because safe stations had been set up and people who had been bombed out were camping on the platforms and tracks. Sra. Rosa would not consider sending Rosa-Laura away, however. If the rules demanded that her daughter vacate the city, she would leave with her. They would not be separated.

An international blockade on aid to the Republic was strictly enforced by England, which didn't want France getting in the ground floor with its old customer, Spain, but word was that Hitler and Mussolini ignored it and generously supplied Franco and the nationalists with money, goods, advisors, and troops. Sra. Rosa couldn't help but wonder, though she said nothing, how such a situation so *sin vergüenza*, so shameless, could have arisen. Some of the neighbors, members of the Communist Party, said that Comrade Stalin and the Russians were going to send the Republic arms and food, blockade or not. Sra. Rosa didn't know much about Comrade Stalin or the Russians and thought they too might be black men, until a huge portrait of a thick-haired, big-mustached white man appeared in the Puerta del Sol. It turned out he was Comrade Stalin. Sra. Rosa thought his expression was hard and his eyes mean, but if he was going to send them food, that was fine with her.

One night very soon after November 7, she awoke sometime after midnight to an unpleasant, booming sound, and boozy with sleep muttered, "Oh Madonna most holy, it's a thunderstorm, I have to get to Emilia's house."

Thunderstorms reduced poor Emilia to hysteria. Sra. Rosa got up and put her shoes on—she had been sleeping fully clothed, and with both pairs of her stockings on because of the cold—and picked up Rosa-Laura just as she was, all bundled up in their only blanket. She shouldered her daughter and went downstairs. It took her nearly ten minutes to unlock the front door, and once out in the street, she had to call a neighbor, a man who before the decrees of August that had abolished his post had been the *sereno*, the block's night watchman. He locked her building's front doors so no one would enter and rob everyone, especially in those days when food and fuel had become so scarce.

She hadn't wanted to wake up the porter, avoiding him whenever possible, and generally handing the rent to his wife. By now the porter knew about Rosa-Laura, of course, but he had never confronted Sra. Rosa, and she certainly didn't want to provoke him. This uneasy truce was reinforced by the fact that the building's owner had fled the city, supposedly because of threats to his life, and all the porter was doing now was collecting rents and waiting. Some of the tenants told Sra. Rosa she didn't have to pay rent anymore, that all those bloodsucking capitalist fiends were gone and wouldn't return, that after this coup and invasion were repulsed, the workers would triumph and the tenants themselves would own the building. Sra. Rosa paid them no mind. "*Unos nacen con estrella, otros nacen estrellados,*" which more or less means that some are born lucky, and some not. The luck of the denizens of this place wasn't going to change any time soon no matter what they believed.

The air outside was icy cold. Sra. Rosa hurried on down the street to Emilia's building, the ex-*sereno* right behind her. The sky kept lighting up in ugly purple and yellow flashes, and there was heavy thunder. They arrived at Emilia's home, and as the man unlocked the big door to the patio, he said to Sra. Rosa, "Better be careful, Señora. I don't think that's thunder out there. Not thunder, no." Sra. Rosa ignored him; he was an idiot.

She didn't want to wake anyone, but as she stepped into the patio, she realized that most of the neighbors were standing outside, looking at the sky. There was no rain, but the air was thick with the cold, and it hurt to breathe it. The neighbors, mostly women and some children, stood staring up and murmuring to each other. Though wrapped in blankets, they too wore what was probably all their clothes because of the cold. Sra. Lourdes stepped forward from this bunch and without a word, took Rosa-Laura from Sra. Rosa's arms.

Sra. Rosa knocked at Emilia's door, fearful because neither her sister nor her niece were outside with the others. They couldn't be sleeping. Something was wrong, and she knew what it was. Behind her, Lourdes patted Rosa-Laura on the back gently. The child was groggy and did not know where she was.

Another boom, quite loud, sounded above them. Emilia's door burst open. Mili stood there in a night dress and a big shawl, looking like a baby ghost, crying. "Oh, Oh, Auntie Rosa, it's so loud, and Mama is so scared!" The sky boomed again at that moment, with a flash of light, but Sra. Rosa didn't get a look at the lightning or she would have realized it didn't look like lightning at all.

Inside the tiny room that was her home, Emilia was crouched up on the table, which was jammed between the bed and the back wall. It was normally folded against the wall when not in use, but now it was half opened and shaking with the strain of carrying Emilia on top of it, though she didn't weigh much more than Sra. Rosa herself.

"Mili! Mili!" she screamed, "Come, here with me, come, it's safer, it's coming through the walls, it's coming through the wires!"

Another loud boom broke hard and the whole building shook. They heard screams and then booms farther off, but more and more. The sky was almost uniformly lit. Sra. Rosa suddenly realized that the *sereno* had been quite right: this was not thunder or lightening at all. She could not connect it to anything she knew.

She took Rosa-Laura, now awake and sobbing, from Lourdes, closed the door unceremoniously, bundled Rosa-Laura and Mili in the bed, and told them not to cry. She hoisted herself onto the table as best she could and put her arms tightly around Emilia, who began to moan, and cough spasmodically.

"There, there, girl, it's all right, it's not going to hurt you, I promise, I promise, it will not hurt you, um, um…" Sra. Rosa said.

Outside an eerie whistling noise began, then sirens, the sound of which Sra. Rosa hated more than the cannons—what use were they anyway, always coming after the bombardments began?—then more booms, now louder and closer. Emilia closed her eyes against her sister's shoulder and fainted dead away. In the lurid half-light filtering in through the door cracks, Sra. Rosa thought she saw reddish stains on her sister's chin.

Emilia fell apart at the slightest hint of thunder and lightning. Once Sra. Rosa was pinning a pattern to a large piece of blue-gray herringbone serge to help her sister out with a particularly rushed consignment, when a thunderstorm broke. Emilia began screaming at her, "Don't touch the pins!" because they were metal and she believed they would surely pluck the electricity out of the sky and into the room, killing them all.

෯෨

The sun rose watery and suffused with dirty fog—or was that smoke? Sra. Rosa got up heavily, her body complaining with creaks at the bad night she'd spent. She got together some bits of scrap fuel and some carbon and started a fire in the stove. She went outside to collect a jug of water from the well. Sra. Lourdes was there before her, and Sra. Rosa glanced at her, then gruffly saluted her. Lourdes drew her water from the faucet, and looked up at Sra. Rosa. She attempted to smile, but the result was sad.

"The neighborhood watch committee was here earlier," Sra. Lourdes said to Sra. Rosa. "The report is, bombs falling from airplanes. Not cannon, or mortar. They bombed us from airplanes. Can you imagine that? What is this world coming to?"

Sra. Rosa didn't say anything for a moment. Finally, she pushed her wits together and said, "Um, what does that mean?" She had a picture in her mind of a man jammed into the seat of a tinny-looking airplane, like the pictures she had seen of Baron Von Richhofen in World War I. How did he drop a bomb? Did he hold the steering wheel of his plane and drop the bomb with another hand? Or did he have a partner in this ugly affair, sitting behind him and dropping the bombs? She had seen pictures of planes with two compartments. None of it made any sense, and her mind was not up to the task of imagining this clearly.

"Where do they carry them? Planes aren't like a car, right? No trunks or such. I mean, there's the big ones that carry muck-a-mucks, and the ones that drop those damned pamphlets on us all the time, just good for starting up a fire, but why—Are you sure of this? There's lots of stories going around nowadays, Sra. Lourdes, and I don't believe the half of them. A cannon barrage makes more sense."

"It wasn't cannon. It was planes. It's true. I don't know how, but it's been written about," Lourdes said.

"Oh," Sra. Rosa said. She did not dispute writing. It was something above her.

She returned to the house and set water to boil so she could make chicory coffee. She told her sister she'd have to go to work. Emilia was back to normal, which included as usual, deep shame at her behavior. "I'm sorry, Rosi, but you know how I am."

"Of course, girl," Sra. Rosa said. "But listen, that wasn't thunder. Lourdes says Madrid was bombed. From the sky. From airplanes."

"Can it be?" Emilia said.

"It's hard to believe, but anyway you look at it, we're in for it," Sra. Rosa said. "Vallecas now, because it's red, but our turn's coming. They don't do it to the rich neighborhoods. One of the neighbors just yesterday was saying they aren't fighting in the northeast. *Madrid va bién, arriba de Atocha.* Madrid is great, if you live above Atocha. And that's how it is."

Emilia shrugged and watched the pot trying to get to boiling with a tiny amount of fuel burning underneath it. A watched pot never boils. "Well, we aren't heroines, so it's harder."

"What?" Sra. Rosa said.

"Heroines," Emilia repeated. "You know, like heroes, only women. Half the girls in this building, they're uptown training to use a gun and defend the city. They asked me if I wanted to help dig trenches."

"You?!" Sra. Rosa said. "Mother of God, Emilia, you've had a cold all this winter, and you're skinny as a straight pin. They've got some nerve asking you!"

"They asked everyone, Rosi. I felt bad I couldn't."

"Ridiculous. Heroes! All these people in the neighborhood running around, 'comrade this' and 'comrade that.' I don't care for the fascists and the monarchists and the Catholics, they're the sons of bitches who began this mess, and they're the ones bombing us out. But I don't understand what our side is doing, fighting on the streets among themselves, fighting in the *Cortes* with the president and his party, and what do we have to do with all that?"

Emilia said not a word to this, but Sra. Rosa wasn't expecting answers from her baby sister. Why did those bastards have to begin with airplanes now? Their cannon fire reached well into the city, by God, as far as the Gran Vía itself. Why did they have to add to that? Everyone was talking about how Madrid would resist, Madrid would not fall. "*No pasarán,*" La Pasionaria said. She was a big leader in the Communist Party. Imagine that, a woman leading things, because her husband had been killed in the uprising in Asturias, and she had taken over his job, just like that famous Aragonese woman who had fired her husband's cannon during the war with Napoleon—well, that's what this Asturian woman had said, "They shall not pass." It sounded good and strong and determined. Everyone believed the Republic would triumph eventually, because it had right on its side. Sra. Rosa was not so sure. *Saben mucho los ratones. Más los gatos.* Mice know a lot. The cat knows more. She figured those guys who had invaded were the cats in this deal; they had the money and the power behind them. Where else would they get planes to bomb the city? Those things cost a lot of money.

She felt tired, very tired. The *corrala* was quiet now, and cold in the sere, gray morning light, and she wanted to stay here with her family, but she had only three clients left in town and had to work. Maybe if she kept their houses spic and span, the families wouldn't abandon them, like the other clients had. Oh, this was all so crazy. She could understand their menfolk running off, afraid of arrests, of midnight executions by the leftists. What she and Emilia were now calling "the other side" had done it too, anyway, and more so. It had happened right here in this neighborhood, where nobody had anything. Falangists had come in the night, kids most of them, and dragged away some union leader or some notorious red. She poured the boiling water over the chicory grounds, waited till they settled, and then ladled out the "coffee" into cups and sat down on the bed next to the two girls, still quite asleep, thanks for that. She held the warm cup in both hands and slowly drank the brew. It tasted like dirt.

"We need sugar," she said to Emilia. Emilia was sitting in the chair, hunched into herself for warmth and still somewhat ashamed of her behavior during "the storm." She sipped from the cup, but then began to cough again, hard. Sra. Rosa got up quickly, put her own cup down, and grabbed Emilia's cup, afraid her sister would drop it.

"What is it, sister?" Sra. Rosa said. Emilia held the end of her sweater up to her mouth and searched frantically in her pockets for a handkerchief.

"Don't touch me, Rosi, don't touch me," she said. She couldn't find a handkerchief and reluctantly swallowed what was in her mouth. "Don't touch me. You'll get it too. I can't even hug Mili any more, I'm afraid to." She began to cry, quietly so as not to wake the children.

"Dear God," Sra. Rosa murmured, more to herself. On top of everything else, this. When would fate have done torturing her family? She put her arms around her sister, because no damned disease was going to stop her from doing so.

Finally, around seven, Sra. Rosa left for work, nodding at Lourdes across the way as she exited the patio. Lourdes was just standing there, while her children pushed around her and nudged themselves into her arms. It seemed as if she had a dozen, all boys, noisy creatures, but there were only three.

As she crossed the plaza, she noticed children and a woman hurriedly scooping up coal that must have fallen from a truck. They checked around, looking at her fiercely as if to warn her off. Fuel was getting scarce. She'd have to do something about that too. Maybe requisition some coal from Sra. de Madriago's house? Why not? Sra. de Madriago wasn't going to give her any *aguinaldo* this Christmas, and was already two weeks late with Sra. Rosa's wages, curse it. Perhaps she'd ask her for olive oil or cheese or butter or something like that. Money was getting to be practically worthless anyway. Sra. Rosa could not work for credit or promises, that was for sure. She had a daughter to feed. Thank God for Emilia's business as a seamstress. That is, if people went on needing clothing. The way things were going, they'd all be naked and starving by springtime.

After that terrible night, more aerial bombing raids came. Living in a besieged city under blackouts and curfews and with scarcity became their lives. They breathed terror and exhaled anxiety until war became the norm.

Every morning on her way to work across town Sra. Rosa would find another building bombed out. The Gran Vía, Madrid's Broadway, which was always a necklace of lights and sidewalk cafés open the whole night long, now shut down by 6 p.m. By 10 p.m., only the militia patrolled, and the city lay pooled and quiet in the blackness. This had no effect on Sra. Rosa, who'd never sat at a table at one of those fancy cafés in the center of the city. But other things certainly did affect her and her family. Food had to be rationed and lines formed to get food. The waiting took hours. At the start of the siege, Sra. Rosa had had no time, but since the siege began, she'd lost another client, and she found she had too much time altogether. Emilia lost customers uptown too, but she could rely on her customers in the neighborhood; soon she found that making a dress for the lady down the street might mean she could trade it for a liter of olive oil or half a kilo of rice or a bucket of potatoes. By Christmas, the government, which more and more began to be run by the industrious organizers of the far left, had issued food tickets and was dispensing supplies; the tickets became more valuable than the Republic's money.

The bombing went on, night after night, and poor Emilia lost sleep and became sicker, although strangely, once she realized the bombs had nothing to do with electricity, she calmed down considerably. Sra. Rosa began to think about the possibility of moving out of her home and in with Emilia. It would have meant sleeping on the floor and moving Rosa-Laura in with a beloved aunt who clearly had the coughing-blood disease, but still, it beat running to Emilia's house in the middle of the night every time bombs fell, which was not only dangerous, it quickly became unlawful. Various military groups, including the Assault Guard, had formed to take the place of the Spanish Civil Guard, which had pretty much defected to the insurgents. The AG patrolled the city at night and expected people to obey the curfew. They weren't going to shoot or arrest a woman with a little girl, but they would demand she get indoors and show some sense.

The thing is, moving out and joining her sister and niece in their home would save money, but it would also mean she'd never move back in to the room she thought of as her and Rosa-Laura's home. Once she was gone, the rent would be raised and some other person would grab it. There was a great need for housing, in that aspect war and peace were alike, and the destruction of many buildings made the need greater anyway, money or not. People who had a house stayed put. To give up her home was not a decision she could make easily. In the end, it would be made for her.

One morning after leaving Rosa-Laura with Emilia she headed across the city once again to get to Sra. de Madriago's house. In the center of town all around the Puerta del Sol and up and down the Gran Vía, the shops were barricaded. Shopkeepers had piled up bags of sand and even erected walls of bricks with the hastily applied mortar spilling out from the spaces, to protect their precious plate glass windows. In between most stores and the windows, a potential customer could still squeeze in and get a look at the goods. The doors would be thrown open and the invitation to enter issued eagerly. Business as usual. Many of the stores in this most central and luxurious of areas carried very fine items, jewelry from Italy, hats from Paris, the latest books, the best gourmet food, the best cigars and tobacco. By now, Madrileños had begun to call the Gran Vía "*la avenida de los obuses,* Howitzer Avenue."

Just as in every other neighborhood, women from the center formed lines to buy goods and pick up food at ration points. Sra. Rosa needed to get in one of those lines very soon, both for herself and her sister, but today she needed more to get to her job, as she was completely out of money. She didn't even have a *céntimo,* that's how bad things had become, and it was possible Sra. de Madriago might not have any money either, though surely she might have some goods to barter with her loyal cleaning lady.

Last week she had given Sra. Rosa one of those damned copper pots from the kitchen wall in fact, which meant Sra. Rosa had to find an exchange center. People said the army needed metals like copper to make weapons and were paying top price. One of the neighbors would take her to the place where metals were bought and collected. The thing is, there was no time at all, what with work (though that was fast disappearing), helping Emilia, finding fuel and food, and then losing sleep, huddling night after night with Rosa-Laura, reciting folk tales to lull her to sleep, listening for the gunfire, the sirens, the booming of cannons, the sound of bombs thudding down from the cold black sky.

She had just left the Puerta del Sol and passed the neighborhood of Tetuán, having glanced at another long queue of housewives and children in front of a grocery shop. As she turned a corner, she heard the lazy drone of planes and without realizing she was doing it, she began to recite the old prayers from her childhood, the ones that had never done her or her sister any good before. The high fog over the city opened up, two planes dropped through, and Sra. Rosa ducked down a stairway and into a shoemaker's shop in the basement of a large building. The shoemaker looked up when she entered, undoubtedly hoping for a customer, then sighed when he saw her. She figured he had to be at least eighty years old, and so decrepit and wrinkled and spangled with age spots that he looked like a dried seed pod split and emptied. A burst of light and a tremendous blast followed her entrance, and they both fell to the floor. When the building stopped shaking, she got up very slowly, because her heart was pounding so hard it hurt to move. The shoemaker lifted his head.

"It's all right, you can get up, it's gone," she said.

He nodded.

More booms sounded, not quite so close but close enough. He shook his head at her as he struggled to get up, and she noticed that he had tears in his eyes. She looked away. He was a complete stranger, but men don't want to be seen crying as if they were women or children, and she didn't want to embarrass him. She looked around at his store: there were quite a few pairs of shoes piled up on shelves and sitting on the floor. Each pair had tags affixed to them. Many were dusty. How long had it been since this poor old guy had had a customer? The shop was dingy, and the small windows looking out right at street level were dirty too. He had no lights on, and his eyes behind thick glasses were rheumy and clouded.

"You get much work?" she said.

He just looked at her, befuddled.

"Because," she said, "if you want to trade one of these pairs of shoes for some clothing or some food or some coal, I might be able to barter with you."

He nodded but did not speak.

"Well, I have to go to work now, but I'll drop by after siesta, how's that? We can talk about this." He nodded again.

She needed shoes and so did Rosa-Laura and Mili. Emilia didn't travel about the city so much, so her shoes lasted longer. Nobody was going to come back and pick up these pairs sitting around the shoemaker's shop, and Sra. Rosa planned to exploit that as soon as possible. Maybe Sra. de Madriago would give her a couple more of those damned pots. Plus, this old guy looked like he could use a meal and maybe she could arrange that too.

When she came out, people on the street were running hard toward Tetuán. She hesitated, then turned back to follow them. It wouldn't take more than a minute to see what was up before she headed out again for Chamberí.

The bomb had hit the grocery line of women and children she had just glanced at a few minutes ago, dead center. At least a dozen bodies lay on the ground. There was moaning and screaming and crying. The sidewalk, a broad and beautifully set platform of octagonal cement plates, was awash with black-red blood; everything else was powdered with white dust from the damage. Sra. Rosa stood there for a moment, staring open-mouthed at the mayhem and trying to catch her breath. One of the bodies was that of a girl with a huge blue ribbon in her curly blond hair. She had no wounds that Sra. Rosa could see, but she lay there with her mouth open, arms outspread, and eyes glazed over, and you didn't have to be a doctor to see she was dead. She was no older than Rosa-Laura.

People were now checking, checking, to see if anyone survived. The moaning and crying continued, louder. Sra. Rosa looked away from the bodies but didn't leave just yet. She heard ambulances; some cars had arrived too, and soldiers were already here to take whomever they could to hospitals or to the morgues, which had been set up all over the city. She looked up at the sky, but it said nothing to her. A tree at the street corner had been split and knocked down by the bombs, and people set at it, tearing and hacking away to get wood to burn. It was a London plane tree, a kind of sycamore, with broad, pale green, fuzzy leaves. Rosa-Laura liked to play with the prickly balls the trees gave as fruit. The pleasantly bumpy toy filled up her whole hand. Sra. Rosa turned and headed again toward Chamberí, almost at a run.

It took her over half an hour to get there, so exhausted that she began to limp. She had not had any breakfast that morning except for a cup of water and a chew of hard bread, and her feet and back hurt from the cold and the worn soles of her shoes. She had put a piece of cardboard inside one shoe; it bothered her now and would have to be removed soon. As she got further into the neighborhood, she saw fewer and fewer bombed out ruins. These buildings were intact and still beautiful, mostly eighteenth and nineteenth century. Halfway up the street as she neared the house with the broad art-deco balcony she saw that its windows were shuttered tight. By now, Sra. de Madriago usually had them opened. Sra. Rosa entered the lobby. There was no concierge, a disturbing situation. She ascended the two flights of stairs to Sra. de Madriago's flat. She never took the lift, because it was tiny and made of open ironwork, and it scared her. She got to the landing, but knew before she rang the bell that they had gone; she rang anyway. To her great relief, Sra. de Madriago came to the door, but relief was short lived.

"There's no work for you," Sra. de Madriago said to Sra. Rosa. She was gray-skinned, still in her silk, maroon-striped bathrobe, she wasn't wearing her corset, her hair was disheveled, and she had clearly been crying. Sra. Rosa stood there, staring at the woman. "But, Sra. de Madriago, I can work for goods you know, I don't mind—"

"They took my husband away last night. I told him, I told him a dozen times, we have to get out, we have to leave, and he wouldn't, fool, fool, fool, I told him."

"Who? Who would do such a thing?" Sra. Rosa said, though she knew who had done it; after all, the man was right-wing, Catholic, monarchist, and a meddler. He had surely been up to something or other, part of that infamous, behind-the-lines "fifth column" helping out the four columns of insurgents who had invaded Spain. Sra. Rosa asked the questions because she thought if she kept Sra. de Madriago talking long enough, the woman would let her in, let her do her job, let her help out, and then she would take some small thing in exchange, something to keep her own family alive. Sra. de Madriago clearly needed some company anyway. Sra. Rosa would make Sra. de Madriago a cup of tea (how she wanted a cup herself!) and they would talk a little, like employer and employee of course, not confidants, and she would comfort Sra. de Madriago too.

"I don't know. Men in a car. No uniforms. They wore caps, not hats. The concierge let them in, the bastard, after all the tips we've given him, all the baskets I gave to his cursed family! They just took him off. They had guns and my husband had a gun too, but he surrendered, because of me. They promised him they would not bother me at all. Oh, I told him, I told him a dozen times, let's go I said, let's get out of this godforsaken communist sinkhole! I have family in Valladolid, we should have gone there even before the blockade, oh, oh. I told him. I told him."

Sra. Rosa stood there at the doorway, her employer blocking the way. She was unable to say anything more, because what she was thinking was exactly what Sra. de Madriago was saying: *Why didn't he go when he could have?* Why didn't he run away to that cold northern town Sra. Rosa had seen once and had no desire to visit again, that wealthy, conservative town that had welcomed the insurgents and whose bishop had blessed them?

Finally, Sra. de Madriago nodding her head miserably and without really seeming to realize that Sra. Rosa had not gone away yet, closed the door softly. It was the last Sra. Rosa ever saw of her. The muffled sound of slippers on thick carpeting retreated from Sra. Rosa into the big hallway behind that powerful mahogany door with the brass handle and elaborate doorbell plate that she had polished golden so that they reflected Sra. Rosa back on herself in bits and pieces. She turned and went back downstairs, her chest heavy with this disaster. Somewhere off to the north of the city, artillery boomed and boomed. Once she was back on the street, she looked up to the sky and silently cursed it.

She began her trek across the city again much slower now, the booming of mortars and the distant gunfire underlining her mood. The sounds were now a part of her life, and she was beginning to feel them like traffic sounds or a passing bus. Every tree she passed had become a possible source of fuel, as had the shutters of abandoned shops, and the ruins of buildings that had received direct hits. She went over the list of supplies she had at home: a quarter kilo of flour, a bag of tea more sticks than leaves, a quarter kilo of sugar, half a liter of oil, six tiny potatoes, one onion, a tin of sardines, a tin of tomatoes, (she could sell the tin cans themselves once they were empty), a package of plain breakfast cookies, a quarter kilo of red beans. Emilia had a similar hoard and maybe a piece of cheese. She wished she had yogurt. Rosa-Laura loved yogurt with a spoonful of sugar in it. She would sell that stupid copper pot this very morning, and get coins for it, not paper. The paper was getting worthless. Good for wiping your bottom now, that was all. She had to decide what to do about the old cobbler she'd found this morning, return and barter or forget him, leave him to die in his shop, old, without use in this world, his life of service gone, perhaps just like hers pretty soon. Maybe he had family he was trying to save, just like her. But if so, why didn't they protect him better, why didn't they keep him at home? Who would have thought it would come to this?

Of course, she never returned to the cobbler's shop. There was only so much you could do in this world, and Sra. Rosa found her life and her family swamped. *Who would have thought it would come to this.*

The war worsened; casualty reports were the first things people read upon going out and the last thing they checked before going home. Night after night and day after day the ordinary sounds of the city became artillery blasts, rockets screaming, bomb explosions, sirens, even machine gun fire. The militias of the less timid political parties had requisitioned the best hotels, thrown their doors open and turned them into hospitals or homes for those made homeless in the bombing raids or some of the thousands of refugees who had flooded the capital from outlying and invaded villages and suburbs. Many of the finer homes, the city's beautiful palaces, also went this way. Their owners had fled, and most *Madrileños*, their patience worn thin with bombings and lack of supplies, cared nothing about property rights. Volunteers kept the schools open, though there were rumors of a drive to send all the children in trains to Russia, where they would be safe.

Walking with Rosa-Laura on the city streets now would have been very dangerous, if not impossible. Many children had already been sent to Valencia, and there was talk that the government was planning to set up an alternate capital there. If they rounded up children to send them away to Valencia or this Russia they always talked about, the "workers' paradise," she'd hide, that's what. No one was taking her daughter away. She could better protect her than anyone.

The woman at the neighborhood dairy store told Sra. Rosa that outside Madrid the loyalists were fighting each other, because some big cheese in the anarchist party had been murdered foully by the communists. It made no sense to Sra. Rosa whatsoever: both those parties were supposed to be allied against Franco and the nationalists.

A little while ago, on a relatively mild Sunday morning, Sra. Rosa had taken Rosa-Laura and gone for a walk down the broad boulevard of the Castellana toward Alcalá Street and Retiro Park, just to walk under trees and show her child the fountains and trees. It was a sobering and informative journey. Most all the fountains had been sandbagged and cemented over to protect them. Many of the Ministry buildings had been bombed. They saw gangs of relief workers and militia opening up some eighteenth-century hundred-room mansion or palace or whatever, its gardens with their statues and carefully pruned greenery now full of men with boots and little concern for flowerbeds.

Right in front of the park, a battery of sixteen-inch guns had been placed. On the arches at Alcalá, huge posters of Lenin, Marx, and Stalin were hung. Sra. Rosa wanted to ask about those guys and why their pictures were there, as she had yet to see food or aid coming from them, but she was nervous about asking, because so many people were being denounced. Old scores were being settled this way, and fresh insults indulged. It was peculiar, the air of extreme solicitude and help from the neighborhood and party leaders regarding supplies, housing, and medical aid, juxtaposed with denunciations and infighting. Rumor was that the newspapers were even more censored now than before the war, though most people said it was all for the good, given the situation. Sra. Rosa kept her ears open to every bit of gossip, but felt it was unwise to ask questions.

Anyway, she had something more important to think about than the sorry political situation. Summer had broken with its usual incinerating heat wave. Sra. Rosa was down to one client only, and one client was not enough to earn rent and buy any food beyond the bare-gones of rations.

This client, Srta. Guillermina, was the ditzy old lady who lived three stories up in a very nice building on Serrano Street in Salamanca, a high-class, newer neighborhood above the Arch of Alcalá. She lived with her brother and their mother. The brother, Dr. Contreras, wasn't home during the day and oftentimes not at night either. He had plenty of work to do in the city tending to the wounded and dying. Sra. Rosa had figured out long ago that he was one of those guys who is more woman than man, which was none of her business anyway. Besides, one didn't talk about such things.

Cleaning and caring for their household was her longest-held job. At barely sixteen years of age she'd gone to their house to ask for justice for her sister. She had fixed her pinched, tired face hard so no one would notice her terror. As it happened, to her great shame she had walked into a funeral, the household full of wealthy guests, and the guy she'd come to confront was the deceased himself. She ended up disguising the original object of the visit with a half-witted, mumbled request for work instead. The brother was busy, the mother distraught, so Srta. Guillermina, as sweet and pretty as a windup doll and weirdly elated despite the somberness of the circumstances, had attended to Rosa and hired her on the spot. *El hombre propone, y Dios dispone.* Man proposes, God disposes, and thus it had worked out for the best.

Now she had worked for the family on and off for thirty years and never had reason to divulge the truth of her first visit. A chandelier hung in their dining room that would entertain Rosa-Laura for hours with its kaleidoscope of colors. It was a pity Sra. Rosa couldn't bring her along anymore. There were twelve chairs for the table, and a huge sideboard. The dining room, like the other rooms of the house, was relatively narrow for the massiveness of the furniture, so that even Sra. Rosa had difficulty moving her skinniness between the chairs, the walls, the sideboard, and the end tables. Pulling a chair out from the table gave you all of a foot's width to slide into it. Srta. Guillermina was hugely fat, and Sra. Rosa had no clue as to how she managed to even get to a chair, much less sit in it.

Srta. Guillermina's mother weighed more than she did. Sra. Rosa figured the old woman was in her seventies, the daughter past fifty, and the brother somewhere in his forties. Both women were about five feet six inches tall, and the brother was hefty too and tall as well, six feet, and over 200 pounds. Healthy, they were. Sra. Rosa would always be one of those people who considered height and a nice layer of fat on a body healthy. It meant they ate, and even during this war they were eating. When Sra. Rosa cleaned their house, she made a point of scrubbing every crevice, of working longer than usual, of being particularly quiet and self effacing to these people who were used to having servants do things for them. They needed her, of course, because they couldn't clean up after themselves, but she understood clearly she needed them more. It didn't look as they were going to up and run off. The brother had his work and seemed dedicated to it, voted for the Republic by the looks of things, and the mother and daughter were shocked at the bad manners of the generals who had risen against their own government. Not that that the grand Second Spanish Republic had gained much by these women's fidelity to its cause anyway, poor things.

They had a cook in during the day, and of course, cooks get to the food first. This cook had generally been fair with Sra. Rosa, but she had her own family to worry about. It made perfect sense she would favor them in the matter of leftovers and tidbits, especially now. Lately, however, the cook had been taking a good many things from the house, like pans and cutlery from the kitchen, and was even branching out into the salon and dining room. Sra. Rosa was deeply worried. What if the family decided to blame her for the little Italian box that had gone missing last week or the smallest shepherd that usually guarded his sheep behind the bigger ones on the long, skinny parquet console in the hallway? As if Sra. Rosa didn't have enough to worry about, now she faced getting blamed for the cook's greasy fingers.

And then one miserably hot evening Rosa-Laura cried and twisted for hours on their little cot, sickly and feverish with a summer cold.

The next morning, Sra. Rosa got up, heated the kettle quickly for a cup of hot water to drink and another to wash her own face, in readiness to leave for work. She had to work, no question there. The real question was, how to leave her sick child with her poor sister, who was not very well these days herself? Mili could not be trusted in these matters either; she was a wonderful playmate and Rosa-Laura adored her, but she was entirely capable of grabbing her little cousin by the hand and taking "a walk" uptown to see if she could find a candy vendor. Worse yet, she was entirely capable of begging the vendor for a handout, with Rosa-Laura observing and learning. Sra. Rosa decided she had to leave Rosa-Laura at home, check in with Emilia and let her know what was happening, then get to Srta. Guillermina's. She would clean faster today than usual and try to get home early.

"Daughter, Rosita, listen to your mother now," She said. The girl opened her blue eyes, which were red rimmed with fever and itching. "Um, I'm not taking you to Auntie Emilia today, because you're sick..."

"I'm not sick, Mama, really I'm not! I want to go play with Mili." But her forehead was still hot to the touch.

"No. Listen. Mind. You stay here. Um, I will tell Doña Pepa downstairs..."

"Mama, I'm afraid of Doña Pepa."

"Rosa-Laura, that's enough now." She threw on her shawl. "Doña Pepa won't eat you. We won't tell her you're sick. But if you need help, you go down and ask her and she'll get Auntie Emilia, OK? Now let's wash your face and comb your hair. Tell you what: you can have a piece of your Papa's candy later. I'll come back at lunch time to check on you."

Rosa-Laura understood her mother's instructions, but she was still afraid of Doña Pepa, the only lady she knew who had a mustache as well as eyebrows as fuzzy and black as the caterpillars that appeared in El Retiro Park in late summer. Doña Pepa always grinned at Rosa-Laura and pinched her cheeks. And it *hurt*. She didn't argue with her mother, though, ever. She did wonder if it would be very naughty of her to eat a piece of Papa's candy right away. Lately, there had been no cookies, no raisins, no apples. She wasn't hungry now though; she wanted something cold to drink. She let her mother clean her up, then, docile and sick to her stomach, she got back into bed.

Sra. Rosa covered her with a soft black old shawl instead of their blanket, cranked the window open but covered the pane with a rag to keep the hot sun off the bed, and left very quietly. As she closed her door, she gave a quick look around the single small room that was their home, never imagining for one moment it was the last time she would ever see it.

Downstairs, she smiled hypocritically at Doña Pepa, told her casually that she was leaving her daughter at home today so the child could rest, the heat you know, one just can't sleep these nights what with the noise of the artillery and all, and having done enough bald-faced lying to get her into purgatory for half of eternity, set off for Emilia's house. Emilia was asleep when she arrived, and Mili in the patio.

"Mama coughed all night," Mili told Auntie Rosa. "I'm letting her sleep this morning."

"Who put your clothes on then, you spoiled girl?" Sra. Rosa said. Her niece was eight years old and still had to be dressed.

Mili giggled. "Sra. Lourdes across the way. I got the dress on backward and she turned it around me and buttoned it. She gave me coffee and bread for breakfast."

"Where's she getting the coffee?" Sra. Rosa said. Shameless, really. The woman probably had a soldier somewhere, now that her husband had run off to war.

Mili shrugged at the question. Where did adults get anything? It just came, and if you smiled enough, looked hungry enough, and asked pretty please, they gave you some.

❧

And she left her niece without waking her sister and walked to the plaza. And the sirens sounded, and the bombs came, and she ran to the metro. And when the all clear sounded, she climbed the stairs again, and she saw the neighbor boys, the live one still holding on to the dead one's hand. And she ran home, her pounding heart slamming her ribs, her head clanging as if all the bells in Madrid had begun to ring in there.

❧

The building just up the street nearest the plaza from Sra. Rosa's was over 300 years old and often people said it should be torn down because the rooms were so small, ugly, drafty, and uncomfortable. Had Sra. Rosa been in a mood to appreciate irony that morning, she might have noted that it stood without a chip knocked off it. She didn't regard that building, however, because she was staring at her own building, which had received a direct hit and was now an eerie carnage of white mortar, yellow stone, beams sticking up like bones, and as far as she knew, her daughter somewhere inside.

The doorway itself was piled with debris, and Doña Pepa was lying there crumpled, bloody, and face down. Sra. Rosa fell to her knees before the doorway, turned Doña Pepa over and began to scream into the dead woman's face. Someone helped her up; she pushed them away and began to dig with her bare hands into the rubble. She pulled away a block of stone larger than her daughter, and where was her daughter? Where under all that? She dug toward the area their home might have been. A haze of dust dirtied her vision, and her throat hurt. It hurt to breathe, in fact. The air was still vibrating with booming and gunfire, but farther off, and the all-clear siren was sounding. At least a dozen people were there, including militia, the AG, neighbors, digging with her into the rubble of her building, her home. She did not notice them.

If once, just once, God behaved and gave her back Rosa-Laura, she would take the child to Mass every Sunday. Without fail. Every Sunday.

It was an impossible task. She was covered with white dust and looked like a fiend, her hair completely loosed from the bun at the back of her neck and standing straight out, her arms and hands bloody with clawing through the rubble. Several times her eyes caked with grit and dust; she closed them hard, blinking out the foreign matter by dint of will, and kept on digging, blind.

Finally, a guard stopped her by holding her arms, and said, "Señora, let us do the digging for a while. You sit down out there. You're in our way."

"She's a little girl. She's just turned six. She's under there."

"We'll find her."

She wouldn't have stopped, even at that, but they led her away. She sat on the narrow sidewalk, her feet in the gutter, her heart blasted. It was hard to remember to breathe, and she was dizzy enough to faint but didn't. She had no thoughts. She was empty. She had never felt such pain before, but could not cry at all.

"Rosa, is that you?"

She looked up at a neighbor standing over her. She couldn't remember who she was, just a neighbor, a tall pretty woman with a name that sounded like miracles, yet was not Milagros. A while ago she had seen this woman's sons in the plaza, and perhaps she had something to tell this woman, but no words came. She could not connect all these terrible, simple things together.

"Where are you going to stay tonight? With Emilia?" the neighbor said. "You can stay with us if she's too crowded. Or," and here she dropped her voice very low in case anyone was listening, "are you going to stay with the nuns?"

Sra. Rosa looked over at her building. No words came.

"It's just a building, *chica*, it's just an old building. We'll all take care of you and your girl," the neighbor said.

"My girl," Sra. Rosa said.

"It was lucky the nuns came when they did. I don't blame you at all, dear, it was probably the best for Rosa-Laura. Poor thing, she must have been so frightened."

Sra. Rosa looked up at her. "What are you saying? What are you saying?"

The woman stepped back a bit, the question was so harshly voiced, almost screamed.

"What is this about nuns?"

"Well," the neighbor said, shifting a shopping bag she carried to the other hand, "I saw her go off with—you know," and here she whispered, "the *nuns*, just after the bomb hit your house. I thought, well, they can serve a purpose after all—"

Sra. Rosa leaped to her feet like an acrobat, and half a kilo of dust flew off her into the air. She clutched the neighbor's arm so hard she hurt the woman, who yelped. *Lourdes, that was her name. Nuestra Señora de Lourdes, grant us a miracle.*

"I'm sorry, Lourdes, sorry, what nuns? I thought she was under the house, tell me about these nuns."

"Ah, no, girl, no, she was standing in front of the building just at the doorway, then up the street, then the sirens sounded, and I was looking at the sky then, and next thing after that, she went off with a couple of nuns. Well, you know, they weren't wearing their habits of course, they don't allow that nowadays, and who knows what they were doing in this neighborhood, but you can tell. The ones that are left, you can tell—"

"Where, Lourdes, which way?"

Sra. Lourdes took a deep breath, and thought a moment. "North, I think, toward Benavente maybe. I wasn't watching too closely at that point, I just figured she was safe. They went away from here. It's dangerous for them in this neighborhood, but they weren't bad ones, were they? I mean, I just thought they were trying to help—"

Sra. Rosa nodded and then turned to go, her mind so focused on Rosa-Laura that she'd totally forgotten the two little boys in the plaza.

Sra. Lourdes's eyes widened at Sra. Rosa's abrupt exit, and she called after her neighbor, "Rosa, Rosa, don't run off! Here, the AG will help you, just report this to them, they'll go get her—"

But Sra. Rosa had already turned the corner.

Lourdes turned away from the disaster and horror in the streets because there was nothing she could do and went home with the meager lunch she had managed to buy before all the bombs had hit. When she got home, only Augustín was there, playing with the girl from across the way, Emilia's pretty child. Lourdes knew Mili was a holy terror. Well, that's what poor neighborhoods produced, anyway. Her mother had a handful there.

"Augustín, where are your brothers?" she said to her son. He looked up at his mother with that implacably sweet and dumb expression that favored his face from the first day he was born, and shrugged for an answer. Mili smiled at her. The girlie had dimples all the way to China.

Lourdes went inside and dumped the contents of her crocheted bag out onto the table. They would have chard and a single potato for lunch, and the boys would cry bitterly. They didn't like chard for one thing, and they needed about two potatoes each for another. If they didn't all die in the bombings, they'd starve to death. Which was worse? She put the chard into a basket and took it outside to wash at the pump. At that moment, Sra. Erlinda came into their patio holding Anacleto's arm to guide him forward. He was sucking his thumb ferociously, a bad habit he had abandoned some years before. Two or three neighborhood women came right behind her, carrying Abelardo's small body.

Most of the Catholic clergy had fled the city. Priests had been beaten and killed, churches burned, and if nuns weren't being harassed or harmed, it was probably because everyone who hated them was too busy fighting. Just before the war the Right had spread countless stories of nuns being raped and murdered by the reds and the anarchists, some of which may even have been true. The sisters who had not escaped Madrid relocated to safer houses through the interventions of the devoted and stayed indoors. When they had to go to the streets they wore scarves, heavy stockings, and modest, tailored, mid-calf black dresses much like widows' weeds. Some kept small orphanages, orphans having been created in great numbers by the bombing and the dispersion of adults. They therefore served a purpose in the troubled times, and the new government, including the de facto governments of the neighborhood committees and communist cells, looked the other way, occupied as it was with more important concerns. Orphans not taken in had to be sent away to Valencia or to Russia, and it was hard on everyone. At war's beginning, the immense, luxurious Palace Hotel in Madrid had been requisitioned by the government as an orphanage for the many children of people caught in the crossfire in Andalucía and Extremadura, but now it was a hospital, like the Ritz.

Sra. Rosa knew about none of this. She had no idea why nuns would take her child, she didn't even know before this that there still were nuns in Madrid, but she was frantic to find Rosa-Laura. As she hurried up the street toward the city's center, she was shaking with a nausea that stopped her in her tracks when she was only a few blocks away. She bent over like a sick dog and heaved up the juice from her stomach, right onto the cobblestones.

By 6 p.m. of that worst day of her life, the sun still blazed fiercely, and the shady parts of the street were just a darker corner of the oven. She'd looked everywhere and had finally found her way to the old Municipal Hospital in Atocha neighborhood. She steeled herself and walked inside.

A corpulent old man sat at an ancient desk made elaborate a century ago with scrollwork and gilding, which was now further elaborated by wood-worms and decades of grease and dust.

"May I view the dead?" she said. He nodded without asking her for identification or plan. Things had gotten to that point that her appearance—haggard face, ragged, dusty, hands scratched and bleeding, hair on end—was enough.

She wandered through a vast gallery of granite with high ceilings and arches open to a wide central patio with a dry fountain. Everywhere raspy piles of brown leaves covered the slate-tiled floor and heaped into what was left of the fountain. She headed for the main salon just to the back of the patio.

What had once been a ballroom or salon a century ago was now a natural refrigerator for dozens of marble tables, and on every table, a wrapped corpse. The sight lacerated Sra. Rosa and brought the aluminum taste of bile to her mouth. She walked down the middle, where only adult-sized corpses lay, and then turned to the right and went back down that row. She found at least six children, none of them hers, and one woman so small she appeared to be a child, so that when Sra. Rosa pulled back the winding sheet she found herself staring stupidly at a gray face at least a hundred years old, the eyes as petrified and milky as a statue's, the head nearly bald, the toothless mouth opened to a purple hole. She continued, but her heart seemed to have stopped beating altogether, and she was afraid to breathe the air. *Thank you Mother Mary Most Holy, that she is not here, and I will take her to Mass every Sunday when I find her alive.*

Outside once again, she stopped, took a deep breath, and then realized that she was not thinking at all, that strange and fearsome ideas were forming in her head, swampy phantasms that stood in the way of figuring things out properly.

She had to calm down, stop bargaining with the Mother of God, figure this out, leave word everywhere, contact the government, contact the police, tell the neighbors in case the nuns returned and tried to find the family of the girl they thought they had saved, and so forth. She must not lose her mind because then she would surely lose Rosa-Laura. But she had to check the morgues and hospitals first.

∽⌢∽

Three days later, having marched from one end of Madrid to another and slept in the entrance ways to abandoned houses at night, Sra. Rosa returned to her neighborhood and Rogelio's apartment, looking like a hag from hell. She knocked on the door, and a stranger answered, a woman in her late thirties or early forties, very pale, gray-haired, vacant of expression. She finally focused on Sra. Rosa, a brush of fear swept cross her face, and she tried to shut the door. It took Sra. Rosa some explaining to let her know who she was and what had happened, especially as she herself wasn't sure she had even gotten to the right house any more.

Rogelio arrived home at that point, asked the woman to make some tea right away, and listened to Sra. Rosa tell her story. His eyes watered during the telling, but they watered easily anyway, and he managed to keep his air of blind dignity in front of the two women. He told Sra. Rosa he too would search and he would get word out and she was not to worry, whatever else had happened, she must be safe.

"Nuns are a peculiar lot, but they don't kill children and eat them, no matter what the reds say, Sra. Rosa."

Sra. Rosa um'ed and um'ed again and listened.

The new wife, if wife she was, offered Sra. Rosa food and a wash, but having gulped down a cup of hot chamomile tea, Sra. Rosa thanked them hurriedly and left to rush over to her sister's house. Emilia had had no word of her sister and niece these past three days and must be thinking the worst.

She limped into the patio at the *corrala*, her back and feet in a rage of pain. Mili saw her and screamed, "Mama, Mama, it's Auntie Rosa, it's Auntie, she's alive!"

It had been many years since Rogelio's blindness had bothered him in any way. He never even thought about it anymore, but the first night of the bombing raids, when the heavens broke into flames, he had been struck with a horrible paralysis and wanted to see so greatly that he thought his sight might burst back into his head like a lost child come home. He found himself outside, half naked, clutching his blanket around his chest, shoeless, his pants on but unbuttoned, not knowing how he'd managed to get there. He heard people around him, screams, everyone running back and forth. He started to run, got totally disoriented for the first time in his life and could not recognize the streets of his own neighborhood. He ended up in a plaza, crouched in a doorway until the hideous noise stopped. A militia man came and said, "Come out now, Señor, tell me where you live and I'll get you home. Or would you like to go the Red Cross? Just tell me."

Rogelio was deeply ashamed. He stood up, took the militia man's arm, and was led home. He wished he could offer the man something besides thanks, but money would have been insulting and anyway, he had no money. He ended up offering tea, but the militia man had said, "Ah, thank you, but I'm off now to find my unit. Good luck to you."

He had said "Good luck" because "God be with you" was reactionary and belonged to the enemy and their priests.

From that night on, Rogelio slept with his clothes buttoned and shoes on, despite the seasonal heat. When his neighborhood's watch committee told him he was eligible to go to Valencia, he agreed and waited his turn, but a few days later he happened upon Constancia, the poor woman who would become his new companion. And now Sra. Rosa had showed up to tell him Rosa-Laura was missing. She had some jumbled story about how nuns had taken the child. How could he flee Madrid then, what with having to search for his daughter and having to care for Constancia?

He offered Sra. Rosa his house, but she said she would stay at her sister's.

That was all right given that he was more or less married again, but he did think it would be easier for them to hunt for Rosa-Laura together. Or, perhaps he was fooling himself. He would probably be of no use and hinder any search Sra. Rosa would make.

The city had become a very hostile and strange place. Every day the surroundings and the streets changed. Just walking around presented dangers he had never had to worry about before. His cane would hit something totally new every few steps: piles of stones and rubble, tiles, cobblestones, bricks in places they should not be. Walls were treacherously weak and could not hold him nor guide him any more. There were very few dogs left, and they were hungry and when he heard them following him, he thought he could hear their hunger too. He believed they would not attack, they were only watching to see if he found food, but it was unnerving.

His beautiful city music was utterly gone, no birds, no horses, no children yelling and laughing, no gossipy women, no motor scooters. In their place, the sound of stones falling, of buildings creaking and stretching precariously, of people walking very quickly—people who bumped into him now, as never before, usually with apologies and surprise, yet still they seemed to be saying, "What, are you still here? Why aren't you dead yet?" But perhaps he was imagining that last part, feeling sorry for himself like a self-indulgent fool.

He also experienced something so disturbing he told no one about it, because he was afraid it meant he was going crazy. He heard people walk by, just walk by, and he heard or felt or knew somehow they were the enemy. He could feel their malevolence, their presence of danger and conspiracy. He knew they were there, watching every one and noting things for the others beyond the city perimeters. He was afraid.

Now maybe he'd lost his lovely daughter. She had never been truly his anyway, he was just the blind man who brought her goodies now and then. Yet, she was all that was left of Laura, and the possibility that the sweet child had disappeared into this alien, terrible, war landscape full of enemies he felt but could not denounce or even touch to see if they were real or not, horrified him more than anything else out there in the city. Never in his whole life, never, had he felt so useless, so invalid.

But no matter, none of these doubts. Afraid or not, blindness be damned, he would be of use again. He would start by notifying every neighbor that was left on his block, and then go to the next street, and the next, and ask any shopkeepers that were left to put up written posters. He didn't know at that point that there were posters and notices all over Madrid, seeking news of lost ones, leaving word for relatives who might show up and find a house transmogrified into a heap of broken gravestones, a monument to the dead.

Everyone in Emilia's building rushed out to see Sra. Rosa. They had all thought she was dead, despite word from Sra. Lourdes, who insisted she had seen both her and Rosa-Laura alive after the bombing. Lourdes hadn't been right in the head before her boy's death and was now even more distracted and strange, so no one listened to her when she claimed to have seen what were surely ghosts or visions.

Poor Emilia was on the verge of collapse, sallow, red-eyed from crying, and coughing so badly she could not say a word. She seemed to have more gray hair than before, and her hands were slightly blue. Sra. Rosa saw clearly she had not done well scouring the city for three days without asking for help or seeking out her sister or letting everyone know she was all right. She had gone off half crazy, and it had not helped Rosa-Laura at all. She must rest now and plan things better.

Emilia boiled water and prepared a galvanized tub and soap for her sister to bathe. Mili for once was trying to be helpful, but managed only to spill the water she brought from the well. Her sister and niece actually had to help Sra. Rosa wash and get her filthy clothes off, so she could fall into bed and a comalike sleep. When she awoke the next morning, almost twenty-four hours later, Mili was asleep and curled into her back. For a moment, she thought it was Rosa-Laura and they were back home. Emilia had slept in a chair, her feet extended onto another chair. Sra. Rosa was wearing one of Emilia's dresses, her own clothing probably hung up out in the patio along with the rest of the laundry. She found a pair of clean stockings from a box under the bed, put them on, then her shoes, then shook her sister slightly.

"Emilia, get up, girl. Get in bed with your daughter. I'm leaving now for a while. Have to go look for Rosa-Laura. Have to go see Srta. Guillermina too. Come on, girl, get out of that damned chair." Somewhere outside, cannon boomed.

Emilia got out of her chair with a groan, and Rosa helped her get into bed. Mili moaned slightly, but did not awaken. In a dwelling like theirs the inhabitants learned to sleep through commotion or not at all.

Outside in the patio, Lourdes was sitting on a chair, her arms folded, her eyes vacant. She didn't even say "*Buenos dias*" to Sra. Rosa, or evidently, notice her presence. Sra. Rosa suddenly remembered the two little boys in the plaza. She left hurriedly through the front door, without looking back. Her daughter was alive and safe somewhere. It might take her days, months, even years, up to the war's end maybe, before she found her but find her she would.

The walk from her neighborhood to her job on Serrano Street had become a trek through a wilderness. Everywhere, people were going about their business through mazes of rubble and fallen buildings, and the city had a ravaged air about it that said as much as the faces of its besieged occupants.

She arrived at Srta. Guillermina's house about 9 a.m. and climbed the three flights of stairs to the flat very slowly, each step a torture on her knees and feet and back. At the landing, she stopped for a while to catch her breath, which was when she noticed two men of about twenty or even younger, watching her from down the hall. She gave them a hard stare. They looked away, and she rang the bell. No one answered. She began to fear her bosses had fled the city. Somehow packed up the old lady and covered the shepherds and shepherdesses with sheets and run away.

Finally, the door opened, ever so slightly. Dr. Contreras peeped out and looked at her blankly, as if he didn't recognize her, then said, "Sra. Rosa? What are you doing here?"

"Señor, I am so sorry I didn't come the other day. My house got bombed you see. My daughter Rosita-Laura is missing, some nuns took her. I couldn't come just then, but I need the work, Señor. I'll make up for not coming sooner. I'll work twice as hard..."

"Sra. Rosa, we have been denounced. I thought you didn't come because of that."

"Um, Señor?" she said, by way of a question.

"In fact," he said, "we thought you had denounced us too."

"Oh no Señor, no, not me, Sir, I wouldn't do that."

He gave a great sigh and opened the door but before she could enter, the two young men at the end of the hallway suddenly marched up behind her.

"Are you a friend of this man, Señora?" one said to her.

"And what business is that of yours, snot-nose?" Sra. Rosa said.

The Doctor winced. The two young men backed off a bit and looked at each other for guidance, like two school bullies checking reactions.

The Doctor said very softly, "Understand, Sra. Rosa, they are watching us now, and perhaps it would be best for you to consider that before entering."

Sra. Rosa turned to the young men and confronted them full face. "This is my job. I must make a living or my daughter and I will starve. That what you want? Back away."

The two young men looked at each other again and finally, one shrugged and they stepped back toward the staircase, to lean against the wall and light cigarettes.

Sra. Rosa stepped into the foyer of Dr. Contreras's house with no hesitation and then gasped at the mess—tables overturned, potted plants disgorged onto the Persian rugs, knick-knacks everywhere broken. "Oh, Mother Mary! What a mess! Sir, please tell me, what happened?"

It was then she saw just how disheveled Dr. Contreras looked. He had his maroon and gold smoking jacket on, wrinkled and the cuffs dirty. He was still in his silk pajamas and tooled Moroccan slippers at this late hour. His long hair, usually combed and pomaded to drape over his balding skull, was mussed and hung lank around his ears and collar, his eyes were ringed with dusky gray circles, and his skin was pale and opaque, not ruddy as usual. When he was upset or angry, he tended to some effeminacy, flapping his hands from the wrists, sucking his lips and pursing them, and walking about as if on tiptoes. He was so now, yet at the same time, he was leaden, distracted. He wrung his hands over and over and looked down the hallway at the floor, then at her feet, then up—everywhere but at her.

"Well," he said, "I got angry at the cook, you see. I shouldn't have, I suppose. It was just that, well, my sister was missing some things, and I was so tired that I really didn't want to deal with it, Sra. Rosa, so I suppose I was hasty, and I blamed the cook..."

"You put the blame where blame was due," Sra. Rosa said. "But she's got family to feed, Sir. Don't be blaming her too hard. I haven't stolen nothing from you, never, I swear on my life. But I'm not saying I wouldn't be tempted if things got too hard to bear."

He nodded. "It was so ugly. I really hate scenes. My blood pressure..."

Sra. Rosa understood. When his sister or his mother got hysterical and he was unable to calm them, he usually abandoned the house altogether.

"Those two boys are the 'Public Investigation Brigade' for this block. They came after the cook brought the militia to search our house. They have been watching us for two days. I have been threatened with arrest. I'm lucky I wasn't shot outright, like another man I knew—ah, but they need doctors. Perhaps they will let me—"

"What?" said Sra. Rosa. She knew what "denounced" meant, but it had not registered before this. She had pictured a scene and recriminations—Srta. Guillermina and her family could be like that, very theatrical—but she had not pictured militia, guns, the apartment tossed upside down, young thugs watching the place.

Dr. Contreras looked so frightened and ashamed she felt truly sorry for him, but her real concern was more basic and selfish: had she lost her last job? It would give her more time to look for Rosa-Laura, but how would she eat, how would she feed her child once the girl was found?

"You see, Sra. Rosa, the militia—the cook said we were fifth column. She said we were sending information to the enemy. But we aren't, I swear it, we are loyalists through and through! I've spent months working with the wounded, and now they say I can't work anymore—"

"Where did these militia men come from? Is there a barracks around here? A station?"

"A military center—Sra. Rosa, you believe me don't you? It was just a misunderstanding with the cook. We'll never do it again, it's just—" He was almost crying now. It astounded her. Here was a doctor who could look at a gaping wound to the belly and stuff the entrails back in, who would dismissively roll his eyes when his mother or his sister told him about all the men who followed them home, who was such a fussy boss he insisted the crystal chandelier be dismantled, cleaned, and polished once a month. Sra. Rosa had to restrain herself from slapping him and telling him to find his damned balls and take courage.

"Look, Sir," she said, "Let's go to that military center, you and me. I'll tell them what I know, and you can help me put in a report about my daughter. My Rosa-Laura. My building was bombed out, I got no home no more. My girl, she was taken away by some nuns. So, you see, I have my own troubles, but you and me, we can help each other, don't you think? I'm just as working-class as the cook. I can say some things about her too. You get dressed now. I'll clean up. When you're ready, we'll go together."

The words worked magic on the despondent man, clicking on his years of discipline and hard-learned restraint. He stopped wringing his hands, he stood up straight, he remembered who he was.

"Well, yes, Sra. Rosa, how kind. And your daughter? This is really terrible, your building bombed? Some nuns you say? Perhaps I can help with that. I can ask around, as a doctor you know, I get all around the city, let me get ready, yes—"

He rushed off to change his clothes, and Sra. Rosa did a quick inspection of the flat while he did. The apartment had been "searched," every room. Broken porcelain spangled the rugs, chairs had been knocked down and broken, entire cabinets of knick-knacks and plates and books pushed over. Disgusting mess. It was going to take her a couple of days to right this, but the thought did not displease her. They needed her. They didn't know how to clean all this up. The soldiers had come more than a day ago and not even a shard of porcelain picked up yet.

The Doctor came out, dressed in his suit and an elegant Italian tie. He looked around the hallway somewhat perturbed, and Sra. Rosa got the shoe buffer brush out of a small cabinet and handed it to him. He smiled, distracted.

"Doctor, one thing—your mother and your sister?"

"In bed, since yesterday," he said. It was almost a groan more than a statement. "They have been broken, stunned. I don't know how my mother will survive this. The shame, the horror, the fear, the shock—"

"Well, um, but you go talk to them a bit, um, let them know we're going to fix it all up."

He sighed, wiped his eyes, and left her in the hallway, working on the mess there. As for the cook, *La avaricia es mar sin fondo y sin orillas.* Greed is a sea without bottom or coastline. How shameless, to save herself from a scolding she deserved by putting the family that fed her into so much danger. Literally fed her, with all the food she'd pilfered over the years, damn her. Some people had no shame, no sense of propriety or honor. They'd steal from children, too, as they did from her and Emilia, and blame it on the vagaries of birth. You could blather on all you wanted about the nobility of the working class, but that cook was a bitch, period.

∞

Dr. Contreras had lived his entire life in a precise, traditional world and learned its hard lessons well. He could handle the worst medical situations with a calm hand and a calm head, drawing upon all his considerable education, knowledge, and experience. He was socially adept, handling servants, police, patients, and other lesser beings with dignity and a certain attitude that came not only from his station in life and his profession, but from his having accepted the rules presented him since birth. Even during that nasty business with his stepfather he had been composed, sure of the justice of his plan, careful in its execution. Rules were rules, and tradition was tradition.

But now tradition had been pushed aside and new rules made. Nothing was familiar. At the neighborhood militia center, because of his class he would be suspect and at the mercy of a group of very young, politically fanatic soldiers. And it was true, his illiterate little housecleaner of all people just might be able to intercede for him.

The neighborhood's military station was located in what had been an upscale storefront before the war. The plate glass windows had been boarded over and the exterior sandbagged. Sra. Rosa felt a run of scorn at all that: what bombs fell in this neighborhood? Waste of time and good lumber.

Inside, the shop-turned-military-center was dingy and ill-lit, and there were kids everywhere. Children in uniforms. Boys and girls hanging around, flirting with each other, serious and proud of themselves.

"*Buenos días, buenos días,* hey, we need to talk to you about a big mistake you guys made," she said as she entered, her bold attitude hiding the fact that she was nervous. Dr. Contreras came in behind her, quietly, intimidated.

"*Buenos.* What is it you want, comrade?" a young man in khaki with filthy boots said.

"I'm no comrade," Sra. Rosa said. "I'm just a woman who cleans houses. I got bombed out a few days ago, and I lost my daughter..."

"Oh, mother, your loss is ours," a young woman said to her.

Sra. Rosa stared hard at her. "No, it's not, *hija.* I thank you for the sentiment, but she's still alive somewhere, and I must look for her, and I must work too, because war or no war, that's how we survive, us who stayed in this godforsaken place. And you made a big mistake here with this gentleman. He's a doctor. He's been helping all of you, and he's a genuine supporter of our Republic. He votes and everything. And he's loyal. And you set the dogs on him."

"Mother, why are you here?" another man said. He had come up behind the first two kids. He had a hat on, a sort of army cap but one Sra. Rosa had never seen before. He had nicotine-stained hands, callused, with a huge angry-red scar across the right one. His face was serious but very young, a boy's face really, dirty, and certainly tired. He had red and gold buttons embossed with a bearded man's sharp profile affixed to his cap and his sweater, which was khaki green and had leather shoulder patches. The sweater was also mended in a hundred places and not very well. His pants were rumpled and boots dirty. He looked as if he hadn't had a good night's sleep since the siege had begun. No surprise there.

"I'm not your mother, so stop calling me that. I'm Sra. Rosa, this man's cleaning lady. He's Dr. Arturo Contreras del Valle, lives over on Serrano. He's no spy, I'd swear to that. You got some nasty types watching him and his family. Don't you need those little bastards to do something more useful than hang around all day smoking in his corridors? Send them to the front."

The young soldier appeared to be the one running things. He looked around and established eye contact with a girl leaning over a desk. She got up slowly, stubbed out her cigarette in a chipped pottery bowl overflowing with butts and went over to some file cabinets behind her. She found a skinny yellow file and brought it to the soldier.

"This is it, Captain."

"Good Lord in heaven, you're a captain? You don't look like you're even eighteen yet," Sra. Rosa said. The young soldier blushed darkly, but the girl who'd handed him the file smiled and quickly turned away.

"Listen," Sra. Rosa said, anxious not to lose momentum, "you must straighten out this business with my boss here. And help me find my girl. She's only six. The neighbors told me she got taken by nuns. To some orphanage. The Doctor here, he can help too. He gets all over the city, because he's a doctor, he's needed everywhere, and he tends the soldiers at the front too, he hasn't run from his duty here. You got some great nerve, you do, setting the dogs on a loyalist. What is this world coming to? Has this damned war made us all savages?"

"Christ, put her in a uniform," one of the other soldiers said. "She's a dwarf but she sounds like she'd make a fine soldier."

"Mind your tongue," the Captain said. He looked up from the file, his face black with fury. "Don't treat a worker, a mother of the revolution, like the damned upper classes do!"

The "mother of the revolution" felt a slight sense of exasperation. Babies with rifles, poor kids, so serious, including that couple of girls over there smoking cigarettes and dressed in pants, (cheeky things).

"You speak for this man, Mother? How can you be sure he's not a spy? He's rich," the Captain said.

"I worked for him for years. He voted for the Republic straight through. He's a good man. He tends to poor people for free. Sure, he's one of his class, I don't deny that, but he's never cracked any whip over me. Always been fair and paid me good. And the cook who denounced him, you got that in that there file? She's a bitch and a thief. She's been robbing his place for years now, and I never said nothing because it's not my business, although I was always scared I'd get blamed too, but I never was. He's got a crazy sister, [The doctor winced openly at this point in Sra. Rosa's narrative and took a deep breath.] and his poor mother's old and not too well herself. He didn't leave the city did he? He didn't even send away his family. He just kept on working, harder and harder, and collecting no money, I can tell you that. Then, he gets into a discussion with that damned cook and she comes running to you to hide her thievery! I tell you, look at the situation here! It's my word against hers, and you can check this all out. You need friends like him, ones can clean up your wounds, like that red mess on your hand, Captain."

The Captain checked over the file again and the girl who'd given him the file said, "Respectfully, Comrade Captain, it wouldn't hurt for the doc to look at that wound."

"It's my hand," the Captain said. "Just a bruise. It's nothing."

"Ecchymoses has set in," the doctor said, in a very low voice. "It could even go to gangrene. Small wounds can develop into bigger ones. Just let me..."

"Enough, I'm too busy for this crap!" the Captain said. "We'll clear your file for now. I'll send someone to remove the men watching your apartment. But don't let me hear about you again from some other of your disgruntled workers. And let me see your papers. Didn't anyone in this place think to check papers? If everything's all right, you can return to your duties as a doctor."

"Thank you, Captain," Dr. Contreras said, noticeably chastened.

"Um, yes, brilliant," Sra. Rosa said. "You let him do what he's good at, as if you don't need him more than he needs you."

"Mother, if we had bullets like your words, we'd win the war today," the Captain said.

"*Son,* haven't you got enough to do without paying attention to every thieving servant with a grudge to settle?" Sra. Rosa said. "You want to put the boys at his house to work, tell them to find my child."

The Captain did not reply. The inspection over, the Doctor very quiet, he and Sra. Rosa left the station and hurried home to present the "Public Investigation Brigade" a signed order for them to desist and return to the station for orders on harassing some other family.

At the doctor's request, Sra. Rosa cooked him something he called an "English breakfast," which he barely touched before he left, probably because she had accidentally broken the yoke of the damned fried egg. She was no cook after all, and who ever heard of eating an egg in the morning instead of in the evening? But, as food is food she ate it herself half-cold. She hadn't had an egg in weeks, and her poor baby loved them so.

The ladies were ecstatic over the good news of their deliverance, not to mention effusively grateful, but were so overcome with emotion they decided it was best to stay in bed. Sra. Rosa swept the flat, uprighted the chairs, pushed the consoles and tables back into their places, and washed the floors. She brought the the Señora and Señorita sandwiches for lunch, which was the best she could do under the circumstances. She made a pot of tea because there was no coffee at all. She also tallied up the damage and reported it to Srta. Guillermina, who burst into tears.

"My Sèvres vase," she said. "I so loved that piece! It was a gift, from the Count of Romanones, worth a fortune, thousands," she said. Sra. Rosa said nothing, absolutely nothing, to that. It was not that she thought the green flower pot, with its pleasant fan-shaped top and painting of flowers and aristocratic girls, wasn't pretty; it was just hard to imagine that a French pot was worth more than the wages of her entire lifetime.

Around 5 p.m. the Doctor came home for a siesta then he went out again for the night, telling her that he had left word at every hospital and morgue and had also asked around to see if any of his colleagues or anyone else knew of more places where orphans were kept. Between Sra. Rosa's loyalty and his own ability to be of use, he had recovered his composure and self-esteem. He hadn't spent an entire lifetime in a hostile and rigid world hiding his very nature just to let something like a malevolent cook destroy him.

"The word is out, Sra. Rosa," he said. "We will find your daughter."

Rosa-Laura thought she had slept for hours and hours after Mama left, but in fact, her feverish nap consumed only a few minutes. Hot, over-rested, thirsty, itchy-eyed, she tossed the shawl her mother had covered her with to the floor, then got up and carefully put it back on the bed, because throwing things on the floor was a bad and dirty habit that made Mama unhappy.

She did not like being left alone. She wanted Mili very much, so much that she found herself at the door, her shoes unbuckled on her stockingless feet, and a couple of pieces of Papa's candy in her hands. Her hands were sweaty and the doorknob was hard to turn, but she did get out. She went downstairs very rapidly for a sick child (the stairwells were dark, hot, and full of whispering creepy things and noises behind walls), and then she snuck past Doña Pepa's doorway, more as a reaction than anything she had planned. The street was brilliantly white with heat and floury dust. She'd passed the portal when she heard the sirens. Suddenly everyone was running around her, and she was so terrified she stood there for a moment and realized she just might have to cry. She ran across the street, not noticing Sra. Lourdes watching her from down the block near a boarded-up shop. A pair of strange women caught her by the arm and stopped her. They were dressed in long-sleeved black dresses that hung almost down to their ankles. They had scarves on their heads, too. Their clothing was not so different from her mother's, yet something was not ordinary about it. They looked at her, then at each other, as if communicating by glance.

The one with wire frame glasses on a pinched, tired, and anxious face said to her, "Child, go with us. The planes are coming. God is punishing us for disobeying him."

Rosa-Laura understood that the street was dangerous and the planes with bombs were coming, that's what the sirens always meant, but the rest of the statement made no sense.

"How did you disobey God?" Rosa-Laura asked. Her mother and

Auntie Emilia always said the planes came because bad men wanted to steal Madrid from everyone living there and thought by bombing it people would run away. Sometimes she wanted to run away too.

The too-close boom of impact began, and suddenly dust and rocks were flying everywhere as people screamed.

The nun with the glasses said, "Let's take her. Hurry."

The other one said, "Isabel, are you sure?"

"She's an orphan. Look at her. She doesn't even have stockings."

Rosa-Laura knew then she was in trouble. Her Mama always put her stockings on her, no matter how hot the weather, and so it stood to reason you could not wear shoes without stockings, and unbuckled as well. It marked you as an orphan, and orphans were sent to Russia. She had heard Mama and Auntie Emilia discussing that very thing a day ago.

"Are you going to send me to Russia? I don't want to go to Russia."

"Oh my poor child, no, never—Mary-Margaret, the planes, we must hurry. Take our hands, child, trust in God."

Did that mean these ladies were God? Surely not. God was a man. Everyone always said "He" and besides, God ran things and was the father. Mili had told her that. At that moment, half her block seemed to disintegrate with a roar, and the ladies ran, ran for their lives, lifting her a foot off the ground by her arms so that she was suspended between them like a rag on clothesline.

They ran from the neighborhood, the ground shaking beneath them. Rosa-Laura remembered that morning for the rest of her life, as if she had been whipped to instill the remembering of it. Buildings moved crazily, the sky vibrated, the planes came very close, maybe they even landed in the plaza because that's how close they seemed, and pieces of everything fell around her and the two ladies. She and her captors entered a world of dust and ear-pounding, flooding noise. Though the fierce grips held her high, she could see nothing through the dust, but one of the ladies screamed, she heard it through the bombing and the haze—it was a jumble and she could find no still center to it.

They emerged somewhere, and then she glimpsed a shop that sold *alpargatas* where Mama had bought her a pair of red canvas shoes with red ribbons and hemp soles once. They were for summer, and though Mama didn't like them because they were poor people's shoes, Rosa-Laura had loved them. "At least they're red," Mama had said later to Auntie Emilia. "Maybe they'll think she's from Aragón and going to dance *jotas*." Both women had laughed at that, but Rosa-Laura didn't understand the joke until years later.

The ladies would not stop. Rosa-Laura was exhausted. She had finally been lowered to the ground so that she ran between them, still tightly held, then suddenly, her legs refused to walk anymore. Though she tried very hard not to, she had to cry. "I want my Mama," she said. Then she was crying, as hard as she had ever cried in her life, and the noise of it shook her as much as the bombs had.

One of the ladies, the one called Isabel, picked her up, with a loud sigh. The lady's shoulder smelled like something that bit the inside of Rosa-Laura's nose. She slept, then awoke, hotter than ever, as the lady was putting her down on a chair inside the biggest room she had ever seen, bigger even than some of the houses where her mother worked. It was also dark, the ceiling *way* above her, the furniture huge, made for giants, but surely not these ladies who weren't much bigger than Mama. In a corner stood a truly terrifying figure all one color like a big dull-colored dog standing upright, with one hand reaching up and two fingers thrust in the air. It was a very still figure, and it would be several days before she understood that it was a statue like the ones in the park. It had a very strangely shaped hat on its head and wore a long dress.

"She has a fever," Mary-Margaret said. "Perhaps we should not have brought her."

"Find a room separate from the other girls. We'll have to keep a watch on her in case it's contagious. God's will be done."

They gave her some water to drink and put her in another dark room, this one smaller, but not much more comforting.

"When can I go back to my Mama?" she said as the lady called Isabel was taking off her shoes. "Can I take off my dress? It's hot."

"It's a sin to disrobe," Isabel said, whatever that meant, "and your Mama's not coming back. She was in the building that was bombed. God is punishing us, and many parents are dying because of their sins. Madrid is hateful to God."

None of that made any sense, and Rosa-Laura began to cry again.

"Courage now! God will protect you," The lady said.

That reminded Rosa-Laura of her mother saying "*Anda, hija*, take courage, take courage. Don't be a big crybaby. You're my girl now, no need to cry." So, Rosa-Laura stopped because it was good not to cry. It showed you were brave and had heart and weren't a baby. Mama would have been proud.

"Who's the man in the big room?"

Isabel looked at her somewhat baffled. "What man? There are no men here, daughter, this is a place for women and girls only."

"I saw a man in a dress in the big room."

"Do you mean the Bishop? He is the founder of our order. He is a saint now. Pray to him for your soul's deliverance."

Again, nothing made any sense whatsoever. The lady tucked her into bed, a cot not much larger than the one she had at home (how she wanted to go back home! If they took her home, she would never, ever disobey Mama again). Above her a window shimmered with slices of light trying to break though the heavy curtains. A very large crucifix hung on the wall in front of her. The face of the Jesus ran with tears because he was in terrible pain hanging on the cross like that but normally men did not cry, any more than her mother did. Sometimes she had seen grown women cry. The sight always shook her, and made her world seem fragile and frighteningly brittle.

She fell asleep again, even though she knew that the lady would leave her all by herself once she did. She dreamed of running through streets until she thought she would choke with the hurt of running, and the red ribbons on her red shoes were coming undone, but she could not stop and get them tied properly. She knew that she had to stop, because if she didn't she would go too far and her mother would never find her, but she couldn't stop running no matter how hard she tried. Then a huge, solid-colored man as tall as the towers on the churches flew out at her and told her she was an orphan now, and if she wasn't good, she'd get sent to Russia, because that was where bad people went.

☙❧

Night at the orphanage brought many nightmares, and when she was awake, she was exhausted and confused and missed her mother terribly. She could not get her bearings, and she did not understand why Mama didn't come and get her. She was terribly afraid she'd done something really, really wrong and this was a punishment, which was what the ladies—there three other ladies besides Isabel and Mary-Margaret, and they called each other "sister"—were telling her all the time anyway. They were completely shocked that she didn't seem to know any real prayers beyond *Hail Mary, full of grace*—and told her that her mother must have been very wicked not to have taught her to pray. That sent her smack down on the floor sobbing. One of the ladies said, "See, she is an uneducated little savage, and it proves her mother was a wicked woman!" So she stopped immediately by holding her breath and pushing her fists into her mouth. And that must have been the right thing to do, because then Srta. Isabel gave her a seed-bead rosary and told her to pray with it for the soul of her mother. At the befuddled look on Rosa-Laura's face, Srta. Isabel sighed and showed her how to use it—*Hail Mary* was useful after all—and promised to help her learn the Credo and the Our Father as well. Rosa-Laura thought the rosary was as pretty as a necklace, and running its beads through her fingers was soothing. The rosary had to be counted at least once a day. She could do that, easily. Counting was fun.

It was then that she realized she could count the days until Mama came and that would make them go by faster. She could even use the rosary to count, but she would not tell them because they might take it away from her if she didn't do it exactly their way. By the tenth day or the first section of the rosary, she was calm and as the fever had long passed and left her upright and hungry, the ladies gave her little jobs to do so her hands would not be left to the devil's devices. Rosa-Laura had heard about the devil before this; her mother had often told her that men were the devil, in fact, but always with a rueful smile as if it were a special joke. Now Rosa-Laura wondered if that frightening statue of the bishop in the big room at the entrance to the house was the devil. She asked just once, and got spanked. Sometimes when she was naughty, Mama would wave her hand in the air with a frown and threaten to swat her but the hand never really connected, not like this. The lady picked up Rosa-Laura bodily all of a sudden, threw her across her lap, and spanked her. It stung and hurt, and Rosa-Laura howled. Afterwards she never liked that particular lady again, but it made no matter, for the woman continued to spank her again and again as the days passed.

Emilia hated to cry around Mili. It upset her girl no end, which was understandable. Mothers weren't supposed to cry, only children. The thing was, she had always been the child before this, her mother's baby, her big sister's baby, then her husband's baby. Now she had her own baby, but no mother, no husband, and a big sister so swamped with her own problems she paid no attention to Emilia any more.

Emilia could not comprehend how Rosi could go on day after day, working at the Doctor's house, searching for her child in the early mornings, during siesta, in the evenings, visiting houses pointed out by neighbors, friends, the Doctor's contacts. Rosi was, as usual, fearless, enduring.

As those next months passed, Emilia tried not to be overwhelmed with depression and wretchedness, arguing with herself that soon this stupid, horrible war would be over, soon Rosi would find Rosa-Laura, soon she herself would be healthy and well, soon everything would be better. She was accustomed to being guided and taken care of, and knew her own weaknesses ruled over her sense of preservation. The nuns, for example, had made much of her and treated her like a favorite, but in a moment of lust, she had fouled that kindness and lost the safety of the cloister.

Little did anyone know what sins she was capable of. That was why God took her husband and their son, her second child, from her so soon, because He loathed her spectacular sins. All the confessions in the world had not cleansed her, no matter what the priest had said. She'd hinted at that once to Rosi a long time ago and had gotten such a scolding she never mentioned it again. But would Rosi have loved her so much if she'd known how Emilia had turned her back on her first baby? How she ignored its cries, loathed feeding it, couldn't bear to hold it—would Rosi have understood that? Even though Rosi hated its father, she had not hated the baby, ever. And the presumption, that awful presumption she'd indulged when her little boy, her husband's true child, was born, that everything would be fine, that she'd been forgiven—gone swiftly, gone forever. Only Mili had been left to her, and she kept her head bowed so God wouldn't notice her anymore.

Emilia desperately wanted to flee Madrid, but said not a word to Rosi. What would Rosi do left all by herself at the hardest time of her entire life?

The government had a sanatorium in a village near Valencia for people like Emilia. It was free and safe. Besides, she was losing work because of her sickness; people weren't stupid after all, they could hear her cough and see her wasting away. Worse yet, Mili was always out, wandering around the neighborhood, possibly even begging or stealing. The girl often came home with a bit of food, a trifle, something that she'd bring to her mother, and which Emilia would often not even taste, until Mili herself ate it, sighing but voracious. The child had a good appetite and no cough. Thank God.

One of these days Mili would disappear too, like Rosa-Laura, if Emilia wasn't careful. Best they left. Best they fled. Rosi had to stay and search for her own daughter. Were Rosa-Laura not lost, Emilia would have been able to convince her sister to leave the capital too even though Rosi had a ferocious dislike of the provinces and the people there.

The women in the neighborhood People's Health Committee were the first to tell her—very emphatically and with a great deal of sympathy even as they kept their handkerchiefs over their mouths and noses and argued with her loudly—that Valencia was a better place for her. They urged her to consider her duty to the Republic and its citizens, given as how her lungs might be polluting the whole building, not to mention the rest of the neighborhood. They emphasized that Valencia was a warmer area, humid, and the sanatorium there equipped to deal with "her problem." They told her that Valencia wasn't affected by the boycott that kept Spain from getting medicine. The committee ladies had powerful and convincing arguments, and Emilia's slight resistance toppled at the moment they solemnly promised her that the area endured no bombing raids. They did not bother to mention that leaving Madrid was, to say the least, difficult. Trains were bombed every day.

Emilia had seen Valencia once. It was a lovely city. She'd passed through it on her honeymoon, a train journey that took her and her dear new husband down the coastal curve of the Balearic Sea from Barcelona to Valencia, and then toward Madrid once again. It was the last journey she had made out of the capital, not counting a few weekends in Alcalá de Henares and Aranjuez. As for her sister, as best as Emilia could recall Rosi had never journeyed outside of Madrid after that first and last miserable trip when she was still just a girl and had to go to the courts in their mother's province to try and get some justice regarding the loss of their inheritance. Emilia didn't know a great deal of what had happened that time. Rosi had returned with the sort of expression you see only on people who have spent the day at the funeral of all their dreams.

"*Somos cabreadas, chica,*" was all she'd said. We're screwed, girl.

The sisters never spoke of it again nor attempted to contact their mother's family. The shame of their situation did not interrupt their lives again until Emilia married and the priest looked long and hard at her birth certificate. She was humiliated, but her husband hadn't cared. He was such a good soul that he didn't even ask any obvious questions when the child was born seven months later. And when that baby died, well, he just shook his head at the pity of it and paid for a decent funeral, but accuse her of anything or remind her of her low beginnings, never. He had coddled her and cuddled her and taken care of everything, a man too good for this world, and then his son was taken from him and look what happened to him as well.

෨ஐ

One particularly awful night Emilia, Mili, and Rosi ran from the neighborhood with dozens of other neighbors, ran and ran until they all reached the outskirts of the city and ended up sleeping in the countryside, or trying to, under a rushing mantle of rocket fire and explosive lights. Huddled together on the wet ground, Emilia admitted to Rosi that she wanted to go to Valencia. That she could not stand it any more. That she was so fatigued from her sickness and so frightened of the bombings she was afraid she was going insane. That she wanted Rosi to come with them, but knew she wouldn't come. Rosi said *um* but nothing more, and Emilia eventually fell asleep, with lurid, obscene dreams lit up like a countryside under bombardment.

The next morning they all filed back into the neighborhood, everyone gray from sleeplessness, exhaustion, mud. In the courtyard, Emilia and Rosi washed up a bit at the fountain. Mili was dancing around the patio, refusing to sit still or be cleaned up. She had her eye on the street outside, and her aunt had her eye on Mili.

"Don't you be running off, girl. I'd be right after you. Believe that!" Rosi said.

Emilia started to say something, but forgot what before she got even a word out, and suddenly began coughing. It hurt to cough, as if someone were scrapping the inside of her chest with a razor. Her sister tried to help her, but Emilia turned away and coughed into her woolen scarf, which was soon a sodden ball of blood.

"Oh Blessed Mother in Heaven, do not touch me, Rosi," Emilia said. "Stay back. Keep Mili away—" as the girl ran up to help her mother or hug her. She finally stopped, but then sat there, clumped down on the patio tiles, bawling like a baby. She wanted to scream but she didn't have the breath.

"Stop that, girl," Rosi said softly. "Stop it now. You're right you know, what you said last night. You got to go to Valencia. You go where there's doctors and everything. I'll go talk it out with the People's Health Committee this morning, before I go to work. I'll stay here at the house and keep it for you. Whatever happens, I'll be here, all right? That's how we'll keep in touch. When this damned war is over, and I get Rosa-Laura back, and you're better, we'll all meet here, right? Right?"

Emilia finally stopped sobbing. Lourdes stepped out into the patio, timidly, and glanced at Sra. Rosa. As if they had communicated telepathically, both hefted Emilia up off the tiles and helped her into bed, Mili behind them. Afterwards, Lourdes filled a bucket with water and half a cup of bleach and soaked the scarf in it and washed down the patio tiles. Sra. Rosa helped, then wiped her own hands off with the bleachy water, commenting absentmindedly to Lourdes that she hated the smell of bleach, even though she had to use it every day cleaning houses. Lourdes nodded in agreement.

"You stay with your mama. I got to go to work," Sra. Rosa said to her niece. "I'll bring food home. Just stay with her, don't go running off. It scares her, Mili. Besides, you and her are going to Valencia. Soon as I can arrange it. No bombs there, girlie, it's nice and warm and safe. Your Mama can have medicines and be cured. You going to mind me?"

Mili nodded. She even meant it.

Sra. Rosa walked across town to Srta. Guillermina's house shuffling, somnambulant, dragging each foot through a swamp of fatigue and depression. Her dress needed washing. It was dusty from the countryside and stained with Emilia's blood. If she didn't watch out, she'd get the lung disease too, and that would make it so much harder to get around town and check the orphanages and schools and the morgues. She didn't have time to go to the People's Health Committee just then. She'd go after work, after she'd searched a few places. Or tomorrow morning.

The worst of it was that despite her love for Emilia, she couldn't stop herself from thinking that her sister had always been a burden instead of a help. Even when they were girls she'd cared for Emilia while their Mama spent hours at a hand-cranked adding machine, or scoured the neighborhood for people anxious to get a loan, or counted her cash in a delicious, dreamy fog of wealth. It was as if Mama ate money and shit gold, Rosa had once said to her sister, who just looked up at her in shock at the realization that Rosi could swear.

Orphaned, she had to do everything to protect Emilia, to get her into the school, to make sure nothing bad happened to her. It had meant so much, that school. Their smart and crafty mother never could get them into a school, but Rosa had gotten Emilia into one, despite the fact that neither of them had a paternal name, and both had a birth certificate with something obscene written on it: "Father Unknown." It had not been the kind of school her mother had wanted, a middle-class, expensive, church-run school that produced ladies, but a small and private convent school for aspiring wives of Christ that had opened its doors to Emilia.

Then, Emilia made a horrible, stupid mistake. She let herself—but where did all that end anyway? She got out of it clean, married to a nice man, one who loved her. Sra. Rosa got no schooling to speak of, she had no beauty to recommend her to a man who could rescue her, no talent, no ability. She just trudged forward like a farm animal, pulling whatever load they piled behind her. It was so unfair.

And now, Emilia would leave her here alone in this horrible war, she'd be safe in a sanatorium, probably eating decent food, with her daughter at her side—ah, but all those thoughts were the miserable envious thoughts of a miserable woman. Emilia might even die of this disgusting disease, not live on butter and cheese. Sra. Rosa despised herself for thinking these vile thoughts, for feeling sorry for herself, and rolling in her misery like a pig in manure. One had to endure, had to make do, had to survive, and had to behave properly. Her mother had ignored everyone else and gone her own way, to the great detriment of her daughters' lives. Selfishness never served anyone, though Sra. Rosa believed she understood how her mother must have felt in that vipers' nest that was her family, in that sty of ignorance that was her village.

She made her way upstairs at the Señorita's house, rang at the door, and once again was face to face with Dr. Contreras. He was on his way out.

"Are you all right, Sra. Rosa?" he said.

"We had a bad night," she said, perhaps gruffly from embarrassment. "I'm sorry I'm late. Did you hear from anyone, Sir, about my girl I mean?"

"I have a place I'm going to check today, Señora. Perhaps we shall be lucky. Anyway—you have blood on your dress. Are you hurt?"

Sra. Rosa silently cursed him for having a doctor's eye. Surely no one else in this beleaguered and battered city would have even cared about a blood stain or thought it odd.

She was too tired to lie and dissimulate. It always took such an effort, keeping up appearances. "Look, Sir, the thing is, well, my sister is sick, but she is going to Valencia, the People's Health Committee will be sending her, probably today or tomorrow, and I'm not sick at all…"

"Of course you're not," the doctor said, very kindly. "What is the matter with your sister?"

Well, here it comes, she thought. He'll not want me back if he knows. She hemmed and hawed and looked down at the marble tiled floor, then looked down the hall and noticed there was a small bouquet of flowers on one of the consoles. Where the hell did the man get flowers these days?! Did flowers even grow anywhere anymore?

"She has tuberculosis," the doctor said.

Sra. Rosa jerked her head up and stared at him. It was scary how much doctors knew. And he had said *that word*, that awful word no one else would use, that shameful word a decent person would not say aloud. Now she would be dismissed, for sure.

"Sir," she said, "I'm healthy. Truly I am. Look at me. I'm a steel wire, I swear it. I'm not tired, I don't cough, I—"

"Of course," he said. "Don't be afraid. But I insist you wash your dress, and in hot water, not cold."

Which showed that doctors don't know all that much: you need cold water to get blood out; hot will set it.

"Would you like me to examine your sister?" he said. She was so astonished at the question she said absolutely nothing. Doctors like him didn't examine working class people like her or Emilia, though now and then she had considered asking him. She had always dropped the idea for fear he might resent having to deal with her kind more than necessary.

"I—well, she's going to Valencia. To the sanatorium. I'm going to arrange it with the People's Health Committee in our neighborhood."

"Good, that's probably best. I'll go see her this afternoon and help make the arrangements through your neighborhood committee. Also, I have some medicine, not much and not even much good, true, but it will help if she is having a bad time. I have morphine too, which can calm the pain. Does she have bad fevers?"

Sra. Rosa nodded dumbly. She was very grateful he was being so good to her, but what she really needed at the moment was to sit down where no one could see her and bawl to her heart's content.

After all, there was something in it for him. He wanted her to remain in Madrid and care for his sister and mother. She wouldn't have left anyway, not as long as Rosa-Laura was lost. Nevertheless, his attending Emilia would be a great relief.

Dr. Contreras told her to wash her dress immediately and while it dried out, wear an old blue flannel robe of his mother's that he gave her. He told her he would return around noon and they would go to her house. He told her not to worry. She wished he would shut up and leave, before she broke down, and finally, he cleared his throat in a very important way and left. She pulled out the huge laundry tub and set water to boil in the kitchen. The doctor had coal, carbon, matches, and running water, and there was tea and chicory coffee. Flagrant luxuries.

His sister and mother were still sleeping when she disrobed in the kitchen and put her clothes first in cold water and carbolic soap and then in hot water with bleach. She wrapped the old woman's huge robe around herself three times, then set to scrubbing. If they had no money to pay her this week, she'd take the robe and ask Emilia to make dresses for the both of them out of it.

☙❧

"This is the ampoule, this is the syringe," Dr. Contreras said. "Understand me now, this is not a cure, but it will help. Someday we will have a cure. You cannot imagine what they are inventing now. What miracle drugs. I have read about something an Englishman..." He looked at them, and stopped talking, embarrassed. Surely they did not understand. But, the two women and the girl all nodded their heads earnestly. He liked the girl. She was quite pretty, olive-skinned but curly-haired and cute like that little American, Shirley Temple, with a lower class attitude suggesting she was one tough little outlaw. He had always liked that type. He was drawn to them, people who knew what they were and didn't care who else knew it.

"The syringe has to be kept clean. Always. No matter how tired you are, once you use it you take it apart like this," and he demonstrated, "and then boil it like this," he set afire the alcohol in the cleansing pan that the top half of the tin syringe case had become, "and then you clean the needle like this—"

The three watched him perform the ritual. On the bed were the ampoules of sulfa he had brought, fragile looking oblong glass bubbles. He filled the sterilized syringe from an ampoule and injected Emilia. Then he sterilized the needle again and filled it from a small bottle he had in his lovely black leather bag.

"This is sterilized water," he said. "I'm going to let Emilia inject herself with it and see how she does." He tapped the syringe expertly.

Emilia had gone pale. He offered her the syringe. "I can't," she said.

"Let me," Sra. Rosa said.

"Aren't you going to stay here when they go to Valencia?" the doctor said.

"Yeah, well, um, we'll cross that bridge when we get to it," Sra. Rosa said.

"I can do it, Auntie," Mili said. "Honest, I can do it."

"Oh be quiet now, crazy girl, *tonta*, don't meddle with this!" Sra. Rosa said.

The doctor kept the syringe for a moment looking from one to the other. "Come here, *hijita*," he said. His voice was very gentle and he was looking at Mili with a certain sort of detached pride. This child wasn't going to fit into society like a well mortared little brick when she grew up. She wasn't going to work herself to death like her mother and her aunt, either. She'd find a place for herself, something comfortable, no doubt. Of course, she might make a mistake too, a fatal one, but that could happen to anyone.

He took an orange not much bigger than a tennis ball out of his bag, without noticing how wide-eyed they had all become at the sight of this rare treat. "Inject this first, Mili. Push the needle into one of the pores, as if it were flesh. Do it, you can do it easily."

Mili took the syringe and injected the orange in one of the tiny dimples on its skin. A light smell of orange oil gently filled the space between them all when she withdrew the empty syringe.

"All right," he said. "You're one smart girl. Now, sterilize it like I showed you and inject your mother."

Mili nodded and complied.

"Do it in her bottom, in her thigh, or in her arm. The bottom is best because it hurts less. There's not much muscle to bruise. Be sure and tap out the air. It can hurt if you inject air. In fact, if you inject air directly into an artery, you can kill a person. The air reaches the heart and causes a heart attack. More or less."

Sra. Rosa shook her head. "You telling us Mili could kill her mother? That's something to think about."

"No, this is not going to be injected into an artery. A little air will hurt, that's all. Best to clear it out. But, child, don't be afraid. It's very simple."

Mili carefully held her breath and put one hand on her mother's bare hip. She injected the contents of the syringe in, cleaned the spot with alcohol, and carefully pulled up her mother's underwear. "I did it, Mama. Did I hurt you?"

Emilia sighed. "Not much, darling. Just a bit. I don't like it, that's all."

"Well, of course you don't like it," Dr. Contreras said. Really, these lower class women had so little imagination. "But you can certainly be proud of your daughter here. Maybe she could learn to be a nurse. That's a very fine job and very good paying. How old are you, child?"

"Ten, Sir."

He was surprised. "You see that? I thought she was twelve. Well ahead of her age. When she's fourteen and finished school, you send her to me, and I'll see if I can get her into a nursing school."

Emilia and Rosa held their breaths. What an incredible opportunity.

Mili turned the orange over and over in her hand and smelled it. "Doctor, Sir, please, can I eat the orange now?" she said.

☙❧

Three days later, the People's Health Committee got Emilia and Mili on a train to Valencia. A large old Mercedes taxi, requisitioned with its driver by the government at the war's beginning, stopped at the door of the building at 4 a.m. and they bundled into it, along with Sra. Rosa and two other neighbors who were also leaving Madrid. All the way to Atocha Station, Emilia took care to cough and spit into a crocheted and lined bag she had made just for this situation. It was small and attached to her wrist by blue ribbons and had a silk tassel on the bottom. She cleaned it in boiling water every evening, along with her handkerchiefs and clothing.

At the station, Emilia and Mili let the soldiers check through their meager possessions which were packed into a single large cloth purse. The ampoules were in Emilia's corset, each carefully wrapped in gauze that the doctor had also provided. No one must know she had them. She was to receive one injection a day until they were all gone, and this Dr. Contreras had carefully explained to Mili. He also told the girl to save the glass ampoules and sell them for refilling at the hospital in Valencia. The gauze should be saved for bandages. The syringe and its kit were as valuable as gold these days, and could be used in the hospital if need be. Mili had listened to him very carefully, once she'd realized all these items were expensive.

The soldiers finished their cursory inspection and let the women go inside.

Sra. Rosa helped them find a seat together, kissed Emilia on her forehead, and hugged her niece. "You be a good girl and don't give your mother trouble," she said. "If I find Rosa-Laura right away, I'll join you, but if not, we'll meet at home when this cursed war is over. You write now, Emilia, and I'll get a neighbor to read me the letters. You hear me?"

Emilia nodded. She could barely contain the tearful emotions welling up inside her. The doctor had explained how tuberculosis brought on excess emotions—how he loved to roll out that word, that ugly, dirty, shameful diseased word!—but the truth was, Emilia had always found crying easy.

Having settled what was left of her family, Sra. Rosa got off the train, pushing past women and children jamming the aisles and crowded together on the seats, past all the boxes and carton suitcases, bags, and carpet purses full of minimal belongings. There were no men, though one car in the middle carried soldiers. Sra. Rosa had not heard about bombs hitting trains, or troops attacking and taking them over, but it was obvious to her that this could be a possibility. The Doctor had assured her that the journey was safe, and Franco didn't need to attack trainloads of women and children fleeing the capital, but that carload of soldiers bothered her. Stolid, unsmiling, weary, she waited until the train left, then began the long walk home.

It was almost February now, and the winter seemed eternal. That was all right. She preferred the cold to the heat, even though the cold could kill outright, whereas the heat just made a body miserable. But then, who cared about such small things as Madrid's lousy weather anymore? She was all by herself, her entire family was gone now, it might be weeks before she found her daughter. Sra. Rosa never drank alcohol, but right now, she would have sacrificed a good cup of the best coffee for a glass of sweet sherry and a moment of dizzy sleep, just to stop thinking.

As horrible and terrifying as the war had been so far, there was one thing about it that brought considerable delight to Mili: she seldom had to go to school anymore. Now and then a neighborhood committee would frantically set up classes in the market place or an abandoned church and people would appear, volunteering to be useful, needing to be useful, to teach for a few days, then, nothing. Blessed relief. The children ran wild, or at least, Mili did. She had friends everywhere.

Of course, she had been sent to school when she was six. What a dousing that was, of the coldest water bearable. No boys, only girls, all uglier than her. And the teachers! Horrid hags of nuns, who didn't like her dimpled smiles, even though everyone liked her smiles. In fact, one day the Sister said to her, "Why are you smiling, Maria-Emilia? There's nothing to smile about here. You are a disgrace to this class." Wasn't that the truth, "nothing to smile about here." The teacher expected Mili to memorize, to read, to do numbers, and to recite. She expected Mili to be quiet all day long unless called upon, and when she called upon her, Mili was never prepared, so that it was a continual humiliation and the cause of laughter in the classroom. Unkind laughter, not the kind she was used to getting. Those other girls were all jealous of her. The teacher would begin her rant about how Mili was lazy, a dunce, a spoiled brat, a wet firecracker—things no one had ever said to her before. Mili tried pouting, smiling, giggling, fluttering her eyelashes which always sent the neighbors into hysterics and guaranteed her a dozen hugs and kisses—and at the latter gesture the teacher let out an explosive sigh, rolled her eyes and said to the classroom, "What, does she think I'm a boy she wants to marry?" and the class laughed *forever*. This same teacher adored Maria-Magdalena, a thoroughly homely and boring girl. Magda sat there in class, silent and sorry, until she was called upon, at which point she magically transformed and recited the lessons just like that windup tin toy Mili had seen for sale in the park and then harassed her mother about until Mama finally found the money to buy it.

Once, when Mili was about eight, she got so disgusted with school that she actually wasted an evening reading, studying, and trying to write out a few mathematical problems and sentences using the spelling words assigned, but of course, not only was it boring, it made no sense. She finally gave up and crawled into bed with Mama, who had the habit of going to sleep hours and hours before she did. She woke her up and persuaded her to tell a story, and later, it occurred to her that if only the teacher were like her mother and could tell stories, school would be so much better. Stories about the beautiful, curly-haired dimpled princess who was rescued by the handsome prince who killed horrid hags.

So, Mili hated school and that was all there was to it. When she was at home, she gloried in the doting care of her mother, who never refused her anything. The other women in her neighborhood were also fond of her and told her how pretty and how adorable she was. They laughed and applauded every pirouette, every funny comment, and awarded dimpled smiles with cookies, or at the very least, a hug and a kiss.

The men were even more wonderful. They loaded candies and compliments on her like it was the day of the three wise men, and like those wise men, they answered her every question. The boys nearer her own age might push and tease, but once long ago instead of pushing back she had just pouted and then flashed a smile at her tormentor, a spike-haired bully almost twelve years old with a really stupid name, "Abelardo." He suddenly turned from torturer into beggar, pleading with her for a kiss, and ended up giving her his banana, all peeled too. It surprised her that a kiss could be worth something tangible and delicious. It was a lesson she never forgot. "Gi' me a kiss," someone would say, and she'd reply, "What'll you gi' me if I do?" It made the grownups or the big boys laugh and laugh and they always gave her something.

Mama had told her that Abelardo was gone forever. He had been sent to the countryside, she said, but Mili was not an idiot after all, school or no school. She had seen them carry the boy into the patio, she had heard Sra. Lourdes scream, and she had watched her crying that afternoon, her two younger boys clutching onto her like burrs, and Anacleto sucking his thumb of all things. Big boys aren't supposed to suck their thumbs, and Anacleto was as old as she was, but then, big boys aren't supposed to lose their big brothers that way either. Mili had a nightmare that night, the night of the day that Abelardo got killed by the bombs and Rosita-Laura vanished.

Now, they were going far away, escaping the bombs, traveling on her first train trip to a place where the sun shone constantly and there was plenty to eat. It did cause the girl to consider that her mother's illness might be one of those blessings in disguise the neighborhood ladies talked about. "*No hay mal que por bien no venga*. It's an ill wind that blows no one any good," they'd say, and then she ask them to explain and they would. Not like teachers. Like nice neighbors.

Rogelio had met Constancia when he stumbled over her while crossing the broad patio in front of some ministry. He had thought to take a short cut home through the gentle rustling of the sycamores in the patio adorning the building's broad front steps. He was very tired because he had not been eating much. He had come to depend upon first the tavern keepers, until they all went to soldiering, and then the women of the neighborhood to bring him cooked food. He'd give his rations to them and tell them to take what they wanted and give him what they could. He really hadn't cared much for anything having to do with living after Laura had died, then found he had enough life in him to become concerned with acclimatizing himself to the bombing, the war, and the things he felt about certain passersby with a markedly evil aura about them as if foul intentions emanated like a stink.

He went through the motions. He was touched how the neighbor women would take his rations and remove very little for themselves, if any at all, making sure he ate even though their own family might be in need. Of course, Rosa was the best, knocking on his door every weekend, gruffly "uming," taking his dirty clothes from his hands without ever entering the apartment and bringing them home to wash and mend. Her goodness did not surprise him as much as had the others'. Rosa was a stringy, tiny, tight-mouthed woman, but she took such good care of his daughter and truly could be counted on for anything. He figured she was one of those women that people see every day with their grand gift of sight and take utterly for granted, a well of sadness and dammed-up love, capable of any sacrifice or any good. He'd liked her from the day he'd met her, the day his brother had married her. He'd felt bad at the time, listening to her repeat the vows in that *castizo* accent, her voice slightly hoarse, a *madrileña* from the lower neighborhoods. After the ceremony he'd congratulated her. She umed a bit, then shyly said, "My man tells me you could see when you were little. You remember seeing things? Ever?" And he'd told her about that gooseberry bush and his mother.

"Well," she said afterwards, her voice a rushed, flinty, whispering rumble, "that's good. I'm glad you have a memory. If you don't let it eat you up it'll console you. I remember my mother that way."

It had surprised him considerably. No one had ever spoken to him so openly about his blindness before. He didn't quite know what to make of it at the time, and his opinions were muddied by the fact that he knew his brother was a selfish and ignoble man prone to violence when he couldn't cope with things. This woman—undersized, because he was only fourteen or fifteen at the time, yet her voice came from well beneath his chin—might have a hard time with his brother, a good-looking brute. Women would just run off once they'd gotten over his pretty eyes or boyish grin, though now and then one would hold on for a while, intrigued and stupid. It always ended badly. His brother couldn't be counted on. At twenty-eight he'd settled late in life on Rosa because though she was homely, she had something permanent and steady about her that suggested she might be a good mother and might endure his womanizing and harsh ways for the sake of their children.

Funny thing, she *was* a good mother, she just couldn't have kids of her own. Such contradictions inherent in human existence absolutely sandbagged Rogelio when he considered them. He kept trying to form opinions of the world, yet found that world to be as liquid as his memories and sorrows. And of course, the marriage of his brother and Rosa galloped inevitably to disaster.

But man needed marriage. He himself, sure in his grief over Laura that he would never take a woman again, had Constancia. He'd found her in the ministry patio, huddled on the steps and utterly surrendered to fear and confusion. She was not thinking properly. There were neighborhood committees for the homeless, the widowed, and even the hungry. People were pulling together remarkably, witness his own situation, but this woman—ironic that her name was Constancia—had just given up after losing her home and gone wandering, waiting for God to come and find her. But it was Rogelio who found her instead.

He had not even sensed her there until he tripped over her, something he would not have done before the war. At any rate, hers was a simple, easy presence, not one of those that disturbed him so.

He had taken her home, told her she could stay and went to get his rations. When he returned, she had cleaned up his house (he could smell the soap she'd used and noticed how nice the floor felt now that the dirt and dust was swept up) and was napping on his cot. He sat on his chair for a while, letting her sleep and listening appreciatively to her soft slightly raspy breathing. She awoke and prepared dinner, they ate, and the next thing he knew, she came over to him, sat in his lap and put her head against his chest, her hand resting gently on his privates. That was all right. It had been over six years since Laura had died. It was nice how affection could always be appreciated, even though love was dead. And, it helped him to forget the people out in the streets—real or imagined?—who troubled him so, those apparitions that were interior feelings only, the notion that the enemy was outside his door.

So, Constancia stayed with him. The women of the neighborhood said, "Well, good! That's the way, Rogelio, you're a man, you have needs, and she can take care of you. That's how it should be." Now that he had someone to cook and clean for him, it was less work for them, but more to the point his having a new woman proved to them that life went on.

He asked Constancia once what had happened to her, where were her people, did she have anyone left, but she didn't seem able to deal with such questions, and wept. He stopped asking. They got along. As the war worsened, he went out less and less. His bookbinding shop had closed up months ago, most of the men off to fight on one side or another. Rogelio missed work. He missed the jokes and gossip of his brother workers and he missed the feeling of the book covers, vellum or cardboard. It would have been heaven to read one. He'd heard about books in other countries written for the blind in a special finger language, but of course, that was for foreigners and probably rich ones. People still read the newspapers and broadsheets in the taverns, but most taverns were closed now, and everyone gone off to war except him.

After Sra. Rosa came by to tell him that Rosa-Laura was lost, he stifled his crazy fears and went out every day without fail, walking all over, questioning people he knew and people he didn't. He knew from the feel of his child and her voice and her manners that she was a real daughter of his beautiful wife. He mustn't lose her. He asked Constancia to help him search, but that was yet another thing that caused her to weep, so he didn't bother her about it after that. Who knows what she had lost before she ended up under the sycamores in that patio?

Of course, he never mentioned to Constancia that he believed the enemy was inside the city, lurking around. He suspected she knew that anyway.

The days held no sunrise nor sunset any more for Lourdes. She barely noticed their passage. When the bombs began to fall and the sirens howled, she gathered her remaining two children and ran for the metro automatically. They slept on the station platform, or even on the deserted tracks. She slept sitting up, back against the cold, tiled wall of the platform or the filthy wall of the track pit, her boys gathered onto her lap, where they scarcely fit any more.

She lost any inhibition about taking things—wood from abandoned houses, food when and wherever she could find it, clothing, containers—whatever came her way she grabbed and if anyone argued with her or yelled or accused her, she'd drop it and just walk away. She felt so little that shame would have been a tremendous luxury, a gift almost. The neighbors watched her and protected their few belongings, but they didn't blame her much. This was how the world operated, as far as they were concerned. Lourdes was a mother first before anything else in their estimation, and if a woman had to steal for her children, well, that was only natural. That the stealing could come quite naturally from desolation and loss of morale, values, or love, would have been inconceivable to them.

She told her boys to stay home when she was gone, though sometimes she'd take them with her too. She didn't trust them to run around the neighborhood. All the children were wandering these days, yet there was a kind of discipline apparent: gangs of children formed, with the hardiest as leader of course, and these scavenged for their families, if they had families. Children's games still existed. She saw all the boys in the neighborhood playing soccer in the plaza almost every day, with a ball made of twisted rags. Once she stood and watched for a long time, marveling quietly that she could miss her oldest boy so much, that boy she'd barely noticed when he was alive, the one with the hickish, embarrassing name, a homely thing, thick like his father, quiet. Anacleto and Augustín were noisier and needier. They missed their older brother too, especially Anacleto. Sometimes Anacleto would stand very still, wherever he was, in the house, in the patio of the *corrala*, on the street, and stare without blinking, as if remembering something. One day Lourdes had shaken him and asked him what he was doing.

"I don't know, Mama," he said. That was all. He'd be like that for the rest of his life. His mother guessed he was drifting back to that day in the plaza when the bomb struck Abelardo but not him, even though he was standing next to his big brother at the time, holding his hand.

One day in late autumn she left the boys with Sra. Erlinda and went walking down toward Embajadores neighborhood, and then she turned and crossed back toward the center of the city, heading northeast. She had a sack with her, but she had no plan whatsoever. She was just walking. The day was cold and clear. She could smell smoke in the air, even dust, but nothing else. The trees were shedding leaves, and as fast as their remaining upper unstripped branches shed, women gathered up the leaves to burn. It was a miracle any trees were left. The fountains in the plazas were bordered up with sandbags and rubble, whatever could protect them from cannon or bombardment. Windows were draped with black as if the whole city were in mourning. There was hardly any electricity or food, and items like gasoline were more valuable than gold. Indeed, black marketers were amassing a fortune in gold jewelry. Sra. Erlinda had removed the outside casing and the gold hands of her husband's beautiful pocket watch to sell them; the watch played music when you opened it. Lourdes's boys had often begged the man to open it and play it for them when they were all alive, before the war.

She passed near an old building that used to be some kind of ministry or government offices. Before that, it had been a palace, of course. It was stripped bare. It had been boarded up, but people in the neighborhood had ripped out the boards, burned them and then scavenged inside for any old furniture or items of value. It was an immense building, and homeless families camped on the main floor, but it was a very cold place too, and stood out because of its size, so that once when someone stupidly allowed a campfire to burn early in the evening, the building became a target and received a direct hit that destroyed the southwest side and killed several families. Since then, no one entered it.

She walked inside easily, stepping over rubble without thinking. She worked quickly, passively, taking whatever she could stuff into the bag, but of course, there wasn't much, just some sticks and bits of wood. She went further in, until she entered a place where the building was still whole. There was a lower level floor, a basement where once a century or more ago the servants of the household had run back and forth ceaselessly, like wasps in a hive. She stepped down a flight of stone stairs as if treading into a cold dark hell, then paused. She couldn't see beyond the next step, yet there seemed to be a bit of light toward the far end, not firelight, possibly daylight through a slit of basement window or something. She resumed her descent. It was very cold, and she shivered but kept on descending, the still, musty darkness calling out to her seductively.

She saw light at the bottom, though she could not see where she was stepping and stumbled, noisily, several times. She passed down a corridor of some sort, her thin shoes making a soft padding sound on the stone tiles of the floor, and then entered a room, a large room that had been cleared of everything except for a cot in the corner, a table and a chair, and a large radio set up on the table.

He came from behind her, of course. She had made enough noise and he was waiting, harboring a rage as cold as the building that sheltered him. He had her down on the floor before she could even guess he was there or register what the radio and cot could mean. He worked very silently, with a grunt now and then, until he was finished. All in all, it wasn't unlike her couplings with her husband, late at night, when he had thought the children might be asleep, in their communal bedroom. She did not struggle at all.

When he was through, he pulled himself on his knees over her, his pants still unbuttoned, and stared at her. There was just enough light in the room—electric light? How?—for her to see him as well as he saw her, in a pool of cloudy yellow, just enough to delineate their forms into hideous misrepresentative shadows flung against the far wall. He was a big man, as tall as she was or even taller, something rare in this age, and square headed, with dark hair cut very short. He had eyes like a demon, somewhat slit, encased in puffy sacks of skin, mean, dark gray, and icy like a sky full of snow. There was a mustache, or a dark shadow. The nose was very finely shaped, long, prominent, patrician. The mouth was tight, as if he were clenching his teeth.

"You were pretty once, weren't you?" he said. He had a raspy voice, a smoker's voice. She had no idea what to reply to him, though she did remember a time before her marriage when she couldn't walk out on the street without getting compliments and low, scary whistles from the neighborhood boys. Her mother or a cousin or a brother had always accompanied her, yet that did not stop the vulgar assessment. Once her brother punched a man who said something. Funny thing was, that particular comment wasn't rude or vulgar at all, nothing to do with breasts or buttocks or bunnies; he'd said something about willow reeds swaying in the breeze.

She sat up, dizzy, and attempted to pull up her underwear. He grabbed her hand and stopped her, looking it over. Then, he did something very strange: he kissed the palm, dirty and scratched as it was.

She couldn't see him very well in that poor light, but she had a feeling he was younger than herself. Or the same age, only women like her aged quickly and were matrons by the time they were thirty. She was thirty-one. She had lost several teeth, but in the back of her mouth, not the front, and her cheeks were hollow from that as well as from hunger. Her eyes were distant and sad. Once they had been light amber; now they looked like wolves' eyes, colorless as water. She was too thin and her height and long legs emphasized that. From longstanding habit she had always walked with good posture, even now in her destitution of spirit, her head held high, as if flaunting her height and her feet and hands that were too big. Her breasts nowadays had no weight anymore, her hair was lank, the dark gold tarnished with dirty gray. Even her hips, which should have widened from the childbearing and padded out somewhat were simply bony, and her buttocks flat. All in all, height or not, she was just another woman from a poor neighborhood, not at all appetizing, which was fine with her after all. Yet her homeliness had not stopped his assault, and now to her surprise, he pushed her back down, yanked her dress even higher over her chest, ran his hands over her belly, pushed her legs wider apart and took her again. It occurred to her that he might kill her when he was done.

When he was finally finished, he sat up again and stared at her. Then she suddenly realized that without seeing him do it, he had a knife in his right hand and the blade against her throat. She was terribly afraid in the second she felt the knife, yet did not struggle or scream. After a couple of seconds, she felt a kind of relief. If she just held her breath and let it come, without thinking, without imagining what it would be like, it was almost all right. It was almost bearable.

The knife was not a pocket knife but a long blade, possibly a bayonet. Where had he held it all the time he was taking her? Was it in his hand that whole time? Had she been a man and not a woman, she would be dead now for sure. He had waited behind that door with all the patience of a beast crouched for the kill. Well, then, do it. Give release. It's too bad for the boys, but it wouldn't be her fault either. Not a sin like suicide or anything.

He breathed raspily, almost panting, and she waited.

"You're not afraid," he said.

"No, I guess not," she said. She wondered at the truth of her words.

"You've lost family? Your husband?" He had an educated accent and was probably from Madrid.

"My daughter. My oldest son. My husband probably."

He actually turned the knife upward and tapped it against his teeth. He got off her and said, "Get up." He was one of those used to giving orders.

She arose, shakily, her back and haunches cold and stiff, her private parts sore and sticky. She pulled up her pants with embarrassment. She hoped he didn't think she was a whore, but these days even some of the most moral women went to the front or hung around the ministries, the committee centers, wherever there might be a soldier or a petty official, someone male, someone with access to food, ration coupons, fuel.

"You have living children?"

"Yes," she said. She patted her hair back and realized it must be sticking out in all directions, and likely dusty. She wished she could undo her bun and run her fingers through it to straighten it out, but that was something she couldn't possibly do in front of this stranger. It was now apparent that he was much younger, this huge, powerful presence. He was no more than twenty-five or twenty-six.

"But you don't care if you die?"

She looked around to see if she could find her shopping bag, then sat back down on the floor and began to cry.

"Stop," he almost shouted, "none of that now! It won't make any difference to me!"

"I'm sorry," she said. "It's what you said then. It's true, I want to die, I want to be with my daughter, but I got two kids left you see, my two youngest boys, so I don't know what to do anymore."

He said nothing to this. She got up again and dusted herself off.

He seemed to be considering something, as he stood in the shadow, the eyes he fixed on her almost feline, assessing her. "Your husband is a red?"

She shrugged. "I guess. I don't know. He's gone, that's all."

"So, you're not a red?"

"No. I'm nothing."

"I need someone who can bring me things and help me out. I'm hiding here, obviously. You see that?" he said.

"Yes," she said. But she didn't, really.

He indicated the table and some food sitting on it. "Eat something."

"I'm not—" she started to say she was not hungry, but then she sat down at the table and ate a piece of bread and drank some sour wine, mechanically. There was actually a sausage on the table, but she didn't dare. "Can I go home now?" she said when she finished.

"No. You can't go until I say. We'll go home when it's dark. Who are your neighbors? Where do you live?"

She was astonished but answered his questions.

⁓⁕⁓

As they approached her neighborhood he fell back behind her about twenty steps. He had already told her he'd do this and she wasn't to think she could run away, because he'd catch up to her quickly and leave the knife in her back straight through the heart. He assured her he knew just where and how to do that, but she hadn't doubted he knew anyway. At the doorway to the house, she looked in. Only Augustín was in the patio, playing next to the well. Some neighbors were home, but it was blackout time so no lights revealed any possible target nor gave the neighbors light enough to see her shame or her companion. She walked straight in, and picked up her boy, kissed him and said, "Did you miss me? Let's go inside. Where's your brother? Hush, don't yell, don't make any noise. We have to be quiet now. I have food. You hungry?"

Of course he was hungry. He was half starved, to be exact. She cut the bread and the piece of sausage in half and put them in a plate. The child drooled watching her. She lit a stub of candle and set it before him so he could see the food, which perhaps was more ritual than necessity. Augustín didn't even ask who the man was when he appeared; the food had taken up all his attention. The man went in back to check out the bedroom. Satisfied there was no one hiding in this house, he came back out, glancing at Augustín gobbling the food, then suddenly grabbed Lourdes by her upper arm, pressing so hard she bit her lip to stop from crying out.

"Anyone else?"

"My other boy. My ten year old. This one's only six. They can't hurt you."

"That's right and neither can you. Now listen carefully, woman. I'll kill them both, both of them, I'll cut off their cocks and slit their throats, you understand? You know I mean business. First them, then you. Slowly. But you do as I say and you'll get food and when this war is over I won't forget you. Understand? I need someone who won't be noticed to go around and see things for me. Things I tell you to watch out for. Understand?"

She didn't but she nodded yes.

"What's your name?" he said.

The day had been so long and gray and fruitless that Sra. Rosa had returned to her sister's home as a man capsized scrambles back into his tiny boat. She had begun by cleaning Srta. Guillermina's house, which she was now beginning to think of as the Doctor's house. Every morning he spoke to her and every morning filled her in on the events of the past night, explaining where there were places she might check out once his house was cleaned and his sister and mother taken care of. This was becoming a fairly agreeable ritual, though at the very first, it had confused and embarrassed her. It was almost as if they were friends, by the exchange of favors they had accidentally begun. Strange friendship, when she thought about it, that of a rich *maricón* and an illiterate working class woman.

The afternoon had been punctuated by a visit to yet another morgue. How many were there in this godforsaken city? This one had been particularly bad: a bomb had hit a school in a neighborhood where rumor had it that another orphanage existed. Dr. Contreras had not been able to go with her to view the bodies because he was needed in another emergency halfway across the city from where she was going and walking was the only form of transportation in this gasoline-starved city, so he'd set out on his direction and she hers.

She had entered the morgue boldly, then suddenly became so seized with fear and disgust that she thought she might actually faint. Once again, she walked down aisles and aisles of small bodies, these laid on the floor, not tables. Little boys and girls, thin and dull eyed, some with fright still etched on their faces, some blank from dying in their sleep.

She didn't want to commit a sin and ruin her chances with God or His Mother to find her girl, but it was so hard not to be relieved that each and every one of those children was not Rosa-Laura. There had been twenty-five of them. She'd looked at every one. When she left the morgue she gone out into the middle of the street and vomited bile, then stumbled onto a curb as some soldiers passed her by, incurious as to her dilemma. Everyone these days had some tragedy they were finding hard to digest.

Now, at home, she stood for a moment in the doorway, looking out into the darkening patio, and watched Augustín for a moment. Poor child. On her way in, she had handed him a piece of bread, and he had swallowed it without even looking at her.

"Where's your big brother?" She asked. He did not reply and just looked up at her blankly.

Question was, where was that great tall half-crazy Mama of his? The woman was so distracted and confused these days that it made a person weep to see her. Sra. Rosa wondered if that was what she herself would become if she didn't find Rosa-Laura soon. A loony old woman walking around with her dress buttoned up wrong, her hair a mess, her cotton stockings crunched and curdled around her ankles. Sad thing is, Lourdes used to be such a lovely girl, prettiest in the neighborhood. One of those almond-eyed, honey-skinned, dark-blond Spanish women, a real knockout. They had married her off at fourteen, too young, but then, with looks like those you had to work fast. If they had waited she'd have been seduced like poor Emilia, laid flat on a kitchen bench by a handsome seminary student who never had had marriage in mind, not that that situation hadn't resolved itself properly.

Y saltó el diablo, speak of the devil, because then Sra. Lourdes walked into the patio, looked around furtively into the gloaming dark, and shuffled over to her boy. She said something to him quickly and pulled him into their house, just as another person entered the courtyard. Sra. Rosa stepped back behind the curtain at her doorway but watched suspiciously. This person was a man, a big man, big enough and young as well, with a cold face, but handsome in his way. Roman nose, finely chiseled cheekbones, high forehead, small eyes, heavy brows, thin moustache, tight stiff mouth beautifully shaped. Handsome like her husband had been handsome, a scary thing. He was dressed in khaki colors with a military haircut, but the clothes were not really a uniform. Something was not right here.

He looked around suspiciously, glancing at Sra. Rosa's doorway, but evidently did not see her there in the dark, peeking out from the doorway curtain. He went into Sra. Lourdes's house and a thin thread of candle glow came from under the curtain at her doorway. It was almost entirely dark now, and no moon. The neighborhood was quiet. No dogs barked, no canaries chirped, no children laughed and screamed in play, no pots clanged in tiny kitchens, no women called out to their families or their neighbors or castigated some errant husband, no men cracked jokes in loud gruff voices and walked in heavy workingmen's boots to the tavern for a beer and some conversation before dinner, no motor scooters chewed up the cobblestones, no bicycle bells, no church bells ringing the evening prayers. Sra. Rosa began to shiver but she barely noticed it. The priests had lied to them again: hell was not a pit of fire, it was Madrid in war, at the portals to a long night.

"So," Sra. Rosa mused. "She did have a soldier after all. It's a wonder these days how low we're sunk. Well, you have to feed your kids. At least she's not as crazy as we all thought. Still, doesn't take brains to figure out how to be a whore. None of my business anyway."

"Mama?" It was Anacleto, in the darkened patio, coming home. He went to the doorway of his house and entered. Low voices moved here to there behind the curtain, woman, boys, man possibly, very low, then silence.

Just the littlest things became the hardest ones, not the terror from the great battles fought in the sky or within the suburbs of the city, but small things that robbed the will and the spirit. Dr. Arturo Contreras del Valle found it deeply depressing he could no longer visit his favorite bar nor pile fresh flowers on the grave of his friend.

He used to visit the bar regularly when it was open. It was a well appointed place on the Paseo del la Castellana, good for hearing the political news and discussing the latest events. But then most of Madrid had always been famous as a good place for discussion: endless, rapturous, opinionated discussion day and night. Discussion among men. Discussion among the men of his class. It was their place to discuss such things. They may not have been the upper class, but they were the mainstay of any society, the intellectuals, the professors and department chairs, the lawyers, the judges, the doctors, the heads of prosperous businesses.

Most of the businessmen had sided with Franco. Dr. Contreras despised the petty urgency of their need for stability and profit—it was a disease. It was ignoble to labor with one's hands of course, but to him it seemed far more disgusting to work with numbers, constantly grubbing to produce worthless material items.

He had an inheritance and a trust fund and didn't have to work. He was a physician because a man needed a profession, a dignified calling, and he believed in helping those less fortunate. He was a good doctor too. He was armored with the pride that comes from learning a complex profession, from doing it well, from saving lives. He mattered. His clientele included some of the best people in Madrid, and because he believed that you never hoarded a gift, he served the poor and working class too. His colleagues were often amazed that he would get up in the middle of the night to tend some poor woman in a bad neighborhood.

He had not gone to the elegant bar on the Castellana solely for intellectual discussion though. He went because now and then in the hours just after midnight, certain young men would come to order beer and sit around the bar, never at a table, and look around them. He was fearful, but he could not help but watch them. He had been one of those boys once, sitting there in golden youth, wondering about the others, exchanging hints, but never daring to leave with a friend, find a private place, express himself. The risk was clear—if one made even the slightest mistake, something that someone might take for an insult to his manhood, indeed, to *all* manhood, one could be beaten, killed even, and no policeman would even question the perpetrator, let alone any judge condemn him.

Once a young man's glance had caught his eye and in that second of recognition, he had risen and left the bar. The excitement stripped his nerves and left him flooded with adrenaline, almost like a diabetic rush. Worse, he was tumescent and humiliated by this lack of control. He paused outside to light a cigarette that he took from a very beautiful silver and gold case—a gift from his mother. The youth appeared next to him and offered him a light, just a wax match carefully lit and then shielded in a beautiful hand. The Doctor felt he could control his nerves, that is, his exterior was calm, so he took the light, very gently holding the young man's hand to steady himself. He offered the young man one of his cigarettes, an American brand, blond cigarettes they called them, *rubios*, with a wonderful smell and a clean draw, the expensive kind he always smoked. He was sure he presented a relaxed mien and thus emboldened, lit the young man's cigarette with his own lighter, which matched the case. The two of them stood there, smoking, saying nothing, the doctor's heart breaking at the loveliness of it. And then, they parted. The Doctor had said nothing, had given no signal beyond the ceremony of the cigarettes, yet he thought the other man might follow him. He didn't, and the doctor was disappointed but relieved.

It was difficult being a physician, seeing death and pain and suffering, fighting the odds and the gods it seemed, insisting that he was more powerful than the diseases and accidents and ill fortune of his patients.

One needed comfort too, of course, but comfort had to come from men and that was nearly impossible, a risk so great he could not chance it. He was sorry to admit it, because he loved his sister and his mother dearly, but women were patently inferior beings unable to carry on serious conversation or understand things beyond the household. It was just a fact of life, that's all, like the location of the heart or the delicate nature of the liver.

He knew that for the sake of his family and its good name that he needed to marry. True, he was past forty, but he knew men who had married at sixty and had children. Surely he could delay a while longer, though if his mother got too old she would not see the wedding, would not see him carrying out his duty, performing this function that he kept putting off, even feared. It exhausted him to think about this. The companionship of a young man, someone not too aristocratic, someone with a set jaw and a way of holding his head high would have helped him remember that he was a man and worthy of respect, no matter what his needs. Of course, that was impossible, suicide.

He missed his mentor, the man who had helped him enter medical school. The love of his life, really, more than a father, so much more. The doctor's own father had died too early, his mother was kind and loving but also frivolous and self-centered, and his poor sister helpless and dependent on him, the younger brother; well, what could you do?

Those were his good old days. The First World War had not yet begun, he was five months short of sixteen and had graduated preparatory school with honors. Schools were more reasonable in those days. No one complained about his being too young. His mother had a house full of friends all week, and parties all weekend. It was delicious, how he used to be able to study all day, take a test, succeed, come home, and stay up all night until his mother, shrieking and laughing, would insist her "baby boy" go to bed and get some rest before he went back to school.

One of her friends was a gorgeous man in his mid thirties whom she called "Ali", as if he were an Arab or something—well, he could have been an Arab. Medium height, the dark skin of a southern grandee, dark eyes, moustache, silky hair longer than was fashionable, the most beautiful custom-made suits Arturo had ever seen in his young life, and he had seen many at his house—that was Alí, Alejandro de la Vega. A name like the poet's. This was years before the crowd at the Royal Academy of Art, Garcia Lorca's crowd, freely roamed the streets of Madrid carousing openly (yet look what had happened to him!)—but still, men like Alí were welcome at good homes, and no one asked too many questions as long as one was discreet, interesting, fashionable.

No one else called him Alí, just Mama. She was so pretty, his Mama, so open minded and loving, and how she loved a party! Alí fit all that well and adored her as much as she adored him. "My baby sister," he used to call her, which goes to show what a gentleman he was, considering that she was many years older than he was.

Alí was a doctor, a cardiologist in fact. Alejandro de la Vega the constant houseguest, the handsome older man who had once, when Arturo was thirteen, held the boy's chin in his hand and said, "What a charmer you have here, Eugenia! He will destroy every heart in his way," —ah, but why even think back to those days? And he, Arturo, didn't grow up so handsome. He was tall and overweight and his hair thin. Not such a heart breaker after all, my beloved. *Would you have cared? Would you have been fickle and loved another, or would you have been true?*

"For heaven's sake, he must be a genius to be able to study here, in all this *jaleo*, this hectic partying," Dr. de la Vega said to his mother when she told him about Arturo's graduating with honors. "From now on, my library is open to him. I will let my butler know. He can come and go as he pleases. And as for his future, I will sponsor him at the university as a pre-med student. If that pleases everyone, of course."

Arturo was ecstatic, his mother was very pleased, and his stepfather had a fit. "You're going to let him visit that house unchaperoned? That faggot's house? Have you gone mad? And how much will medical school cost us?"

His mother had laughed. "Us? You mean me, *cariño*? And as for Alí, he won't touch Arturo. I can trust him with my son's life. I wish I could say the same about you and Guillermina, you damned old Herod!"

His stupid, disgusting stepfather had called Alí a faggot. *Maricón.* After that acrimonious exchange, the stepfather shut his mouth. Dr. de la Vega ushered Arturo through the procedures and got him enrolled in the university on a pre-med curriculum just after his sixteenth birthday, and Mama paid for everything without a qualm. Well, he and his sister both had inheritances, and Mama was richer yet, thanks to her first two husbands and despite the depredations of the great love of her life, her third husband, his stepfather Montero. As for the business about "Herod," Arturo realized years later that he had blocked out the possibility of his mother's complicity in what was going on in that house. Tragedy and destiny, really. *Nadie puede huir de lo que ha de venir.*

Yes, it was true you could not run away from what has to come. He had trembled every time he entered Alí's magnificent old house, a palace on Princesa Street. He saw Alí now and then, and he knew the man was watching him. Yet, though Alí was kind and very generous with the scholarly advice and presents of medical books, he kept his distance.

Around that time, events forced Arturo to come to grips with his feelings not only about himself but also about his abilities, his capacity for action, his scruples. This had all culminated with the rotten, greedy criminality of his damned stepfather. Guillermina was in her early twenties, a beautiful girl with droves of suitors. Friends had begun to tease her about becoming an old maid if she didn't decide on a husband soon. Arturo didn't think much about his sister's reluctance to pick a suitor; it had always seemed to him she was afraid of men. At first he'd simply relegated that suspicion to his growing impatience with the entire female species. Then, it began to make him uneasy.

Arturo had just turned eighteen. One night, he had been studying and came home quite late; he found his stepfather leaving Guillermina's room. He pretended not to notice and saluted him then apologized for the late hour. The stepfather was so rattled he smiled and patted the boy on the cheek and told him to go to bed and not concern himself. It was the first time Arturo had ever caught the old bastard, though he had begun to suspect something was wrong in their household, especially when his mother would lock herself in her room and cry for hours, even before a big dinner party.

"It's nerves, just nerves," his stepfather would say when Arturo would ask why she was crying. "All the women in this damned family are nervous, including you, you little prick."

Having put his stepfather at ease that late night when they'd bumped into each other unexpectedly, Arturo went to his own room and waited. When he was sure everything was quiet, he went to his sister's room. She was half asleep. His eye was already that of a doctor, and he saw immediately she had been crying, violently. He felt a very strange thing just at that moment, something he let pass immediately and then never dared think again: he was almost jealous of his sister. He wished his stepfather, a big hairy man with heavy-lidded eyes, large well-manicured hands, and a constant knowing smile, had visited him instead of her.

She told him she hated the man but was too ashamed and terrified to tell their mother. Besides, he had ruined her, ruined her years ago, in fact, right after he had married their mother. What man would want her now? Arturo became the doctor right then and there and examined her, which was as disgusting to him as it was to her. She had been treated quite roughly over some time. He comforted her and told her not to worry. It would not happen ever again. And, no man would ever know, especially since the son of a whore had been using "overcoats" the entire time, the premeditating bastard, and even if she did get pregnant, as a medical student, he knew how to correct such a situation. When she married, he'd even ensure that something would impede the entrance of her husband's passion on the wedding night. No one would ever suspect she was not a virgin, let alone so fouled. Of course, their mother must never know. He would take care of it. And her. And their mother, for the rest of their lives. When he finally left Guillerminia, she was no longer crying, she was sleeping peacefully.

The next day, he went straight to Alí's house after his last class, and told the butler that he wished to speak with Dr. de la Vega the minute he got home, whenever that was. He would wait, even if it took all night.

"It's a serious medical matter," he said to the butler. It didn't matter what the butler thought, but Arturo did not want to compromise his friend in any way or behave ill-manneredly.

When Dr. de la Vega returned, there was some muted discussion in the hallway downstairs, then he went straight to the library where Arturo waited. Arturo loved that library. It was everything a library in a grand old house should be, high ceilinged, framed with polished oak and mahogany, its thousands of books stacked across the shelves, and four long, elegant sliding ladders to bring a reader up to the last of them. The room was insulated with tapestries, gold curtains, and plush Turkish carpets in red and green. Arturo knew that green Turkish carpets were rare, and genuine ones hard to come by; Alí had told him so.

Dr. de la Vega entered the library and Arturo, who had been sitting on the green rug of all things, fighting tears, got up and said, "Doctor, Sir, I need your help. I need your wonderful discretion and your help."

"Ah," the Doctor said. "Are you in love, my poor boy? I suffer for you."

"It's not that," Arturo said. "I want digitalis. I'm going to kill someone."

✑

Dr. de la Vega listened without a word as the ugly story unfolded, and he did not blink an eye. (Arturo had the distinct feeling that the doctor had already guessed at what was happening in Eugenia's household.) The story finished, Dr. de la Vega told Arturo to wait for him. He left and came back almost an hour later. When he returned he had a small, carefully wrapped pharmaceutical package, and was accompanied by his butler, who carried a tray of *merienda,* coffee, wine, sherry, and plates of pâté, cheese, olives, bread, sliced sausages. He waited until the butler settled the tray and left. He told Arturo to sit down and eat. "Do as I say, young man. Do not insult me by arguing with me."

Arturo did as he was told and demolished the *merienda* tray with an appetite befitting a man preparing to murder someone or a kid who hadn't eaten since last night. Alí sat watching him with a big smile, as if it delighted him to see the boy's appetite, but he ate nothing, only sipped at a glass of *fino*. Arturo kept glancing at Alí's hands. They were much more beautiful, much finer, much more elegant than his stepfather's. They could operate expertly on a beating heart, in more ways than one.

"You know," Alí commented quietly at one point, "I knew you and I would be friends, from long long ago. I knew when you were six years old. I looked at you and knew. What do you think of that?"

"Am I so obvious?" Arturo said. It scared him, that everyone might know when he wasn't even so sure himself.

"Not really," Dr. de la Vega said. "But people like you and me—we look for each other, don't you think? Don't tell me you haven't thought of this before."

"I have a friend—I had a friend, that is, who killed himself when he was fifteen. Just before I graduated. He didn't want to shame his family. They were devoutly Catholic, and he was in great despair. I always wanted to talk to him, but I never dared. I wanted to say something to him, but I never dared. I still cry late at night thinking about him."

"Yes, I would too," Alí said. They were sitting at the long table, close to each other, and Alí leaned over slightly and touched Arturo's cheek.

Arturo blushed and became totally confused, not to mention embarrassed at his body's immediate and fiercely heated reaction.

"Do you believe that suicides go to hell, Sir? Do we?" It was best to know these things, even if at that point, inflamed and urgent with desire, Arturo didn't care anymore about sin or death or propriety.

"Hell is here on earth, my darling boy. When we die we leave it behind. And please call me Alí. But only in private, of course. Do you want to take this package home now?"

"Let me stay tonight," Arturo said. "Please. I want it so." *Lo quiero tanto.*

❧

A few days later, his parents hosted another of their huge dinner parties. When the guests had left and his stepfather had drunk at least a bottle of brandy and another of champagne all by himself, Arturo gave him a nightcap. It was four in the morning, and they were in the salon.

"When you awaken, Sir, we'll all eat French pastries for breakfast," he told the man. "I'll go out and buy them myself from that shop you like on Serrano."

That afternoon, the stepfather suffered a massive heart attack. He was still in bed and had not any chance to take up Arturo's offer of French pastry. It was no surprise to anyone. He had been overweight, of large stature, and prone to arrhythmias and angina. The weather was warm, so he was buried almost immediately.

After the funeral, Arturo asked his mother not to marry again. She acquiesced to her son's wishes. This last marriage to Sr. Montero had been hard on her. She had a suspicion that as men go, her luck was pretty much over. She had so adored Montero. She had fallen so hard. This was what it had been like to lose all control, to not be the most beautiful one of the two, to be at the mercy of someone heartless. Now she knew how her other lovers and her other husbands had felt.

Arturo was grateful his mother was obedient and sensible. And, he was grateful that what was on the surface of it all a crime, had actually been a cleansing experience that had guided him into the arms of his dear friend.

Alí died of liver cancer, but they had had seven beautiful years to love each other and become the best of friends. A family friend commented that the man had died relatively young at forty-three, because he was a sinner, but the comment did not frighten Arturo. He believed what Alí had said about hell and regretted not one minute of their passion. He visited the grave at least once a month and kept it covered in flowers, until the war stopped such gestures altogether.

The night Emilia and Mili arrived at the sanatorium, the sirens sounded just minutes after they had been ushered into their room. Emilia got hysterical—"They swore to me, they swore, they said no bombs here! They swore to me!"

Mili tried to comfort her, but she had no idea how to do it. When her mother finally collapsed on the clean white hospital bed, asleep, Mili snuck out.

People were everywhere on the streets, and no one noticed her at all. She just followed where they were going, then hitched a ride on a wagon full of furniture. It stayed on the outskirts of the city, but she could see that Valencia was pretty and citified, with big buildings like Madrid. She didn't like the looks of the village where the sanatorium was very much, no fun there, and people in small places watched you too much, but Valencia looked very promising. She managed to get all the way down to the harbor.

The sea was amazing, dancing and lit by flares and explosions red, blue-green, and gold all the way across the water to the horizon, and Africa on the other side or so people said. She watched ships and fishing boats moored at the wharves snap and flash into flame, one or two at a time, like toys in the pond at El Retiro. She thought of fireworks and fiestas and could scarcely relate this bombardment to those of Madrid. It was almost fun, this.

The next morning, back at the hospital, she grinned her charming grin and walked past the old guard in the lobby with no problem at all, got upstairs, found their room, entered softly. Mama was sound asleep, snoring wetly, her chest sounds somewhat deep yet muted, coming as they were through all that liquid and rot. Mili climbed into the cot next to her mother's bed. What a luxury to have a bed all her own. This was going to be great. They should have left Madrid as soon as the bombing had begun. They could have taken Rosa-Laura too, and now she wouldn't be lost.

Emilia got sicker and sicker. Mili was usually left on her own, but now, her mother was so quiet and out of her head most of the time she didn't care if Mili stayed out all night or visited Valencia during the day, or visited other patients and helped feed them, which meant she could finish up what they couldn't eat, so she didn't starve at least. It was a sin to waste food, and these folks had no appetite at all, none. Sometimes she would sit by her mother's bed and talk to her about Valencia, about the harbor, about the other patients and Mama would try, she'd say, "That's nice, my love," or something, but she wouldn't say much more, and Mili needed stories and conversation and diversion. Sometimes, a nurse would read to Mama and Mili would sit and listen, but after a while, a lot of the nurses and doctors left, ran out, the pigs, going to France people said. France was a place somewhere on Spain's border, far away, not as far as America. Mili wished she could go to France, because Paris capitalized France, and in Paris, you could buy pretty dresses by the dozens.

Once she was sitting with her mother on the hospital terrace, overlooking the broad, dried-out, brown lawn. Lunch had been eaten, but not without a shiver of disgust: chard and cabbage, boiled to pus, heavily salted. An old woman, a patient, came and sat with them. She had orange-brown makeup caked on her face, amazing enough, but she also wore the hugest ring Mili had ever seen. The girl couldn't take her eyes off of it.

"My girl likes your ring," Mama had said. She had that embarrassed sound in her voice, the one that came when Mili was being naughty. But the old woman was all right about the staring.

"Well she might. It's coral and gold, and worth a lot." The women held out her hand to Mili so she could see the ring better. Mili ran her fingers over the smooth, large, dark orange stone. The old lady was wearing gold bracelets too, which made agreeable jingling noises, like a pocketful of coins but so much prettier. Earrings with brilliants stuck into their filigree dangled from her wrinkled earlobes.

"I like silver better than gold, it's prettier," Mili said.

"Like what you want, but silver's worth nothing, *niña*. It may be prettier, but gold is better than cash and gets you through hard times. I don't even care about this ring, but my man gave it to me, and it's worth money. That's what's important, not pretty."

"Your husband give it to you?" Mili said.

"Naw, child, I never had a husband. Let me tell you something: you're a pretty thing, and you'll go far, only make sure you get something for it. Fun and a bracelet or two, that's what you want, don't give anything away."

"Mili, we have to go inside now," Mama said. She had a look on her face that said "angry," but she was trying to smile at the lady. Mili wanted to stay and balked. Then she regretfully let go of the old lady's hand and pushed Mama's wheelchair to the front entrance.

"Nasty old whore," Mama had said, as they returned to her room. "Don't let me catch you talking to her again, Mili. She's full of diseases, and not just the one we all got either. She's disgusting."

But Mili wasn't listening to her mother, because she liked the old woman, she liked the ring, and she very much agreed with what the old woman had said. Showing a boy what was in her pants or even letting him put his hand on her privates so that afterward he had to give her something was well worth the sin. Sometimes it even felt good, but that was the least of her needs.

Sra. Rosa arrived at the Doctor's house just after sunrise. All-clear warnings were sounding throughout the city. Her head pounded from the shrieking ululations of the sirens and the terror that she kept packed down hard in her chest, where it constantly threatened to break upward choking into her throat, the urge to scream. For the very first time, she could not bear to climb the stairs but allowed the concierge to put her in the lift and send her upstairs in its wobbly iron grill cage.

She rang at the door. The Doctor answered, fully dressed, his face somewhat animated despite its sallowness and tired, pouchy eyes.

"Sra. Rosa, we are going to the North Station, now. We'll take a tram. I tried to get a taxi through the emergency services, but of course, there are none for us. But we'll be there in time, I'm sure."

"Señor?" Sra. Rosa said. She hadn't even stepped into his house but stood outside the door, her mouth open, her heart now pounding harder than her poor head.

"They are sending children to Russia this morning. Perhaps your daughter will be among them. We'll go there and look together."

Sra. Rosa very deliberately stretched out her hand and gripped the door frame.

"Dear Mother Mary, I've shocked you. Come in and have a cup of tea—"

"No, Doctor. I'm fine. Let's go now."

He saw she was in charge again and nodded at her. They went downstairs together in the awful little elevator.

She thought it took hours and hours to get to that station. It was near the Plaza de España, and she remembered it from the last time she'd taken a train to her mother's province, a wretched memory of wretched meanness and shame. She hated trains and she hated travel.

The Doctor was excited and hopeful, but when they entered the station about an hour after they'd left his house, he became instantly dismayed at the sight of hundreds and hundreds of children amassed in groups all across the huge waiting room. Thin children, with sharp, stressed faces, the youngest no more than three or four, the oldest perhaps twelve or thirteen. Little girls with amazing huge loops of ribbon perched atop their heads like daffy, drunken birds. Little boys with chopped, ugly haircuts, some with caps, most without. It was a cold day and it was colder inside the vast, high arched ceiling of the waiting room and vaulted platform area. The children all had coats, flannel or plain wool, brown, blue, black, worn and often too small. He could see these were the children of the poor. Or children whom the war had made poor.

How were they going to find just one little girl in all this? And the din in the cavernous place was deafening and dull.

Anxious mothers or relatives hung around the groups of children, Women putting one last final pat to a shoulder or cleaning off a stray hair on a coat lapel. The only men were militia and authorities; no fathers were there to say goodbye to their sons and daughters. The Doctor looked around, trying to regain his composure and keep his outlook properly hopeful.

"Papers?" A militia man had approached them. They each removed their documents from their pockets and presented them to the man. He was perhaps in his thirties, even more worn and thin and exhausted-looking than the children. His rifle was old, but shiny clean, and he had a small pistol tucked into his coat belt. He checked over their papers and said, "Where is your child?"

"No," the Doctor said, "we are not bringing a child. We are looking for a child."

"None of that allowed. These children are on their way to a better place and no one is taking them away."

Sra. Rosa made a little choking sound.

"My relative here," the Doctor said very, very gently, "has had her daughter taken from her by accident. During a bombing raid. She only wants to look around and say goodbye, if the child is here. We certainly do not want to cause trouble or concern. She is just desperate to see her child again and make sure she's all right."

The militia man nodded and waved them on. Perhaps he was just too tired to assert his authority or dispute with them.

Sra. Rosa said, "Let's start with that bunch. Or maybe we should each go separately, more ground covered that way?"

He was astounded at her composure. If they found the girl, he was sure she would not allow her daughter to be taken from her again. "We'll go together for now," he said.

The Doctor and Sra. Rosa spent the whole morning searching the waiting room, then the train platforms, talking with the relatives and other adults, describing Rosa-Laura, moving as fast as possible from group to group of children. Hundreds of little girls turned up their expectant, lovely faces to them, but though one or two had blue-gray eyes or a tiny overbite or a spray of freckles across her nose or rich auburn-colored hair, not a one had all those beauties come together, not a one was Rosa-Laura. Finally, they watched the train pull out.

Some of the children inside were hanging half out the train windows, waving wildly. Other children stood behind those, looking out, but their eyes and bodies still. They were all going to Russia. To an earthly paradise far, far away where there was no war, and good people would care for them until this war was over, and Franco dead, and their parents ready for their return.

Dr. Contreras and Sra. Rosa walked home. He was saddened but not surprised that his little housekeeper did not cry or complain.

All in all their time in Valenicia passed by pleasantly enough, even though so many people died or ran away, and worse, the bombardments always sickened Mama to an alarming point, until some days she would cry and cry and beg God to take her. Mili felt sorry for her, but there was, after all, another important consideration here: "If God takes you, Mama, then what will I do all alone? And I don't think Auntie Rosi would like it either, so there!"

One night was particularly bad. No one was around to help nurse Mama, who was coughing blood and spit and pus so that Mili had to run up and down the hallways with a basin. She was tired, and this time she was crying, like a little baby, like Rosa-Laura or something. Then, she stopped, just too damned tired to go on, and crept into a linen closet to curl up and sleep on the towels and sheets. When she awoke and pushed open the closet door, the sun was sending long shafts of light through the dirty, high-up corridor windows. No one seemed to be around, yet it must have been at least ten in the morning.

She crawled out of the closet, straightened her hair a bit by combing it with her fingers, dug a few bits of sand out of her eyes and yanked a hard snot out of her nose, then picked up the basin discarded in the hallway last night, and went to see her mother.

When she got to the room, no nurse attended Mama, no breakfast tray sat on the narrow window table, and some fool had pulled a sheet up over Mama's face. Mama certainly wouldn't like that. She lifted the sheet, and said, "Hey, Ma, where's breakfast? Wake up. Come on now, don't be that way, wake up."

Even as she said it, she knew what that hard, lavender-gray skin, the half open mouth, and those no-look eyes meant. She'd seen plenty of deaths in this hospital, including the death of the old woman with the big gold and coral ring.

But she wasn't about to let death have its way, not yet, and she shook her mother hard. "Enough now!" And shook her again. A nurse turned up and Mili screamed at her, "You fucking whore-shit, where the hell you been? My Ma needs you! Look at this. Look at it! Look what you've done!"

The nurse pulled her away and Mili punched her belly hard, then the nurse slapped her, which astounded Mili. No one slapped her, no one. She kicked and screamed and the nurse yelled for help, until a guy finally came, a doctor, or an intern, or a helper, who knows what the hell he was. They pulled her out of the room, and the guy took her for a walk on the terrace and promised to buy her some lunch. Only then did she cry a little, because that is what you are supposed to do when your Mama dies, and because it felt good. Really good.

⌒⌒

She had to get back home. She had to find Auntie.

Mili knew Valencia like she knew her breakfast plate and was well acquainted with the train station. She had often gone there to watch the trains come in, to beg from soldiers, who were such nice guys, to offer help to new kids arriving in town.

She asked about trains going to Madrid and then snuck onto one, leaving Valencia forever. She never wanted to come back now. No one on the train even noticed her or asked her where she was going. She had a large handbag with her clothing and some of her mother's things, not much, but she would have died to keep it. She didn't get on in third class, even though she knew that would be easiest. She climbed up in first class. Some soldiers sat in the compartments, playing cards. Everything was filthy, and the toilets stank. She wondered if the train would even get out of the station, because she'd heard someone in the station say that coal was scarce and why should they even waste the fuel on trains to Madrid any more?

"Send 'em to the border, that's where we all ought to go, and fast," the man said.

She was disappointed at how sad first class was, but that was the war for you. It spoiled everything. She found a nice compartment with no one in it and curled up on a seat and waited. She needed to cry, but not just yet. She had a way to go before she could enjoy a good long cry. Maybe when she found her Auntie Rosa. She wondered if Rosa-Laura was home yet, if Sra. Lourdes and Anacleto still lived across the way, if Madrid really was still there or if it had been bombed into the ground.

She heard a noise in the next compartment, pushed her bag out of sight under the broad upholstered seat, and crept out quietly. The door to the next compartment was slightly ajar, and she got down low and peeked in. The conductor, in a scruffy, stained, and much-mended uniform, was sitting there on the seat, drinking wine from an unlabeled green bottle. His pants were unbuttoned, and he was rubbing his big prick slowly with the other hand. She watched and smiled. This was something she knew about, something secret and wicked. She had seen boys in the neighborhood at home do this a thousand times, and men at the sanatorium too. When she was still just a baby, it had scared her, but then she had figured out that it was something she could use to get a bribe or a reward.

"Hello, *niña*, you watching me?" The conductor said.

She nearly jumped out of her pants, but quickly controlled herself and got ready to take over the situation. "I'll tell on you. I'll tell. Or else you give me something nice to eat. Or something. Or else, I'll tell."

"Come here, cutie, I'll give you something nice."

She wasn't that dumb. "Yeah, right, old man. You wait till I tell on you."

"You want a drink, girlie?" He held out the bottle.

She didn't like wine. "You got something else?"

He put the bottle down and fished out a coin. "Here. It's not going to be worth much too much longer anyway."

"I want that nice watch you got there."

"*Chica*, you'll have to do a lot more than not tell on me to get that," he said. He smiled, put the bottle down, and held out his pocket watch to show her. His other hand was working faster now.

❧

The train was halted by a barricade with a tank some kilometers outside

Madrid in a village that was now an enemy headquarters. Soldiers boarded the train yelling and swearing, and half the occupants of the train were taken prisoner, including the train conductor who'd given her his watch and some coins and then half his dinner. She slipped out easily, however, and found a truck loaded with coal near the railroad, across a swath of filthy tracks.

She was sad, scared, and tired of bargaining, so she didn't let the truck driver know she needed a ride. He might not have been so nice as the conductor anyway. She was twelve years old and knew that some day some guy would want more from her than a bit of work with her hands and some peeky-boo. She wasn't eager to begin that game yet. It led to babies, and although she liked the idea of a big soft live toy to play with, she had been told often it hurt to give birth and one needed a real husband to pay for it. It was also a huge sin if you weren't married, bigger than most, and God was not friendly to women who did it. God had an annoying habit of watching, seeing, and knowing everything, and though prayers and confession could get you off the hook, fooling an old priest in a confessional box might not be quite the same thing as fooling God.

She had climbed up the back of the truck and slept in the *carbón* until she'd felt the vehicle lurch somewhere around late afternoon and head for Madrid. It was stopped once on its way in, and two men in civilian dress got on, one of them getting into the cab and one hiding himself in back. He never even noticed her, which was good, as she thought he looked hard, cold, and mean.

The truck entered the city and then stopped near Atocha. The man in the back climbed down without ever noticing her just a pile of coal away, and she watched him, then climbed out herself, quietly. The truck driver was talking to a man about the price of the load, arguing in a low voice over his black market treasure. She escaped the Atocha train yard, and then walked till she was numb with fatigue, down streets she knew and remembered until she found her plaza, then her alleyway, then her building. Midnight streets, not a light anywhere, all still and no bombs, though there was distant cannon fire. No one had noticed her at all as she traversed the dark labyrinth of streets and plazas. She figured it was because she was a clever girl, but truth was, their minds were on surrender and survival, and she was covered with coal dust. No one was looking around for a pint-sized, baby-doll Abyssinian on her way home.

The big door to the *corrala* was actually open, as if expecting her. She entered the patio and ran to the door of her home. She stopped, caught her breath, and pounded on the door but no one answered. She wanted to cry now, but it was such a waste to cry alone, without someone to comfort her and feel sorry for her. She pounded harder. Finally, someone said, "Who's there?"

"It's me, Mili," she said. "I've come home, Auntie Rosa. Let me in."

Auntie Rosa didn't move fast enough. Mili began to cry and then sob, and then she *howled*. "You fucking son of a whore, let me in! I shit on your grave, I shit on your mother, I shit in the sea..."

The door opened in a rush, and Auntie Rosa said breathlessly, "Mili, I'm going to wash out your mouth! Where did you learn—oh my God, you're black! You're black!"

"Dear Mother in Heaven, hush, hush," someone called "Sra. Rosa, please shut her up! We'll all be arrested!"

Sra. Rosa grabbed Mili into her arms and held her very tightly. "All right, *hija*, hush now. Hush. It's like the neighbor says, Mili, we'll be arrested. You can cry later, you can—hey, why are you so black? It's coal, isn't it? You covered in coal? You in disguise or something? Damn, girl, I'm so glad to see you. Yes, I'm glad to see you—but—where's your Mama?"

And Mili cried harder now, but kept her voice down.

Sra. Rosa finished off the torn seam, doubled the stitch to make a knot, then bit off the end of the brown thread. Mili sat on the cot, wrapped in a blanket, her hair still wet, her face scrubbed and cream-colored again, her eyes red from tears. She looked older somehow. The dimply smile was still there, but the delightful gleam in her eyes had disappeared like blossoms on a little fruit tree before the second week of spring.

"So, only two days ago, then?"

"Yes, Auntie. I fell asleep, just a while, but I was so tired. And when I woke up, Mama called me, and told me she was a goner, and she loved me, and then the nurse was there, and Mama left me. Mama was really brave about dying. She was awfully sick, coughing lots of blood all the time. It was too hard, Auntie. It hurt. I think she really wanted to die. She wanted to be with God and Papa and be taken care of again. We talked about that some times."

Sra. Rosa was threading a needle with white thread for the torn collar. Mili's dress looked as if the child had rolled down a rock slide, then slept in a mud pit. Or hitched a ride in a coal truck. At Mili's last words, she looked up at the child, pained and somewhat shocked.

"But, she was taken care of, wasn't she? They were good to her?"

Mili nodded assent. "But she was tired, Auntie, I told you. She went bravely to her death, the nurses said so. She showed courage in the face of death. That's what they said."

Sra. Rosa shook her head. "Too often the courage about dying is a cowardice about living," the Gypsies said. They say when a Gypsy faces death, he thrashes and fights and wails and begs for a minute more. When he's buried, his family carries on with screams and laments, then holds the biggest party you ever saw. Funerals and other fiestas, it was how they saw life, and Sra. Rosa could not deny that. Life is something to hold on to, isn't it? Emilia was never much of a fighter. From the day the doctor told her she had the disease, she prepared for her death and prayed for release from pain. Well, who wants to feel pain? But then again, just to be able to feel— even pain? Sra. Rosa shook her head again. Poor sister. Poor little girl.

Mili slept now. She had eaten everything Sra. Rosa had in the house, even fighting Sra. Rosa about washing up first before eating, making enough noise so that every neighbor left in the building knew she was home again. At dawn, a few of them came by to see what was happening and ask how Emilia was. Lourdes brought some food. Mili ate it all immediately and without a thank-you, which Sra. Rosa would have to talk to her about. The child had an appetite, unlike her mother. For Emilia everything had been tragedy, regret, mistakes, close calls. For Mili, life was food to be seized and devoured. And for her, for Sra. Rosa? What was it all about for her? First find her child, then find out whatever else she needed to know as the question presented itself. Philosophy was for university swells.

The war had become so much a part of their lives that few could remember when there had been no war. The time before it, when food riots and violent debates filled the city streets with angry demonstrations, was forgotten, and people remembered what they wanted to remember: a just and abundant world flooded with the scent of narcissus and hyacinth in springtime and everyone happy and hopeful about the beautiful future the Republic would bring them.

Every day now, three years into this hell, Dr. Contreras visited the front, scarcely knowing whether he was in the north or the south, the east or the west. It was all a vast, yellow-brown and gray plain, treeless, dry at times, muddy at others, but stripped of vegetation and dotted with ruined houses or villages. A washed out hell of their own making. Stepping into the trenches, he remembered being told a little story at the beginning of the war: the civilians of Madrid themselves had done all the digging, and they were mostly women and old men who wanted to participate in the heroic defense. The story omitted the fact that the amateurs' trenches were too narrow, had no drainage, and had to be redug, deeper and wider. Muddy in winter, dusty in summer, they stank of dirt and blood and piss and sweat. They stank with rumors too. The war was nearly over, the International Brigades had been sent home, soon there would be a cease-fire, soon there would come executions, roundups, settling of scores. He didn't know what to believe and as he seldom was able to visit the ministries and had few friends left now in high places who were still in the capital, or alive for that matter, he had no way to corroborate the stories he was hearing.

Passing through a dozen guard points, hitching a ride whenever he could since walking was extremely dangerous, not to mention tiresome— he'd make it to some area just outside Madrid and do what he could. Then he'd return to the city alive, and he'd head for his hospitals. He had no medicine, not even morphine. He needed bandages and gloves and alcohol and ether. He had the skill of his hands, a bottle of brandy now and then, and the elegant tools in his black leather bag. His desperation was near hysteria these days, but he would not let himself break. He wanted to scream, "What do you want me to do? I check their wounds, I see if I can sew them up a bit, I tell the nurses to smile at them, to talk to them, I operate on gangrene without anesthesia—God in heaven, what do you want me to do? This is insanity!" But he kept this all inside and said nothing aloud.

After the battle of Brunete in 1937, he had protested bitterly to people who insisted the valiant and ineptly led forces of the loyalists had "won" that monstrous event. He understood then he must shut his mouth, not only because he might be denounced again but also because it was futile to say anything anymore. Thereafter he silently attended the battlefields, the trenches, the hospitals, the bombed city streets, and carried his silence home to his mother and sister. He pretended, he dispensed what comfort he could, he pondered. He separated the ones that would surely die from the ones that might die. He believed he was going mad, but not just yet, not just yet.

His major assignment now was a huge luxury hotel, a main hospital full of wounded. One morning in winter he walked into the front lobby and wiped his feet on the filthy straw spread across the front of the huge carrousel entryway as a score of nurses ran to report to him. These days the news was always bad. This one died last night after the amputation Dr. Contreras had performed with such care and speed, minimizing the shock of the pain, cutting as little as possible, promising the boy, who was deliriously drunk on the grand hotel's best brandy, that after the war he would be able to get a good prosthesis with which to work just as hard as before the war. Another one died after midnight. Another at 4 a.m. Another just before he arrived. Had he found any source of morphine, any supplies?

He listened to his nurses dully, grunting now and then to let them know he heard them. Girls. Children, really. Teenagers frantic to save lives. Growing up and wearing out, fast. He looked up at the gorgeous lobby ceiling. Didn't they design these things to emulate heaven? And wasn't that ruined storefront where they stored the cadavers once a candy shop full of marón glacés and cherry chocolates that his sister and mother loved? The rug beneath his feet was filthy and foul. He could not see the flamboyant leaves and colors anymore. Why did the best hotels have such garish rugs? Orange-red, lime-green, emerald green, caramel yellow, panther black. He smiled at the recollection and his nurses said, "Comrade Doctor? Señor? Orders? Señor?"

One nurse, a ruddy, still-plump girl with beautiful teeth (what a miracle that was, in all this misery), said to him, "Doctor, I mean, Comrade Doctor, one more thing, there was a patient last night, and a very strange man—"

"Stranger than all the rest?" Dr. Contreras said. He was hard put to keep the tired sarcasm out of his voice.

"Yes, Sir, just before eleven. He visited the patient with peritonitis, the older man. The patient died soon after the visit."

"I was not expecting him to live, Nurse. And why are you concerned about his having a visitor?"

"I, uh, well, Sir, the patient was alive and lucid, then he had this visitor, a very fierce looking man, cropped hair, strange clothes, not a uniform—"

It took all the doctor's reserves to keep from screaming at her to get to the damned point. He bit his lower lip.

"He was lucid, Sir, awake, then the visitor came, and when I next saw the patient, his face was blue and he was dead—"

"Blue? Contorted? Tongue—" His voice had risen.

"Yes, comrade doctor."

"His visitor suffocated him. He was dying a horrible, horrible death, and his visitor put him out of his misery. Call the authorities and denounce him, if you wish. As for me, I hope if I ever sustain such a wound and there is no morphine, I hope, *comrade* nurse, mark me, that you or someone else will do me such a favor. "

The other nurses were staring at the girl now, and she set her jaw stubbornly, embarrassed but refusing to be cowed by a man everyone had been telling her for two years was her equal. "The patient was a minister, Sir. He had lots of visitors. This one was different, and I believe he murdered him. I will tell the authorities."

"Good," Dr. Contreras said. "Murder is a crime of highest magnitude. Sending boys off to die in war is patriotic, smothering a dying man in horrible pain is murder. Thank you for enlightening me. The world is tip-top again. And incidentally, nurse, we have no ministers in Madrid any more. They're all in Valencia. Or, France, if they have half a brain and can sniff the wind. The man who died last night had some military title. Colonel, perhaps."

The nurse twisted her hands on her blood and pus-stained apron and struggled to keep her revolutionary equilibrium.

Dr. Contreras strode off without dismissing his nurses or further acknowledging them. He had not gotten halfway across the filthy carpet when sirens began keening and the artillery hammering. He pretended to ignore the assault even as he realized with a sickening fear that it was close again, very close. Up the street from the Hotel were the the chambers of the *Cortes*. Ministries bulged from every corner of this neighborhood. It and Vallecas were favorite targets, ripe and inviting. The army had placed anti-aircraft guns and artillery on the rooftops to protect the area, but had had no ammunition to load them with for some time now. *Da Dios pañuelos a quien no tiene narices.* God gives handkerchiefs to those who have no noses.

The hospital managed to get through two hours of bombardment without a direct hit. At one point, ambulances began to bring in more wounded. He wondered briefly at the miracle of the ambulances having enough gasoline to get down the block. He wanted to shout, "Enough! It's not a damned warehouse!" but of course, it was a warehouse, and of course, once again he restrained himself.

When the pounding stopped, an elderly man who'd worked at the Hotel as a bellhop before the war and now served the hospital as a kind of majordomo for the doctors and nurses, brought him a glass of wine.

He didn't ask the old man where it came from; throughout his service the old man had brought him and the nurses wine and also served it to the wounded who could take in fluids. At the war's beginning, Dr. Contreras had issued instructions that the wounded were not to be served wine, especially if they were being given medication. When the medication ran out, he finally realized the utter idiocy of his trying to manage this place as if it were a normal hospital under normal circumstances. The old man had emptied the hotel's cellars, watched over the premises, advised the nurses where sheets could be found and how to use the massive laundry apparatus—until the gas and soap and even the water ran out, that is—as well as how to haul the heavy curtains across the vast windows during a blackout, which pots in the kitchen could be sent to the front to make bullets and which would be useful for boiling bandages.

Dr. Contreras drank his wine slowly by habit, pinky slightly extended. He was well trained and had exquisite table manners. Some of the other doctors had lost their veneer of good manners and their hold on sanity as the war had progressed. Dr. Contreras was regarded as an example of grace under fire, but that did not necessarily earn him one hundred per cent respect. The old man had once remarked to the nurses, "He's a gentleman, our Dr. Contreras, girls. A pleasure to serve. He's a butterfly too, and that helps."

The nurses had screeched in delight at this assessment and held their hands to their mouths glancing at one another to see who was sophisticated enough to understand what was actually being said.

"Don Rafael," the Doctor said, "Tell me: do we have any more 'important' people here? Government people? Officers?"

"Some may have come in now with this last batch, Sir," the old man said, "but since the government fled to Valencia—"

"Keep an eye on any that come in. We may have someone going round trying to end this war his own way."

"Yes, Sir. Incidentally, Doctor, I found another of those places—an orphanage. In one of the best neighborhoods. Not too far from here, but a very safe area. No bombing at all there. The owners of the house fled, but left it to the sisters when their convent was burned and they sought refuge just at the beginning of the war. They have been very discreet. Most of their girls are daughters of the upper classes, and the neighbors are in on it, the ones still around. I saw a little girl there once like the one you described—I would advise some caution in this matter, though, if I may presume to advise you. A denunciation could cause such havoc that the children would suffer or be shipped away. Or, if the sisters suspected they'd been found out, they might try to move again, hide."

"I am not in the habit of offering denunciations, Don Rafael," the Doctor said.

∾⳿

The next morning, he told Sra. Rosa he'd visited a certain palatial house on a broad boulevard northeast of Sol after his shift at the hospital. She wanted to go immediately, yet he'd managed to calm her down and he'd managed to convince her to wait. Things were changing, very fast, and Rosa-Laura might be better off there for the time being.

"I know this is hard, Sra. Rosa, but you must trust me in this. We don't want denunciations and some fanatic authority entering into this now. We have to find the right time to contact them and get her back. We don't want to scare them or cause them to send her away or hide her or argue with us. We really can't force our way in. They fear us, but things are changing fast, and we don't want to anger them either."

He didn't tell her that he'd seen a strange thing happen in the middle of the night at that house, that he was sure it was a safe house for more than just little girls, but he did tell her he'd glimpsed her daughter there, and the child was well.

It was agony and hard to understand. Sra. Rosa sat in the kitchen all day after that, cleaning the same spot on the table over and over. She was miserable but Rosa-Laura was alive and safe, that was the crux of the matter, and she must trust the Doctor's wisdom in this terrible trial.

Nevertheless, after work she walked to the big house he'd told her about and then again many times over the next months, and stood outside its iron fences for hours, like a little wraith, staring at the granite façade, at the broad French windows, hoping to get a glimpse of her daughter. Once or twice she thought she saw a girl inside, but none who looked like Rosa-Laura. No one ever came outside.

But then, things really were changing. The war was nearly lost.

Sra. Rosa took her kettle off the stove and added two heaping spoonfuls of black tea to the bubbling water.

"Ah, I can smell it now," Rogelio said.

"Um," she said, pensive. She'd gotten the tea from Dr. Contreras and had considered using it to barter for oil or flour. She'd left it at home for a day, and when she'd returned, most of it had been pilfered. She knew that Mili had taken it and the thought was hard to bear.

"There's not much of it, Rogelio, so it'll be weak, but never you mind. I'll give you the rest to take home to Constancia."

"No, too generous," Rogelio said.

"Either that or Mili will sell it," Sra. Rosa said. She hoped the frustration and disappointment she felt wasn't too apparent in the sound of her voice.

"She's just a child, Rosa. Maybe one of the neighbors stole it. That one across the way who consorts—what you said."

"No," Sra. Rosa said. "Lourdes wouldn't steal from me. Especially now she's got someone to take care of her. Only Mili knew I had it because I gave her a cup as a treat."

The night Mili had arrived, Sra. Rosa went through her things after giving the child a good wash. The girl had brought back all she could of her mother's belongings: Emilia's only pair of earrings, a wedding present from her husband; her wedding ring; two beautiful lace collars; a pair of old suede shoes with metal buckles once fine but no longer stylish; a steel pocket watch with a railroad insignia on the back. Sra. Rosa looked at the watch and wondered where it came from, as she had never seen it before. Mili's father hadn't worked for the railroad. From the black velvet purse with the lace trim that Emilia had sewn for her earrings, something else fell out: a large, heavy gold ring with a huge coral stone, dark orange, smooth. A very expensive ring.

"Where did you get this, child?" Sra. Rosa had said.

"Oh that. It's mine. A nice lady at the sanatorium gave it to me. Because I was so cute and so nice to her too. I read to her in the afternoon when Mama slept. She wanted me to remember her."

"Child, no one gives away rings like this."

"Auntie, she was dying. She had no use for it. I helped her. When I wasn't with Mama I was with her all the time and I fed her and read stories to her. She wanted me to have it. And she had other stuff too, but the nurses kicked me out and got them."

∞

Rogelio shook his head. "Rosa, maybe she was telling the truth."

"Mili can't even read a menu or a street sign. Lazy. Lazy student. As illiterate as me and not so much reason for it. Bad things happen in war, and I know Mili did what she had to. But she's learned bad lessons. This war must finish and then the Doctor will help me find her a good school. She'll become a nurse and forget the rest.

"Anyway, I have much bigger news, Rogelio, and I don't want to leave you out of it any more. Don't shout now, just be quiet—we found Rosa-Laura."

He almost dropped his cup. He couldn't believe he'd sat here in Rosa's house for nearly half an hour now, gabbing about that little Gypsy of a Mili without Rosa revealing the news.

She explained the situation as best she could, describing the house, her waiting in front of it, what the Doctor had told her.

Rogelio was flabbergasted. "We can't have her then? I'm not sure I understand. She's ours. What right have they—" He was abstractedly savoring the warmth and scent rising from his cup, resisting the temptation to drink while the tea was still too hot.

"Not a question of right," Sra. Rosa said. "Maybe they would just give her over if we marched up to the front door and asked. More likely they'd deny it all, deny they were nuns, deny they have orphans since they probably have kids from important families they are guarding, blockade the door. And then we'd have to go to the militia or the police—we'd have to denounce them. They haven't hurt us, Rogelio. They tried to do the right thing with a child they thought orphaned. And the Doctor says if we scare them, they'll pack up the girls and run to another—what'd he call it? A safe house. They have friends in that part of the city. Maybe all over the city. She's fine where she is, safe, and I can't risk it."

"Nuns are strange creatures," Rogelio said. "Maybe they'll convince her to be a novice."

Sra. Rosa actually smiled at that. "Now then, you were the one said they wouldn't eat her. She's still a baby. Just a baby. They feed her. She's in a zone where no bombs fall. Wait and when it's safe, I'll go get her. Nothing will stop me then. And um, I'm watching the house. So's the Doctor, no time these days but such kindness to us."

Rogelio raised the cup to his mouth, ungratefully wished he could have some sugar and even some milk in it after all, and finally slurped at it, surprised at how thoroughly he could enjoy the almost bitter taste. "I'm upset with you, Rosa. You should have told me."

"Um, I had to be sure. The Doctor asked me to be quiet. But I knew it was unfair."

"I can't believe you're so calm about it, Rosa," he said. "I always knew you were constant, but this surprises me. Any other woman would have given over to hysterics. Fallen apart, like my poor Constancia. Your name should be Pilar, not Rosa. You're a pillar of strength, you are, not a rose."

"Well, um, um," Sra. Rosa said, embarrassed. "I guess no one ever thought I was a flower, but plenty have felt my thorns." They both laughed at their silliness.

Sister Isabel was the one who gave her the rosary beads and taught her how to use them. She was also one of the two ladies who had taken her away from her neighborhood and her Mama and her Auntie and Mili. She was usually very nice. The one who spanked her was Sister Asunción.

Counting from the first day to today, it had been 593 days since she had arrived here. That was almost six rosaries, each day rolling by beadlike, smooth, round, unchanging. She'd gotten up this winter morning same as every other winter morning, said her prayers, washed at the too-tall stand with the basin of icy water, put her dress on over her cap-sleeved under-slip, which was also her nightdress, and which she had embroidered with cross stitching. She had learned the cross stitching from Sister Isabel, and she did it so well she was now the one making all the handkerchiefs for the sisters. She had begun to make pillow cases too, and Sister Isabel had promised she could embroider a tablecloth by summer.

She had been born in 1931, the same year as the Republic her mother had said, though she could not mention such a thing in here—the Republic was a horrible, sinful thing the sisters said, and the reason everyone was suffering so. She had been here 137 days less than two years. She had arrived just before her sixth birthday. Six years is 2,190 days—so very many days.

She did not know that a few more days of patient waiting were to pass as a cold and cruel winter slithered into a blood-red spring and another, forty-year-long wait.

She went downstairs to the kitchen to help with breakfast. There were five sisters and ten girls. There had been fourteen girls, but four had left very late at night, wrapped in white sheets, their faces hidden, and the next day everyone else had to pray for them a long time. Sometimes Rosa-Laura had nightmares that she was the girl under the sheet and other times she dreamed of her mother finding the sheet and lifting it and crying out, "Well there you are, girl! I've been looking everywhere!"

The kettle was already on the stove and Rosa-Laura said a prayer of thanks that there was fuel for the fire. Fuel meant heat and hot food and bits of crushed coal for the irons. Rosa-Laura loved the irons. Little cast-iron towers embossed with leaves and deer and rabbits. You filled one with a couple of hot crushed coals, and you waited until the plate on the bottom was good and hot, you sprinkled water carefully over the cloth (once she had tried to spray the water more finely by blowing it from her mouth like Mama did, and a sister had slapped her and called her a pig), and you ironed out the wrinkles on the dresses, the cuffs, the collars, the handkerchiefs, the pillow cases, and the sheets and towels. It was heavy work, but Rosa-Laura liked it, at least in winter. It kept her hands warm and helped her forget that Mama was taking so long to find her.

Sister Isabel came into the kitchen as Rosa-Laura was setting out the cups for breakfast. The kettle had begun to steam. Rosa-Laura was not allowed to lift it from the stove because she was so small and the kettle big and heavy, bigger and heavier than even the iron, which Rosa-Laura managed by standing on a stool at the ironing table. Sister Isabel lifted the kettle and brought it to the table with both hands. "Darling girl, do you know what has happened?"

Rosa-Laura shook her head. Sister Isabel smiled at her.

"No, Sister Isabel."

"The war is over."

Rosa-Laura considered this news. "Does that mean I can go home now, Sister Isabel?"

Sister Isabel frowned. "Girl, haven't I told you many times that you are going to stay here until you are a nun, or else, go into service with some nice, Christian family? I've told you that a thousand times."

"No you haven't, Sister, a thousand times is a lot of times. You've told me only twenty-eight times. I'm sure."

"Rosa-Laura, you are a very wicked girl this morning. But I will not be angry at you [Rosa-Laura didn't worry about Sister Isabel's being angry; it was Sister Asunción whose anger she feared] because today is such a wonderful day, a great day, a day for God, a triumph. We have won the war. Our soldiers have already begun to enter Madrid. Of course, they must be careful, there are still devils inside this capital that won't stop until they're removed. But we have won."

Rosa-Laura didn't know what to say. The sisters weren't fighting the war, so how could they have won it? They weren't soldiers. What she had overheard the sisters call "soldiers" were men she had seen from her window many times, and she had also seen soldiers come to this place late at night. Sister Isabel meant that *her side* had won the war. Rosa-Laura wasn't sure that meant anything good for herself. She had been told enough times that her own neighborhood was almost as bad as Vallecas in this matter of refusing to take the *right* side, and Rosa-Laura was not pleased with her old neighborhood being singled out like that and placed aside. She had spent many happy days in that old neighborhood.

More soldiers entering Madrid? What did that mean? Soldiers came late at night and were scary; none of the other girls had seen them, but the other girls didn't stay awake late as she did (a very naughty habit and one she had to confess if they ever had a priest again for the sisters and girls to confess to, though she did not understood why it was a sin. Much worse sin, she was angry at God for not loving the people she loved). These nighttime visitors were dressed in different uniforms from one time to the next, and they brought things for the sisters, and the sisters gave them things too. It was scary but thrilling, sitting up on the third floor, peering through the balustrades, being careful not to be seen, watching the sisters, who stood in a melted puddle of yellow candlelight downstairs, just enough to see lumpy, peculiar shapes that might be Isabel, Asunción, Mary-Margaret, Angelica, or Adoración, then the big shape of the man who had been at the door, the hurried whispers, the exchange of goods, papers, money even. The men never stayed, because this wasn't a place for men, but once a man was carried in by other men and the sisters had him brought to the back of the house. Rosa-Laura never saw him again. The next morning though, there had been dirty smears all over the kitchen, sticky black, or brown, and smelly. Rosa-Laura had to help Sister Isabel scour and bleach the floors and table before breakfast. Rosa-Laura asked the sister what the stains were and why they smelled so bad, and Sister Isabel said it was dirt. When Rosa-Laura protested that was not true, Sister Isabel slapped her, the first and last time. Hard to bear that betrayal from one who was closest to being a mother to her in this place.

It was four in the morning of an inhospitable spring, a spring that had begun not with rain and flowers but with detentions and summary executions in the streets. Sra. Rosa had stayed the night at the Doctor's house sleeping on the sofa in the cubicle off the front entrance. She had been concerned about leaving Mili at home alone, but this was important, and the girl could certainly take care of herself. She and the Doctor had decided it was the time to fetch Rosa-Laura from the nuns, and for her to go walking through Madrid's inhospitable streets at 3 a.m. would have been madness. The nationalist troops had occupied the capital for a month and a half now, and citizens like Sra. Rosa hadn't breathed a breath of peace since the troops had begun to filter in, carefully and secretively, in the late night of March 31, the early morning of April 1.

"We have to move fast now. There is to be a parade today. We'll go to the house and get her, they won't be thinking of anything but that, they won't care if we take one little girl, they can't be denounced or denied now, it's all official, they are feeling safe, victorious. The arrests have been terrible. Perhaps I'll be arrested—hush, say nothing! My mother and sister are not to know. You must return here if that happens and take care of them. Promise me."

Sra. Rosa nodded. She was going to get her daughter back. This cancelled the fact that the war was lost. Rosa-Laura home and no more bombings, good things, the best possible things. Supplies from the provinces, food, coal. But the new government, what about that? What would he do, this dumpy, short, sour-faced general who had beaten their best forces, and destroyed their Republic? He was a *gallego*, that general. She knew a saying about Galicians: *Gallego con mando, ya estoy temblando.* Galician with power, now I'm scared. She'd never actually known a real Galician, but there was no disputing old sayings, was there?

The Doctor was fearful for his fate, but she could not believe anyone would imprison a physician. He would be needed, surely. Perhaps now the family would have real money too, and could pay her. All the other rumors, the bad things that had happened since the surrender had been signed—that had nothing to do with them did it?

Before the sun rose, Sra. Rosa and Dr. Contreras hurried out into the cold May morning. The air was still, the sky dark gray but striated with cream-colored light on the eastern horizon, and the boulevards damp. Not one car was on the streets, nor any carts, nor any other pedestrians either. Sra. Rosa was afraid they might get stopped by a guard, but there was no one. It was the kind of weird stillness one feels just before a storm or an earthquake.

Sra. Rosa pushed herself to keep up with the Doctor. Being so tall he took long strides; he had lost a lot of weight during the war and had a kind of demonic, unnatural energy. They hit a rough patch in the street where cobblestones had been uprooted to help brick a small fountain, and she stumbled, nearly pitching herself into the rocky clay of the under-street. The Doctor caught her arm and held her, then helped her back onto the cobblestones. "Careful, careful," he said.

Sra. Rosa's head spun. She had eaten nothing, and suddenly, her right knee buckled and gave out, she lurched to the curb, scarcely aware of what was happening, and sat down. An avalanche of emotion, hunger, fear, shame flooded over her. She felt ill and put her head between her knees. With a grunt, the Doctor squatted next to her and took her pulse.

"It's not far now, Sra. Rosa. Let's wait a second. Breathe deeply now. Just take a deep breath."

"I'm scared she won't remember me." The tears that she had dammed up back when her house was bombed were very close to overflowing now, too close. She took a deep breath, as he had told her to, obeyed him, got hold of herself.

"I'm very proud of you, you know," he said to her.

"Um?" she said.

"You didn't go barging in, much as you wanted to. You waited and trusted me. You're the most patient woman I've ever met, Sra. Rosa. Courageous too. A real woman of Spain. Strong as a lioness. You won't regret it."

He helped her stand up and they continued, the Doctor and the lioness, walking more slowly now.

They came to the house and for the first time, she passed through the gate of the severe, seventeenth century fence of black iron bars rising eight feet and topped with spears. They rang the bell. No one came out. The Doctor made a mew of impatience, nothing vulgar, but impatience nevertheless, and rang the bell again.

"Oh, Señor, they've gone to see the troops. The victory parade." The woman who called out to them across the gardens from another house looked like a maid or a housekeeper; she wore a high buttoned black dress, a brilliant white, starched apron, and over this uniform a black cardigan.

"Are the children here?" Sra. Rosa said to her, raising her voice as the woman was so far away.

The woman glanced at Sra. Rosa, crossed her arms, and kept silent. Clearly she did not regard Sra. Rosa worthy of a reply.

"Did they take the girls with them?" The Doctor said, loudly and with authority.

"Yes, Sir," the woman said. "They've all gone. They took the children, with flowers in their hands, to give to the soldiers."

A picture of surreal strangeness flashed in the Doctor's mind: soldiers, guns, girls, flowers, blood, a boulevard covered sidewalk to sidewalk with a carpet of bloody red flowers. He controlled his breathing and ignored the vision.

"You see, Sra. Rosa, all for the good. They'll be in the open. No need to argue or bully them into bringing her out, she'll be right there."

Sra. Rosa nodded but hadn't the presence of mind to offer an "um" in assent.

Lourdes slept late and so did her boys. It was such a luxury to sleep until eight, to let the light and the need for a glass of water or a piss or boredom with the bed direct the events of one's rising. She stretched and shivered. So cold. She had some carbon. Bernardo had brought it last night. He had stayed only an hour, and to her astonishment the reason he came was not for news of the neighborhood or to take her to bed, but so that she could brush and iron a uniform he'd brought. He was deeply excited and even happy, if that simple, pretty word could be used to describe any emotion he manifested. She had cleaned the uniform with a brush dipped in water and ammonia, ironed it, wrapped it in the muslin cover he brought with it, and asked him what was happening.

"I'm wearing it tomorrow," he said. "There's to be a parade. Uptown. Down the Gran Vía, our men marching, asserting our victory over this communist stink pile, as we said we would."

"There's been parades every day," Lourdes said, confused. Trucks, troops, more and more and more. People running out to give the fascist salute. Others tremblilng inside their houses, waiting for their doors to be broken down.

"You don't know what you're talking about. Troops moving into a city are not a parade. This is a victory march, a grand celebration. Are you sure the uniform is clean? I'll beat you to death if there's a spot on it, woman. You know I mean it."

The threat was casual and as common to his conversations with her as hello and goodbye and do-this-now. It didn't worry her. She carefully began to dismantle the iron, transferring the fuel left in it to the stove. He had brought enough carbon for the iron and for heating the stove in the morning. Perhaps one day he really would kill her, but for now, she was useful to him, even desirable, and he always brought them good things, things so hard to find since the war began. The war that was already over.

Besides, she had already told him about her pregnancy. He had mumbled something about her being too old for more babies, which was what she felt too, but fact was, she was thirty-three and pregnant with his child. There were women in the neighborhood who'd had children in their fifties. She hoped it might be a girl.

She got out of bed and checked on Anacleto and Augustín sleeping on a cot in the kitchen, where Bernardo had removed them after his first night here. He didn't like being with her and the boys sleeping in the same room. It was something savages did, he told her. People from the country-side, not civilized people. "You're animals," he had said. "I can't live like that. In my home, we had a bedroom for everyone, including the servants. My parents slept in separate rooms." She could barely imagine such luxury.

"Get up now, boys, we're going to clean up and go uptown. There's to be a parade. With soldiers and tanks and maybe horses," she said to her two sleepy sons. She went outside to get some washing water from the well pump. Mili was there with a blanket wrapped around herself, her thick curly hair a tangled mess, her sleepy face puffy.

"Morning, Sra. Lourdes. How's things? Auntie didn't come home last night. Hope she comes soon. I got nothing to eat," the girl said.

Lourdes realized that Mili was naked under the blanket. It offended her, but given the state of her own belly, it would be a hypocrisy to criticize the girl. What could you do these days? Still, it must have been cold to sleep that way. And the girl wasn't even worried about Rosa's not showing up all night. Poor Rosa. She was probably working somewhere, cleaning a house, washing floors, doing whatever she must.

Mili was developing breasts. Lourdes hadn't developed breasts before she'd been pregnant, and afterward, they had never been very large, even when she was nursing. Mili's breasts would be large, and the girl would be plump, until she was old enough to be fat. She was pretty in that way, plump, smooth skinned; she smiled easily and loved to lower those long lashes and stare. Well, there was pretty and there was pretty. Lourdes may have been too tall and too thin, but she had been the prettiest girl in the neighborhood until they'd married her and her husband had filled her belly up so quickly. She had barely reached fifteen when she gave birth to Abelardo. Pretty didn't get far in this place. And her poor Abelardo didn't even get to the age his mother was when she delivered him.

"Mili, cover yourself, girl. It's chilly out. You'll get sick. If your aunt doesn't show up soon, come tell me. I'm going uptown, and I can look for her."

Mili nodded. "Hey, you got some coal? I need to heat up some water."

Lourdes said, "Well, wait here, I'll get you some." She didn't want the girl going into her home and the boys seeing her undressed like that.

She got two pieces of coal, enough to crumble into a small fire and brought them out to Mili, who took them but said nothing, certainly not thank you, just turned and went into her home. The girl had no manners, but then, what could you expect? Poor child.

Much to Rosa-Laura's surprise, the sister wore a strange contraption on her head, a heavily starched white bonnet that Rosa-Laura had ironed just yesterday, thinking it was a decoration of some sort for the statues.

"What is that, Sister Isabel?"

"It's a sort of hat, my child. We call it a cornette. This is a day of celebration. We are all going to a parade today, to welcome the soldiers," Sister Isabel said.

Rosa-Laura didn't know what a parade was, but she didn't ask either, because they had told her so often it was rude to ask questions. One just waited for the sister to explain and if there was no explanation, then God would provide one eventually. Sometimes "eventually" meant after a person died. Her Mama might get annoyed at her for talking too much and asking too many whys, yet Mama always answered her. Was it possible her Mama was more reliable than God? After all, Rosa-Laura couldn't believe anyone loved her more than her Mama loved her, but she kept that opinion to herself.

One by one the rest of the girls and the sisters arrived downstairs. The girls were all from well-off families and good neighborhoods, and being orphans now didn't change their class. This distinction had been made clear to Rosa-Laura from the start of her stay in the house. She was not allowed to sleep with them or play with them. The other girls did not wash and sew and iron. They were allowed to do some embroidery, but clearly they could not embroider as well as Rosa-Laura did, and she was given all the choice work. She loved to embroider. It was not hard to be working class if you were allowed to embroider and didn't have to sit at the big dining table in the hall and eat slowly and be so very careful of which fork went where like the other girls did. Rosa-Laura liked eating in the kitchen with Sister Isabel. Sometimes though, she wished she could have a girlfriend. She missed Mili almost as much as she missed her mother. The other girls were mean to her. They said that after the war, their parents would return and punish people like Rosa-Laura. How was she supposed to like the *right* side if what it meant was that she would get more spankings?

Once she had asked Sister Isabel why they didn't bring more girls like her, so she could have someone to play with, and Sister Isabel had said something about having gone to that horrible neighborhood only once and not to look for orphans, but to get a message to a friend. Then Sister Isabel paused, looked pale and scared, and told Rosa-Laura very harshly to keep on sewing and stop talking so much, because God hated women who talked all the time. Rosa-Laura obeyed. Perhaps her mother might be beloved of God after all, because she was mostly very quiet.

"Here, try this coat on," Sister Isabel said.

She had never had a coat before, and this such a nice one. It was a navy blue sailor-style wool coat and big for her. The cuffs and collar were slightly worn. One of the older girls had outgrown it, surely, but Rosa-Laura didn't mind at all. In fact, she wondered if she could open the seams and make it temporarily smaller. She had seen Auntie Emilia do that many times. Would she ever see Auntie Emilia again?

"We have some flowers for you to hold," Sister Isabel said. She was terribly nervous and shaking and kept clutching at her rosary and pressing her hands to her chest. "They were very hard to get, let me tell you, so you just be very careful with them and don't shame me in front of the other sisters, because they would have given them only to the little girls upstairs to carry. I interceded for you, so you can have the honor as well. When I tell you, you are to give them to the soldiers in the parade."

Rosa-Laura had never held flowers in her hands before. They were shiny and felt like velvet and satin. Red. Nested atop dusty gray-green spiky leaves. *Claveles*, Sister Isabel said. Carnations. *Clavel* meant nail too, like the ones in wooden boards and stuck through the hands of Jesus. These didn't look like nails at all. They were so beautiful.

∽⚬∾

By the time they arrived at the Gran Vía, Sra. Rosa felt as if she had been dragged by two dray horses over a hundred kilometers of cobblestones. Dr. Contreras had tried to slow down for her, but she hadn't wanted him to slow down; she wanted him to hurry, faster and faster. She had this feeling, this tremendous, painful, ecstatic feeling. She was done with patience. Exhaustion and the lack of breakfast, or dinner for that matter, could not slow her. She was operating on iron wires, scarcely aware of their existence, the iron weave of her will and her need.

The Gran Vía, or Broadway, the heart of the city, looked fair after three years of bombardments and scarcity. The boards and sandbags had been removed from the shops, the streets washed, the barren winter trees hung with ribbons and banners. Wealthy women who had not left their homes since the war's first shot, dressed mostly in black and as finely as they could, now stood along the street waving silk lace handkerchiefs in their gloved hands. Priests and friars dressed in cassocks for the first time in three years held up placards and crucifixes and rosaries. Nuns wearing the elaborate habits of various orders also for the first time in three years gathered together in sleek flocks, fluttering and chirping. Newspapers would later declare 100,000 people were out to welcome the new order. Yet, Sra. Rosa and the Doctor found it easy to walk behind the parade watchers on the sidewalk, going in the opposite direction of the parade, northwest up toward the Plaza de España.

☙

Rosa-Laura, her guardians, and the other girls had come down Princesa, passed the Plaza de España, and found a fine spot just on the Gran Vía. They had arrived in time to see the start of the parade, soldiers, tanks, even horses. Every soldier and every animal was blowing steam from nostrils abused by the cold spring air. Rosa-Laura loved seeing her own breath, this wonderful proof of her existence. She blew on the carnations in her hands too, until Sister Isabel tapped her on the cheek and motioned for her to behave.

Sometime after the parade had begun and for no reason she ever remembered, Rosa-Laura turned and looked behind her, though everyone else was looking at a passing contingent of soldiers in bright red berets. She saw Dr. Contreras, a very nice man whose house her Mama cleaned. He had given her chocolates and sometimes chucked her chin. He was a huge man, taller than anyone else, like a soft old bear standing upright, and he was smiling at her. She smiled at him, and then saw that his bulk obscured someone behind him, a very tiny woman, all in black with a shawl wrapped tightly around her, nothing but an old shawl in all this cold. Rosa-Laura dropped her flowers, looked down, picked them up, and moved decidedly toward her Mama. She held out the flowers, but her Mama didn't seem to see them.

And then Mama was hugging her, and Rosa-Laura was so happy that she was home again.

"*Hija, niña mía, ¿me recuerdes?* Daughter, my child, do you remember me?"

"Oh, Mama, what took you so long? I needed you!"

"Oh my baby, I'm sorry, I had to wait, I don't know why now."

At that point, though Sister Isabel's eyes were as myopic as a mole's, she saw what was happening and screamed. Dr. Contreras moved forward to talk to the sisters, but Sra. Rosa in a fit of terror that she might lose Rosita again, hauled the child through the parade watchers in front of her and out into the street, running right into the middle of the contingent of soldiers with red berets. She slipped and went down on one knee, the same knee as before, and grunted with the pain. Her daughter cried out, but she rose up quickly if shakily and said, "Run, daughter, run, keep going, get home."

Rose-Laura did not move from her mother's side. Whatever happened, this was where she wanted to be.

"Stop them!" Sister Isabel yelled.

"No, Sister, you don't understand," Doctor Contreras said.

A soldier wearing a red beret reached out, almost automatically, and gripped Sra. Rosa with his left hand. His right held a rifle to his shoulder.

"She's mine, soldier, she's mine. I lost her, but now I found her. She's no nun's girl, she's mine." It was almost a howl.

The loud and uncouth accent of the *madrileña* actually brought a slight smile to the tired face of the soldier. He looked to be no more than seventeen or eighteen, his eyes bloodshot, his skin grayish and dry. He let go of Sra. Rosa's arm. "Get on with you then, Mother, and God save you." he said.

In later years when the story was retold, mention of the red berets of the fanatic Catholic far right-wing of Franco's forces brought a sour smile to listeners' faces. *Requetés* could have been the laughing stock of the army with their relentless religious beliefs and loyalty to the ideals of the Spanish inquisition, had they not been so lethal and so fearless. The fascist commanders used them as shock troops, sending them in first to die by the thousands for their faith, and they went first gladly, true believers to the last. Sra. Rosa always remembered that particular red-hatted soldier affectionately, however, and when she was of a mind to pray, she included him in her modest supplications.

They ran as far as the Plaza de Canalejas, toward the shop that sold candy violets, and then Sra. Rosa's breath deserted her entirely. She stopped to catch it again, but didn't waste any time: as she caught her breath she ran her hands over her daughter to make sure she was all there, that nothing had been removed or tampered with. She noted the tiny bones lumping up hungrily under the fine downy skin, the awful choppy haircut, the scissors' nick behind the right ear, the earlobes emptied of the tiny golden dots that had been put there when the girl had been baptized, a present from her godmother, Auntie Emilia.

"Damned bitches," Sra. Rosa said. "They took your ear studs, the thieves."

"Ear studs are for the vain, Mama," Rosa-Laura said. Even as she said it, she noticed that Mama wore two gold drops hanging from each ear. She didn't know that they were plated brass and thin metal at that, but the sight of those earrings that she could not remember from before, when she was just a little girl, did make her reconsider the edict she had just pronounced.

"And gold is for those who got it," Sra. Rosa said to her daughter. She smiled and stared at the child greedily. "You are so pretty, my little one. Why'd God make you so pretty, eh? Just to torment the rest of us or to make us happy in the sight of it? Think about that, if you want to think about things vain. Ah, my beautiful child, I can't tell you how happy I am to get you back!"

And her Mama hugged her so hard you might have thought she'd flatten her, yet all the same she felt so filled up with happy she wanted to cry and yell and jump, things she had not been able to do for 638 days. "I'm happy too, Mama, happy as a saint come into heaven."

Sra. Rosa kissed her daughter's face loudly and then kissed each of her hands and began all over again with the face. She rubbed the robbed ears to warm them up and then rubbed the naked skinny legs poking out from this fine coat that needed the seams taken in. She had to get the girl home right away, it was too dangerous for them here. Had to get her fed a bit, too.

"Saints in heaven," eh? What trash had they dumped into her head these past two years? Prayers no doubt, and guilt at being alive. A few days in the patio playing with the other kids will help her forget all those old things.

PART TWO · AFTER THE WAR

CHAPTER ONE

The sky above was quiet, the walls stood still, and he could hear people walking past his house during the day again. Constancia was still afraid to leave their home; she had headed underground like a field mouse, cuddled up with his mole of a self, and there they were, two half starved creatures, awaiting the war's end. Rogelio knew this life would have to change or they'd both die. He was not going to drag her out into the streets though. He'd wait for her to get better, for some clarity to push through that fog of terror and bad memories that caused her to wake up whimpering and weeping in the middle of the night. He was sure warm food and sunshine would help greatly.

One day he emerged from his burrow and felt a certain breeze on his face. The air still felt cold, sharp, with an edge of brick and mortar dust smell, but he recognized the freshness floating in behind it. Springtime. The best time of the year for Madrid. Certainly better than winter or summer, horrible times with their extremes of cold and heat and filthy air, but also better than autumn, the air of which always had a pungent and not entirely pleasant taste of smoke and decaying leaves. Spring brought buds to the trees and birdsong and every now and then the buzz of flying insects. The sounds and the smells of spring sang life. Drifting in this clean air, the war just over seemed feeble and impotent against the movement of the earth.

The streets were still cluttered with rubble, though cleaning had begun now that it was safe. Women carted away baskets of their own buildings and dumped them in vacant lots or else just swept the building back up into itself. He loved the sound of clattering bricks and rocks being chucked about. "When the men come back, then the real job can begin," the women were saying. Rogelio was sure some of the men would never return, and also that some had already, the ones that had been stationed just outside the city. They'd snuck back into their own homes terrified or angry or both, the uniforms—if they'd had any—torn apart for the cloth and hidden, the empty guns discarded as too dangerous even to try and sell. Posters appeared in every neighborhood soon after Franco's victory parade, one on Rogelio's own house. One of the upstairs neighbors read it to him: Houses would be searched, neighborhood by neighborhood, and if weapons were found, *immediate consequences* would follow.

That spring morning he visited Sra. Rosa and his daughter, who had come home four months ago much bigger since he'd last touched her delicate face and searched for Laura in her hair and her eyelids. Rosa-Laura was playing in the patio with her cousin Mili, who had also returned, who had also grown. Their voices resonating like glass bells in the background of his discussion with Sra. Rosa and her neighbor, Sra. Lourdes brought a fullness to his throat and his heart that made him want to cry out with delight.

Yet despite his happiness, the discussion he had with his sister-in-law and her neighbor about the doings of the new authority in Madrid unnerved him.

"Vallecas. You think they're going to take this above Atocha? No, they started in Vallecas. They just hauled them out. Shot them there on Presilla Street, right in front of the women and kids. Others were arrested. Maybe we're next on the list. The war wasn't enough, now there's more?"

He noted the rage in Sra. Rosa's voice as she repeated this news. Sra. Lourdes, in that soft and hesitant voice of hers, added that the city's soccer stadiums were full of prisoners, that roundups and purges had begun. The use of the word "purge" confused Sra. Rosa for a moment. She associated the word with powerful laxatives. Rogelio would have laughed had the reality not been so ghastly.

When she realized what Sra. Lourdes actually meant, Sra. Rosa said she felt offended beyond reason, as if the men who had defended Madrid were shit and needed to be flushed out.

"Ah," Rogelio paraphrased, "Like the ox, not only deballed but also shot to death." The real saying was "(A laborer is) like the ox: not only deballed but also beaten to death," but a little wordplay never hurt a true saying.

Sra. Lourdes coughed slightly and cleared her throat. She said, "Rogelio, Rosa, be careful. It's not the time to complain. We have to repair the damage and get things going again. Who knows what the new government will be like? Maybe it's all for the best." That shy voice of hers had dropped to a near whisper. He had to lean forward to hear better. Her voice always came from above him, tree leaves rustling in the breeze, poplars, he thought, or white birches.

Neither Rogelio nor Rosa commented on Sra. Lourdes's terrible advice. He was safe because a childhood illness had already deballed him, more or less. That's what they would think. He wondered if he had made a terrible mistake not reporting what he had felt during the war, the sensation of enemies walking in the city itself, behind the lines, the feeling that now and then he had passed a vicious creature ready to attack. What would they have said, You're crazy, blind man—or, would they have listened? The former. The word for a man like him was *invalido* or *menosvalido*. Invalid, or less than valid. Cripple. Useless, without purchase, not worthy.

Sra. Lourdes said something about going out to look for some food and left. Sra. Rosa told Rogelio she had chamomile, foraged from the spring soil around the Puerta de Toledo, and she'd make some tea for them both. Rosa-Laura came in for a moment, put her arms around his neck and kissed him, then went off to play in the plaza with Mili and Sra. Lourdes's boys. Sra. Rosa grumbled to him that she did not like her girls playing with the boys, but what could you do? Soon they would be in school. He could hear the delight in her rough voice as she said that, the pride. She sat him down on the bed cot inside her home and gave him a piece of cloth that his daughter had embroidered, so he could feel the beauty and quality of the work.

"Real good work, that. The girl is talented. Even the sisters at her new school said so. They were pleased to admit her, you bet."

He smiled at the air around him, his fingers carefully skimming each French knot, each looped leaf, each fine cross stitch. Sra. Rosa tapped his hand gently to let him know that a cup of hot tea had been placed next to it. He drank the infusion slowly, careful not to burn his lips, warming his hands on the cup. Sra. Rosa was sitting across from him, almost out her door, rustling a cloth every now and then. Sewing. His Laura had made that sound too.

"Some day when you go shopping, when we all have something to buy and money to buy it with," Rogelio said to her, "I would very much appreciate it if you would take Constancia with you. She's frightened about going out, but now that the bombing is over, perhaps I can convince her. Be good for her."

"Um," Sra. Rosa said by way of assent.

"The neighbor down the street from us, Isabel García, you know her?"

"Um," Sra. Rosa said.

"She has olive oil. Her son-in-law ran a butcher shop before the war, he knows truckers and farmers. See if she wants a dress or a shirt for one of her sons now they're come home, and maybe they'll let go some of that oil."

"Um," Sra. Rosa said. She wished Rogelio could see her nod her head so that she wouldn't have to talk so much. Then something important occurred to her. "Look, Rogelio, the black market business, careful those you talk to."

"Why, Rosa?"

"Lourdes's man. He's a copper. Fifth column, it's certain. He'll want to know about black market stuff. "

"Lourdes's man?"

"The new one. Got him months ago, um, uh, about nine, if you know what I mean. Been parading around the neighborhood, setting up this block chieftain stuff. A lot of contraband she gets from him, but he doesn't care for us to have it. If she slips and says something about someone else in the neighborhood with too much stuff, well..."

"I see." Rogelio finished his tea. "That was good tea, Rosa. I'm going to go home now. Tell Rosita-Laura the next time I come, I'll try to bring her something nice. You can send her over to see us any time you need someone to watch her for you, you know. Constancia likes her."

"Um," Sra. Rosa said.

Rogelio tapped himself out into the patio, brushing past Sra. Rosa and through the edges of the heavy curtain she used for privacy and to keep the warmth in during the daytime when the wooden door stayed open and thus announced to everyone she was home. He took a deep breath, hoping to get another joyful feeling from the spring air that had so elated him that morning. He smelled greens boiling in someone's pot, a poor lunch but a good sign. People had fuel again, if not meat to cook over it. He smelled the whiff of rankness emanating from the communal latrine at the far end of the patio. He heard children playing, a wonderful sound. A pigeon flapped by overhead, the heaviness of its wings reminding him of wet clothes and sheets hung on a line over the street and yielding in the wind. How had that poor pigeon survived the war? He himself had tasted pigeon stew. Tough and gamy, just like you'd expect, *Sí, Señor*. But he delighted in the sound of flight. Crows and pigeons, heavy sounding; a bat now and then, barely any sound at all, just a whisper like paper blowing in the wind; sparrows sudden and soft; swallows, noisy, swift little creatures.

His tenderness toward birds was not shared by his neighbors. Spaniards seldom romanticized their flying friends; they ate them, not just in wartime but as a delicacy of spring migration. When the goldfinches flew over Spain headed for Africa, many of them ended up roasted and piled on big platters, set on a thousand tavern counters from north to south, east to west. Well, what could you do? Finches were delicious. Yet, it was bread Rogelio craved, not crispy birdies. The bakery across the street from his house had been closed these past years. He yearned for it to open again, for the warmth and smell of the ovens to fly to him clear across the street and down his basement, before sunrise.

He passed through the short narrow tunnel that was the entranceway of the building and ran directly into someone who had been standing there in its recesses, quietly, perhaps watching him. He yelped in surprise, and the man cursed him, "Son of a whore, cretin, cripple, get out of my way," and Rogelio mumbled some kind of apology without thinking, though it was the other man who should have apologized.

He exited into the street, stumbling on the cobblestones, disoriented and frightened. He hadn't felt the presence of the man lurking there, but now that presence permeated Rogelio's skin. A young man, a smoker (but then everyone was a smoker), tall, broad, educated accent, good woolen coat, brass buttons, behind the tobacco (and the tobacco'd voice) the smell of expensive soap, and, musky masculine power. He wore gloves too, leather ones. Rogelio felt for the wall on the narrow sidewalk across the street and stopped for a moment to catch his breath and make sure he was facing in the right direction. What had happened to his "sixth" sense? He had felt this kind of presence before, why not now? The war was over and his abilities over too? Or had his momentary happiness cancelled out the rest?

So that was Lourdes's man. Poor woman. What had he been waiting for there, in the enclosed entranceway? She was in her house, why had he not gone directly there?

Announcements had been posted. No one was talking but everyone was gossiping in whispers. Every neighborhood now would have its "chief," a *sereno*, the reestablished night watchman, who would be expected to report on comings and goings, particularly late at night. He would be expected to know who had weapons and who was pilfering from the neighbors. It was no longer a matter of who was a drunken lout and who was cheating on her husband. Besides the tips a neighborhood's *sereno* customarily got for escorting people home late at night, and kickbacks from the brothels, the tavern owners, and the market vendors, now he could expect a small but regular government salary to keep tabs on "his" area, and if he failed to do so, he could expect to pay a heavy price.

Beyond the *sereno*, the cops, and after the cops, the Civil Guard, *la presencia*. The Spanish Civil Guard was a border and country patrol, originally formed to combat smuggling, but Rogelio had heard that until everything was completely "secured" in Madrid and people were clear that they dare not form an underground or resist the inevitability of the dictatorship, the guards would stay. Rogelio felt sorry for himself and his neighbors. The siege and the airborne death might be over, maybe they'd even have a drop of milk and a piece of bread before long, but he surmised the worst was yet to come, and the presence of the man—police or secret service?—in the entranceway emphasized that.

Every Sunday, they attended Mass. Rosa-Laura was used to Mass after her sojourn with the nuns of course, and she didn't question her mother on this new custom. Years later, Mama would explain to her daughter that she'd made a deal with Mother Mary, and you didn't cheat on a deal made honestly or otherwise dishonor your word. At first, they attended Mass at San Francisco el Grande, a dour, dark, gloomy old building on the way to the Plaza Mayor. Later, they attended Mass at the Church of San Lorenzo in their own neighborhood, which had been carefully rebuilt, as Sra. Rosa had suspected it would be, and reestablished as the neighborhood's chief place of worship.

Sra. Rosa also began the arrangements for Rosa-Laura and Mili to attend school. She gathered together the papers proving their legitimate birth, a letter for the mother superior from Dr. Contreras, which cost her a fair amount of face to ask for, and samples of Rosa-Laura's embroidery. The embroidery business was a godsend, truly. Days after Rosa had brought her daughter home, she discovered her girl busily repairing an old pillow case with a pretty overlay of sequin-sized brown and blue roses. Brown and blue were the only colors the child could find in the sack of twisted satin threads that Auntie Emilia had left behind when she went to Valencia. Sra. Rosa had said nothing as she watched her clever daughter. She just got up, walked to a shop in the plaza, and used a couple of *céntimos* she had saved to invest in new thread, tiny twists of red, green, yellow, pink, and white. She walked back home and gave them all to Rosa-Laura without a word about the expense or caution against any possible wastage. Her daughter was a treasure; you did not begrudge a treasure some thread. Rosa-Laura had been ecstatic.

All this activity made for lovely neighborhood gossip. The women left in Sra. Rosa's building, down the street, in the plaza, found it wonderful to be able to talk about a talented child instead of death and bombing and food shortages, not to mention the intense fear that the new regime inspired, not the sort of ghostly fear that some distant evil might occasion, but the fear bestowed by the house-to-house searches begun in Vallecas and probably coming next to their neighborhood. So much better to talk about Rosa-Laura's skill with the embroidery needle.

Mili was disgusted with all this bustle and embroidery. When she realized Auntie Rosa was preparing to put her back in school, she protested with screams and foot-stamping. To her amazement, Auntie did not rush to placate her and back off the plan. The woman just stood there staring at her niece, her jaw stiff, her eyes steely. When Mili finally quieted down, Auntie Rosa said, in a still, tight voice, "There'll be no more of that, girl. You'll go to school. And you'll do well. It's the least you can do for your mother and for me. You're lucky to be in school. Some people aren't even allowed there."

"Whatever that meant," Mili muttered to her cousin later on, as they sat once again in the patio playing with the pincushion, a daily entertainment now, especially since the weather had become as peaceful as the cannons. Mili jabbed each pin in the fat velvet heart of the pincushion as if it were a real organ that she could kill bit by bit. She was thirteen. In another year, she could work. She wanted to work in a beautiful store on the Gran Vía, selling pretty things and meeting people. She did not want to study stupid boring things that would do her no good nor offer her money or freedom.

Rosa-Laura listened to her cousin without understanding any of her complaints. She herself was happy to be here in the patio, with her Mama in their home (which was Aunt Emilia's home, only Auntie was in heaven now), with Mili, playing *bonis*. Love and companionship, her Mama and her cousin. As for school, the idea of that excited Rosa-Laura so much she felt her chest would burst. She was astounded that Mili didn't like school. What did Mili mean by "boring"?

After ten minutes of this activity, Anacleto came out and stood there, watching them, without a smile or a word. He was a solid fellow, with short, spiky brown hair, dark brown eyes, dirty clothes.

"Hey, lump-of-coal, you going to say hello?" Mili said. She giggled and then she winked at Anacleto. He kept on staring at her and finally approached closer, but said nothing.

Rosa-Laura felt a little uncomfortable. She wasn't very used to boys, and they scared her somewhat. The nuns had told her a thousand times they were devils and good girls avoided them, but truth be told, she felt sorry for Anacleto. Mili had already told her about the day Abelardo died and how everyone said that Anacleto hadn't been right in the head since then. Mili always knew more about what was happening in the neighborhood than Rosa-Laura. "People like me," Mili had said to Rosa-Laura. "I can talk to anyone. I got a lot of personality."

Mucho personalidad. Rosa-Laura didn't even know what that meant. She was embarrassed to ask, but she knew that Mili was adorable and assumed that was the kernel of the thing. Look at Anacleto standing there, staring at her, like he was in love. Maybe they would get married some day. Rosa-Laura felt no jealousy of her beautiful cousin, but she did feel cheated in the matter of personality. Clearly, she was an uninteresting person. A *mosquita muerta*, a goody-two-shoes, her cousin called her, and (even worse) someone who liked to work and study, an *empollona*.

At least those names were better than what Maria-Sofronia had called her. Maria-Sofronia was a sour-faced, mean girl that Rosa-Laura had approached one day soon after arriving at the eorphanage. Rosa-Laura approached her not because she was looking for a friend her own age, but because Maria-Sofronia had a kitten, a miniscule thing no more than a month old. It was mewling horribly, a sort of kitten-sob, probably because Maria-Sofronia was twisting it ruthlessly with both hands and poking its eyes and nose.

"Can I play with it?" Maria-Rosa said.

"You're the new kitchen help," Maria-Sofronia said, emphatically. "*I'm* a guest. You're low class, a servant, a drudge. You're not supposed to talk to me, and I'm going to tell Sister Asunción on you!."

Rosa-Laura stood there a moment, staring at Maria-Sofronia and the kitten. The girl was seated in a chair in the cool foyer of the orphanage, probably to escape the heat in the upper floors or the inner patio. She was nearly at eye level with Rosa-Laura even though she was seated, because Rosa-Laura was a small child. Maria-Sofronia was tall but thin and had eyes muddy-colored with hunger and rage. Her skin was yellower than the kitten's.

"I'm not a servant. I'm waiting for my Mama to come get me."

"Your Mama's dead and in hell, because she was a nasty communist. I heard Sister Asunción say so. And you mustn't talk to me any more!" And with that, Maria-Sofronia flung the kitten at Rosa-Laura's face.

Rosa-Laura caught the kitten and ran to her room, crying. She nursed the tiny creature as best she could, but all she had for it was water, which it could not drink. It showed scant life and finally died later that night. The next day, Sister Isabel had taken it away, but would not tell Rosa-Laura what she was going to do with it. She did tell Rosa-Laura not to speak to the girls from the upper floors any more.

"Will the kitty-cat go to heaven now?" Rosa-Laura asked Sister Isabel.

But Sister Isabel said it could not. Neither could her Mama, evidently. Why did God make people and other creatures he didn't like?

The old blind woman who before the war had sat at the doorway to the market on Tribulete selling parsley and lemons and every now and then a few twigs of fresh laurel appeared there again one early summer morning, holding up her produce to passersby like a Vestal blessing the air. No one asked her where she had gone during the war after the first time when she'd mumbled imprecations and crazy words. Things no one wanted to hear these days. Who needed to know anyway? It was just a way of being neighborly, that kind of questioning, only now, everyone began to see that being neighborly would be different since Franco had won the war.

Folk wisdom was still important, of course. For instance, *Antes mujer de un pobre que manceba de un conde,* Better a poor man's wife than a count's whore. Some of the neighborhood people despised Lourdes for her alliance with that man whose presence shot fear through them and sometimes a thrill of perversion. Handsome son of a bitch he was, handsome and cold and utterly without respect. Yet, if you wanted something, if you had a really big favor to ask, the release of a man from some arena or soccer stadium, you could ask Lourdes, and she'd ask him, even if it meant he'd rack the back of his hand across her face for the presumption. Lourdes never said no to any request, but the neighborhood women learned to ask only for dire need, life and death, because clearly, it brought more hell to Lourdes, poor whore that she was.

❧

The school Sra. Rosa found for her girls was in Embajadores, Rodas Street, *El Colegio del Ayuntamiento,* a simple five minute walk from their home. It was on the second floor of a huge old building. She presented her girls' papers to the nuns, proudly. Beautiful birth certificates, family booklets, and baptismal certificates, on tissuey paper criss-crossed with delicate red silk ribbons and stamped with gilt seals. Papers that proclaimed the names and occupations of both parents, proof of legitimacy. Sra. Rosa's hands trembled as she handed over the provenance of her two precious children.

The day before, she and most of the women in her building had gone uptown to get identification papers. Lourdes went with them, as they all believed it would be safer with her along. A dull, swampy terror saturated their every movement, their questions, their long wait in line, but it went well after all: no one was denounced nor appeared on any sinister list. From now on, they and every other Spanish citizen would carry an identification card with their photo and have their fingerprints on file. Children would carry student papers until they were old enough to work, at thirteen or fourteen, then they too would have to carry national identification cards everywhere they went. Life under the dictatorship had begun. No one at the time suspected it would last forty years and end very quietly, the whole country holding its breath, poised to stumble out into the sunlight of a burning, bright release.

❧

Quickly it became evident Rosa-Laura was a wonderful student. Her teachers adored her, because no teacher can resist a child that loves to listen and learn and understands easily, enthusiastically. When she set those big blue eyes into a powerfully serious look and pursed her mouth pondering a problem, particularly a mathematical problem, the teacher observing her would thrill with pride. Sister Pilar doted on her and let her cross-stitch her personal handkerchiefs. Rosa-Laura shot from levels *pequeña* to *mediana* to *mayores* like a baby goat jumping from peak to peak, and soon was two classes ahead of Mili. Mili dealt with this minor treason in her own way: she disparaged, ridiculed, and laughed at Rosa-Laura, making the little *empollona* the joke of the schoolyard. It humiliated Rosa-Laura so that she would have done anything to please her cousin and make Mili like her again.

❧

One day in early spring, more than a year after the war stopped and when the world had begun to seem normal again, Mili casually invited her cousin to skip classes and accompany her and Anacleto to a park near the royal palace, a pretty place on a hill with a view of the Sierra to the north. Rosa-Laura was sick with fear at the wickedness of it all, but did not dare refuse.

The park was forested and a few civil guards watched the place. Anacleto joined them only after they'd passed the Plaza Mayor where he'd been waiting for them. He glanced at Rosa-Laura. Mili took his hand, but she ignored him and talked volubly to her cousin. Rosa-Laura still ached about ditching school, but she paid strict attention to Mili and tried to laugh knowingly at all her jokes.

They entered through an elaborate iron gate, pretending not to notice the civil guard there with his machine gun. He in turn barely glanced at them. They walked until they found a bench and sat down, looking out over the deep green forests of the north that inclined upward into the mountains. Mili opened a paper cornucopia she was carrying and dispersed a pile of individually wrapped fruit candies. Anacleto gave Mili a cornucopia of fruit candies for her to disperse. Anacleto's new stepfather, a truly frightening man who seemed to be very rich, had brought it to his mother.

A herd of sheepish clouds lazily ambled across the vast sky and cut the glare of the late spring day; the air lay warm and still on them but not hot. Mili kept on talking to Rosa-Laura, quite normally, telling her some story or another, and when Rosa-Laura turned from the view to reply to something Mili had said, she noticed that Anacleto's hand was underneath Mili's skirt. Mili didn't seem to notice. Rosa-Laura had no idea what to do. This was something the nuns talked about now and then, and she knew that a sin was being committed. Finally, she asked Mili timidly if they could go home.

"Sure," Mili said. Then, "That's enough, kid, we all got to get home now." Anacleto removed his hand. He stared at it for a while, then rubbed his nose with it appreciatively. He never smiled. People seldom saw him smile.

"I got to piss first," the boy said.

"Look here," Mili said to him. "Rosi doesn't know what boys look like, do you Rosita?"

Rosa-Laura was very indignant. "I do too! Anacleto's a boy! I know what he looks like!"

Mili giggled. "I mean in his pants, silly, you got no idea what's in his pants!"

Then to Rosa-Laura's absolute astonishment, Anacleto unbuttoned his corduroy britches and pulled out something that looked like a thick finger with no nail. She'd seen a baby boy, Lourdes's new son, Anacleto's brother, and she knew boys had little half-thumb pissers instead of baby girl splits, but this thing really looked different from the baby's. Anacleto proceeded to bathe a tree, aiming the finger like a fountain spout, an accomplishment that left Rosa-Laura speechless. Mili burst out laughing so hard she could barely control herself. Anacleto put the finger back in his pants, buttoned them, and looked up calmly at the guard that both Mili and Rosa-Laura had not seen approaching because they were watching Anacleto instead of watching out.

"*Hijo de puta*, you get out of here now, or I'll take you uptown. Pissing in public is against the law."

Rosa-Laura almost wet her own panties she was so terrified, but Mili just sighed gustily and said in a loud voice, "Anacleto, you're just disgusting! I'm sorry, Mister Guard, he's just a little boy you know, and my Mama's told him, but we're just his sisters and he won't listen to us at all."

"Get out of here," the guard said. "Bunch of Gypsies, little animals, and I should herd you all to jail but I have more important things to do. Get out of here. Parks are for nice folk, grownups."

Rosa-Laura hated the way he looked at the both of them, up and down, up and down, but then he shrugged and walked off, yet still keeping an eye on the girls.

Anacleto reached for Mili's hand. "Oh, you're really nasty, you know," Mili said, pulling her hand away. "after handling that thing of yours! You find a fountain and wash your hands, Mister."

"Isn't as if you haven't handled it yourself, 'big sister'," Anacleto said, gruffly. He seemed offended, but then he sighed and went down the incline to a copper fountain where he washed his hands.

All of this was mystery and embarrassment to Rosa-Laura, and she had no idea what to say to her cousin or Anacleto. She felt like such an idiot, but she did know she couldn't tell anyone about this, not her girlfriends or her mother even, and certainly not the nuns or a priest at confession. Besides, was it her sin as well as Mili's or only Mili's? Was it something she should confess or should Mili confess or both of them?

Of course, Sra. Rosa found out about their skipping classes. The very next day Sister Pilar sent for her, and she had to walk down to the school and miss her morning at the Doctor's house. She came home two hours later, just before siesta, her ears burning, grabbed Mili by the arm as the girls were playing in the patio, and dragged her inside. She slapped Mili hard about the shoulders and even aimed at the girl's face. Mili was already a head and a half taller than her aunt and twice as heavy, so she dodged the assault easily. But she was enraged, and screamed, then pushed her aunt down onto the cot. She ran out the door, out the patio, and down the alleyway before anyone could stop her. Sra. Rosa stood at the doorway, exhausted with passion and despair.

"I should hit you too, you know, I should, because you're so stupid to do what she says, you are, you like school, Rosa-Laura, so why ditch it?"

Rosa-Laura sat on the patio stones, sobbing not only in shame for her transgression and the spectacle her mother had made for all the neighbors to see and hear, but also because she had never seen her mother assault anyone. She had been spanked when she was at the orphanage, she'd seen other mothers slap their children, she had seen fathers beat their sons many times, and she had seen her teachers time and again bring down a ruler hard on some offending girl's palms, but her own mother? It was unthinkable.

Wails broke from the street doorway, and Lourdes entered the patio with her baby boy, Bernardito, in her arms. Augustín tailed behind her, holding onto the skirt of her dress. It was a nice dress, blue, with flat blue and green mother-of-pearl buttons up the front. Lourdes's breasts were full now, as they had never been before in all her other pregnancies. She had time, food, and finances to sit for hours holding her baby and feeding him. He was all male, it was true, and she had prayed for a daughter, but what god or mother of god would listen to such a disgraced supplicant as her?

When the baby was born his father told her that he already had three girls from his wife—the first time he'd mentioned a wife—and he was glad to have finally produced a son, even if the kid was a bastard. In the glow of his achievement, he'd promised Lourdes he'd get proper papers for the baby, none of that "father unknown" business for his son. He had not mentioned to Lourdes that those papers would have his own wife's name on them as mother, not hers, but she wouldn't have protested even had she known.

"What's this, now, what's this?" Lourdes said to Rosa-Laura. Sra. Rosa had turned her back on the whole scene and was facing her doorway, her arms tightly crossed, her face black with shame. Several of the neighbors from upstairs were standing in the gallery looking down at the patio. Others were peeking out their doorways. Sra. Rosa was utterly humiliated. *Fine time for the neighborhood hussy to come home with her bastard in her arms and—*

"Rosa, please, tell me. It can't be that bad."

Sra. Rosa pursed a gusty sigh. "They skipped school yesterday. Both of them. Shameless, shameless. They get to go to a real school, and now look."

"Oh, Rosa, that's nothing, nothing. It just happens now and then. Rosa-Laura is a good girl, you know that—" Lourdes said nothing about Mili, and Sra. Rosa noticed the omission.

Bernardito stopped fussing and crying and belched, primitively, lustily. Augustín snorted in derision. He hated his new brother, but at least Papa Bernardo didn't hit Mama or yell at him and Anacleto as much now that the baby had come. He edged closer to Rosa-Laura and tentatively touched her hand, gently trying to get her to hold hands with him. Rosa-Laura snatched her hand away and stuck her tongue out at him.

"Oh well, look at that! A lady never sticks out her tongue! You'd never see Srta. Guillermina do that!" Sra. Rosa said.

"He touched me! I don't like it. He's a baby, and I don't like it. Mama, Mama, I'm sorry I skipped school. I'll never do it again!"

"See," Lourdes said, as she shifted her hefty child from one side to another. "She didn't mean it. And you Augustín, don't think I didn't see that. You leave the girls alone."

"Anacleto holds Mili's hand. And she lets him."

Both women blushed and looked away from each other. "Well," Lourdes said finally, "he's not supposed to. And Mili is just trying to be polite, but she shouldn't let him. Here, take your baby brother and go in the house. I'll be in soon."

Augustín hefted the big baby clumsily into his arms and slogged across the patio to his home, hauling the kid like a sack. The women took the drama inside Sra. Rosa's house. Lourdes set some fuel to burning and prepared a pot for chicory coffee. Rosa-Laura huddled on the cot, sniveling and utterly miserable. Loudes sat awkwardly on a stool, her long legs folded almost up to her chin, and Sra. Rosa sat next to her daughter, wringing her hands. Finally, Sra. Rosa reached out shyly and patted Rosa-Laura on the arm.

"Mama, I just didn't want Mili to think I was such a, such a *mosquita muerta*! I hate being so uninteresting! Was it so bad to miss just one day? Two more years and I'll be working, won't I? And I know all the work now, I get a four-plus in mathematics, and Sister Gloria Hosanna says there's no more mathematics for me to learn, I know it all! And I can read better than any of the other girls, too, and I sew better, so why can't I go to the park for a day?"

"*Nadie es tan ignorante que no sepa algo, ni tan sabio que lo sepa todo.* No one is so ignorant that they don't know something, nor so wise that they know everything," Sra. Rosa said. "You think you know everything? So much? You know enough to be a teacher, maybe? Then teach!"

Lourdes poured the mess she'd brewed into three cups and added a heaping spoonful of sugar to each. Rosa winced at the expense, but Lourdes had plenty of supplies now and shared liberally with all her neighbors, so how could Rosa be stingy to her?

"You know," Lourdes said, "Rosita-Laura, maybe you are so smart you can take a day off now and then, but can Mili? She's behind isn't she?

And when you give in to her like that and go off, well, it's doesn't help her much, does it?"

Rosa-Laura sighed and set to whimpering again. The two women watched her quietly. You could complain all you wanted about being uninteresting, a *mosquita muerta*, but what good came of defying convention, of breaking rules, of running off and making powerful people in your life mad at you? That sort of thing might work for a boy or a man, they might get some fun or even some benefit from it, but not a woman. Even Lourdes, with her new dress and her new baby, and a pantry full of things, knew that she was the disgrace of the neighborhood and lucky that the other women would even accept her sharing her ill-gotten wealth or still say *Buenos* to her when she passed them on the street.

"Look," Lourdes said, "You want Mili to end up a beggar or a whore? Is that what you want? Mili has to go to school and make something of herself. You have to help her. You're smarter than she is, and that's better than being 'interesting' or whatever—besides, girl, a woman don't get to be *interesting* until she's a lot older, until she's real experienced, and experience costs. Believe me, it costs."

Sra. Rosa sniffled softly. She was afraid for Mili, very afraid. She was afraid for Rosa-Laura. She had to confide in someone, and she didn't want to worry Rogelio and she couldn't bear to make Lourdes feel any worse. She would consult with the Doctor. She hated to bother him, but after all, maybe now was the time to divulge the secret about that first day she had appeared at his house looking for a father for Emilia and finding a funeral.

Dr. Contreras met Mili at the metro stop nearest his house, as he had promised Sra. Rosa, and walked home with her. He ushered her into his dining room, and pulled out a chair and held it out until she sat down. Her eyes widened at the courtesy. She sat down, glanced around the room and then, of course, up at the chandelier.

"It's every bit as gorgeous as Auntie Rosa said it was, Doctor," she said. She smiled grandly at him. Her teeth were crooked but clean, and none were missing. Her skin was clear and the color of cream sherry. She ate well, that was sure.

She pretended to keep her eyes on him, but she was checking out the room with a glance here and there, at the green vase full of calla lilies in the middle of the table, at the heavy lace tablecloth, at the multitude of cabinets with their brilliant gimcracks and porcelain figurines, at the paintings crowded at both ends of the room, and at the side board with its gilt and platinum bordered China dishes and large mahogany box where their best silver was stored.

The Doctor saw that he would have to struggle for Mili's attention. He took his time and used it to look her over thoroughly while she was diverted. She was tall and looked much older than fourteen. Her breasts were thoroughly developed and stuck out far enough to make his walk with her from the metro to his house a joke. He had never seen so many males of all ages unable to move their eyes from an object—a pair of objects—in his life. Her clothing was unnecessarily tight; surely Sra. Rosa had enough cloth to make the girl a dress or a blouse and skirt more appropriate and comfortable? She was chubby, and plump-bodied women were considered very lovely in this day and age of near starvation and rigid morality. She had pitch black hair, large brown eyes (probably myopic), prominent cheek dimples, and a slightly receding chin and low forehead, both latter attributes ugly to the doctor, though clearly his opinion in such a matter didn't count for much.

"Do you know why your Aunt Rosa asked me to speak with you, child?" He said. He used his best doctor voice, the soft-but-with-authority voice that he used on frightened patients.

Mili forced herself to look at him and away from the cabinets. She knew she had to do well at this interview, or at least, give everyone the impression that she was going to be better, or else they'd punish her. Or something. How could they punish her? She hated school, so if they took her out of school a little early, well, so much the better. She frowned at the difficulty of all this contradiction.

"Really, Sir, it's not such a big deal like Auntie Rosa says. I need a job is all. I'm of age. I'm nearly done at school anyway. I can work at a store. I'm really good with people and people like me."

"Do you think," Dr. Contreras said, "that any decent store would hire a girl to serve their clients who speaks as badly as you do? Who is lazy and who can't be trusted to come in on time or show any kind of self-discipline?"

Mili blushed furiously. How dare he talk to her like that? He talked to her like her fucking teachers, so mean, so rude, so *untrue*. She took a deep breath. She certainly could not show any anger in front of this powerful man, this rich man. The family needed him; indeed, she needed him. Best not to burn bridges, best to show him how smart and clever and cute she really was. He liked her anyway. She knew that the first day they met, that day he let her inject her Mama. Why, if she played her cards right and flirted with him just so, he might even marry her. Of course, he was way too old, and he wasn't the kind of guy she liked the looks of, tall but no muscle at all, pudgy, and though his hair was nearly blond, light brown at least, clearly he'd soon be bald. He had nice eyes anyway, brown with lots of gold and that peculiar resin color, so that was OK. Guy that big had to have lots in his pants, and that meant he was a real man. Best of all of course, he was really, really rich. If she just got a chance to lean into him, let her breasts brush his arm or something, he'd drop everything and get all fluttered, like other older men she'd gotten the best of.

"Sir, I know I've been bad, but I'm not a school girl, really. My cousin Rosa-Laura, now, she's really good at all that, a regular *empollona*. But if I don't speak good, I can learn, fast. I'll listen to the shop girls next time I'm in a nice store."

"When do you go to nice stores?" Dr. Contreras said. He pulled out an elegant tooled red leather case and took out his sunglasses and began to polish them. His eyes had been bothering him lately, and he needed dark glasses when outside in the brilliant, hard, city sunlight. It had taken him weeks to find this pair, imported of course, because things like this were not yet made in Spain. He found them in a very elegant gentleman's shop off Alcalá. And thinking of that, he decided he would take Mili uptown later, after the siesta hours, and bring her to a few shops, where she could see how impossible her dream was unless she settled down and learned a few things. He had not yet given up on the notion of making her a nurse, either. With just a little discipline, she would be a wonderful nurse. She certainly had a good bedside manner.

Mili did not answer his question. She was staring at the sunglasses.

"Mili, listen to me. When do you go into nice stores? Would they even let you in by yourself, a girl with poor clothes and dirty hands?"

Mili blushed again, harder. A vein throbbed in her temple. She set her mouth hard, clenched her teeth. "Sir, this isn't nice at all. You can't say such things to me."

"I'm saying it for your own good, Mili."

Well here it comes. All the grownups said stupid things like that. Lecturing know-it-alls. "Sir, school is dull. That's it and you can't convince me different. They go on and on, those old women with their ugly faces. No wonder they had to become nuns! No man would look at them! And all right, I don't talk like I should. But I can listen. I'm smart, smarter than anyone gives me credit for. I can make myself sound just like anyone I want to. I can be an actress I'm so smart, and in fact, that's what I'm thinking of now, being an actress! You should see me imitating Sister Pilar! I got all the girls in the schoolyard laughing to burst I'm so good at it!"

This was going to be difficult. He certainly wasn't very good at counseling young girls. The truth was, that Mili, for all her cleverness, for all her native wisdom and sharp ways, didn't appear to have much in the way of intelligence. The Doctor sighed.

"Mili, I can get you into a nursing school, if you'll just apply yourself now and pass this level and the next one. It shouldn't take you more than two years to catch up, and then I'll get you into nursing school. It's a highly respectable career, and there's money to be made as well. Your Aunt would be so happy and so proud. Your poor mother too, were she here, would be so proud. This acting thing—well, it's ridiculous, really. And acting isn't just imitating people, after all, even acting requires you to study, requires some academy training. Such places are expensive, and unfortunately, often disreputable as well. On the one hand, you'd need a sponsor, and on the other, acting is hard work, child, believe it or not. And the more talent a person has, the harder they work."

Mili said absolutely nothing and looked toward the balcony. The Doctor saw he had lost her, utterly. Well, he'd suspected he might not get very far with this. He'd done it for Rosa's sake, that's all. Mili would survive or she wouldn't. That was the cold truth of the matter.

"Can I look at those things?" Mili said.

She surprised him with this odd request, but he handed her the case. Very delicately she opened it and lifted out the sunglasses. She put them on. They were too big for her and rather masculine, but still they flattered her round face and disguised the fact that her forehead was low. She smiled broadly and her dimples blossomed. "What do they look like?"

"Go look in the mirror," he said, wearily indicating the huge gilt framed mirror on the wall facing down the table and the balcony. She got up, carefully, and walked over to the mirror. She had a very accomplished walk. She'd learned it somewhere. Perhaps after all, she was destined to be an actress. Or a chorus girl.

"Ooo, they look so nice!" She giggled, turned right and left, then said, "I don't suppose you want to give them to me!?"

He simply stared at her, shocked. She laughed. "Oh, I was just kidding, honest. Are they real expensive, these things?"

"Considerably," Dr. Contreras said. All he wanted at the moment was to get her out of his house. "Listen, let's take a walk and go look at the shops on Serrano. We can go inside a few, and you can observe the sales-girls. Listen to them a bit."

"Phenomenal," Mili said. He stood up and held out his hand. She smiled and gave him back his sunglasses, stroking his hand as he took them. He popped them into the case, snapped it shut, and pushed it toward the vase of lilies in the center of the table, automatically. He took a very deep breath.

"Of course," he said, "if you started working in a smaller, neighborhood shop you wouldn't have to be so polished. You could begin in your neigh-borhood, then later try another, until you got the experience. I certainly would be willing to speak with a shop owner there on your behalf."

"I won't work in that neighborhood, so those lousy people there can laugh at me and put me down. I'm going to be somebody and you'll all see that soon enough. I do really appreciate you helping me out here, and speaking with someone in a nice shop, because I call tell you, Sir, if you talk to them, they'll hire me, and they'll be so surprised how fast I learn."

How absolutely awful she was. He knew he had failed in his effort to help out his housekeeper and her family, and it troubled him because he liked Sra. Rosa and did not want her to be perturbed. It was also discon-certing how contemptuous he felt, how appalled. A fourteen-year-old, still just a child. But lost, lost to everyone, even herself. And he doubted Sra. Rosa would find this one as she had found her Rosa-Laura. He rubbed his eyes nervously with the back of his hand, took a deep breath, and held open the dining room door for her. He had a splitting headache, blood pressure up again surely. With all that, he forgot to take his sunglasses—and had he remembered, the leather case was no longer on the table anyway.

"It was a complete disaster," the Doctor said. He stood in the doorway of his kitchen, trying to catch the eye of Sra. Rosa, who was polishing a marble countertop with a maniacal energy. She avoided looking at him as if she were afraid such a sight would burn her to a crisp.

"I truly am sorry, Sra. Rosa, but I'm not the person for such a task, you see, I'm just an old bachelor—"

"Oh, it's all my fault, all my fault," the tiny scrubber said. Her voice cracked. "Ashamed I even asked. I just, well, I just don't know what to do with the girl, you see, I love her, and my poor dead sister—"

"Sra. Rosa, she's at an awkward age, that's all. And please, it does not bother me that you ask me for help. In fact, I feel good when I can do you a favor. You have been so loyal, stuck with this family through thick and thin, and my mother and my sister, they quite adore you, really, and I like you too. You're a perfect housekeeper, no one else could keep this wretched cluttered antique shop of a house so clean, and that means much to me, it does. I loathe filth, I loathe disorganization." He started to wring his hands in distress, then realized how silly the gesture must look and stopped. He rubbed his eyes. He couldn't find his damned sunglasses, couldn't remember where he last put them, and his eyes hurt. Not sleeping well added to the grainy, burning sensation. He wished he could just lay down in his room with the curtains drawn, an ice pack on his head, and stay there until all his thoughts loosened and floated.

Sra. Rosa shrugged and still would not look at him. She shook the cleaning rag out the kitchen window, frightening a pigeon squatted on the ledge, and set to cleaning another counter. "Yes, Sir, I'm so glad you think I'm a good housekeeper, but still, I asked too much this time. I did. I thought I had a right, you see, I don't know how to say it, and I don't want—I don't want to offend you, no Sir."

He waited. He needed to sit down, but he had been unable to convince her to come sit with him in the dining room or even the salon. She was really in a whirl this morning, full of her usual nervous energy, but fitful and agitated as well. He was used to this with his poor sister, but not Sra. Rosa. Was his housekeeper getting senile? She was old. Was it the change of life? That business had driven his sister nearly mad, and his mother too.

"Um, she's so tall and pretty, outgoing, Sir, and boys like her so much. She takes after my mother, Sir, her grandmother, that's where these things come from just like that's where the looks come from. It's what I worry most about. My ma, her grandma, she left the village when she was scarcely sixteen and headed straight for the city. She'd had enough of the country life."

"She was very brave to do something so bold in those days. Even today, that would take courage and resolve. Was she a suffragette?"

"No, she wasn't any educated woman and she wasn't brave at all. Bold maybe, but not brave. She didn't think it out at all, she never thought out much at all, she just didn't like things in the village. I sure can't blame her on that one. So she just ran away. It scares me to think of it. Then, she got herself set up with my father, but you see, well, they never made it to the church, if you catch my drift—"

"Sra. Rosa, please don't insult me. I'm not the kind of person that judges people by the family they're from—"

But he was. He was exactly that kind of person, and Sra. Rosa's story was embarrassing him.

"And then he took off or died or something, or maybe she just kicked him out, because he was a homely guy, a head shorter than her she said. I took after him one hundred percent. She never explained her story properly, of course, but then somehow she got money and set out to lend it, at high interest. She even bought herself a house, all in just a couple of years, that's how quick she was at such things. Then, there was Emilia's father. Um, that's it, you see. I followed him home once, when I was still a child. I wanted to see why he couldn't stay with us and take care of us better, and why Mama cried when he left. I saw him come to this building, but it took me a while to figure out he had another family and other people he was responsible for."

He waited, patiently, observing her as if she were an ill person describing symptoms that would lead him to brilliantly define the clinical disease. Physician that he was, not to mention a student of life, he had already guessed just what disease she was about to present.

"My Mili is your Mili too, Dr. Contreras. I am so sorry to tell you this way, and I would never, never, never shame your family or shame your poor mother, but Mili is your niece, really. My sister Emilia, her father, well, your father—"

Dr. Contreras tightened his jaw and made an angry O with his lips. *That damned devil. How many other lives had the son of a whore fouled before he was finally put down like a dog?* "The day you first came to see us, Sra. Rosa, you were actually here to speak with my stepfather, then?"

"Stepfather?"

"Yes, Sra. Rosa. The man in the pictures on my mother's dresser. The man whose funeral we were observing that day you first came. Mother has other pictures too, you know, two full sets, in her drawers. Photo albums full of pictures of three different men. My father was Mother's second husband. The man you are talking about, Emilia's father, was probably Mother's third husband, the last one, Montero, my stepfather. He was mother's favorite, her true love I guess you might say, just as he was probably the grand love of your mother. As you can guess, he was something of a womanizer. Mili may well be his granddaughter, Sra. Rosa; nonetheless, she is not my niece, as I was not related to that man except by my poor deluded mother's unfortunate alliance. But I do not blame you for thinking so or hoping to gain something for the child that way. Truly, I do not blame you. And as for the rest of it, well, if Mili can see her way to finishing her level and passing the exams, I will try to help her get into nursing school, or at the least, get her a job in a shop, as she has told me she wishes. The business about being an actress, though, that is much too awful a thing, and I will having nothing to do with it."

Three husbands was shocking enough, but at the word "actress," Sra. Rosa sat down on the floor. She didn't plan to do so, but suddenly the floor came up and met her as her legs slipped out from under her.

"My God, Sra. Rosa, please," he said. At that moment his sister, fanning herself with an elaborate blue and gold fan and thinking to find as if by magic a pot of bergamot tea on the kitchen counter, happened by.

"Oh my God, oh my God, Sweet Mary, Mother Virgin, Oh, Oh—help her, Arturo, the poor thing, oh—"

And then he had two crazy women sitting on the gleaming checkerboard tiles of his kitchen floor.

As Mili sought to free herself from school, discipline, and anything else that didn't suit her, Rosa-Laura provided counterweight in the family by embracing discipline as if it were the feet of the Blessed Savior Himself. By the autumn she turned twelve, she was sewing for all the sisters, making handkerchiefs, embroidering sheets, repairing their habits. Then one day Sister Pilar, who favored her even more than the other nuns, spread out some tissue paper on a big table in the sewing room and with a ruler chalked out a rough pattern for a skirt. Rosa-Laura watched her and immediately understood.

"Is it for you, Sister?" she said.

"For my mother. She's thinner than I am, but we're the same size otherwise." Sister Pilar said.

Rosa-Laura changed a few lines so the finished product would fit together better and then helped cut out the pattern, pin it to some dark gray serge, and cut the cloth.

From that moment on, whenever she saw a pattern she could imagine it finished easily, filling out the flat levels and constructing a three-dimensional picture of the finished garment in her mind with no problem. Soon she could quickly construct a garment in her head by extrapolating a photograph in a fancy magazine into a mental pattern, then she would rapidly sketch that pattern with chalk on tissue paper or newspaper or whatever paper was at hand, and then cut out the cloth from it. If someone was wearing an interesting garment and passed her on the street, she began to deconstruct and reconstruct that too. Garments on mannequins in shop windows proved even easier because they were still and allowed for staring. Finally, she discovered it was great entertainment to imagine buildings deconstructed and laid out flat, or certain items like horse carts and kiosks in pieces. She pulled them apart and put them back together, all in her head, standing up the flat drawings and popping them into place as if they were the magical, perfect, and elegant puzzles of geometry. She never told anyone about her quirky little habit. Who would have cared anyway? It was just something peculiar she could do, and it was fun. She did get praise for the garments she sewed, of course, and that made her very happy. Everyone said she would be a superb seamstress, which pleased her Mama no end.

As time passed, she willed herself to forget the orphanage, never realizing for a moment how it had shaped her and honed her beliefs. Some of the girls in school reminded her of the girls upstairs at the orphanage, but most she liked. She wasn't a favorite among her peers, being far too much a favorite of the teachers, but she had friends, three good ones and one very best friend, and that meant the world to her. She no longer loved her cousin as much as before. Mili made her sad now. Worse yet, Mili made her Mama sad.

Carmen-Victoria was the best friend. Such a lush, splendid name for such a choppy stump of a kid. Carmen-Victoria lived behind the neighborhood market, in a tacky, leaky, three-room shed on the roof of a washed-out yellow-gray building, the roof being the worst, cheapest place in any building, worse even than the basement, and harder to reach. This tilted, skinny building was so narrow its apartments seemed more like tiny corridors to somewhere else. It was a slice of a building entirely smashed in by its neighbor buildings, an afterthought of a building squeezed in to a space of necessity rather than design or good planning. But Carmen-Victoria defied her skinny surroundings: she was a chubby, merry child with a square, homely, freckled face, a snub nose, dishwater-colored hair, and an easy laugh. She never missed a day of school, though perhaps her teachers wished she would now and then. She had a genius for breaking up a serious scholastic session.

"Did Jesus love Mary Magdalene?" she asked Sister Pilar, in catechism class. "You might think he would fancy such a hot number, you know. Even if he was a bit of a butterfly." She started a riot with that one, and Sister Pilar had to dismiss the class.

Rosa-Laura adored her. Carmen-Victoria was like Mili without that scary way Mili had sometimes of looking at you as if you were a complete dunce and beneath contempt. She didn't try to order Rosa-Laura around like Mili did, either. After the debacle in catechism, Sister Pilar whacked Carmen-Victoria ten times across her ink-stained knuckles with a metal ruler and then washed out the girl's mouth with soap at the pump in the school courtyard. Rosa-Laura traded her lunch to the Gypsy who ran a candy stand near the school's front gates for four pieces of coconut nougat and gave them to Carmen-Victoria to cleanse the girl's palate of gritty, gray laundry soap.

∽∾

The afternoon of Sister Pilar's soapy lesson in religious respect, Rosa-Laura brought Carmen-Victoria home with her after school because her friend's mother was giving birth to yet another child. "We're twelve already in that penthouse," Carmen-Victoria said to Rosa-Laura with a certain air of pride at the awfulness of the fact. "I think she'll just have to pitch it over the roof when she's done delivering it, and herself too."

Rosa-Laura swallowed her giggle like gulping air and said, "Carmen-Victoria, that's dreadful. Your mama would so mad to hear you say that."

"No she wouldn't. She said it herself, to Papa. She told him he could sleep outside atop the chimney from now on. Said he could hump that if he felt like it, because its hole is just about as big as hers after ten kids. Say, you got any more of that candy? That was so good!"

For some reason that Rosa-Laura never understood, when Carmen-Victoria said things like that they were hilarious, but when Mili said similar things, they were filthy.

"We got chamomile tea, and we got rice pudding. Mama made it yesterday. It sat outside on the patio tiles all night. Pretty soon the summer will come and then we won't be able to keep anything. I wish I was rich. If I was rich, I'd buy Mama an ice box."

Rosa-Laura had unlatched her door, then pulled down the curtain after they entered. The little room that was her home was dark but somewhat warmer than outside. Sra. Rosa wasn't home at the time, not unusual, as she was probably still at Srta. Guillermina's. Lately she had begun to bathe Dolores del Valle, Sra. De Montero, the mother of Srta. Guillermina and Dr. Contreras, every afternoon, as part of her job, and she was paid extra for it.

"I don't know how she does it," Rosa-Laura said to Carmen Victoria as she lit a small kerosene lamp. "Sra. de Montero is huge, really huge, so huge I think she might weigh 200 pounds. Srta. Guillermina is huge too, and Dr. Contreras is a mountain. But they're all tall besides, so I guess it works out. My Mama is a small woman, but she manages Sra. de Montero, and doesn't complain at all."

"Is that your bed?"

"It's mine and it's Mama's and it's Mili's when she's home. Sometimes she stays over at my Papa's house. Sra. Constancia, that's my Papa's new wife, likes her. Mili likes to talk and Sra. Constancia likes to listen."

"You bet," Carmen-Victoria said. "We all just love to listen to Mili. She's such a firecracker."

Rosa-Laura suppressed a giggle. Firecracker, *petardo*, was not exactly a huge compliment: it sounded as if it meant smart, crackly, explosive, but what it really meant was idiot. "Carmen-Victoria, Mili's my cousin, understand? And she's made Mama worry a lot lately, so watch what you say when Mama's around, all right?"

Carmen-Victoria considered all this. It was entirely understandable. Mili was Rosa-Laura's family. You did not quarrel with blood lines, you defended them.

"I'll be real careful, but you should know, kid, the whole neighborhood's talking about her. My older brothers talk about her all the time. Even my Dad, but not when Ma's around, if you catch my drift."

"What are they saying?"

Carmen-Victoria squinted at her friend and then dropped her gaze to search the floor for clues to how to squiggle out of this messy topic entirely. "Boys like her, you know, like *that*, you know? I figure it's justice in a way. Me, I'm not pretty enough for them to notice, but then, no one talks bad about me either. Mili's pretty enough, but they say bad things about her. So it's kind of fair, if you catch my drift. Look, it's just the way things are, it's baby-making stuff."

"Do you know what a boy looks like, Carmen-Victoria? I mean, in his pants?"

Carmen-Victoria looked up at her friend sharply. "Well, I live with five of them, I'd have to be blind, no offense to your father, but Holy Mary of the Angels, Rosa-Laura, you sure surprised me asking that. Why do you want to know?"

"I don't know. I'm sorry, really, I shouldn't have said that. It's just that, it doesn't seem right the way boys get to do things and everyone laughs when they say stuff, but everyone speaks badly about Mili when she acts that way or says stuff. It's not right."

Carmen-Victoria shrugged. "Excuse me, friend, but you're crazy. Boys are different. Frankly, I'd rather be a boy than a girl, but this is what I got. Mili had better shape up and watch out, and you got to watch out for her too, because family is family, and that's one thing I know for sure."

She was taking inventory of Rosa-Laura's home now, searching earnestly for a change of subject. "You know, this place is smaller than mine. Only mine seems smaller because they're so many of us. Don't you just dream of the day you get a bed all to yourself? I don't think I'd know what to do if I had a bed all to myself."

"And a water-closet and a sink in your own house, too," Rosa-Laura said. "And a brand new dress every Easter, right?"

"Wow, yeah, and—

This game they could play all afternoon.

One day back in 1939, well into the autumn of the year of the General's victory march down the Gran Vía, Rogelio had found himself rounded up and hauled uptown. A bunch of men had surrounded him and told him to get into a bus and not to worry, he would be very happy at the outcome. There were many others in the bus too, evidently all blind. No amount of questioning the driver or the men who'd pulled him into the bus had gotten any answers. Rogelio had thought he and the other men were all goners and seriously readied himself to fight like a cat in a sack if they tried to handcuff him, though more likely they'd just question each of them and then put a bullet into the back of the neck. The bus had disgorged the men at a broad plaza with no fountain or pigeons that he could hear and marched them inside into a high vaulted hall.

Then someone had entered from far in front, ascended some kind of pulpit or stage and announced, "*Compañeros*! A new and better society has begun. Our grand leader, Generalisimo Francisco Franco, taking into account the needs of all citizens, even *invalidos* like yourselves, and especially veterans wounded in the glorious war against communism and atheism, has decreed that the blind have the right, indeed the privilege, of taking a job and thus being a useful contributor to our new society."

It turned out that from that point on, national lottery ticket vendors would all be blind people, and that was how the government was going to take care of a portion of its multitude of cripples.

Rogelio had listened to the spiel and said absolutely nothing, but he was steaming inside. He had already heard of the formation and recruitment of the *ONCE* last May and had ignored the call. He wanted to be a bookbinder again. He wanted to touch one of those vellum covers and run his callused fingers over the gold lettering. Some months earlier he had gone back to his old shop; a store selling religious articles nested in its place like a magpie in a robin's nest, and no one knew where the old owner had gone or even if he was still alive.

"Spain doesn't need books," the salesclerk had said to him. She was female by voice, just barely, taller than he was, younger, and hardened. "That sort of thing won't do here at all. We need religious guidance, we need to pray for forgiveness and pray thanks for our deliverance despite our evil natures. You want to bind books, you immigrate to some other country. You want something decent to do day or night, then we have rosaries here, at all prices."

So, as Rogelio stood there in the big government hall he realized that like it or not, he had to make a living. He signed up that same day and became one of those people selling lottery tickets on every corner in every Spanish city. *Las ONCE*, the "eleven", they are called, an acronym for *Organización Nacional de Ciegos Españoles*. Insurance that the blind will have employment, of their not being beggars, and serving a highly useful function, because the proceeds from the national lotteries served as taxes, collected with no grumbling from a population that loved gambling, taxes paid by the poor and working classes, as the rich had casinos in which to indulge their illusions.

He loathed the job at first, eaten with regret and longing for his old employment as he was, but then, he began to converse with the people he met every day, not about politics, as that was dangerous, but some gossip, some philosophy, some bullshit, some jesting. Soon, he learned to enjoy his occupation, even looking forward to taking his place on his corner, where he made many friends. He became the particular lottery salesman who stood at the southwestern corner of the neighborhood plaza. The one who sold the winning ticket in 1949, in fact, and therefore a "lucky" seller, one from whom it became good to buy.

Every morning he would leave his basement apartment, his burrow, and walk uptown to the *ONCE* building to get his tickets for the day. It tuned his hearing and enthused him, this trek from his neighborhood down to Almirante Street to report in and exchange pleasantries with other blind people. Better yet, he made a good living at it during a time that many Spaniards had no work at all.

By 1943, the year Rosa-Laura was twelve, the international blockade against Spain and the aftermath of a civil war with a million casualties, not to mention the world war raging just outside Spain's borders, had left the country exhausted, demoralized, and isolated. The dictatorship locked down the nation, and most people just turned up their collars against the cold wind in the jail yard of their lives and kept on walking in circles until they dropped dead. The winners gloated over their victory and kept on settling scores. There was little food and no medicine, neighborhoods were still being purged now four years since the civil war's end, but churches were open day and night, lottery tickets were selling as if they were food, and there were bullfights on Sundays. Rogelio knew by now he was damned lucky to be blind, innocent of soldiering, and in possession of a decent living.

Constancia on the other hand kept on withdrawing further and further into that hole that the war had driven her. She took no interest in anything, with one notable exception: she was very fond of Mili. Rogelio would come home and find the girl there, chatting away with Constancia, saucy, self-involved, lively. She frequently ate dinner with them, and though he obviously wasn't supposed to notice, he knew that Constancia ate less so that Mili could eat more. He didn't know what to say about that, because he was glad Constancia had something to live for, though he didn't figure she'd live for long if she got any skinnier.

He put no sexual demands on her these days, not that there had ever really been much of that anyway. He'd never deluded himself that she truly enjoyed their infrequent couplings, though she had at first been the one to initiate them. He now realized that was probably just a way of making sure he kept her. She did not like him to touch her breasts, even at first, and had never taken off her clothes with him, even during the worst nights of August. Now though she never refused him outright, clearly she merely endured his caresses. It hurt his feelings, especially when he remembered how beautiful an act it had been with Laura, and so he gave up altogether and stopped bothering her. Truth was, they were two sad beings thrown together by chance and certainly not the Lovers of Teruel or some other star-crossed pair. It saddened him that he could offer her so little solace. When they lay in bed at night, she'd curl up in her lamentable thinness and almost disappear against his chest and belly, like a wood shaving fallen between the cracks of a work bench. She had a peculiar smell about her too, nothing disagreeable, but definitely off, too sweet, like a soft ferment.

He mentioned this last thing to Sra. Rosa, as delicately and indirectly as he possibly could, one day when they sat in a tavern, he drinking a tiny cup of red wine and she drinking a bubbly sweet drink known as *gaseosa*. She said nothing but "Um, um," as usual, and finished her glass. A few days later she showed up at his apartment just before he was to leave in the morning for Almirante Street.

"Got to go to the Social Security Clinic and register for health care," she said to Rogelio. "Those folks make me nervous. Constancia, you come along with me—keep me company."

Ever since Rogelio asked Sra. Rosa to take Constancia along when she went shopping, the two women had gone to the market together. Constancia always held onto Sra. Rosa's arm as if she herself were a child and allowed the older woman to select and barter for everything they bought. She seemed to enjoy being with Sra. Rosa, or at least, she never refused. But, now at this request, Constancia murmured, "I don't know, I'm not feeling so good—" then she halted, caught her breath, and fumbled with her handkerchief.

"You'll like it, you'll get out some," Rogelio said. He dug in his pockets and came up with a *duro* and gave it to Constancia. "There now, buy your-selves a vermouth at the tavern when you get back, chat a bit, it'll vitalize you. Be sure to stop by and say hello to me when you come back through the plaza."

"Um, we'll have a fine time of it. Don't be timid now, I can't go alone, Constancia," Sra. Rosa said.

Thus encouraged, or coerced, Constancia pulled out her shawl and wrapped it around her shoulders and head, as if to hide herself like a Moor's woman. There seemed to be no sense in it, but on the way down the gray, cobbled street to the clinic, the two women passed a car full of police, unmarked and the coppers in civilian clothes. Constancia grunted in fright at the sight of them, and Sra. Rosa had to pull her into an alleyway and prop her up against the wall of an ancient brick building so she could compose herself.

"What's this now?" she said to Constancia.

"They scare me."

"Woman, they scare anyone with common sense."

"They took my family away—they'll take me away. They'll take Rogelio for being with me."

"Tell me, Constancia, I'm not afraid to know it with you."

But the woman wouldn't say anything more. Sra. Rosa could guess, though. Husband, father, brother, or all three. Once in Sra. Rosa's patio, when Constancia was there to bring Mili a collar she'd sewn as a present, Bernardo had come swaggering in as if he owned the whole place, daring anyone to look at him askance or trouble him about so brazenly visiting his mistress. Constancia caught a glimpse of him through the doorway curtain and suddenly nudged past Sra. Rosa and tried to hide under the bed, but the boxes and stored items underneath it prevented her. It took Sra. Rosa half an hour and two cups of chicory coffee to calm her down.

The clinic was housed in a musty building now being rebuilt after crumbling from two stories to one in some bombing or another. The construction workers had been at the building since the war's end and still hadn't finished it. They were on government pay, and government time, so they were in no hurry. The scaffolding was constructed like a child's vacant lot toy, disorderly and poorly nailed sticks of trash wood hand-hewn; the buckets full of stucco and mortar were made of rubber cut from old tires. The gloveless and hatless workers wore their neck kerchiefs over their mouths when they were tired of eating dust; squinting sometimes kept out the debris from their eyes. When they had to hammer something, they hammered in unison and counterpoint, sounding for all the world like a chorus of Gypsies at a midnight flamenco celebration. Every now and then, a worker would burst into some drawn-out wail of a couplet, and if he was any good at it or had half a voice for that matter, the rest would shout *¡Olé!* and continue to accompany him with the hammering. The musical play delighted the passersby, but made trying to engage the attention of the staff in the clinic a feat of endurance, patience, and much mime. The receptionist was an exceptionally frazzled young nurse, with no aptitude for clerical ceremonies and clearly beaten down by the all-day construction symphony.

When the two women entered, no one paid them any attention; then, the receptionist glanced up at them standing there before her, planted firm like two crooked little trees used to wind and rain storms and whatever else the weather blew at them. One of them, the smaller, scarier one, grinned at her. She quickly handed that one a long form on cheap paper with lots of blank lines.

"Say," said Sra. Rosa to Constancia, very casually, as if the idea had just occurred to her that instant and wasn't it such a good idea? "Why don't you register too, Constancia. We all need these medical cards. Then if some day you need to come here, you won't have to wait to fill out forms and stuff."

"I can't write," Constancia said. Her voice was so low the hammering quite pounded it into dust.

"Well, course, me neither. You'll help us out now, won't you, dearie?" Sra. Rosa said.

The receptionist scowled at the suggestion of such a further outrageous waste of her time. Sra. Rosa slipped her the *duro* that Rogelio had given them, and with a sigh, the girl set to work interviewing them and filling out their forms.

"Well, after the folks at the clinic looked her over, they told me it was—you know." Sra. Rosa said.

The Doctor nodded. She was just releasing the sorry news of a sad yesterday, that's all. They had gotten into this strange routine years ago. When he got up early in the morning, or else came home early in the morning after an exhausting night running from household to household, netted like a pike in a pond by their diseases and woes, soothing and lying to some old man dying of prostate cancer, arguing with some head of a wealthy household that drinking a bottle or two of brandy every night was turning his liver into a lace doily—when all that was over, come early morning he sat in the dining room with Sra. Rosa, drinking strong coffee cut with sugar, or saccharin if the sugar ration had been used up that week, and canned milk.

"Do you want me to look at her?" He said.

"No. Thank you, Sir, but um, no. She's had enough looking at. She knows. Knew before we got there, I suspect. Asked me to keep quiet—you know, she doesn't want me to tell Rogelio. Now, this will be his second one. He just can't seem to keep them."

Dr. Contreras finished his cup and let Sra. Rosa pour him another. He dropped in a tablet of saccharin. He really hated the nasty aftertaste of the stuff, but his mother and sister used so much sugar in everything there was never enough, even with the extra coupons he got as a doctor, not to mention the coupons he collected as payment for his services now and then. He always took sugar coupons for payment, but not flour or oil coupons. Most of his patients were wealthy and had supplies, but nevertheless, he wanted to be sure they ate and were well nourished. His poorer patients he just put on the tab. Those owed him enough to buy a new apartment on the Gran Vía. He made up for it by overcharging the richer patients.

"They're renaming the Gran Vía. They're going to call it José Antonio Primo de Rivera," he said to Sra. Rosa. She just stared at him, unable to digest this bit of news.

He smiled at her. "I'll bet you that the taxi cab drivers will be calling it the Gran Vía twenty years from now, no matter what fascist's name they put on the street signs."

She pushed a grim smile onto her face and held her coffee cup, warming her hands. From the main bathroom behind the Doctor, they could hear Guillermina singing. She had a passably good voice and kept her tune well. This morning it was a *jota*, an Aragonese folk dance. She hit a high note perfectly, and they both smiled at each other. If they were lucky, next she'd try a theme song from some *zarzuela* or another. It was better than the radio and with no scratch or static.

> *Por una moza del barrio,*
> *Por una moza del barrio,*
> *Patricio está si se muere*
> *No diré cual es su nombre*
> *que ella lo diga si quiere.*
> *Que ella lo diga si quiere,*
> *por una moza del barrio.*
> Because of a girl in the neighborhood,
> Patrick is dying for love.
> I won't tell her name,
> let her tell it if she wants.
> Let her if she wants.
> All for a girl in the neighborhood.

"She's in good voice," the Doctor remarked. He was proud of his sister's voice. His own sounded watery to him, weak and not male enough. When someone said to him, "You haven't much voice," it meant that there was no power behind the sound, no projection. No depth. He had once looked at a few books on the subject, medical books, and decided that despite his height and wide chest, he really didn't have much in the way of lung power. If he had the time or the inclination, he could study with someone, practice, and exercise with breathing techniques. But of course, for whatever reason would he do that? To sing at parties? He hadn't attended a party in years.

"She gets it from Sra. de Montero," said Sra. Rosa. "I always thought your mother should have sung in the opera."

The Doctor laughed gently. "In a bourgeois family such as ours, the stage is not an option. Mother sang at parties, of course. They were such glamorous affairs, those parties. There was always someone to play the piano or the guitar and plenty of people to sing. Mother sang French songs," he said. "She has a fine accent; one can barely tell she's not French." He smiled broadly. Those certainly were wonderful parties. They pretty much stopped after his stepfather died, though his mother and sister had organized afternoon card parties, luncheons, a soiree now and then. Since the war, there had been almost no parties at all. That must be killing to the two women, though neither had ever asked him to arrange an event. He should host a dinner party some evening, but he knew he hadn't the time, the talent, or the patience to deal with the bother, Guillermina couldn't handle that kind of chore and its stress anymore, and his mother was almost bedridden these days. It was a supreme effort just to get her up and walking around the flat. Her mind had drifted back to those days when she was much younger, and she didn't have much interest in forcing herself to take note of what was happening in the present.

He finished his coffee. "Will you be giving mother a bath today?"

"Yes, of course, Sir."

"I don't see how you manage it. She's too heavy for you. I plan to call in workmen to remodel the main bathroom as soon as I have the time to consult some friends of mine who did something similar in their flat. Provide a built-in, step-down sunken tub and maybe a sit-down shower."

Sra. Rosa's eyes widened slightly. It sounded messy, exacting, expensive.

"Ah, Sir, not on my account, surely? I hate the mess remodeling makes, I do. Your mother's not decrepit, you know. She can get up out of the tub as long as she has something to lean on."

She meant *someone* to lean on. The Doctor waved aside her argument with his left hand and delicately touched his napkin to his mouth with his right. Sra. Rosa stood up slowly and somewhat regretfully and began to pile up the dishes to take to the sink. It was time to go to work.

Well wasn't this just a fucking whore-son of a day. Twice last week stayed at that lousy shop late, half an hour after closing time, mind you, just trying to help out that old pig, who never smiled, not once, not at me or anyone else, good God, you'd think a joke or two—but joke with him and all you got was a stare as if you were an idiot or something. He's the idiot. Didn't appreciate what I brought to the job at all. Should have taken that other scarf too, and all my being good about that, so honest, what did it get me? Fired for being late a few times. Stayed late twice, so what did it matter arriving this morning fifteen minutes late and yesterday ten? It wasn't as if he had any customers at that hour, damn him. And the whore-son customers loved me!

Anyone would rather talk with a cute girl than some old sourpuss— oh, shit, shit, shit, now I have to go looking for another job. Auntie Rosa isn't to going to take any of this without a scene, that's for sure. The day they kicked me out of school—well, hadn't been in school for months anyway, so actually, I left school—Auntie threatened to kick me out of the house and send me off to a boarding school, as if the old donkey could have afforded such a thing! And who was she to kick me out of my own house? That house is mine by law. It was my mother's and now it's mine. I'm the one ought to kick Auntie Rosa and that damned goody-two-shoes daughter of hers out.

I'm so upset, having to listen to that bastard shopkeeper. Once Auntie hears how unreasonable that old sourpuss was, how ridiculous, and as soon as I get another job, and I'll get one fast, people like me, I'm pretty and I'm fun to be around—Auntie can never be mad at me for long. She adores me. I remind her of Mama, even though I'm prettier than Mama ever was.

Mili strode down Atocha Street, her head high, her hands in the pockets of her new sweater. Auntie Rosa had knitted the sweater. It was navy blue. She would have preferred finer, silkier yarn, and she would have preferred

red, but yarn was expensive and red was a hard color to obtain these days. Besides, Auntie Rosa didn't complain about navy blue but she would have complained about red. Navy blue was close enough to mourning. Mili was so heartily sick of black. Black skirt, black blouse, black stockings, black shoes. She had a black and gray and green scarf, but she didn't wear it on her head like some old Gypsy. She wore it carelessly thrown around her neck and shoulders, like a woman of style. She walked with her head high and her black hair hanging loose about her shoulders, and more than one man turned his head.

That's right, bastards. Look and look hard. Make all the compliments and cracks you want to. Won't get a look or a nod or a smile or anything at all. I have plans.

Past noon she finally stopped walking and window shopping and went home, tired, sad, ready to face the music. Rosa-Laura was there, reading and studying with Carmen-Victoria. What an ugly little kid! She had to be twelve, like Rosa-Laura, but she looked like she was ten, positively a dwarf. But then, Rosa-Laura looked younger too. Rosa-Laura was sweet looking, angelic. She would always be that way, poor kid, and it would get her nowhere. Even those pretty blue eyes, what wonders Mili could accomplish with such eyes! Eyes wasted on Rosa-Laura, but she was a good kid just the same.

⁓

Sra. Rosa didn't arrive until almost three. By then Rosa-Laura and Carmen-Victoria had to return to school for afternoon classes. Sra. Rosa was surprised to see her niece. She kissed her daughter and sent her off and managed a smile for Carmen-Victoria, whose mother, as best anyone in the neighborhood could recall, had never been seen in any other state but that of full-blown pregnancy.

"Well, Mili, let me get a bite to eat, and tell me what's happened."

Mili divided up the bread left over from lunch evenly, saving some for dinner. Best to get this all over with at once, since Auntie probably had already guessed and it would do no good to putter around and make up interesting stories. Auntie didn't appreciate stories at all; she had no imagination.

"That son of a whore fired me, Auntie. I came in late this morning, just a few minutes, mind you, I mean, it's a hell of a long walk to that damned store..."

"Ah, Mili, please can't you think again about finishing school and getting into a nursing college? It would be such a good career! You could make something of yourself, someone your mother would have been proud of."

"Auntie, you don't understand. I really don't have the time to bore myself silly at that school. Besides, they won't take me back. Anyway, I guess if I really asked nice, your Doctor could get me into nursing school without my finishing first. But I don't need to bother him for now."

Sra. Rosa said nothing. She had glimpsed a pair of peculiar glasses in Mili's purse a few nights ago just as Mili was closing it to go and have dinner with Rogelio and Constancia. Glasses like movie actresses wore. Sra. Rosa thought she recognized them, but hadn't the heart to confront the girl. If they were what she thought they were, Mili had ruined her chances with the Doctor. Accusing Mili would have brought on a terrible row, and what if she was mistaken about them? She wanted to be mistaken, but Mili's comment about not bothering the Doctor sounded fake. Mili never had problems "bothering" people if she wanted something.

"Look, girl," she said, "how about a shop here in the neighborhood? A way to start anew? Just for a while. You'll get some experience, make money, then move on to a better place."

"You just don't understand. I'm fifteen, now, I'm not some fourteen year old apprentice. I have to be seen. Frankly, I'd rather work at a really nice, high-class bar. That's where I'd shine."

Sra. Rosa sat on a stool with a small knife and a bit of cheese wrapped in gray shop paper. It was Manchego cheese, gone just a bit hard, and that was how she'd gotten it so cheaply. It would taste good anyway, hard or not. She had tomatoes, three of them, she had bread, cheap because the government kept the price regulated and subsidized. She looked at all this nice food spread out on the tiny table and had the weirdest idea: she wanted to hug it and kiss it and cry for all she was worth.

Mili watched her aunt slice the tomatoes and make a little *bocadillo* with the bread. "Look, Auntie, I've been thinking. [Sra. Rosa groaned; Mili *thinking* was usually cause for running to the church to pray fervently for divine intervention] I'm going to apply at a few of the nicer bars, uptown, of course, some of the nicer ones by the Puerta del Sol, that have girls as waitresses or hat check girls or cigarette girls."

"What are you talking about?" Sra. Rosa said. "You think it's so easy to work in those places, you think those places are so refined? Dear God, Mili, you'd be one step away from a whore."

"Auntie, you don't understand things very well, really. I know what I'm talking about. You're just a bit old-fashioned. Don't you worry about me!"

Sra. Rosa looked at the paring knife she was holding and wondered if it would hurt if she just pushed it into the palm of her hand. Would it be soft like that tomato? Or hard like the cheese? Or in-between like the bread?

"Mili, you remind me of your grandma. Too much. I don't fault her for trying to live well, for being different from other folks, but the end result was two kids who didn't have a father or a name. A lot of troubles just surviving, and my poor mother didn't live long either."

Mili snorted and rolled her eyes. It was a very old, stupid, boring story. Auntie Rosa had tried to explain the whole history of their sorry grandmother to her and Rosa-Laura. Funny, but Rosa-Laura was such a dunce she never understood a word. She didn't even understand how a woman could have a kid without having a husband. Family of cretins, this one. No wonder they had no money, no style, no talent, except for Mili, and clearly, it was up to her to get to work and get them all out of this mess. That way, she could take care of them and they could take care of her. It would be a very beneficial arrangement.

Rosa-Laura graduated when she'd just reached thirteen instead of fourteen, because she was way ahead of everyone else and clearly had a profitable profession cut before her like a broad, clean road leading right to heaven. Sister Pilar spoke with an estimable and very religious master tailor who on Sister Pilar's respected references agreed to apprentice the girl tailoring men's clothes and making uniforms. Tailoring men's clothes was where the money was, and it was where the talent was too. This tailor took only the best apprentices, mostly boys. It was an amazing honor to be apprenticed even before she was fourteen, and at such a grand establishment. At first, she worked as a *pantalonera*. Part of that job entailed her and another female apprentice or the master's wife herself as chaperone walking twice a week with finished goods from the master's shop on Arenal Street next to the Church of San Ginés to some of the best shops on Recoletos.

The best education she ever had was that biweekly hour or more it took to walk briskly down those fine streets, careful to drape the pants in their muslin bag without a single wrinkle over her arms, observing other people strolling, observing the cafes and their clientele, observing the hordes of police and guard and army men, observing the working people who looked so different from the higher-ups, with their shabby, old, much-repaired, and well-ironed clothes, and their heads down, not a very Spanish custom, and apparently not observing anybody around them. Rosa-Laura soon realized they were all very aware of where they were and who was there. It had to do with the glances thrown now and then at a policeman, with the tightening of the jaw, with the blinking that became so rapid when one of the *presencia*—a word now used to mean anyone like a cop, a guard, a soldier—walked by, gun at the hip or machine gun carelessly and comfortably leaning against the shoulder.

Rosa-Laura didn't understand politics and could never quite pinpoint what made her neck prickle and her skin go goosebumps when a man in a uniform walked into the shop and she was called downstairs to write measurements. She had a wonderfully legible cursive, as elegant as a monk's, perfectly straight across the small, creamy, unlined page of the master's leather-bound notebook. No one else in his establishment wrote so well and so clearly. The subject being measured seldom looked at her, but as she got older and taller, now and then one of them would look at her, hard, or even worse, leer, pinch her cheek, wink, and then resume standing for the fitting, hands on his hips, a sneer on his lips. When such occurred, the master clenched his teeth and concentrated on the task at hand, as he manipulated his tape from the back of the middle of the neck to the wrist, around the waist, from inner leg to ankle, and so on. But when the client had left, he would rebuke Rosa-Laura sternly. She never knew what to do to stop the unwanted attention and wished the master would just not call for her anymore, but she hung her head and said nothing.

The twice weekly walk to Recoletos Street presented a long array of fine shops to look at, but Rosa-Laura didn't have much inclination to window-shop. The displays offered her no dreams of Arabian nights and opulent possibilities. They showed her what she could not have and—the peculiar part—did not want. She did dream of nicer clothing—clothing in colors, at least—and she dreamed of making that clothing, but walking into a shop and picking out some item she hadn't made left her somewhat bored, not that there was much in the shops of Madrid these days for women. Clothing had to be made to order or by oneself. Length of skirt was crucial, none of that prostitute's short skirt length it was rumored they were wearing in other countries, and certainly not pants, like American women wore, but then, Americans in general were creatures as fabulous as lions and giraffes. Men's clothing was displayed in shop windows, coats in particular and ties and jackets, but more often, one saw cloth, dark or neutral colors, draped and flowing elegantly and tastefully—and dully. Leather goods, jewelry of fine gold, mostly religious in motif, but also earrings of bright coral she did scrutinize now and then, but still, these things left her empty.

The ornamentation on the buildings themselves, that was another story, though not the elephant heads that underpinned the cornices of one particular building on Carrera de San Jerónimo just past the Puerta del Sol. The elephants at the zoo in the Park had died during the war. So had most of the other animals.

She liked the statues on top of the buildings like the god Mercury at the reins of a gorgeous, full-size chariot with horses, bronze and brilliant in the sunshine. She liked the caryatids in the portals, the bas relief ribboning along walls. She loved the fountains, Neptune and the Sybils, anything that showed that Madrid was not dour, cold, fanatically religious, full of uniformed men.

She tried to keep up with changing styles, though things seemed to change very slowly in Madrid. A way to keep up with fashion was to read the magazines the master got now and then from rich customers. French magazines in particular were spectacular, and also the Italian ones. Spain did not produce such magazines. It did have a genius called Balenciaga; he was a Basque from San Sebastián, though, and had escaped to live in Paris at the war's beginning. His creations were often featured in the foreign fashion magazines. He was as good as a sculptor, in her estimation. Trying to work out his patterns was a huge and absorbing challenge, though no one ever asked for them.

She liked working in the shop. The boys in the master's establishment worked on the ground level of the building, in the back of his shop, itself a very fine place with nice display windows and a brass lined doorway. The girls in his establishment, basters and hemmers mostly with a few seamstresses, worked separately, under the observant eye of his wife. He owned the whole building, from the elegant, understated gentlemen's store on the ground level, the warehouse of cloth and other supplies and inventory on the first floor, his own ample apartments on the second floor, and the third floor, the roof studio, where the girls sewed. One climbed three flights of high, narrow stairs to get to it, the last flight the steepest and narrowest of all, to reach a wide, low-ceilinged, long garret that was frozen dry in winter, blast oven dry in summer. But it had a wonderful view of the rooftops of other buildings and the courtyard of San Ginés. Rosa-Laura always felt as if she were wrapped up in that studio, separate from the windows, the drafts, the doorways, encased in a billowing cold or a blasting heat as if in sheeting. She didn't like the garret's weather, but she loved the view and she liked sewing, every part of it, from the basting to the final hidden hem. Everyone said she did beautiful work, fit for a marquis. Now and then she was allowed to make an entire vest. Jackets, of course, rested in her rosy future. She felt proud. She might not be a very interesting creature, but she was useful.

The boys in the shop smiled at her, when they could, but they were always under the master's eye, and he and his wife made quite sure teasing or flirting or other such scandal did not occur. Rosa-Laura didn't mind. She had no idea how to tease and flirt anyway, and when Anacleto or even Augustín tried to do that with her, it tended to rile her into a fury of embarrassment and shame. At the same time, she envied Mili's easygoing ability with boys and men. How did she manage to be so unafraid, so casual, so sure of herself?

Sra. Rosa offered to knit her a navy blue sweater like Mili's. Rosa-Laura thanked her mother and accepted the offer; she needed a sweater, after all, and Mama so loved to do things for her. The thing was, well, the black. She herself was still in mourning for Auntie Emilia. It was supposed to last longer for Mili, because Emilia was her mother, not just an aunt. Mama wore black for Emilia too, but then, Mama had worn black ever since Rosa-Laura could remember, because she was a widow. Most men wore black, though their time of mourning was far less than women's. Rosa-Laura was sick of black, and she wasn't very interested in navy blue. She wanted to wear something light blue, with embroidery or smocking or faggoting. She wanted a skirt in custard yellow, with a white silk blouse and green leaves of ivy embroidered up and down the front twining around pearl buttons. She wanted stockings spun of silk, though most of all she would have loved to actually take off her shoes, like people did at a beach or in the country, and walk barefoot. It was a silly idea she never shared with Mili, though once she had mentioned it to Carmen-Victoria.

"Hey," Carmen-Victoria had said. "Be thankful we got shoes now. I have to wear my older sister's when she's done with them. She's got stinky feet too, it's a family curse. Use your noggin, Rosi. Look at you! Your shoes are leather and you walk to a good job every day!"

Rosa-Laura's feet never stank, and even when she sweated, she smelled like talcum and fresh-cut green citrus leaves. Boys had commented on that. Rosa-Laura hated those comments. Whatever is someone supposed to say when a boy presumes to tell you how you smell? What would Mili say?

Once she had asked her mother if she had to marry and if she did, when would it happen, and how would it all come about? Did the attention boys paid and the *piropos* or compliments that annoyed her so much really have to do with all that? Her mother had sighed loudly and said nothing. Often when her mother wouldn't answer a question, she would quit asking, because she knew the question had troubled Mama. This time, Rosa-Laura didn't let it go at that. "Mama, answer me, please. I know you don't like to talk about these things, but who else can answer me? Shall I ask Mili about things like this?"

Her mother smiled, grimly.

"I got asked to marry once, Rosa-Laura. I thought it a kindness from heaven. He was handsome, your uncle, handsome. More handsome than your poor father, though for a blind man, your Papa's not so bad looking. But his brother was the devil, half-crazy, mean for no reason, moony. I'd thought he'd done me an honor marrying me. No one else ever asked, much less a good-looking man. But I think it would have been better if I'd said no to his proposal and stayed a virgin. I couldn't conceive. He got meaner and meaner. He said it was my fault, I didn't love him enough, that he should have married another one who did love him, and he'd have thought an ugly little thing like me would be happy to have a man like him. The thing is, he'd had lots of women before me. They'd given him diseases, but not a one of them gave him a child. One day he hit me, not the first time, but I was so furious I yelled at him that no woman could give him a child, and it was his fault for whoring. He threw me to the floor and from there I bit his leg so hard I loosened a tooth—oh, it was disgusting. He took a few days to think about it, then just packed his bags and left. He died in Soria. Your Papa went to the funeral, not me. I was glad to be a widow. I pray you marry a man who loves you and treats you well. Don't marry until you find one like that. Never mind if you don't love him back. Just be sure he loves you, like a dog loves a kid. Understand?"

Rosa-Laura nodded, but she was horrified and depressed for days afterward.

One day she got home late from work, very tired, to find Anacleto lolling in the patio as if waiting for someone. She glanced at him; he looked straight at her, into her eyes. He had a dozen carnations, garnet red, a color she thought exquisite. He'd undoubtedly gotten them from the Gypsies who sold flowers on the corner now and then, a dozen for a peseta. It was a sign of good times, Mama had said, that Gypsies were selling flowers again.

"Those for Mili?" she'd said to him. Why she even spoke she'd never know. What did she care if they were for Mili? They could have been for his sweet, dear Mama just as well.

"They're for you," Anacleto said. He scratched his cheek and held them out to her. She had been told often enough he was nice looking. Mili told her, Carmen-Victoria told her, others too. To her he was thickset, square-headed, taller than most thanks to his Mama, hair brown-blond, longer now and better cut, his eyes dark with heavy lashes, and never a smile on that scowling face *ever*. Homely or handsome, it didn't matter. She had no feeling for him.

She said nothing to him, of course. Nothing at all. But she held out her hand and took the flowers. She smelled them. She thought they had a slightly musky, rank smell, but they reminded her of the day Mama found her, and that was a wonderful memory. She wanted to keep the flowers and knew she could not, knew that any decent girl would throw them back into his face. A song sprang to mind—a low class, vulgar, Gypsy song, one of those flamenco couplets men sang in bars:

Les tiré al pozo, olé, les tiré al pozo,
Los claveles que me distes, olé, les tiré al pozo,
Que no quiero claveles de ningún mozo.
I threw them down the well, down the well.
The carnations you gave me, I threw them down the well.
I don't want flowers from some little boy.

Mama had told her the song meant that "she wants love from a man, not a moonstruck boy."

Carmen-Victoria's explanation was even more curious: "My ma says love from a man makes you crazy. Like her, always getting pregnant, even though she knows better. She just can't tell poppa to stop and leave her alone. She likes what he does. I think with a boy it's not so expert and they can be dumb as lead."

Mili told her that the woman singing wanted something "a lot nicer than some cheap flowers, something you can bite, and I don't mean a loaf of bread!" Rosa-Laura gave her such a questioning look that Mili laughed and said, "Gold, stupid, she wants gold. Don't you know anything?"

Rosa-Laura did not know, did not have a clue, and she was sick and tired of not knowing. She clutched the carnations, gave Anacleto the coldest stare she could muster and said, "These are for my mother. I'll give them to her. Thank you," and she turned her back on him without another word.

Anacleto, also wordless, was ecstatic, though no one would have ever guessed from the scowl on his face. She'd spoken to him. She'd taken his gift. And properly too, accepting them not for herself but for her mother. Like a real lady.

Bernardo visited Lourdes often nowadays, especially after his son was born. He didn't wear a uniform, but everyone knew he was police, someone high up, a captain or some other such title, and he drove a car, a prototype sedan like the new ones that were going to be produced in Spain itself, a type of Fiat that would go by a Spanish name, *Seat*, and bring lots of jobs to the country. Proof that the government was supplying its people with employment and wellbeing, that the war had been won not just by the Right, but by the right people. Bernardo's car was black, sharp, scary, a cop car, though it had no siren. It just felt like one with him in it. Bernardo drove it as if it were a racing calash and he the lord of the manor, only Madrid, with its ridiculously narrow warren of sixteenth century streets, was his demesne. Bernardo drove fast and didn't care if he hit a curb or an old wrought iron hitching post taking a corner too quickly.

His unit eventually assigned him a driver, and they were always together after that, though sometimes Bernardo would drive, and sometimes his officer. The day they assigned the man to him, he bragged about it to Lourdes and let her know just what kind of a guy this driver was. Of course, Lourdes mentioned it to someone else in the building, and pretty soon, the whole neighborhood knew, which was what Bernardo had wanted.

The driver's name was Silvio, and his rank sergeant. He was from Extremadura, a beautiful and lonely province on the border with Portugal. One of its towns was Badajoz, Silvio's home town. It had a large bullfighting arena, as did most provincial towns of any size or importance.

Lourdes told the story and as she told it, it got worse and worse, not because she was given to exaggerating, but because she wanted people to understand that Silvio was not to be tampered with. Historians later clarified all the rumors, but as everyone heard the story in the few days after Bernardo bragged about it to Lourdes, Silvio had been one of the officers assigned to deal with the refugees rounded up into the arena. They were loyalists, mostly men, but also women and children, who had all escaped over the border into Portugal at war's end. Portugal's dictator ordered his army to send them back at gunpoint. The people returned to be slaughtered by Franco's soldiers, and Silvio was one of the men who gave the orders. The ending of the story was the crowning touch: when all the killing was done, half a meter of blood soaked the sands of the arena, and Silvio waded through it until his boots were caked.

No one doubted the story or wanted to interfere with Silvio, even though he was rather an indiscriminate creature, short, not too stocky, taciturn. He shaved his hair nearly to the skull and had a very plain, unassuming face with a thick long nose and wide nostrils above thin lips. For a while, he wore the uniform of an army sergeant, but soon he was wearing a tailored suit, like his boss's, and very expensive, elegant shoes, one hundred percent Italian leather. The heels were built up to give him some extra height and had tabs nailed on the back, so that his shoes clicked on the cobblestones of the street. The sound of those shoes unnerved everyone in the building, because though he seldom exited the car, when he did he would walk the streets or enter the patio of Lourdes's building almost militarily, his head facing forward always, but his eyes moving everywhere and seeming to see everything. If any of the neighbors had been asked which of the two, master or driver, frightened them more, no sure answer could be given.

No neighbor begrudged Lourdes her misalliance, ugly as it was, and that was not so much because they were afraid (which they were) of her lover. The woman had suffered, no one doubted that at all. She was alone except for her children, and she had to feed them somehow. Her husband would never return—he was either dead or in prison. No one had heard from him since the war, not even the few members of his family that still resided in Madrid and called on the boys (but not their disgraced mother) now and then. Besides, Lourdes always helped everyone whenever she could, even if they had been unkind or snotty to her. Bernardo brought presents when he visited, nice stuff other people couldn't get, and she shared with everyone.

Lourdes and her boys now had meat and fish, coffee, candies, sometimes cookies. The boys were nicely dressed and she wore nylon stockings and even lipstick. For an old woman in her thirties with so many children, she was still a beauty. She held her head high out of habit, but she was not at all proud, and somehow that also softened the feelings of even the most rigid and proper of the neighborhood women. Poor whore.

Some of the things Bernardo brought her were amazing. The neighbors didn't even know how such goods could be gotten into their blockaded and boycotted country, though clearly the smugglers in both the north and the south were having a field day. Take that lipstick for example. Lourdes didn't like to wear makeup; her skin was translucent, fair, glowing, especially now that she was eating well, but lipstick Bernardo brought her and lipstick she wore. It made her finely proportioned lips glow on her pale face.

Mili had first instructed Lourdes in how to apply the lipstick. The saucy girl was almost seventeen now, looked more like twenty-five, and went uptown every day. She was in between bar jobs at the time and could visit the finest stores often enough to see both pictures of how lipstick was used and observe salesgirls and clientele who used it. Sra. Rosa didn't allow her to buy it, of course, and anyway, it was horrendously expensive, but plenty of boys or a bar patron would buy her a present now and then. Makeup could be wiped off just before a girl got home, and if a girl stayed overnight with Constancia, no one commented on or complained about some paint on a girl's face.

One day Mili had been hanging around Lourdes's house and saw her neighbor take out a tube of lipstick from a box of things Bernardo had given her. It was a wooden tube, not metal. It might have been five years since the Civil War had ended, but outside Spain's borders, in that year of 1944 another war still raged and metal was scarce and expensive. The newspapers carried little word of the war, so whatever anyone knew of such a war, they knew mostly by rumors, letters from the Russian front where Franco had sent a few men or word from someone who had crossed the border and managed to get back.

"You know how to use lipstick, kiddo?" Mili said.

Lourdes frowned just slightly at the disrespectful slang, but she hadn't the will to reprimand Mili. What could she say anyway? She was the neighborhood whore, and that sort of woman didn't tell young ladies how to speak, even if those young ladies waggled their asses when they walked and flirted openly with your sons.

Mili showed Lourdes the best way to put the lipstick on, including a reminder to wipe her teeth if any color got on them, then tried some on herself.

"Please," Lourdes said, "wipe it off before you go home. Don't be disrespectful to your Auntie." But, Lourdes was too preoccupied observing the effect of her own colored lips suddenly jumping out at her from the mirror to notice that Mili had only lightly blotted her paint.

Leaving the house, Mili saw Bernardo enter the patio. He seemed surprised to see the girl exiting Lourdes's place, her lips pursed and pouting and bright red.

"You look good, kid," he said in passing and then watched her walk slowly across the patio. She glanced back at him, just like she'd seen girls in the movies do. He smiled at her.

Later that evening, she was leaning against the wall out by the front entrance, watching as he came out, settling his hat on his head. She liked those hats. They weren't workers' caps, they were real hats.

"You look like a movie star with that hat," she said to him. He turned and looked at her and smiled. His coat was cashmere and the maroon and blue tie silk, a little wide.

"You ever been to the movies?" he said, glancing back.

"Sometimes the boys take me," she said.

"Your mother lets boys take you to the movies?"

"I don't have a ma. My aunt doesn't know. Anyway, it's boys like Anacleto. Nothing I can't handle there, right? You want to take me to a movie?"

He smiled.

"I'm hungry too. Can we get something to eat? I won't tell Lourdes."

"Of course you won't, kid," he said.

∽⚬∽

Silvio drove them to an upscale cafeteria on the Gran Vía in Bernardo's fine car, which the driver parked where he pleased so he could nap while his boss conducted his business. They ate English food in the cafeteria, something called a "sadvich," which was something like a *bocadillo*, but instead of meat or fried fish stuffed into a roll, it was boiled ham and mayonnaise between two slices of American style bread, grilled and served on a plate. You ate it with a fork and knife, not your hands.

After that elegant meal, Mili and Bernardo strolled to a nearby movie palace. It was a magnificent theater, just renovated, gilded, mirrored, and soft with plush red carpets and red velvet seats. He didn't take her downstairs though. She should have asked, or demanded, but she was so happy he'd actually taken her there that she hadn't complained when he guided her upstairs. The usher put them in a more private area to the side, took the generous tip that Bernardo gave him, and made sure no one else came near that section for the rest of the movie. Mili never did remember what the movie was. Something from Hollywood, dubbed, all the best parts cut out, from the late twenties or early thirties from the looks of the old-fashioned clothes they wore. What she did remember was that as they sat down after Bernardo had conducted his business with the usher, he shoved his hand right up her skirt, without a by-your-leave, and pulled her panties down past her knees.

"Hey," she said. "Not that I mind, honey, but you can slow down, you know." Usually guys went for the breasts first.

He unbuttoned his pants, staring at her in that gentle penumbra before the house darkened and the curtains opened, saying not a word.

"Oh, OK," she said. A nice little rub. She was expert at that. She started to put her hand over what was a firm, well-sized cock, but he said, "Sit in my lap, baby. Put it in."

Mili was a virgin, more or less, but no novice. It was time for her to explain the rules. "I don't go all the way," she said. "But I'm a Vaseline wonder—*frota y basta*." It was a vulgar joke making the rounds of the city, from a Vaseline commercial that announced, "Rub and that's enough."

He didn't laugh. "From now on, baby, you'll do as I say. You're not dealing with a little prick like Anacleto here."

She took a deep breath. Well, it had to come some time, and this guy clearly had more to offer than anyone else she'd ever met. He had a lot, in fact: he drove a car, he dressed well, he spoke like an educated guy from a good family, he had money, he was a cop—

"All right then, but let's get this clear. You have to give me a present. And it better be nice. Lourdes is my friend. I don't want to hurt her feelings."

He laughed now, and he wouldn't stop. She hated that, it made her feel as if she'd lost control. The guy was supposed to slavering all over her and begging her for a kiss, anything, not telling her what to do. She finished removing her panties, and he took them and shoved them in his coat pocket.

"I'll let Lourdes sniff them later on," he said. "And perhaps you've still got a bit of skin down there, baby, but not much, so don't whine about it."

This guy was no sucker, he meant business. *Vergüenza y virginidad, cuando se pierden, para toda la eternidad.* Shame and virginity; when you lose them, it's eternal. She'd never felt any shame, that's what everyone said, and no one believed she was a virgin anymore either, so, since she liked this guy, why not?

As if reading her thoughts, he reached over and hauled her onto his lap, her legs spread, her skirt up to her waist, his hands holding the cheeks of her rump firmly, just as the theater went dark, the huge red curtain rose, and the music swelled. She was surprised at how easy it was and how thrilling. A little painful too but not as much as everyone said.

The usher standing far back at the very top of the balcony stretched his neck and observed as best he could by the light of the movie screen how the big tipper was definitely getting his money's worth from the cute little tart.

Dr. Contreras took Sra. Rosa home one day. He hailed a taxi, of course, because he certainly had no time to walk to that neighborhood so far away. The gesture surprised her considerably, and then as the Mercedes taxi chugged gently up Valencia Street, he suggested they stop at Miguel Servet Street and walk down a side alley to Rogelio's house. They could then drop in for a visit with Constancia. Once again, he had paid attention to her concerns, he had listened, and it touched her deeply.

The visit did not last too long, as Rogelio was not home, and the big doctor who had to duck his head just to get in the doorway clearly frightened Constancia. Afterward, they strolled toward Sra. Rosa's home down the cobbled streets between the narrow buildings that tipped gently toward each other as if just about to kiss. Some balconies now sported pots of geraniums. The city was still glum and still in black, but there were geraniums and carnations to be had. Just last month Rosita-Laura had brought Sra. Rosa a bouquet of carnations. The lady at the fruit stand in the market had volunteered just two days ago that by summer, she'd have melons. And now that Rosa-Laura was bringing in a bit of money, they could afford a melon once in a while.

As for her daughter, Sra. Rosa could not help herself bragging about the child, though she knew full well that could bring on bad luck. But Rosa-Laura was such a gorgeous child, serious, wide eyed, elfin, so intent upon everything, as if she were studying each and every stone in the street, each and every face that passed by, the curve of a bloom of smoke from a chimney, a tree full of new leaves and one dead branch. She might comment on things she saw too. Sra. Rosa didn't always understand, but just listening to her daughter speak so seriously on some subject—yesterday it had been about bas relief carvings on the buildings uptown, imagine!—brought intense joy to her.

So, life was a real, tenable proposition again, and as it had to be, to balance out all that sprouting joy lay the grim worm feast of Constancia's condition.

They did not go to Sra. Rosa's house after visiting Constancia. That would have been improper anyway, and who wanted to have a guest at a house that was one room crowded with a tiny bed and cheap furniture folded against the wall and chipped cups and covered dishes of yesterday's food? They passed her building, walking slowly and relaxed, and found a nice tavern in the plaza instead. The Doctor ordered sweet vermouth with seltzer and a twist of lemon for her and a brandy for himself. He also ordered a tableful of appetizers: bite sized tuna pies, some fried cod, a plate of vivid-green, thumb-sized peppers deep fried—Sra. Rosa was awfully fond of those peppers. *Pimentos del Padrón* they were called, because of they came from Padrón, one of Galicia's most beautiful villages. The peppers had the wicked tendency to be sweet and amazingly delicious so that you ate and ate like a pig until whoom!, you got to the hot one, tucked beneath all the others, the one that seared your mouth ferociously, the "surprise," as everyone referred to it. She loved getting a surprise, loved filling her mouth with a crispy combination of sweet and piquant. She was getting too old for it, of course, and it hurt her stomach and the holes in her gums where her teeth used to be, but still, what a pleasure, to bite and have your food bite back.

"All I can do for Constancia is give you a good supply of morphine," the Doctor said, after he'd drunk his brandy and ordered another. He hadn't begun the conversation with coy euphemisms and bourgeois diplomacy. One thing he liked about his discussions with his housekeeper was that he believed she expected him to speak as he felt and did not fault him for lack of delicacy.

"Sir, you know I appreciate your help, as always. I owe you a lot—"

He rolled his eyes and waved his hand as if to toss her words aside. "Really, Sra. Rosa, we have discussed this before. I often visit poorer patients. It's part of my job. Do you know that I am required by the government to serve in the Social Security clinics at least one day a week now? I don't mind. I did it anyway, before they required it. My private practice is very good these days. The rich seem to be collecting a heavy debt on their lifestyle and their abuse of our country. They present with ulcers, impotence, the most arcane cancers, tuberculosis—"

Sra. Rosa almost choked on the crusty bite of codfish in her mouth. It was bad luck to say those words, didn't he know that? Sometimes higher-ups were utterly ignorant of the most basic truths of life.

"Sir, the morphine won't cure her, will it?"

"Morphine only takes away the pain. Her disease was terminal to begin with, given that, well, in this country, at this time, no medicine, blockades, such a profound disease—what can I say, Sra. Rosa? It's sad, but someday they'll find a way to cure it, I am sure of that.

"Even if she had been wealthy and come to me early, well, I would have operated, but still, that's an unlikely cure anyway, with lots of pain. No wonder she wouldn't let her poor husband touch her breasts. But you will be good to her and so will he. She is loved, what more can a human ask? I will get you the morphine, but let's be clear, soon she will drift and lose her sense of time or place, then she will pass. But tell me, has she ever told you her story? Or Rogelio? Or is she one of those poor wraiths that float out of the fog of the war and now returns to the nether world?"

Sra. Rosa was befuddled by his phrasing, then she suddenly found the "surprise" in her peppers and let out a yelp at the heat. Dr. Contreras raised his eyebrows and smiled.

"Ooo, that's good. My mouth's going to burn for days. I don't really know her whole story. Got bits and pieces of it, mostly from neighbors, and, you know, her reactions to things. She's terrified of cops and the civil guard especially. Story is, someone came one night. Truth, no one knows if it was them or some of ours. It was just before the war ended, and her old man snuck home to rest a bit and heal from a wound. They had a boy and a girl, both under twelve. So you can see, months of bombings, months of protecting those kids, and where did it get her? The old man goes home one night, he's snuck off from the battlefield to check and make sure his family is all OK. Then, some hours later—like someone informed, you know?—a car pulls up, they pile out and grab him, and the children scream and carry on, and they grab them! The kids! And she runs.

"I think that's the heart of it, and the beginning of the—well, of the sickness. She ran. Out of the house and down the street. Never looked back. That's what's eating her from inside, that she ran. They're gone, and she didn't go with them. Maybe it would have been better to go with them. Anyway, that's the gossip, that it's the 'witness sickness,' what's killing her."

He nodded. There was a lot of that in Madrid these days, the "witness sickness."

"Look, Sra. Rosa, one more thing: this medicine I'm giving you, it's very, very valuable, and it is a narcotic. Do you understand?"

By the look on her face, he could see she did not.

"It can be used by addicts, people who like drugs, who use drugs, or even people who sell drugs. It is worth a great deal of money. Do not under any circumstances allow anyone but yourself and Rogelio to administer it or see it or even know it exists. Are we clear on this?"

In other words, don't let Mili know about the drugs. Sra. Rosa nodded, her heart heavy.

He saw that she understood, and he was sorry to have to have said such things. He looked over at the bar, wondering if there was more food he could order. Food was relaxing, it made people happy, it made him happy, or at least, it helped him endure the lack of other things in his life. There was a poster over the wall in the back announcing a *zarzuela*, to be held uptown at a theater in the Plaza Santa Ana. He loved the Plaza Santa Ana.

"Do you see that poster?" he said to Sra. Rosa. "We're getting some entertainment back in the capital. It's about time. Nationalist stuff, of course, only our own product nowadays, and frankly, I prefer operas to operettas—"

Sra. Rosa was looking at him completely blank.

"The poster—oh, I do apologize Sra. Rosa. I forgot."

She said nothing, but blushed deeply. Now he felt like a graceless fool, rubbing her face in her illiteracy. There was a long pause as they both recovered their dignity.

"Listen, Sra. Rosa," he said, wanting to chose his words carefully and not make a worse mess of it, "Rosa-Laura, she's done quite well in school, hasn't she?"

"Oh, yes, Sir, she's a wonder, my girl. And now that she's apprenticed, well, the tailors like her a lot, they're not paying her yet, but next month she's fifteen, and then she gets a salary. As for now, she gets nice tips all the time, and it looks to be a very good profession."

He had forgotten the child was already graduated. Girls didn't go on to preparatory schools for the most part, because girls didn't go on to the university. He cleared his throat and signaled the bartender for another brandy. The bartender was wiping a glass and nodded to him, casually and with a firm gaze. It was his way of letting his well-dressed client know that he was no servant, he'd come when he damn well felt like it, and no civil war was going to keep him from being just as proud as any representative of the upper classes. The Doctor knew the game well. It was a thoroughly Spanish game and sometimes he relished it and sometimes he despaired for his poor, deluded countrymen.

And speaking of carefully nurtured Spanish delusion and elaborate charades, a Gypsy walked into the tavern, looked around casually for the most likely client to alleviate his needs, and walked over to the table where the Doctor and Sra. Rosa sat chatting. He stood there a moment, regarding them both, deciding whether or not to honor them with his business, and then he held out his hand, toward the Doctor, of course.

Sra. Rosa was shocked; the regime was rounding up Gypsies encampment by encampment. They hated Gypsies almost as much as Jews. Yet here was this character standing straight-backed, head high, hand out, and proud, as if he weren't even begging but demanding his fair share. If a cop happened by, the fool was a dead man. The Doctor smiled and gave the man a peseta. That was the Doctor for you. No money sense at all. When the well is deep, water can be wasted.

"Hey, you son of a whore, get out of here!" The bartender said, seeing the Gypsy for the first time. Head still held high, the Gypsy left the tavern without hurrying.

"I can't believe it, son of a whore, I don't know what's worse, their whining females or their arrogant males, *desgraciados*," the bartender said, bringing over the bottle of brandy.

"If you don't mind," the Doctor said to the bartender, "there is a lady here."

"Oh, of course, sorry, Sra. Rosa, my apologies for the language."

When the bartender had returned behind the counter to wipe and rewipe his wine glasses, the Doctor said to Sra. Rosa, "I was thinking, you know, does Rosa-Laura still have her school books?"

"Um, no, Sir, we had to return them when she graduated."

"I see. Well, I have some at home. We saved all our books, my sister and I, as souvenirs of those lovely days—ah, what I mean is, I could loan Rosa-Laura some of them."

"Sir?"

"Well, how shall I say, Sra. Rosa—you are certainly an intelligent woman. I have had proof of that time and again. And a tenacious one. You know, like one of those sayings of yours, *'El que madrugó, un billetero se encontró!'*"

Sra. Rosa sighed. Leave it to one of his class to forget the rest: *"Más madrugó el que le perdió.* The early riser finds the wallet, but the earliest riser was the fool who lost it in the first place," she said.

Dr. Contreras groaned inwardly, but didn't correct her—it was the fool who stayed out *late* the night before who lost the wallet, but— "Look, what I'm trying to say is that, I'll loan you some books and your daughter can teach you how to read. She'd like to, I'm sure. You could do it in the evenings, when you're at home sewing together or whatever you do in the evenings."

Sra. Rosa didn't tell him that Rosa-Laura got home past 8:30 p.m., ate some dinner, and they went to bed by 9:00 or 9:30. Besides, what he was saying was interesting. It didn't offend her at all. It was just the sort of thing a good person who had just offered to get one's poor sick friend a lot of expensive medicine might suggest. It was amazing, astonishing even, probably impossible, but such a nice idea.

When Rosa-Laura came home the next evening from work, the books were there.

"Oh, Mama, it's marvelous! What beautiful books! Look, they're so much better than mine were! Mine were cardboard, and all marked up, but look at these, leather-bound, pictures, so beautiful—oh, Mama, this is so lovely! And he gave you a notebook and a pencil too? Mama, what a wonderful man! We'll start right now!"

"Yeah, well, eat something first, OK? And try not to forget how old I am, *hija. No es la miel para la boca del asno,* You don't feed honey to a donkey."

"Enough! I'm sick of those stupid *dichos.* What, are you calling my own mother a donkey? These books will teach you something else besides old sayings."

Rosa-Laura's day at work had been exhausting. Client after client to measure, run up and down those stairs, three flights, time after time, the walk to Recoletos with the master's wife, who was so fat she was slow as a snail cooked and stewed in cumin sauce and set up on the bar counter for an appetizer. Then there were the pants for a general that had to be cut and basted, Rosa-Laura's job, because it was becoming very clear to the master that she was the best cutter and baster he had, and—well, she was tired, but these presents were so beautiful and the idea of teaching Mama to read wonderful.

She couldn't touch and feel and open and close the books enough. One book was a primer for learning to read, another was a book of simple tales, moral lessons, and allegories, and the third a book on how to speak properly. The leather covers were red or blue, with gold lettering and the names of the owners inscribed on delicately engraved plates inside. One plate showed a knight in armor on horseback, pike at the ready, another a girl with fat curls seated beneath a tree reading, another an owl with glasses on its huge eyes, a clapboard on its head, and a professorial pointing stick clasped in his claw, chalk board behind him.

"It's so easy, Mama, don't you worry. You already know a lot of letters, and that's how a word begins, by sounding out the letters. Soon you just have the words memorized, and it's even easier. Let me show you—"

∽৹

On Rosa-Laura's fifteenth birthday, her Papa gave her a lottery ticket. It made sense, though she wasn't really very impressed by the present. When four of her numbers came in, however, she was very impressed. Hysterically impressed in fact, and gave over to screeching and shrieking so that her mother, half the block, and her whole building all found out at the same time that Rosa-Laura had won a hundred *pesetas*. It was 1946, and though now she would be a full-time salaried employee at her master's shop, one hundred pesetas was three times her monthly wages.

She cashed in the ticket, with Mama's help as she was underage, and turned the money over to her.

"Hey, this is your birthday money," Sra. Rosa said to her. "I don't want it, girl."

"I don't know what to do with it, Mama. Keep it for me."

Her Mama considered this and realized the girl had a good idea there, so keep it for her girl she did. She had a new hiding place in their tiny apartment, a loose brick behind the stove. Mili didn't know about it, nor did Rosa-Laura for that matter. A good deal of things fit behind that brick.

"Why didn't you buy yourself something nice?" Carmen-Victoria asked Rosa-Laura the next day as they ate pastries and drank coffee in the neighborhood plaza. Rosa-Laura was footing the bill, as the birthday was hers, and that's what you did on birthdays, you treated all your friends. Besides, Carmen-Victoria had something else to celebrate. Her third cousin, a quiet boy from Navarre who had come to stay with her family so he could work in Madrid, had gotten her a job in a kitchen at a small restaurant uptown, not more than three blocks from where Rosa-Laura worked. Now they could walk to work together and walk home together as well. Rosa-Laura didn't know what made Carmen-Victoria happier, finally finding a job after graduating almost a year ago, or getting to work alongside the quiet boy from Navarre, who made Carmen-Victoria's usually acerbic mouth go quite soft and caused a moony unfocused shine to slip over her usual unfazed, sarcastic gaze.

"What could I buy? Cloth for a fine dress? That and this bill still leaves me ninety pesetas, girl."

Carmen-Victoria considered the possibilities. "We could go to the Plaza Oriente and eat at that fancy café there, and then we could go see a review or a *zarzuela*, and then a movie too, and then go dancing. I could get my, uh, cousin to come with us and watch out for us. And then, you'd still have enough to buy a bed!"

Rosa-Laura laughed. "I'd surely like a new bed, but where would we put it? The place is barely big enough now for the one we got."

But shortly thereafter Rosa-Laura would go shopping for a bed.

Her father asked her to help him find some furniture, and in particular, a bed, a nice one, he said, with a headboard and a comfortable, modern platform so that the mattress would have something solid and reliable and supportive under it. In other words, not a stingy cot with leather straps or a creaky wire mesh to hold the stuffed mat and the poor sleeper.

Rosa-Laura said, "Certainly, Papa, I'll ask my boss for the morning off right away." That was all she said, but she knew. Papa wanted something comfortable for poor Constancia to die on. He could afford this luxury by now. He was making a very respectable salary at the *ONCE* and getting plenty of tips back from the winners of his tickets.

His request came the first week of September, right after the Saturday he paid the priest at San Lorenzo to come to his basement and marry him to Constancia. Sra. Rosa, Mili, and Rosa-Laura were there, as were two of his blind cronies from the *ONCE*. Rosa-Laura brought flowers, orange blossoms, which cost her a fortune. Her mother made no comment on the extravagance. "They smell nice, daughter," was all she said.

Constancia wore a new black dress that Rosa-Laura had made. She could barely stand for the ceremony. She was skinny to the point of emaciation. Her gray hair, despite its thinness, had been carefully combed by Mili into a very presentable and elaborate figure eight bun, and she carried the bouquet of orange blossoms, frequently sniffing at them. Though all the street level windows in the apartment were open to let in some summer air, the smell of orange blossoms and decay filled the room. Rosa-Laura, for the first time in her whole life, was glad her Papa was blind, so that he could not see how she fought not to bawl aloud. As it was, tears streamed down her face and she gripped her mother's hand so hard the poor woman had to fight herself not to yelp in pain.

Rosa-Laura and her Papa went uptown Tuesday morning to buy the bed. Rosa-Laura offered to help pay for it from her winnings, but he refused. "I want to buy you a wedding present, Papa," she said.

"No, my lovely one, you paid for the flowers. I couldn't have asked for more. I think Constancia liked them very much," he said.

She led him to a shop on a street of furniture makers, and they picked out a very serviceable and well-made bed. They also purchased a second cot, at Rosa-Laura's suggestion, so that Mili would not have to sleep on the floor when she visited. She was seldom at home these days, so Rosa-Laura assumed that she spent all her time at Papa's, helping poor Constancia and comforting her.

Then her father checked out some chairs, one by one, running his hands over the rattan and the carved backs and underneath to see if they were sturdily built and had good cross-bars and finally settled on two chairs that he thought would make good companions to his table. It was a shopping spree that quite delighted all the participants. The shopkeeper promised a delivery by the next morning, which undoubtedly meant in a week or so. Rosa-Laura promised the shopkeeper that if her stepmother weren't in that bed comfortably settled by next Saturday, she would come back herself with a policeman.

After they exited the store Rogelio told his daughter he was shocked that she had exhibited such crass manners. After all, one has to trust, and her such a young girl to be so cynical.

Rosa-Laura said, "Like the Moor said, Papa, 'Trust in Allah but tie your camel.'"

"Ah, dear God, that comes direct from your mother. Such a depository of *dichos*, that woman!"

Rosa-Laura laughed. "Mama is learning, Papa, she is learning. Every day she learns to spell a new word, and she can read simple sentences already. By the way, is Mili going to be at your house tonight?"

Her father suddenly lost his aura of good humor and said nothing for a moment. "Well, I suppose so, daughter."

Rosa-Laura felt the chill. "Papa, tell me. Please. I won't tell Mama, if you don't want me to, unless—"

"She comes when she comes, daughter. She has another place these days. A pensión in Embajadores; in the plaza."

Rosa-Laura paled but with ease in her voice said, "OK, Papa, no problem, no problem. Don't worry about all this. It's not what it appears, really. She'll be all right. Mama probably knows anyway. Don't worry."

Unless her mother were to ask her right out, she was not going to repeat this information. She thought about confiding in Carmen-Victoria, though. She went directly to work after leaving Papa at home and got a stern lecture from her boss about taking time off in these days of so many consignments. She worked six days a week, eight to ten hours a day, with a short lunch and even shorter siesta, and that was how things were. She accepted the scolding with head down and many promises not to take further advantage of his kindness.

"That's what I get for listening to nuns and hiring a girl," he muttered.

Rosa-Laura nodded and went upstairs. She felt no anger, just a clear and realistic awareness that she was the best tailor he had and the most conscientious as well. If and when Constancia got sicker, or God chose to take her, Rosa-Laura would ask for leave again. And if the master dared to oppose her request for a decent time to help her family and mourn, maybe even a whole day, she'd leave and find another position. She was good at what she did. She was very good. A damned *mosquita muerta*, wasn't she now?

Someone else Sra. Rosa knew was called to meet her God shortly thereafter, but it was not poor Constancia.

Dr. Contreras came home late one afternoon looking to eat a quick snack and take a siesta. He was so busy and had so many patients nowadays that he seldom had time to rest, and often ate at restaurants instead of going home for lunch. Nor was the food at home as good as when his thieving, treacherous cook had been employed. Sra. Rosa could prepare sandwiches and make a soup, she more or less knew the ingredients to a bland garbanzo stew with salt pork or rancid ham, and could even fry an egg now without breaking the yolk, but not much else. Once he had asked her for scrambled eggs, which name she did not recognize, and when he explained how one scrambled an egg she had said, "I know how to do that. You start with an omelet and ruin it, that's how."

When he walked in his doorway that day, he noticed at once that everything was quite dark. The curtains had been drawn in all the rooms. He supposed that was because his sister had one of her migraines and the house had been darkened and stilled so she could rest with an ice pack, Sra. Rosa by her side, holding his sister's hand and replenishing the ice when it melted. He checked the salon, and to his astonishment, his sister was lying on the chaise lounge, dead drunk, a half empty bottle of his best brandy at her side. Sra. Rosa sat next to her, her eyes wet, rosary in hand. Without realizing that he already knew, knew when he saw that rosary in the hands of a woman not much given to piety, he whispered, "Sra. Rosa? Tell me what has happened."

She said nothing but stood up, checked to make sure Guillermina was quite insensate, and led Dr. Contreras to his mother's room.

It had been peaceful. He was grateful for that. But the peace of it did not assuage his devastation. Ensconced blithe and pampered in her own special world, queen of her realm, his dear, beloved, capricious, useless, wonderful, exotic, beautiful, sophisticated, amusing mother. It was inconceivable, a world without his mother. And he hadn't even married and given her a grandchild, though she probably didn't really want to be reminded of how old she had gotten anyway.

His head was pounding so much it seemed that Sra. Rosa must hear it as if it were a drum beat emanating out of his occipital region.

Sra. Rosa, of course, had been spectacular. She'd found the old lady that morning, closed the bedroom door quietly, drawn the curtains, picked the lock on his liquor cabinet, and fed Guillermina brandy and pastries until she'd passed out. Guillermina didn't ask why Sra. Rosa was being so lavish with the goodies her brother usually refused to let her have. Just as she had never asked her younger brother how it was possible their stepfather could die so conveniently. The Doctor hoped Guillermina hadn't gone into a diabetic coma. For several years now, he had checked his sister's blood sugars and fought to keep her from gorging herself on pastries. But today, an awful, awful day, his sister clearly could do with anesthesia. Once Guillermina had passed out, Sra. Rosa had taken Guillermina's rosary, a crystal rosary blessed by the Pope in fact, and sat with her, watching her and praying for the soul of Sra. de Montero.

There was a phone in the apartment, and though Sra. Rosa did not really know how to use it, she clumsily dialed the number the Doctor recited to her. She got it right on the third try. Then, she sat and waited for the director of the funeral service to come and take his mother. She hadn't even disputed with the Doctor by insisting she could prepare the body herself.

Ordinary people didn't use funeral services. Women cleaned and dressed the corpse, the family had a home viewing as long as was decently possible, depending on the weather and season, and everyone brought the corpse to the graveyard themselves in a hired van. Masses in neighborhood churches were purchased for the swift flight of the soul to its Maker. But people like the Doctor did not clean and wash and take care of their corpses. They called a mortician, a peculiar and very expensive employee not much in demand in Spain. They would hold a funeral service in a special hall, pay for high Mass at a big church, maybe Los Gerónimos, a cathedral his mother liked very much, and probably give a reception at home afterwards. By that time, the body would have been deposited in an elegant crypt at the Cemetery of the Almudena. The family still had friends and acquaintances and relatives in the capital, though there had been no party at the house in years—and how the Doctor wished now that he had held one, just one, maybe on her last birthday, but he hadn't, he was too busy.

After Sra. Rosa hung up the phone, she sat with the Doctor, put a cold compress on his aching head, held his hand, and let him cry as long as he wanted. Days later, when the reception took place, she refused to be one of the guests, though he had requested it. He was so distraught he never thought about how she might feel as a guest among a crowd of rich mourners. Instead, she came early, neatly dressed in her best black, and helped Guillermina into a very elaborate ruffled black dress of satin, beautiful patterned French stockings purchased long before the war, and platform pumps of black suede. Having done that, Sra. Rosa then oversaw the hired waiters and caterers serving the food and drink. She felt better being useful, she told the Doctor. Afterward, he recaptured his wits, thanked her, and told her that she meant a great deal to him, that she was more than his housekeeper, she was like a surrogate mother to both Guillermina and himself.

Sra. Rosa blushed. "Now, Sir, really, you're just upset is all. I did what I always do, that's it. I liked your Mama. She was a good sort. Never gave me any trouble, always had a joke to tell."

That gave him his first smile since his mother had died. His mother had a stock of risqué jokes that went back sixty years as well as a way of telling them that could make a person piss himself laughing. The Doctor could not even imagine his mother telling Sra. Rosa any of those jokes.

The horrors began not because Sra. Rosa first figured it out, but because Carmen-Victoria did; she told Rosa-Laura who let the cat out of the bag without even realizing what the consequences could be. But at any rate, no matter who started it, the start was inevitable.

"You seen your cousin lately?" Carmen-Victoria said to Rosa-Laura one morning as they dipped greasy churros into bowls of coffee boiled with milk and sugar. They were at a well lit *churrería* on Esparteros Street, just a few blocks from their respective work places. It was 6:30 a.m. and work began for them both at 7:00 sharp. Everywhere around them waiters and clients came and went quickly to the sounds of orders and clacking shoes, the slosh of dipping, drinking, licking chops smudged with custard-thick chocolate or slurping strong coffee, paying, laughing, talking, voices louder and louder. Now and then a waiter would skid or slip on a floor dredged with discarded tissue napkins and bits of churros. And the smell!—pastry, grease, coffee, chocolate, sugar. The girls sat at the bar, as it was cheaper than sitting at a table and having to tip the poor waiters a *real* or two *céntimos* more than the *céntimo* they could leave for the barman.

"My brothers saw her at Embajadores yesterday," Carmen-Victoria said.

"So?" Rosa-Laura said. She did not want this comfortable breakfast to end, and she had a weird premonition it was going to end very, very badly.

"Look, Rosa-Laura, it's not my business, I don't care, but you know how the guys are—I mean, it's not real obvious yet, but they saw our ma so many times, and they know—"

"*Miel da,*" Rosa-Laura said, "Honey given," two words that were not shit, *mierda,* but certainly close enough to give Carmen-Victoria an idea of how exasperated she was by the hesitancy and hinting. "Tell me what you are talking about, because I do not understand. Just say it, Carmen-Victoria. Say it."

"She's with child," Carmen-Victoria said. "Even my brothers, dumb shovels that they are, knew. And it won't be long that no one will have to guess, it'll be right there at belly level, sticking out to the suburbs."

Rosa-Laura suddenly had an urge to throw up. Sort of a morning sickness by proxy.

She had to work that day too; there was no way she could ask her boss to let her go home and talk to her mother. Besides, if she'd gone home early or walked over to Dr. Contreras's house to visit her mother at work, whatever could she have said? "Hi, Mama, hey, Mili's gone and gotten herself a fat belly, and that surely comes as no surprise, right?"

At 12:30 p.m., contrary to her usual custom of eating a light lunch and then either taking a short walk or resting during the siesta on a cot in the back of the attic workshop, Rosa-Laura advised the wife of the master tailor that she was going straight home for siesta and would be back by 3:30 p.m., as was to be expected. Downstairs, she caught a bus, an indulgence to her need to make haste so she could return to work on time. She got off at the Plaza Glorieta de Embajadores stop. The question was, where would she find Mili? She had no clue as to which pensión her cousin was staying in or even if she were there now. Or maybe the whole damned thing was a lie, and there was no pensión, and no belly.

She circled the plaza slowly, keeping her purse next to her tightly so she wouldn't become a target for some pickpocket, keeping her head up and her eyes straight ahead so she wouldn't become a target for some randy guy. Rosa-Laura always got *piropos*, compliments, from the boys and grown men too, when she walked alone or with Carmen-Victoria. There was a law against kissing and hugging in public and strict rules about talking to females you didn't know, but it hadn't stopped the harassment and the longing, it only made it worse. Rosa-Laura hated the way the men looked at women, she hated the exchanges of suggestive compliments then angry retorts from the woman targeted. She hated being followed by some idiot who was expecting to wear down her resistance. She hated the way Mili acted around men. She hated how her own mother feared and despised most men. She even hated being female at times, because boys had it so much easier and freer, or at least, it seemed that way. All this glut of hatred, boiled to syrup from the poisonous recipes that divided men and women, boys and girls.

She managed to walk a block around the wide plaza with its rundown fountains and honey locust trees in full bloom. One block and then the barrage, from a group of young guys hanging out in front of a bar.

"Hiya, doll-face, how come you're alone? You want a companion? You want a drink? Beautiful blue eyes! Wow, you're better than the home team on a winning streak, you're better than four ears at the bullfights on a warm Sunday!" and so on.

I want to find that damned cousin of mine so I can slap her as hard as I can, and I want all of you to cut your balls off and stuff them in your mouth. If anyone ever guessed how foul her thoughts were, maybe then they wouldn't think she was such a *mosquita muerta*. She set her mouth hard and made no reply to the boys. She wasn't witty anyway, like Mili. Whatever could a girl say to undignified and foolish comments? Did these boys think she was going to run right over and lift up her dress or something?

Dear God, when Mama finds out about Mili she's going to kill her or die of shame herself. Mama is so—

A boy positioned himself right in front of her so that she couldn't pass him, and when she tried he began a stupid game of blocking her, hands on his hips, his companions laughing riotously at the clown act. She stopped. Looked him right in the eye and said, "Get the hell out of my way, you fool, or I'll yell for the cops over there in that car—"

Which was when she realized one of the cops was Bernardo, and Bernardo had seen her too.

He got out of the car, leaving the driver inside smoking, and walked over to her slowly, head high, hat rakishly tilted, eyes amused, hands in the pockets of his elegant long coat. The boys who had been goading on their friend sidled back into the bar behind them. The boy directly in front of Rosa-Laura jerked from a half-second spasm of terror, then immediately composed his visage and hardened it.

"*Lárgate, jilipolla,*" the cop said. The "asshole scrammed," without a reply, walking away with his head up and his hands hooked onto his belt loops. Bernardo flicked his cigarette at the boy's receding back.

"What are you doing here this time of day?" Bernardo said.

Rosa-Laura clutched her purse to her right side even more tightly and scanned the newspaper kiosk directly to her left. The kiosks sold not only the regulation government approved newspapers, but also a few local magazines and certain types of comics which were actually photographed with models, real people, not drawn, and depicted the exploits of various heroes in maudlin or highly romantic adventures. Candies, sunflower seeds, and peanuts were also for sale. Rosa-Laura counted the different kinds of snacks for a minute, then faced Bernardo, composed.

"I'm here because I'm here. You can tell my mother, or I'll tell her myself. But I'm doing nothing wrong."

"Yeah. You and your cousin, you're a pair all right."

What did he mean by that? Did he know where Mili was? Rosa-Laura struggled to maintain some composure, and she did that by remembering the day a few years ago that she saw Bernardo hit Anacleto, in the patio of their building. Lourdes had been standing there, and it shocked Rosa-Laura unimaginably to see the woman throw her hands over her mouth to stuff back any protest. Bernardito was crying in the house, and that's why the cop hit Anacleto: he thought the boy had bothered the little one. The neighbors said that Bernardito was Bernardo's son, which made sense, though at that time when she was just a child, Rosa-Laura had not understood at all how Lourdes could be married to another man yet produce a son by this one. She'd finally figured that one out, but to this day she still couldn't understand how Lourdes could let this man hit Anacleto.

Now Rosa-Laura wasn't a baby anymore. She knew exactly what was going on with Lourdes, and it was difficult for her to understand why she still cared for Lourdes as much as she had before, especially when she witnessed daily how Anacleto and Augustín were treated in contrast to how Bernardito was treated. Not to mention how she felt about Bernardo's treatment of Lourdes herself.

"Sir, I need to get going, because I have to be back at work by 3:30. So, thank you for getting those boys out of my way, and good day."

But like the kid who had teased her, Bernardo was not moving out of her way.

"I asked you why you're here. Answer me."

"I'm looking for someone, I just don't know exactly which house, that's all." Rosa-Laura didn't want to talk to him, but no one refused to answer a policeman. Ever. The only person more of a loose pistol than a cop was a civil guard.

"If you're looking for Mili, she's in that pensión above the butcher shop."

He grinned at her and walked back to his car. Rosa-Laura paused a minute, swallowed her spit and her bile and her terror, then walked to the crosswalk. When the traffic permitted, she crossed the broad street and headed for the butcher shop on the southwest corner of the plaza. She couldn't see if the two men in the car were watching her, yet she didn't doubt they were.

⚬⚬⚬

She had found the pensión and seen Mili, but her cousin was on her way out, in a hurry, and had simply brushed past her with no more than a "Sorry, kid, I got to run. No time." Rosa-Laura stared after her, and Mili turned just before leaving. She saw Rosa-Laura's expression, frowned, glanced down a little nervously, then laughed, and left.

Rosa-Laura arrived home late that evening, having stayed after work to finish a job and to make up for returning from the siesta fifteen minutes late. Rosa-Laura still walked home with Carmen-Victoria and her third cousin, Eduardo. He seldom spoke with the two girls, but guarded them quite proudly, then ushered Rosa-Laura to the outer door of her building, generally unlocked until 9 p.m., watched until she had entered the patio safely, and left with his cousin. Rosa-Laura could see from the first day how happy Carmen-Victoria was to have the next five minutes alone with Eduardo as they continued across Tribulete and down the street to the family's home.

Shortly after Eduardo had first met Rosa-Laura, he'd asked her if she'd like to walk with him in the neighborhood plaza on Sundays. She told him no, firmly, and also told him not to ever ask her again. She never told Carmen-Victoria about Eduardo's request. If she had to chose between loving the serious Navarrese and loving her best friend, clearly Carmen-Victoria was the winner. She knew this decision further branded her as a *mosquita muerta,* and she never told either Mili or her mother about it.

Inside the patio of their building, Anacleto sat at the side of the well, fumbling with a child's wooden toy, of all things. It was a cup fixed on a stick with a small ball attached to the contraption by a string; the object of the game was to flip the ball into the cup while holding the stick. He seemed deeply engrossed in this childish trick, yet she could see that he was a hundred kilometers elsewhere, sullen, quiet, unhappy.

"I was waiting for you," he said very softly, just as she passed him. Whatever was the matter with all these boys? Had they all gone crazy? She wanted to ask Carmen-Victoria, but that might mean mentioning Eduardo's proposal. And she certainly wasn't going to ask Mili and get laughed at. Besides, suddenly Mili wasn't looking so wise about the ways of the world any more.

"Why?" she said. Well, that was a brilliant riposte.

"I've liked you for ever so long, Rosa-Laura," he said. "Why don't you like me? Am I too ugly for you?"

"I thought you liked Mili," Rosa-Laura said. She tried to keep the evil out of her voice, but it was there. Who else could be the father of Mili's child, if child she truly had, but this stupid boy sitting here and playing with a toy like a kid? They had done something dirty, and Mili would pay for it, unless he married her, but Anacleto was younger than Mili, and both were too young to marry without permission. Twenty-one was the age of consent. And there had been far too much consent going on here.

"Mili's not my girl. She's just—available, that's all. I've always liked you best. You're so pretty, the prettiest girl in this whole neighborhood. Maybe in all Madrid."

"Prettier than Mili?" Rosa-Laura said. She couldn't believe he didn't taste the poison in her voice. He had used up Mili and now wanted to begin on her.

"You were always the prettiest. You look like one of those dolls in the shop windows, perfect. The most beautiful blue eyes. Mili's just a loud-mouth. Everyone has to look at her and listen to her, that's all."

"You miserable dog," Rosa-Laura said, resisting the easy insult of "son of a whore," keeping her voice down, keeping an eye on her mother's doorway. Any minute now Mama would come out and hear something Rosa-Laura did not want her to hear. "You got my poor cousin with child, and now you're trying to seduce me. I hate you. I hate you so much! Don't ever talk to me again, or I'll—" she had to think about that one. What was the worst possible thing she could threaten him with? "I'll tell Bernardo, that's what I'll do."

Anacleto stood up so suddenly she thought he was going to strike her and she jumped back. He just looked at her, looked at her so strangely and so hard he terrified her.

"What do you mean, she's with child?" he said.

Rosa-Laura couldn't dredge up any words. She felt sick. She was a stupid loudmouth, an idiot. Anacleto was not looking at her though. His face was white and he was staring at past her at his mother's house.

"*Putas, las dos,* Whores, the two of you," he said and ran out of the patio to the street.

She thought he meant Mili and herself. Years later she would realize she had not been included in his imprecation; he'd meant someone else.

Rosa-Laura hung her head in shame and turned toward her own door, when her mother parted the curtain shielding the doorway, where she had been standing and listening anxiously. "Rosa-Laura, what were you saying to Anacleto? What has happened?"

"I can do whatever I want," Mili said. "Men like me because I'm so pretty and happy-go-lucky. I don't need to get married, and as for this, well, OK, so I'll have a baby. He can't marry me because he's got that ugly wife he don't love anyway, but he loves me so much I know he'll pay for the kid, don't you worry. I'm going to get a house and money and lots of nice things, Auntie Rosi. Why should I marry anyway? Husbands just treat you mean, you said that yourself a million times. I can get more this way, playing hard to get."

Sra. Rosa sat across from Mili at a café in Embajadores. She had found the girl quite by accident but it was lucky she had. It was nearly midnight. Curfew was in effect. Sra. Rosa had no idea how she was going to get home, but the café was open and they were there and that was that. Madrid was a city of night cats, and everyone accepted that, even the police. Curfew just meant a person could get arrested or beat up or both if a cop felt like it. Every now and then a man entered the café and glanced at the odd sight of two women out so late, one an old woman with steel gray hair in a tight bun at the nape of her neck and dressed in black, of course, from toes to chin, and the other a very hot young tart also in black, her dress quite tight, the top button undone, the second straining to follow the first, the girl's breasts underneath all that as full as cream cakes. She was smoking, cigarette after cigarette, while the old woman pleaded with her in a whisper. The guess would be a prostitute and her poor old mother trying to save the girl's soul.

Sra. Rosa was still recovering not only from the shocking news of who her niece's paramour really was, but also from Mili's brazen, bragging attitude about the whole affair.

"What are you saying? Are you listening to yourself, girl? Pretty soon the results of your playing 'hard to get" are going to be out there on display for the whole neighborhood to see. You got dust balls for brains. Dear

God, why'd you let him do it to you? What were you thinking?"

"He gave me stuff. He took me to movies on the Gran Vía. I got the prettiest dress you ever saw, and I got a new coat and a beret and a scarf. It didn't even hurt much the first time, not like you all said it would. He's going to get me a job too, not a hard dirty one like yours either, and not one where I got to pinch my fingers with needles and pins and sit sewing all day like a drudge! I'm going to dance in a night club, and wear beautiful costumes, and everyone will look at me and see how pretty I am!"

"A night club? A night club? Oh my God, are you mad, girl, have you gone off your head? You'll be a whore! Do you know what a whore does? And who'll take care of your kid when you're working at this wonderful club? His wife?"

"He'll take care of everything. And don't worry about the gossips, I'm going to use another name. I hate my daddy's name anyway, so it don't matter. I need a name that has to be artistic."

Sra. Rosa stared at her niece. The kid was an absolute donkey, an idiot. Not wicked, not conniving, not anything sinister, just stupid.

"Artists like me must have artistic names, and Papa's name ain't artistic. I'm going to get another one, and he'll get me one for the kid, don't you worry.

Sra. Rosa managed to muster up a few words, scarcely realizing what she was finally admitting to, finally saying aloud. "Your mama and me, *I*, your mama and I, we didn't have patronymics." She lingered over that fine word. "We weren't allowed in regular schools, because we had no fathers to speak of. We were," she cleared her throat, remembering a finer word, though not much better, than *bastards*. "We were illegitimate. Your grandmother went up against her family and tradition and all the rules. That was her way, and I guess it's your way, but your mother and I, well, we suffered. It was hard. I would have so liked to have had a real name, my father's and my mother's, like everyone else."

Mili giggled. "My God, Auntie Rosi, that's just so old-fashioned. My kid's birth certificate is going to say the same as Mama's, 'Father

Unknown.' Too bad. I know who its father is, and he loves me, and he's going to care for us. I'm getting a lot of money out of this, Auntie, and everything will be fine. You'll see. Bernardo's a big cheese with General Franco. He'll protect us."

Sra. Rosa made a noise between a snort and a moan. She turned away from her niece and started to leave, then she sat down again. "Listen, girl, I know you don't want to hear this, but he's no favorite of his big general! He's just a cop, that's all, and he has a wife already, and the General doesn't like bastards any more than the government he threw over. Franco's a Catholic, not a *facha*, he just uses the fascists for his own ends, and between him and the priests, bastards are bastards—"

Mili stopped giggling and said, "Oh shut up, you stupid old woman. You don't know anything at all! Bernardo's secret service. He's gonna take good care of me. I got him by the balls, and no man pulls away from that. And if I want, I can make lots of money on my own. I can dance at the Red Mill, I can dance at any club I want, and I'll make 400 pesetas a month just from that, I can live high, and he knows that too! So, if he doesn't want me in there shaking my pretty tits at other men, he'll pay. He loves me."

Sra. Rosa shook her head and got up to go.

"Come home with me tonight, Mili. Come home now. We got to sort this out. Please. Listen to me for once."

"Auntie, I'll hail you a cab. You get on home, it's past curfew. I got money now, I can ride in cabs, see?"

Sra. Rosa allowed Mili to hail her a cab. It was nearly one in the morning. The pensión above the butcher shop was now Mili's home, that was clear, but Sra. Rosa still hoped that the child would come home with her and they would somehow correct this mess, but she also knew she was completely crazy to be thinking these things. Argument was useless, words of wisdom were useless, begging was useless. There was nothing she could do to stop this wagon from rolling downhill to its destruction. Then again, perhaps Mili would survive, as the women of this family often did, perhaps she would even triumph.

The real sadness came from knowledge, knowledge not to be denied, finally. Sra. Rosa understood for a certainty that Mili was not a good person. The girl was stupid, useless, bad, so that even if she did survive or triumph, it didn't matter. And that was why Rosa wept as she got into the cab. Mili gave the driver some money and the address, and walked off, the driver watching her ass recede into the night. Sra. Rosa in the back seat stuffed her fist in her mouth to muffle the sobs.

~⚬~

Sra. Rosa got home and summoned the *sereno* with weak clapping. He sauntered up, realized who she was, and said, "Woman, what are you doing out so late! It's dangerous! Hurry up now, get in here. Next time let me know, and I'll have someone accompany you."

She forgot to give him a tip. She tiptoed into the patio and managed to get her door unlocked without much noise, but Rosa-Laura was waiting up for her anyway.

"I found her. We talked. No good. No good at all. Poor Emilia. It's almost a blessing she's dead and can't see this."

The worst of it was the words, flooding back now molten and hideous, all of them, everything they'd said to her, things she had refused to think about for years:

"Your mother's a whore, you can't inherit! That house is your uncle's now, and you'd better believe he doesn't want any little bastards like you and your sister living there! Neither one of you's got a father. The daughters of a whore and bound to be whores yourself! That's what comes of her being a slut, a shame to the family, a disgrace, that's what comes of it, two more sluts with no future. Go on and find a convent or a corner, because no one else is going to take you in!"

Rosa had defied them as best she could, a girl so young that when she went to the provincial courthouse to try and register her complaint and get her and her sister a lawyer, the authorities just stared at her and laughed, then called for a jail matron and told her to wait in the hallway until they could find a proper escort to take her home. The escort, a serious policeman who looked at her as if she were trash he had been made to step in, took her to the train station, as she insisted. She'd escaped the provincial town that her mother had escaped years before and returned to Madrid, third class, in a slow train.

When she got to their house, the police were already there overseeing their eviction and the possession of their household goods in the presence of her uncle's lawyer. Emilia was huddling in the kitchen, sobbing and whimpering. Rosa packed what she could snatch and ran away down the back stairs like a criminal fleeing the scene of the crime, dragging her sister with her. They slept in the railroad station that night and later, a friendly station worker directed them to the convent where after much persuasion she cut a deal to clean and cook and sew for a room to sleep in and schooling for Emilia. She had worked there like a slave until the day Emilia came to her crying and told her that she was dying for love of a handsome seminary student named Esteban, but he had refused to marry her.

"So what," she'd said to Emilia, not yet understanding what had happened. "Why do you want to marry anyway? Better you're a nun and stay away from men altogether." And then Emilia had told her what Esteban had done. What she had let him do.

Years after that debacle, Rosa herself gave in to holy tradition gratefully when a man appeared who actually wanted to be her husband. She married a handsome man, in a church, was a good wife, and tried to do as women were supposed, and all she got for it were beatings and contempt. She'd never wanted a husband, someone to boss her around, she'd just wanted a family to love, children, people she could trust, a normal life like everyone else. And look how that had ended.

Now, her sister was dead and her niece as bad or worse than her grandmother, and Rosa-Laura, the light of her life, what would happen to her with this example right in her face? How could she protect her? Was this destiny, their destiny?

Rosa-Laura listened to all this without a word. She had heard a good bit of it before. Her mother hadn't lied to her or tried to keep the truth from her, though she had given it up very slowly and sugar-coated a good deal. She had wanted them to be on good terms, mother and daughter, and she wanted Rosa-Laura to understand why school and job and respect and name were so important. Rosa-Laura nodded at her mother's words and put her arms around her.

"It's OK, Mama. It'll be OK. There now. It'll be all right. Let's sleep. Tomorrow's another day."

What her mother had neglected to mention was the appalling fact of who the father of Mili's bastard was. Rosa-Laura fell asleep still believing it was Anacleto and hating him with all her heart.

At 3 a.m. of the same night that Sra. Rosa had confronted Mili and then gone home to be comforted by Rosa-Laura, Constancia too finally found peace. It was just a few weeks after Rogelio had bought Constancia the new bed. The neighbors who had been helping Rogelio out with the death watch had left around midnight to catch some sleep. He sat with her as she expired, soul and self and anguish and guilt all dissipated with a gurgling last breath. He wept, then whimpered like an animal, then he remembered his lovely Laura and wept some more.

Later that morning, by 6 a.m. when everyone was likely to be up and about, he took his cane and gently tapped on the ceiling, at a certain place close to the back wall. Five minutes later, the upstairs neighbor, the building's porter, came on down.

"She's gone, Don Jorge," Rogelio said. "Would you send for the priest? She had confession and extreme unction yesterday, so he won't be surprised, but I'd like him to say another prayer."

"Sure, Rogelio, don't you worry now. I'll get the women too." The porter left, glad to be out of that room that had stunk of putrefaction long before Rogelio's woman had died. He summoned his wife and some of the women in the building and sent his son to get Sra. Rosa. His wife was a good woman, and she brought down a clean sheet with nice embroidery, a generous and beautiful gift. She had liked Constancia, especially after Rogelio had married her and put their situation to rights in the eyes of God. No one was surprised she'd died, of course; not only had it been obvious how sick the woman was, the sight of the priest yesterday with two altar boys and the monstrance rushing down the street toward the house had been clearer than a government radio broadcast.

Sra. Rosa had barely slept at all so that when the porter's son came to get her, she was up and dressed and came right away. Rogelio was sitting by the bed, leaning on his cane and staring at the wall above Constancia's body. Sra. Rosa touched his shoulder lightly but said nothing.

"She was very brave about the pain," Rogelio said. "She died without a complaint."

Sra. Rosa wasn't thinking very clearly or precisely at that point, her head a complete jumble what with Mili's mess, but the old Gypsy saying regarding the cowardice about living did occur to her once or twice that day.

She was so tired. And that policeman, that frightening, wicked man, would not leave her thoughts. Had Mili even told Bernardo yet? Worse yet, could it be possible he might not be the only candidate for the position? How would she ever face Lourdes with this scandal? Sra. Rosa felt directly to blame. It would have been actually a relief if Anacleto were the father. At least then she and Lourdes could conspire and pressure the two delinquents to marry.

She helped the women wash the body, her gorge rising at the smell. Constancia's corpse displayed harsh evidence of the path of the disease, and it was horrible to contemplate. The women moved fast, some with tears falling onto their handiwork, all tightlipped, sighing, a prayer now and then. "It's good she got the priest at her last breath," one said, by way of injecting some relief into the ritual. No one replied.

They placed laurel branches and candles around the bed, Sra. Rosa swept up the floor and helped move the table to the center of the room where it could hold some food; someone had sent for a Spanish omelet and some wine from the tavern down the street, and someone else had brought in little tuna pies. Rosa-Laura showed up eventually, cried for a while, and then led the rosary. She was a wonder at praying, that kid. That's what she got out of two years with the nuns, rote blathering. Sra. Rosa got down on her knees with some difficulty, as this was not like the easy work of kneeling down to clean a tile floor, and old rag nicely tucked under your knees, not at all, and mumbled her Hail Marys along with the rest of them. She glanced at her daughter now and then, but Rosa-Laura's distress at the discussion of last evening seemed to have been completely overcome by the present sadness.

And speaking of all that, where the hell was Mili? Why wasn't she here yet? Constancia had favored and pampered the girl, and Sra. Rosa still believed that Mili visited every day, like a good child, because believing anything else would have added to her pile of anger and disgust and shame more than she could have borne at the moment. "...Mother of God, pray for us sinners now/and at the hour of our death."

Right in the middle of the rosary, Lourdes entered the room, ducking her head under the low lintel of the doorway. She looked even paler than usual. Sra. Rosa marked how lovely Lourdes looked these days. Sin had plumped her up a bit and put a shine in those strange, light-colored eyes. She also looked slightly mad, and that Sra. Rosa marked too.

Dear God in heaven and Mother Mary, especially you, Mother Mary, because you must have more sense than the rest of them, make sure Constancia gets to heaven, she's had enough of hell down here, and make sure Mili is OK, please. You know what it's like to have a baby and no husband to explain it. And if Emilia's up there—surely she is, she wasn't a bad woman at all, not really—if she sees all this, please intercede for me and tell her I'm so sorry I didn't take better care of her girl, but I won't abandon Mili either. And you, you been good to my dear daughter, please keep that up. I do thank you for that. I thank you so much.

Of course, Sra. Rosa had been very late getting to the Doctor's house that wretched day Constancia died, and only Srta. Guillermina was home, upset at being left all alone. Her brother was attending a birth, Srta. Guillermina informed her. Sra. Rosa shook her head. Life and death. God spat in their faces, he did. She hoped that Mother Mary had listened to her at least and would intercede with her son, because men do love their mothers.

To placate Guillermina, she spent half an hour telling her about Constancia. Guillermina liked to cry, and she wept copiously for Constancia, whom she had never met. Guillermina needed conversation, stories, gossip, she needed company. Sra. Rosa often wondered where their family was, what had happened to their friends and visitors, why there had been so many people at the funeral of Sra. de Montero but no one here during the day or evenings to pay this woman some attention, but that was none of her business anyway.

She swept the floors, dusted the consoles and tables and cabinets and lamps, swept off the debris on the balcony—Madrid was getting dirtier and smokier these days, and grime coated the blue and green tiles of the balcony flooring, so she washed them too. She polished the dining room table, and uttered a foul imprecation at the chandelier. The crystals were getting clouded and it was almost time to take the damned thing apart and clean it, but she wasn't going to go through that today, not today. She put a kettle on the stove, lit the gas, and waited for the water to boil. The kitchen was still clean from yesterday. Evidently the Doctor had not had time to dirty up everything by trying to make himself a midnight snack as he usually did. She checked the icebox. Time to do some grocery shopping at the Mercado de la Paz. The way life was now, if she bought enough at a good stall, the seller would give her something to take home for herself and Rosa-Laura. It was the custom and not looked upon as a bribe, more as a tip. Life was definitely less hard, though she would not go so far as to say it was as good as it had been before the war, which was odd, because before the war, she had been poorer.

The iceman would come by eleven. The gas man would come when he damned felt like it. There might be a delivery or two, and for that, the doctor always left money for the tips in the iridescent Venetian bowl on the cabinet near the front door. Guillermina needed her tea and something to eat. Maybe she'd like to take a walk down Serrano street, holding on to Sra. Rosa's arm. It would take her at least two hours to put on her makeup, then her clothes, her fine high-heeled shoes, her big hat, a fur stole if the weather was brisk. After their mother's funeral Dr. Contreras had absentmindedly suggested to his sister that she change her bedroom to that of their mother's now, but the suggestion had brought on one of Guillermina's episodess of hysteria. He hadn't meant to be brutal, he was just a man, that's all, and he had wanted to be nice to his sister, whose bedroom didn't have a balcony as their mother's did. It was larger too, his mother's room. Now it was closed up, and Sra. Rosa would have to help him sort through it all one of these days and get rid of some things or pack them away. She wondered about the pictures in the silver frames and wondered if she should save one of the photos of his stepfather for herself. After all, the gent was Emilia's father. Maybe Mili would want to see what her grandfather looked like.

Mili. Sra. Rosa heard the teakettle whistle. She turned off the gas and filled the tea pot. She sat down at the kitchen table to think and wait for the tea to steep. From down the corridor, Sra. Guillermina began to call her, querulously at first, then louder and more insistent.

"Coming, Señorita, coming," Sra. Rosa said. The funeral would be that afternoon, and it occurred to her that it would not be at all a bad idea to have Srta. Guillermina attend it with her. They could go in a cab. It was a poor person's funeral anyway, so it wouldn't last long, just the procession to the cemetery, the sermon, the men pitching a fistful of dirt into the trench, and then a light supper at Rogelio's house. Srta. Guillermina would feel so important, too, because everyone would stare at her. Sra. Rosa would stay by her side and talk to her and tend to her every need, and thus she would not have to think so hard about Constancia, and she would not have to think about Mili at all.

Late that afternoon and into the evening, as people in the neighborhood would discuss for days and weeks and months and even years later,
a tremendous yelling dispute occurred between mother and son in the
patio of the building where Sra. Lourdes and her two boys lived. Screaming and cursing and breaking pottery. Someone called the police—some
idiot who hadn't lived long enough to realize that calling the cops always
made things worse—and the cops called Bernardo. They always kept him
advised about the neighborhood and the extra "comfort" he kept there.

The car pulled up, shortly after that, and as usual, Silvio settled back
to light up a cigarette and wait for his boss. Bernardo burst out of the
car like a man who knew everyone would move out of his way fast and
marched into Lourdes's house right into the argument. The shouting got
louder. Eventually, Anacleto—the oldest boy now, as the neighbors later
explained to the officers—left in a hell of a hurry. Augustín, crying and
sobbing, followed him begging him to return. Everyone saw them go. Yet,
the row continued, which was peculiar because Sra. Lourdes never crossed
her lover, never argued with him, never challenged him, but this time
everyone heard them continue the row, punctuated by Bernardito's frightened wails. It would have been unthinkable to interfere, not to mention
suicide given who Bernardo was and how he was.

There were a lot of words like "whore" and "son of a whore" and
"disgraced"—both *desgraciado and desgraciada*—and worse even. From
what people could cull from all the shouting, it had to do with young girls,
old women, children, wives, situations, lack of shame, lack of dignity, lack
of respect, ugly, stupid, old, and so forth. Finally, Bernardo stormed out,
his expression terrifying. But, he didn't leave the neighborhood at once.
Instead, he stood at the driver's side of his car, conversing with Silvio, or
whispering with him. Silvio said little, but nodded his head many times.

Though no one heard—or wanted to know—what Bernardo and

Silvio were saying, everyone in their building heard Sra. Lourdes and her youngest, Bernardito, sobbing together. Finally, Augustín returned for a moment. Lourdes's middle son was a boy of working age now. He didn't seem as enraged as his older brother or his stepfather, more as if he were stunned or hurt. He spoke to his mother, softly, no shouting, then he walked out again quickly and didn't come back until two days later, but by then, it was too late.

Arriving after Augustín had left, and thus unaware of all this drama, Sra. Rosa had came home at 9 p.m. Then Rosa-Laura came home just before ten. She had stayed late at work to make up the time missed when she went to Constancia's funeral. They barely said a word to each other, so leaden with sadness about Constancia and worry about Mili, who had not shown up at the funeral even though both of them had gone to the tavern to telephone her pensión and leave word.

The building darkened quickly thereafter. No one wasted kerosene or candles, much less electricity or gas. By 10:30 p.m., the neighborhood was quiet, except for some soul walking down to the plaza to find a bit of noise in one of the taverns. Rosa-Laura and her mother fell asleep without eating, both spiritless and exhausted.

In the middle of the night, Rosa-Laura woke up suddenly, startled and confused. That awoke her mother.

"What, you having a bad dream?"

"No—I, well, yes, I guess so. I heard the building crack. Or something. It was a strange dream."

"Daughter, sleep."

At that moment they both heard someone running across their patio.

"Who's that?" Rosa-Laura whispered.

"One of Lourdes's boys, maybe," Sra. Rosa murmured. "Go to sleep." She was too worn out to reason out why she knew it wasn't a big man crossing their patio, but someone smaller in stature and not very heavy on the cobble stones. The thing was, and this she never thought about or ever remembered, the smallish person running across their patio wore shoes that clicked, not the cheap hemp-soled shoes the boys from across the way usually wore.

∽⌒∾

"It's done, Captain."

"Good. Where's the car?"

"Downstairs in your space."

"Anyone see you?"

"No, Sir."

"And the child?"

"As you ordered, Sir."

"I have some unfinished business here. Leave the keys and go home."

"Yes, Sir."

If the older man felt any insult at the brusqueness of this exchange, his face registered only its usual cold impassivity.

∽⌒∾

The loud old clock that ticked from a box under the bed, where they'd put it wrapped in a towel to muffle its noise, rang at 5:30 a.m., too early for Rosa-Laura. She heard her mother groan and felt her get up heavily, her bones creaking with morning and bad sleep. She got up herself without a word, shook her head to clear out the bad dreams and headache. She pulled a wool shawl around her shoulders and went outside to get some water from the patio faucet. As she filled the kettle at the pump, Sra. Erlinda, the ironmonger's wife, entered the patio with a pile of groceries and packages. The market had opened only half an hour ago, and this woman had already done shopping for the day. Rosa-Laura smiled at her with some effort and said, "*Buenos días*, Sra. Erlinda."

Sra. Erlinda nodded at her. Upstairs, two more neighbors were up, and other neighbors were moving in their houses and calling out to children and husband to get out of bed. The whole building hummed with wake-up and get-going. Rosa-Laura finished with the pump and turned, her right side sagging with the heavy kettle. Sra. Erlinda went to Lourdes's door and called out, "*Oye*, Lourdes, wake up, *chica*. I got a deal on some ham just in from Estremadura, and I can share it with you if you like."

No one answered at Lourdes's door, and then Sra. Erlinda saw the door was not truly shut, so Lourdes must be up and about already. She pushed the door open and went in; she was close to Lourdes and familiar enough to take liberties. She had no fear that Bernardo would be there. His car was not parked right outside as it always was when he was present. Anyway, he almost never spent the whole night there and never came early in the morning.

"Hey, boys," she called out, "make yourselves decent, I'm coming in! Lourdes, you there?"

Inside, the house was still dark. Surprised, Sra. Erlinda put down her packages and lit a kerosene lamp with the matches Lourdes always kept right by the stove. She turned around to look, the lamp in her hand, and saw Bernardito's crib overturned on the floor, his blue and white blankets tossed aside, his toy rabbit stuck underneath. A few things had been knocked aside, almost as if someone had moved stuff very roughly on the way to the door. Anacleto's and Augustin's bed had not been slept in. The baby was no where to be seen, though she knew he could easily climb out of his crib now; he was much too big for it, but there was no room for another cot or bed in the space. She heard no sound except for those of the neighbors outside. She took a deep breath, unsure of what she was really seeing, and then pushed aside the curtains to the bedroom.

In her house, Rosa-Laura hauled the heavy kettle onto the stove, now lit. Her mother had already finished dressing and was filling the coffee pot with grounds. She sat down on the cot and reached down to find the box with her stockings and underwear when they heard a high-pitched, shrieking scream from across the patio. She looked at her mother, who was looking at her, and they both rushed outside. So had everyone else in the building.

Mili showed up at the Doctor's house that same night as the argument in the *corrala*, ringing repeatedly and as hard as she could on his bell at the front entrance. The porter answered, but did not want to let her in; however, the bell rang upstairs as well, and the Doctor called down to the porter to find out if it was a patient in need ringing at this late hour. He was told of the appearance of his would-be visitor, and after a moment's hesitation, asked the porter to send her upstairs. The porter was incensed. The girl looked like a common prostitute, and a somewhat harshly treated one at that. He put her on the elevator with much grumbling, but there was nothing to be done about it. The Doctor had lived in this building longer than even the porter had and gave extremely generous *aguinaldos* at Christmas time and Easter as well.

The Doctor was used to being awakened in the middle of the night, and in fact, hadn't even gone to bed yet. It was about 2 a.m. The girl standing before him in the dimly lit hallway wore a torn dress and ragged sweater, and her face was luridly rosy as if it had been slapped hard. The long mirrors hanging in the richly wallpapered hallways reflected her to the Doctor from all sides, and no side looked unabused.

"Please, please, Sir, I got to have some help, please!"

"Mili, what is this about! Has something happened to Sra. Rosa?" He imagined a break-in, something rough that could happen in a neighborhood such as theirs, and this girl run clear across the city to bring him to help.

She stood there in the corridor catching her breath in sharp rasps. "No, no, not her, she's OK, it's me. Me. I need help. I couldn't go to Auntie, he'll find me there. He's going to beat me to death, he said so, he said lots of awful things, and I'm scared now, and I can't go to Auntie's house, and now who's going to take care of me? Because he said he'd kill me! Please, Doctor, please let me stay with you. I didn't know where else to go, and it's so rich here, he wouldn't dare just come and drag me out!"

He let her stand there, frantic, for a moment. He was careful that she saw how he looked at her, his mouth tight and angry, his eyes cold, his posture rigid so that he looked down at her from a great height. His appearance might have been slightly mussed from long hours with no sleep, but he had patted some cold water on his face and wore a dressing gown that covered himself decently. His hands were in his pockets, and he waited a good long time before asking her inside.

"You may come in, but you are to be very quiet. My sister is not well, and she is sleeping. If you raise your voice, I will put you out at once and ask the concierge to call the police."

It was a cold speech, but not as cruel or frightening as the one she'd just heard an hour ago, and she nodded her head in understanding. He let her into the hallway, but did not invite her to the salon or even the kitchen. They stood there, and Mili began to cry.

"I told you not to wake up my sister. Please tell me what has happened to bring you here at this time of the night."

She controlled her sobbing with some effort. She was beyond being angry at him for his disrespect. She was terrified, and whatever it took to appease him and make him help her she'd do.

"I, I got into trouble, with my, my fiancé, and he's a big important guy, and he got mad at me, and he's going to kill me, he said so, then he said I was to get rid of the baby, but I don't think he meant it, because he..."

"Baby?" The Doctor said. Of course. That's what happened to them. They were stupid creatures and they got pregnant and had stupid children. He was so angry he could barely control his thoughts. This creature was in his house once again only because he respected and revered Sra. Rosa. That was all that kept him from throwing her out.

"Are you here to get an abortion? Is that it?"

"A—a what? You mean get rid of the baby? No, I want it. He wants it too. It makes him mine, that's what, it makes him responsible, and he is responsible, and he is the father, not like he said, I haven't done it with someone else. He's got to take care of me. But, I meant to tell him nice, and have him be happy, and instead, my stupid cousin told the whole neighborhood, the bitch, and then someone, another bitch told him, and he got into a big fight with her, and the whole neighborhood—"

"Enough," the Doctor said. He was so disgusted and repulsed by this vulgar behavior and her moronic story, not to mention very tired from a long day, that all he wanted to do at the moment was sit down and have a brandy. He did not want to know any more about this mess, but if nothing else, he owed this creature some civility for Sra. Rosa's sake. She would certainly want him to take care of her niece and not let her get into any more trouble.

"Come in here," he said. He indicated the salon. She hadn't been in there before. It was smaller than the dining room, but had a very comfortable blue velvet sofa and two huge stuffed chairs with ottomans. The coffee table was twice as big as Sra. Rosa's kitchen table and covered with bric-a-brac. Mili settled on the sofa and picked up one of the knick-knacks, a rainbow colored glass paperweight full of flowers and butterflies and began to turn it over and over, as if inspecting it.

"Put it down," the Doctor said. "The last time you were here my sunglasses and their leather case disappeared. Do you think I'm an idiot? You got the glasses, and for that you threw away any hope of ever getting anything else from me. Do you understand?"

"Oh, Sir," Mili said, blubbering now, nearly dropping the paperweight, "It was an accident, I just forgot I had them and I meant to bring them back, but I got so involved in this mess I'm in that I forgot and—"

"Do you think I would believe such a stupid lie? Do you think I'm an idiot?" The Doctor said.

She took a deep breath. This was going badly, and she needed him on her side. She had to rethink her tactics here or those damned stupid glasses were going to cost her dearly.

"Does this policeman of yours not want to marry you? Is that it?"

She sighed. "He's got a wife. He loves me, not her. It's a mess, you can see, but I was completely innocent in all this, I was just a child, and he made me do it! I love him, I do, and I had to do it. He forced me. My Auntie Rosa wasn't home that day to protect me, and I was so ashamed afterwards, and now I just want to have my baby and he can pay for it like he should, that's all. But he's really, really mad at me, because my cousin, Rosa-Laura, is such a stupid little loudmouth, always jealous of me ever since she was a kid, you know, and he came tonight because she spread it all over the neighborhood so I'm disgraced, completely disgraced, and my poor Auntie will just die when she finds out and I'd rather die myself than hurt her like that, you know? He roughed me up a bit, but he'll calm down and then he'll do the right thing, I'm sure, but I have to have a place to stay until he calms down, that's all, and if I stay with Auntie Rosa, he might hurt her and you wouldn't want that, would you?"

Now it was the Doctor's turn to sigh. He had the beginnings of a bad headache. A clock struck three. He fought for a clear thought and stared at a water-color of Montmartre on the wall, something his mother had picked up on a trip to Paris decades ago. Mili certainly could not stay here with him and his sister. Period. She'd clean him out of house and home in two seconds. She might be related to Sra. Rosa by blood, but she reminded him more of his ex-cook than his housekeeper. Or worse yet, she was a true descendent of his stepfather. He looked at her closely. It was true she resembled the man now that he thought of it. The headache bloomed, full force.

"You certainly cannot stay here; however, I can take you to a pensión on the Castellana that a patient of mine runs, and we can get you a room for a few days. And, I will tell Sra. Rosa where you are, because she will be very worried. Did he come to your house then? Did he hurt your aunt or your cousin?"

"They weren't home. They were out, having coffee in the plaza or something. I didn't feel like going."

That didn't sound like Sra. Rosa, but then, he didn't know his housekeeper's routine or habits, either. On the other hand, this whole story sounded—well, strange, forced, incomplete. It was time to get her out of his house. He stood up.

"You wait outside for me. I'm getting my jacket and we will take a taxi to this pensión."

Mili's face darkened with rage. "What? I got to wait outside? I'm not some servant here—" She stopped herself with some force. She must keep calm. Let him throw her out. Damned glasses. It was all their fault. They ruined everything, and she hadn't even worn them in months.

∽

Downstairs, as they came out of the elevator they ran into the porter, who was standing in the entranceway next to the open door of his office, smoking a cigarette. The Doctor barely acknowledged him; it was none of the man's business after all.

Outside, the Doctor started toward the Castellana, but kept his eye out for a taxi. Mili walked behind him, as fast as she could, furious that he wouldn't take her arm or wait for her like a gentleman should.

From inside the building the porter watched them go, considered the whole episode a while, tightened his bathrobe more closely around his thin body against the cold, then went inside his little office to call his contact at the police station nearby. Not to have reported this somewhat suspicious situation and then have something happen to the Doctor would bring down the authorities on him, hard.

Dr. Contreras did not understand there was a highly complex and efficient system of information-gathering operating in Madrid. When he had heard stories about this elaborate net, he'd dismissed them as paranoid fantasy and hardly believable. One could not go about suspicious of one's own concierge, every taxi driver, *serenos*, and one's own neighbors. Besides, how could a police force possibly keep track of such a vast yet primitive system of snooping on one's citizens? Though it was true that half the people in Madrid these days seemed to be authorities or government employees of one sort or another.

A taxi came by soon after they left the building, the Doctor hailed it, and they were on their way to his patient's pensión. They did not speak to each other in the cab, and the Doctor sat as far away from her as he could, which she noticed with some bitterness. Men liked to cuddle up close to her, whether she wanted them to or not. This high class bastard acted as if she were dirt.

They arrived at the address the Doctor had given the taxi driver. He paid the man and led her to a modest but very respectable establishment after the *sereno* permitted them to enter the building and got his tip. A porter came out and called his tenant to see if this early morning visit was acceptable to her, then called the elevator for them. Every one of the men, the taxi driver, the *sereno*, the porter, reported to the police after their business with Doctor Contreras was finished and the tip collected. The pensión was on the second floor. A middle-aged lady in a dressing gown opened the door.

"Sir, Dr. Contreras, this is so unusual!"

"Sra. Fernandez, I greatly apologize for the hour. This young woman is, uh, well, she has been assaulted, as you can see, and needs a place to stay until I can contact her family and—" It hadn't occurred to him up until that moment how disgusting this all looked. He took a deep breath. He had saved Sr. Fernandez's life by treating his hypertension and convincing him to leave off drinking. Sra. Fernandez was just going to have to accept this situation and think what she would.

"May she stay here? I will cover the charges while I am searching for her family."

Sra. Fernandez glanced at Mili with a slight surprise, her eyes widening, her mouth tightening. She didn't appear to think much of Mili and Mili wasn't helping matters by standing there sullen and bruised. But, the landlady must have remembered her manners, not to mention the good treatment of her husband, because she stepped aside so they could both enter and went to a desk in the entry hall where half a dozen keys hung on a board. She got one, and nodded for them to follow her, but then her phone rang. She answered it and frowned.

"Yes? What? Well, I don't understand, well, are you sure? Well. Yes, of course, right now, yes, no, yes."

She hung up the phone and said, "I'm sorry, Doctor, but there's some business with the police downstairs. The porter says you are both to go downstairs immediately."

Downstairs, an ordinary policeman, a cop on the beat, waited for them with the porter. They exited the lift, Mili behind the Doctor and fidgety, as if she needed to urinate. Pregnant women had to urinate frequently, the Doctor remembered.

"May I ask—" the Doctor began.

"Documents," the policeman said.

"But, Señor..."

"Documents," the policeman said, this time louder.

The Doctor reached into the pocket of his overcoat for his wallet, his hand shaking somewhat, his jaw tightened, teeth clenched. Mili's mouth was slightly opened, and her eyes glazed. She sniffled, then reached into the pocket of her torn sweater and sidled in the direction of the porter's office, as if to look for something to sit upon. The policeman took the Doctor's identification and studied it seriously. The Doctor opened his mouth to snap at the man, then got hold of himself and decided then and there to shut up and wait patiently for the outcome of this ridiculous ritual.

"Yours, Señorita?" the policeman said.

Mili had fished out a wrinkled little card that she handed it to him. She was off to his side now, almost behind him, with the Doctor and the porter facing him directly, their backs to the elevator, the policeman's back to the front door.

The policeman studied her card, frowning slightly. Then he said to the porter, "Let me make a phone call." The porter nodded.

And Mili bolted for the front door.

☙❧

Later, in the station as he thought about it all, the Doctor believed that had she not run, not much would have happened. After all, the policeman was just doing his job, and Mili had no record on file. It was just that she was so terrified of this lover of hers she accorded him supernatural powers and assumed he was on the other end of that telephone. A colleague of that policeman had been waiting outside the door, smoking, and Mili had run right into his arms. He grinned at the catch, expertly avoided the knee she attempted to shoot into his groin, and quick as that had her kneeling on the ground even as he managed to get a squeeze of breast and a handful of buttock. The Doctor was appalled at Mili's moronic behavior and the policeman's quickness to take advantage; then the policeman next to him grabbed his arm and said, "Not you, Mister, don't you try anything."

"Señor," the Doctor replied, grinding the words out over a spit of fury, "I am not the sort of man that 'tries' things."

They all ended up at the nearest station. They took Mili to a cell right away but not the Doctor. He was too well dressed and looked too prosperous for them to act precipitously. He sat on a bench in a cold room with appalling green and brown walls and harsh lighting. Despite their caution and courtesy, he was humiliated. He could not believe this was happening. It was worse than when the cook denounced him. He was a highly respected physician. The only thing in his life that might leave him subject him to unpleasantness or even danger, he had avoided, hard and lonely as that had been. He was a physician. A respected member of society.

"Sir, if you wish to call someone, that's all right with us, but we have to check out th e girl you were with," a sergeant finally said to him. The Doctor had been sitting on the bench in front of this sergeant's desk counter for at least an hour and feeling worse by the minute.

He got up heavily, feeling his age and weight on his body like boulders. As he was about to dial a number on the grimy phone that the sergeant passed across the counter to him, a man walked into the station and stood in front of the sergeant, right next to the Doctor. The sergeant stood up. The man, of medium height and strong build, very well dressed, with heavy brows, a thin moustache, and dark gray eyes as cold as the North Sea, flipped a document toward him, a leather-bound, more official-looking booklet than an ordinary ID. The sergeant inspected it, and very carefully and politely handed it back to the man.

"This here is the gentleman she was with, Captain, Sir," the sergeant said to the man. The Doctor, still holding the phone receiver in his hand, turned to look at the man.

The man gave his name, smiling at the Doctor. He held out his hand, which was gloved in gray kid. "Perhaps someone has mentioned me to you?"

The Doctor shook his head, then shook the man's hand. The Captain had a powerful grasp and was pleased to let the Doctor feel it. The Doctor in turn felt as if his own hand grew from some source too far away from his brain to give it much instruction; it lay limply in the other's grip.

"Well, I'm glad to hear no one has been shooting off their mouth needlessly, but still, we need to discuss some things. Please come with me."

He turned down a hallway; the Doctor could do nothing more than hang up the phone and follow him.

Lourdes's body lay on her bed, her back facing from the doorway, her right arm flung outward, the other arm reaching toward the wall and a picture of Saint Mary Magdalen. Her face was turned slightly back toward the doorway, in what appeared to be something of an awkward twist for the neck. The blanket and sheet were halfway down the bed, covering only her hips and legs. She wore a light cotton nightgown, cap-sleeved, embroidered with tiny roses.

All this Sra. Erlinda saw as she entered the bedroom, the kerosene lamp held out before her, softening the room with ripples of smoky yellow light. She also saw, and all of this she saw at once, that the one eye visible from that angle was slightly opened and Lourdes's mouth as well. A very small red smudge flowed sticky from just under her braided hair, at the very bottom of the back of her head, and the bed at that place was stained, but not much, as if the position of the head kept the blood from flowing outward. And that was when Sra. Erlinda began to scream.

ↁↂ

Everyone in the building had run out into the patio, most, like Rosa-Laura, barefoot, and found Sra. Erlinda, still holding the lit lantern, outside Lourdes's house shrieking and shaking as if undergoing a fit. The women of the building had attempted to calm her while the men entered Lourdes's house and found the body, rigid yet still lovely even in that terrible pose. Her boys, including the littlest, were all missing.

The police were sent for and arrived relatively quickly. Rosa-Laura, her mother, and the rest of the neighbors spent the morning being interrogated by one cop after another. It was the worst day of Rosa-Laura's life, even worse than the day she got lost, and she scarcely remembered what she said to the police.

In the thick diseased ground of all that mystery lay buried another question: where was Mili? As soon as the police had finished their questioning and left, both Sra. Rosa and Rosa-Laura rushed to the plaza to find Rogelio and tell him what had happened (he had already heard via the express service of neighborhood gossip), and then rushed off again to the pensión in Glorieta de Embajadores. The owner, a florid woman with dyed red hair and armfuls and earfuls of cheap jangly jewelry nearly threw them out. It seems that Mili and the man who was paying for her room had a fight very late the evening before and the girl had run off, the man close behind. Another scene had ensued in the street, and then the girl escaped and had not come back.

"And if she does, I got all her stuff. She owes me money, she does," the woman said. "It's clear the boyfriend's not paying any more."

"And what kind of woman runs a place that allows a man to pay for a girl's room?" Sra. Rosa said. Rosa-Laura grabbed her mother's arm and hauled her out of there, without so much as a "Thank-you-good-bye" to the hennaed horror.

What could Rosa-Laura and her mother do after that? Where could they look? And, both of them had to get to work as well. By that time, it was well past the siesta hours.

Sra. Rosa finally left her daughter at the bus stop and went to work. She arrived at the Doctor's house to find that he had not been home all night, according to his hysterical and frightened sister. "Where were you? What took you so long? I needed you!" Srta. Guillermina had cried to her. It was not an accusation as much as the wail of an abandoned child.

Rosa-Laura arrived at work quite late and got a severe scolding by the master tailor himself. She was no longer his favorite, that was for sure, and she would never forgive him for saying in front of everyone, all the apprentices, the other tailors, his wife, "You do nothing but make the situation worse! You are of no use at all, and haven't the courtesy or the manners even to call if you are going to be late."

As if she could have run out to a tavern or the metro to make a phone call with police in the patio and half the neighborhood outside their building in the street.

Over the next two days, Rosa-Laura made so many mistakes at work that her boss threatened to send her home without pay and maybe suspend her for a week as well. Even worse, it seemed that everyone at work was delighting in her discomfort. It turned out the boys considered her a snob because she wouldn't tease or flirt with them, the older tailors were jealous and glad of "that child's" disgrace, and the master's wife had had enough of what she called Rosa-Laura's snotty manner and way of insinuating that no one but herself could cut a pattern the right way.

Rosa-Laura had to think long and hard about all this, and given her distress and shock at what had happened at home, she simply could not fret over whether or not she had been snotty to a bunch of gossiping, lazy dullards like her fellow workers. She allowed she had been distant, cool, and shy. She allowed that she was unable to praise a cut badly made, and she allowed that she didn't like to flirt, barely knew how. She didn't like to socialize with the other apprentices either, but by her second year there she had been the only girl apprentice left anyway, and it certainly would have been inappropriate to socialize with the males. As for the master tailor's wife, well, the woman didn't like to cut patterns and it was reflected in her work, though Rosa-Laura allowed it was no business of hers nor her place to comment. Beyond all that, this unpleasantness at work was unfeeling and ridiculous, coming as it did after the terrible and distressing events at home.

She said all this and offered to resign the morning of the third day, shaking and in tears, standing before the master tailor, barely able to articulate that cobbled speech of faint apologies and huge grievances. She had not slept at all since that hideous morning when the body had been discovered, and the sight of Lourdes's door across the way, an ordinary sight almost every day for the past nine years, sickened her so that when she arrived home now, she had to rush through the patio to her own door, her eyes downcast to the flat gray stones, breath heavy, heart wild. Her mother wasn't in any better shape, especially since she also had the disappearance of the Doctor and Mili to worry about as well, and they had taken to sitting up in bed together, hugging each other and weeping and trying to pass the long hours of the night that way.

To her extreme surprise and confusion, the tailor and his wife took her aside, gave her tea, cookies, and soft words, and talked her out of her resignation. She was sent home "to recuperate" from her shock and was told to take a week of vacation, without pay of course, but her job would be there when she returned and not to worry. Rosa-Laura walked home dreading having to face that door across the way. She had not eaten much in those three days and the tea and cookies kept rising to her throat as if to spew out of her mouth.

Most of all, she was afraid that maybe Anacleto had killed his mother, though she believed, like everyone else, that Bernardo was the likeliest suspect. Sra. Erlinda had told everyone who cared to listen that Lourdes had been *shot*, cleanly in the back of her head as she was sleeping, and the baby's bed thrown over as if someone had grabbed the kid and left in a hurry. Nothing else but that child had been taken from the house, as far as the residents could see, but the police investigators who had entered after them said Lourdes had been stabbed and the place robbed. Rosa-Laura herself had heard something that could have been a shot in the middle of the night, then footsteps (there was something about them that she could not remember), and she told all this to the policeman who questioned her, but later another cop told her that she was just a child and should not repeat stupid, untrue rumors, that Lourdes had been stabbed, that if she saw Anacleto she was to inform the police at once, and that any disrespect she might show to the police by fomenting lies or hiding criminals would be severely punished.

"This is a crime for the garrote, just don't you forget that, *niña*," the cop said. "And we'll be looking at accomplices and those giving false testimony, like that ironmonger's wife."

She had asked her mother what a garrote was, and Mama told her it was a way of strangling someone. "That's how they do it to a murderer," her mother said. "The death penalty, what you get for killing someone. And I hope they catch him and do that to him, and I'd watch it, for what he did to Lourdes. But it won't be that way. Heaven's got to find its own justice in its own way, because these cops are more interested in framing that poor kid than catching the real killer."

No, Rosa-Laura could not go home. She went to the Church of San Lorenzo, emptied all her pennies into the box and lit as many candles as she could purchase for Lourdes's soul, for Mili's, for Anacleto's, and Augustín's. She didn't light any candles for Bernardito. She hoped God didn't get angry at her just for assuming the child was all right. God could be an awfully demanding, cruel, and insupportable supreme being, who allowed murder and hated know-it-alls, and she knew she'd better confess all that as soon as she could figure out how to be sorry for believing it.

After the candles she still could not bring herself to go home and stopped instead at her father's house. He wasn't back from work yet, but she had a key and let herself in. She sat down on one of the new chairs, and just stared at the high basement windows, counting the feet of passersby.

Sometime after one, he tapped home for the siesta, slipped his key easily into the lock with no fumbling like a sighted person, and entered his house. "Who's there?" he said.

"It's me, Papa. I'm home for the day. For a week in fact. They gave me leave."

"You poor kid. Let me make some coffee and stuff a bit of bread with ham for you. I've heard some news, but no word about the murderer. There's lots of talk about that argument she had with her sons, though, and lots of talk about Mili."

"I can imagine, Papa."

Besides hearing a great deal of interesting gossip over the years, Rogelio also came to know a slew of strange characters, low types he'd met in the plaza when selling his tickets. After all, if a person couldn't trust his blind lottery ticket vendor, who could he trust? Besides, unlike the *serenos*, the ticket sellers were generally wary of the police and tight-lipped about their customers. No one wanted to lose a good customer, no matter how unsavory his way of making a living (and those types were often the ones who bought the biggest lot anyway), and as for the police, how could they with a straight face ask a blind person what he or she *saw*?

Among these low lives, Rogelio became friendly with a taxi driver who frequented the neighborhood and bought tickets every week. Rogelio knew he didn't live in the neighborhood and didn't have any relatives or a woman there either. He never asked the taxi driver what he was doing in this poor neighborhood where fares would be less likely than, say, on the Gran Vía or Recoletos. This driver was about Rogelio's own height, as he spoke and breathed fairly directly on Rogelio's face. He never played around or attempted to steal a ticket, and he never joked with Rogelio. A cautious, serious guy. He disappeared promptly when a cop or a guard was around, but when he was buying a ticket, he'd talk with Rogelio, pleasantly, and Rogelio knew he was checking out the plaza and whomever was around, because his voice came and went as he turned his head, and his concentration was studied. Sometimes he smelled of kief, fairly reeked of it in fact, yet his voice was steady, his words unslurred. He spoke with the rough accent and slang of a Gypsy, so much so that one day Rogelio had ventured to ask him if he was a Gypsy. The guy wasn't offended, in fact he laughed, the first time Rogelio had ever heard him laugh.

"No, none of that, but I bunked with them now and then. Not bad people once you get to paling around with them. You just got to realize they won't be letting you in any more than they want to, and you're not family, and no matter how much they like you, you're nothing but a *gabacho* and they'll kill you for a penny and they'll kill you for sure over matters Gypsy."

Rogelio nodded. Gypsies stuck together. If they hadn't, they wouldn't have survived all these centuries. Downright tribal, they were, and inbred. Most people hated or feared them or both. The police and civil guard could kill them without worrying about writing up any official report. That was generally true in most cases, but with Gypsies, it was truer. Rogelio didn't fear or hate them. A few times in his blind life, he had cautioned a woman about trying to take advantage of his pockets as he stood somewhere or waited, but that was all. Mostly, they'd respected his inner eye. Or feared it.

Earlier the same day he'd gone home for siesta to find his daughter waiting for him, this client had come by in a very good mood. "Tell you what, give me a hundred today. I feel lucky. You got some good numbers?" The taxi driver said. "I'm going out of town for a few days after tonight, but I'd like to have something to return to."

"Most men return to their family, or a woman at least," Rogelio said. It wasn't a question, but it was a form of query. He knew better than to ask why the man had to leave town for a while after tonight.

"Yeah, well, when I travel I carry no baggage and no regrets, Sr. Rogelio," the man had answered.

As the driver walked off, Rogelio briefly considered the fact that sometimes it was good to have an acquaintance like him.

While Rosa-Laura had prayed that morning at the Church of San Lorenzo, Sra. Rosa, having managed to calm down Guillermina, left the house and spent two hours and a lot of the household allowance at the Mercado de la Paz, as well as a pastry shop down the street on Serrano. She was loaded down and tired, but the household had no food and she had to replenish the larder. Guillermina left on her own had eaten up everything. Sra. Rosa boarded the lift to the flat just after one, even though she usually climbed the stairs, being somewhat nervous of the glass and brass birdcage and the way it danced as it brought a person upstairs. She got into the house and put all her sacks and bundles down in the kitchen. The house was very quiet. Srta. Guillermina was probably napping. She often took a three or four hour siesta and hadn't shown much interest in going out to look at shop windows since her mother had died.

Sra. Rosa had bought a bottle of anís to replenish the one in the liquor cabinet, per the Doctor's instructions (*and where has he been all this time?*). She carried it into the dining room. The curtains that she'd opened that morning had been drawn, which was when she realized the Doctor had come home. In the yeasty, stuffy darkness, he sat quietly, draining a bottle of his best cognac. He looked thinner, as if he had managed to lose weight these past three days, as if he had not eaten at all. His skin was yellow and pasty and his eyes already glazed over from the liquor.

"Good afternoon, Sra. Rosa," he said, though his back was to her.

She came around to face him and stood there, staring at him. "Sir, we been, we have been, worried. Your sister—"

"Yes, I imagine so," he said. His words were slurred. She had never heard him speak like that nor observed him to drink like that. He kept looking at the curtains as he spoke to her.

"I've been detained at the police station, Sra. Rosa. I think you might want to go down there, the one on ___ Street, because Mili is there. I didn't dare ask for her, you see. Do you have any idea what has been happening with her these past months? I dread having to tell you, so you will, I trust, forgive me if I say that I hope very much you know already."

He then glanced at her and said, "Please do sit down, Sra. Rosa. You're going to swoon if you don't, and you'll hit your head and break that good bottle of anís as well. Sit now."

She sat and he poured himself another beaker of cognac. He always poured just the right amount, without looking, enough so that if she had tipped the snifter on its side, the liquor would have reached the lip of the glass without a drop spilling out.

"May I offer you some?" he said.

"Yes, but please, much less than that. A swallow."

He turned slightly and with great ease took another snifter out of the open cabinet behind him. She held her breath, afraid he might break something, but it was amazing how graceful he was, even now, half-potted. He poured "a swallow" looked at it, nodded, and handed it over to her.

Sra. Rosa then consciously thought for the first time in all those years that he and his whole family were very graceful people. Srta. Guillermina walked beautifully, despite her great weight and height, Sra. de Montero had done as well or even better and when the old woman had unfolded a fan it was as if an angel were spreading its wings. They were beautiful people, fat and all. Sra. Rosa thought about this and forgot her usual reaction to alcohol, which is why she tried to drink the cognac in a swallow instead of sipping it.

"Be careful now, that's the real thing, not as sharp as our Spanish brandy, more perfumed. And quietly lethal. Fine stuff," the Doctor said.

Fine stuff or not, Sra. Rosa coughed and her eyes watered. It burned her throat considerably, and made her stomach heat up as well. Feeling somewhat more loquacious immediately, she said, "Sir, enough now, please, what has happened? Are you all right? How did you know about Mili? How is she?"

"She came here," the Doctor said. "Oh," as Sra. Rosa's eyes widened and she seemed about to utter a protest, "don't worry, I know you didn't send her here. She came in the middle of the night. My concierge called the police. He thought to do me a favor, but it didn't turn out that way. We were picked up, taken to the station, and she was put in a cell and I detained."

Sra. Rosa felt the tears well up in her eyes, this time for shame and grief. "Sir, I don't know what to say."

"Not much to say, Sra. Rosa. I don't think they've harmed her, at least, I pray not. Evidently one of the policeman, a captain, somewhat of an animal, but from a good family—" and here he began to chuckle at this bizarre assessment, then he lost some control and laughed, then he recaptured his control, finished off the cognac and reached for the bottle.

"No," said Sra. Rosa firmly. She took the bottle, capped it, and put it to her side, away from him. "You need food, that's what you need. What were the charges? Why'd they do it? Because of Bernardo?"

He stared at her a moment, somewhat nonplussed. "You know him, then?"

"That dog killed my neighbor, Lourdes, three days ago, I'm sure of it. But no one cares at the police headquarters, we can all can be sure of that. She was his, well, his, I mean, like a wife, they have a child, but he has another wife too, and evidently, well, now I guess he likes Mili too—"

"That man likes no one, least of all himself. He eats and drinks hatred and force and control. He has gotten Mili pregnant—I'm sorry to tell you—"

"I know," Sra. Rosa said. She wiped her eyes and settled back in the chair. It was hard to bear that Mili had dragged the Doctor into this. And speaking of which, "Why did she come here? What did she ask of you?"

"Not to end the pregnancy, don't be alarmed. She simply was running away, and she had nowhere to go. She remembered me and this house and thought she could make use of it, a safe place, somewhere the police couldn't come. Not much thought in all that, but she was a little animal fleeing the herder and fleeing the butcher. And I managed to lead her right to the slaughterhouse."

Sra. Rosa looked at him sharply. He saw the look, took a deep breath, and said, "No, don't worry, I didn't sense that he was really going to kill her, just give her a hard lesson about obeying him, that's all. And give me a lesson about interfering in his business. Are you sure he's guilty of this murder of your poor neighbor?"

She nodded in the affirmative.

"I guess I'm lucky Mili didn't ask me to arrange an abortion. Or maybe he would have liked that. Whatever the reasons he had for his behavior— he made sure to let me know he would brook no interference. You'd better get on down to the police station. I'm sure they'll release her to you, but from now on, she has to think about what she is doing. She has gotten involved with a very dangerous, very sick creature. If you have anywhere you could send her, out of the city, out of the province, you could try, but I warn you, he might then come after you and Rosa-Laura, and frankly, your niece is not worth that price. But of course, you must do what you feel is correct, and she is family."

Sra. Rosa nodded again. "All right, I'm going, but first, I'm making some lunch for you and Guillermina. Why don't you go clean up, Sir, and put a good face on this. For your sister."

This time he was the one to nod. She got up, picked up the bottle, and pointedly waited for him to get up and out of her way so she could put it back in the cabinet.

It was testimony to her place in the family that he did as she suggested, very humbly in fact, and went off to his room and private bath.

He bathed carefully. He was in pain, but the cognac, not to mention the dose of morphine, was at work. Thinking of good people and different times helped to soothe his disturbed thoughts, and so he ruminated boozily on two patients he had at No. 1 Hermosilla Street. He had attended those ladies for years. They trusted him entirely. Everyone called them sisters, but they were not sisters in the familial sense of the word. Neither were they flamboyant or foolish. What they were was rich, the both of them, daughters of wealthy bourgeois families, and that enabled them to survive. They both tended to embrace the stereotype, the older one, Isabel, being somewhat stocky and having to watch her blood pressure constantly. She loved wearing pants and comfortable clothes, but of course, never did so in public. It was unthinkable for a woman to wear pants on the streets of Madrid, then and now. The younger one, Maria Francisca, or Quica as everyone called her, liked dresses and skirts, and wore the latest Parisian fashions, albeit tailored ones. Neither woman tended to lace or ruffles or flounces like the Doctor's sister, though Quica wore lipstick when she went into public and kept her hair long. Isabel's hair was short. Both were discreet, elegant, well educated, and well mannered. Both smoked richly perfumed foreign cigarettes, in long holders.

On Thursday nights, they held soirees. They invited six or seven friends, more on special occasions like the holidays, and had card parties with a long, relaxed, late Spanish dinner. Even during the war they held their card parties. It was whispered that they were fifth column, but the Doctor knew their democratic sympathies. All of them were inured to secrets, had even learned to relish secrets, and felt themselves to be above vulgar politics. Beyond that, at the heart of the thing, they knew to the depth of their souls that democracy or dictatorship, they were an anathema, a perversion in society, and would survive only by being utterly cautious.

After the war, Isabel invested her considerable fortune in a toy factory and a scissors factory, which were profitable and served the women's financial interests as well as had the family monies that had preceded these investments. They both loved children. Each of them was godmother to the children of several of their friends.

He liked them, and he liked that though none of them discussed their "situations," they were all comforted by the others' presence. They had told him about clubs for men like himself, and before the war he had even gone to a couple of them, especially during the heady days of the Second Spanish Republic when it seemed that liberties had dropped from the sky like divine indulgences, and everyone was dancing and reading and debating and blooming in the rich sunlight of their new but quarrelsome democracy. One night he had danced with a young man and realized he hadn't felt so happy since Alí had died. Just dancing, that's all it took to unwrap the gift of happiness. At that club he could behave just as he pleased, he didn't have to watch his gestures or his nerves. In fact, he got a bit theatrical, even made everyone laugh. A quiet dullard like himself, a professional man, a proper bourgeois, had loosened up enough to make other men laugh at his jokes and his gestures.

Another night a few months later something magical had happened, something he would always remember. He'd gone to the theater, to see a brand new play by the Andalusian García Lorca, the toast of the town. Everyone in Madrid was talking about the man, a charming creature with big eyes and a seductive mole on his face. The Doctor had seen him at the theater, watched him on stage during the standing ovation at the play's end. The playwright was short, wore a dandy bow tie the size of a tropical butterfly, and had a certain amount of theatrical affectations, but he also stood straight and proudly, and clearly knew how brilliant he was.

Afterwards, Arturo had waited in the street until the man came out the back of the theater, signed a dozen or more autographs, and walked off, surrounded by a crowd of admirers, mostly handsome young men. They headed straight to the club, that same club, and Arturo followed, too shy to present himself or insinuate his presence. He spent the rest of the night watching the man and his admirers, and realizing that what he had always read about, that the stories he'd always heard, about art and genius and ability and grace, were true, true, true, and though he might not be of that milieu or that talent, yet he was part of a generation and a type and he did not have to be ashamed. Some months later, the playwright returned to his home in Granada. Just at the outbreak of the war, the news of his assassination sifted in from the province.

Since the end of the war, many of the clubs had disappeared, though once Quica had told him there were others, one simply had to be careful. He hadn't the heart to even look.

All of which led right back to what he could not bear to think about, but then perhaps the best way to handle bad memories is not to try and concentrate on good memories but to end the memories altogether and not with good French cognac either. The answer was close by.

He hauled himself out of the bathtub wearily, not bothering to put on his bathrobe. He pulled out his shaving equipment and regarded his razor pensively and affectionately. Such a fine implement, such a beautiful straight edge, the ivory and amber handle. Just stroking it gently once across his throat or each wrist, then getting back in the warm water of the tub and letting himself go to Alí. In the immortal darkness or in hell, wherever. Yet, he had just been in hell, and Alí wasn't there, only Bernardo, with his sick smile and his feral eyes.

He shaved carefully, his skin well softened by the bath. He finished, laid his razor down on the side of the bathtub, and got back into the water gingerly, then turned on the spigot again to add more hot water. The whole bathroom was steamed over, the glossy copper-colored and blue tiles dripping with moisture, and he liked the atmosphere that way, cloudy, warm, transient. He should have gone and seen his own physician as soon as he had been let out of the station, but he was afraid the old man— who certainly hadn't ever discussed with Arturo anything but the most respectable of patient needs—would think he had gone carousing and gotten what he deserved. Maybe that was not such a bad thing to have him think. *Let him give me a lecture, let him think I had some fun.* He pressed gently on his side, where the ribs hurt the most. He was positive none were broken, just badly bruised, possibly cracked. His chest under the fine gold and gray hairs was bruised as well, deep red bruises now, purple and yellow soon. Worst of all, of course—he shifted his buttocks. He couldn't face his own doctor and wouldn't unless the bleeding got worse. God knew what an ironwood baton could do to one's internal organs. There was just so much anger and evil you could take in this world, and he'd about had his limit for now so he would not be seeking the sour repressed anger of a righteous soul like his physician unless he absolutely had to.

As for the rest of it—it was so bizarre how most men assumed that as long as they were the ones penetrating, they were different and better than the one penetrated—they were men, and not women or sissies or girls, or even sheep, he supposed. What they had done, the pleasure they had gotten out of gratuitous cruelty had not marked them in any way, just him. *Maricón. Mariposa. Jodida mariquita.*

He sat a while longer in the bath, then turned the spigot again to get more hot water. It would overflow soon, and that would mean more work for Sra. Rosa. He remembered how much Guillermina needed him. In fact, Sra. Rosa needed him too, and he was glad of that, despite her cursed pig of a niece. You cannot abandon family. He pushed his razor off the tub's edge; it clattered to the floor. He would not kill himself, not while Guillermina was alive. What would they do with her, old and crazy as an owl? They'd steal her money and put her in a mad house, and all of it would break Sra. Rosa's heart not to mention take away her only employment.

Maybe there was another reason for him not to kill himself too. Maybe living was a way of shoving their shit back into their damned faces. They didn't want him to live, so he would, fuck them all, the inbred bastards. And with that surge of defiance he decided he would go to his own doctor too, and tell him what they'd done. Let the old prude be shocked. They all deserved to be shocked.

Sra. Rosa found Mili in the front hall of the police station, leaning insou-
ciantly against the granite walls, looking like any other young whore just
released from jail. The corridor of the building was more than a story high,
deeply vaulted, and the sounds in it—policemen passing, clerks coming in
and out of tall wooden doors—made a stony yet high-pitched echo. There
were no other sounds; the walls were so thick no voices or street sounds
penetrated, though the vast double doors were wide open, and the street
visible from where they were standing.

"You OK?" she asked Mili.

Mili nodded briefly. She'd been roughed up, her hair was a mess and her
blouse dirty, disarranged, and part of the collar torn, but the only evidence
of an actual beating was an old bruise on her jaw. The lovely young face was
hard and the makeup smudged, but the eyes were not blackened.

"They put me in a separate cell. They knew. It was on his orders," Mili
said.

Sra. Rosa stifled an urge to weep, she felt so sorry for her niece. A cop
passed by them.

"Hey, Big Guy, got a ciggie for me?" Mili said to him.

He stopped, looked her up and down, glanced curiously at Sra. Rosa,
and pulled out a pack of *Ideales*.

Mili didn't protest at the cheap brand. She took one, held his hand
when he lit it, inhaled deeply, and fluttered her eyelashes at him.

"Thanks, cutie."

The cop winked at Mili and left.

"He just wanted to scare me. Wanted to show me who's boss."

"Is that why," Sra. Rosa began then stopped. "Let's go outside, Mili."

"Hey, I have to go see him, Auntie. I have to talk to him. Get this
straightened out."

"*Someone*," Sra. Rosa said, "shot Lourdes three days ago. Walked in, shot her. In the head, while she slept. From behind. The baby is gone. His brothers are gone. The cops are out for blood, they're going to pin it on Anacleto. It wasn't him. I know it wasn't him. They're saying she was killed with a knife, but—" she took a deep breath. She mustn't let out too much. She didn't trust Mili with the information. "Well, that's the official story anyway. I was told pistol, and we all heard the shot, but that's not for talking about."

Mili stared at her for a moment, her face pale, her mouth slightly open. She pursed her lips and took another drag of the cigarette, blew out the smoke, then threw the foul smelling stick away and walked out the front doors, her heels clacking and echoing on the stone floor. Sra. Rosa followed her, silent now. The girl was not a quick study, but she knew what a pistol shot meant. There might still be guns around after the war, but it meant decades in jail to be caught with one, and few people dared. A gun had to mean police, army, *la presencia* were involved, not citizens. Citizens beat, strangled, stabbed, or wept in frustration. They did not shoot.

They walked down the street for a block, Sra. Rosa struggling to keep up with her niece's brisk walk, then Mili stopped and without looking at her aunt said, "Look, it's nothing to do with me. And if it is, if he did it, he did it for me. To clear up the way for us being together."

"Are you completely stupid? He did it to settle accounts and warn you! To remove a mess he'd made, that's all! She threatened to go to his wife over you, that's what set him off, that's what got her killed! We all know that, the whole neighborhood knows it! It has to do with power, Mili. Why are you so stupid!?"

Mili whirled toward her aunt, her right hand raised as if to strike her. Rosa held her ground, daring the girl to commit such an affront.

Mili dropped her hand and said, "Fuck it!" She took off down the street, Sra. Rosa right behind her.

"I don't like being called stupid, Auntie, that's really insulting. No one likes to be called stupid. And all you loudmouths in the neighborhood, that's what got me into trouble, all you loudmouths. Things were fine before Rosa-Laura got to talking."

"I have money," Sra. Rosa said between gasping breaths. "Go somewhere. Aranjuez, that's a pretty town. Have the baby and give it to someone who can raise it right. Get a job. You're nice-looking. Work in a cafeteria. Learn how to work in an office."

Mili snorted. "So, you're not talking any more about me being a nurse, eh? That hot shot of a doctor of yours. Lot of help he was. I don't need him, and I don't need Bernardo, either. I can make 400 a month dancing at a club, that'd show him."

Sra. Rosa made a small, mewling cry of disgust, desperation, anger. She had heard this 400 a month routine before, and she didn't believe it then any more than she believed it now. Or rather, she knew it might be possible for someone like Mili to earn that much, at least at the beginning, but not by dancing. "Mili, my God, think of your baby at least. What do you want Bernardo to do? He can't leave his wife, he can't risk a scandal. It would ruin his career in this right-wing, Catholic country! He's a horrible creature. He doesn't care about anyone but himself."

"I want money! Lots of it! I want 1,000 pesetas a month and I want to live on Serrano or Princesa and wear furs! He's got money. I got his kid. It's not fair. You can't even imagine the stuff I do for him. Stuff he taught me, too, lousy pervert, no matter what he says! No one else."

Sra. Rosa had nothing more to say.

Anacleto and his brothers had completely disappeared, and everyone in the neighborhood feared asking after them, because genuine ignorance in the matter of a police suspect was best for everyone concerned. People assumed that Lourdes's son was with his father, certainly a fair surmise. No one in the neighborhood now had any doubt that Lourdes had been the loveliest woman who'd ever lived there. And no one had any doubt that her very beauty had condemned her to a horrible existence. Lips pursed, heads shaking, they let fly maudlin speculations, not to mention discussion of serious messages about feminine virtue and what happens to women who abandon it. Little by little, the gossip died down and the sadness set in.

Thus, three years passed after that horrible week. Rosa-Laura was now a de facto head tailor at the establishment. She made entire suits and had an apprentice, a boy, to measure the clientele. Of course, a young woman could not be a head tailor in any master tailor's shop, he'd be laughed out of town and lose business. The older men who had been at her shop many years were all above her, and the one had been there the longest time held the title of head tailor, second only to the master tailor. He also made the most money of all the employees, as was to be expected. Rosa-Laura didn't think too much about the situation. It was just the way things were and as far as she knew, had always been.

Despite her seriously professional standing in the shop, the boys and the men still flirted with her. No one ever caught the entirely ungirlish look that now and then would pass over her face, a look that said, *Take me seriously or else.* Who expects life to be brewing behind the porcelain perfection of a doll?

She sewed a beautiful jacket for her father and made dresses for herself and her mother. She had also begun to sew for some of the ladies in the neighborhood, for extra cash and because she couldn't say no when they asked. Now and then she'd sew very elegant dresses for Mili.

Mili would show up with her son, Emilio, and bring along nice cloth for dresses and skirts for herself, with extra to spare for Rosa-Laura, as well as expensive foreign fashion magazines like *Vogue* from which to pick styles and design patterns. Mili kept to black, like everyone else, but it was hardly the neck to foot-sole rusty woolen black of women like Sra. Rosa who buttoned themselves past the esophagus and down to the wrists, and wore their skirts to the mid-calf. With that fashion statement came nasty black cotton stockings in winter as well as summer, pulled high and held up by rolling them round and round cheap elastic garters that constricted the legs and popped out veins like string beans.

"Which, you must know," Rosa-Laura commented to her mother one day just as the long, heated summer was beginning, "is why you don't like summer, because of all these awful black clothes."

"Do you expect me to wear nylon hosiery, daughter? It's expensive, and I'm no young girl to put on airs at this time of my life," her mother retorted.

"Mama, I go bare leggéd in summer."

"And complain constantly about the boys who comment on your legs."

"Mama, they'd comment anyway, even if I wore workers' overalls."

"Maybe so, my daughter, but at least you wouldn't advertise yourself as well."

Sra. Rosa spoke like Srta. Guillermina nowadays, with good inflection and good grammar. She liked it. She didn't presume while in the neighborhood, but she thought this new, educated way of speaking, assiduously practiced with her daughter from the books that came on loan regularly, was nice in her mouth and suited the soft new voice that danced it through conversations. Now and then gutturals would intrude, but then, *madrileñas* are *madrileñas*, lower class or upper, and even God can't change that, much less grammar lessons.

Rosa-Laura and her mother had moved out of their building and into Rogelio's home very soon after the murder. Neither could stand to live in that building anymore, the sight of that door across the patio like a black hole straight to hell.

Rosa-Laura braved the crowds at the *rastro* on Sunday and bought a nice screen, a painted one with six panels of scenes of rabbits and deer in gardens where girls picked roses. She put it up at the end of the long room so that she and her Mama would have some privacy. She would save up her next two wages and buy another one at the flea-market to make a separate room for Papa too.

"Do you know, Mama, I've never seen a rose, except once in the florists' when I bought Constancia her bouquet." So, the curtains they put up over the windows had a fine print of rose sprays. The curtains let in the sunlight, the cloth being fairly thin, but they kept out the street a bit, especially nosy boys that would trot by and then squat to peek through the windows at street level and stare.

❧

Rosa-Laura crafted dresses for Mili that were low cut, flounced, tiered, and ruffled, with peplums to stand out over her fetching buttocks, and blouses with polka dots, black and white. To dress up the dismal color of mourning, Mili sported red scarves and velvet-black sweaters with fake leopard fur collars. Whenever she showed up, Sra. Rosa would let out a loud sigh, because it always meant she was going to leave Emilio with them for a few days. He was a hefty boy with his mother's beautiful eyes and black hair, but his father's big head, as well as strange, long fingers sprouting off hands that could pull a pot off a table in no time and rip up a bedsheet right from under the covers. No one had the time to discipline him nor the force to say no to him, so he was spoiled, and when Rosa-Laura and Sra. Rosa babysat, they gave in to his every wish. What was the use in trying to discipline any child of Mili's?

The first year after Emilio's birth, Mili came back and forth between their apartment and her home in Embajadores, sometimes afraid, sometimes angry, sometimes replete with presents and money. She told them that "he" had threatened to take Emilio from her, "like he did to Lourdes," but as it turned out, his wife had had some say in all that. One bastard to take care of was evidently quite enough for that woman, and who could say what she had suffered over the years or not.

Mili had birthed Emilio in Rogelio's basement, in a corner opposite to where Laura had birthed Rosa-Laura, that farthest away spot chosen by Sra. Rosa so as to rest her own superstitions. Mili gave birth with barely any fuss or screams, which astonished everyone. Within only four days, she climbed out of bed, took her baby, and left, despite Sra. Rosa's protestations that she needed ten days of rest to recover.

When Mili visited them with cloth, presents, Emilio, and gossip, she also brought laughter and fun. Mili might have been a selfish girl and she might have been a self-serving girl, but she was Mili, and they couldn't really be angry with her for too long. Indeed, mostly what both the cousin and the aunt felt about Mili was fear for her life and her wellbeing. Though Mili managed to escape paying her dues year after year, her aunt and cousin believed she could not avoid some inevitable reckoning. They waited anxiously, Sra. Rosa held her breath and Rosa-Laura lit candles for her cousin.

Bernardo surely would never be called to answer questions about the murder. The very notion of a policeman being questioned for a crime, let alone arrested, was ludicrous. In fact, no one in the neighborhood had seen him in three years, though someone started the rumor that Silvio was running the "investigation" into Lourdes's death. Mili seldom mentioned her son's father either. She knew that everyone was disgusted with her for still having dealings with him in the first place. Now and then when Rosa-Laura went to light her interminable candles, Sra. Rosa would ask her to light one to keep people like Bernardo at bay. Negative wishes weren't the purpose of the candles, but Rosa-Laura chucked an extra fifty *céntimos* into the box anyway and requested deliverance from foul presence. Unfortunately, the entire country rested in a foul presence in those days, and prayers proved useful mostly for distraction.

∞

Carmen-Victoria stopped criticizing Mili to Rosa-Laura and was even friendly when she saw her at Rosa-Laura's house. After all, she herself had gotten pregnant at sixteen and had to marry her third cousin Eduardo four months later in a somewhat hurried ceremony. The bride wore a pretty white dress with a very high waist that Rosa-Laura made her as a wedding present. Rosa-Laura also sewed Eduardo Jr. his baptismal dress, with a skirt of hand-made lace that hung down to the ground, and served as his godmother. By eighteen, Carmen-Victoria had her second child, a boy, like the first. She was quite happy with the arrangement, though it appeared to many that Eduardo had been left reeling in shock. It was just one of those neighborhood things: what could anyone expect from a family who all slept in the same room? Anyway, either it served the boy right for taking advantage or, it was a shocking shame how the homely little hussy had seduced the poor guy, take whichever side you preferred.

∞

After the affair at the police station, Dr. Contreras became pensive and sad, and he and Sra. Rosa didn't sit in the dining room and converse over *café con leche* as much as before. It hurt Sra. Rosa deeply, but she blamed Mili not him. Clearly some sort of enormous *desgracia*, unmentionable and unimaginable, had occurred that night, and it had sliced off a slab of his soul like ham in the butcher shop. He went about his business and closed off that part of him that remembered. She understood those kinds of maneuvers well and treated him as gently as she was capable. Guillermina was becoming something of a problem for them both anyway, and that and the household needs were what they discussed these days, usually while she stood in the kitchen and washed or cooked and he stood at the doorway, distracted, polite, overwhelmed.

They were worried about Guillermina because though she had finally stopped sleeping all day in honor of her mother's demise, now she arose early every morning to dress herself to the nines. She got herself buttoned up properly and all that, but her dresses became more and more outlandish and girlish and she insisted on violent combinations of bright colors. She lathered her face even more heavily in makeup of rice white, baby pink, beetle black, and cerulean blue. The Doctor and Sra. Rosa had finally realized her lifelong makeup preferences were a clear attempt to imitate the facial markings and color scheme of a two foot tall Japanese porcelain doll she had in a huge glass case in her bedroom. They got the connection after she topped off her paint job with rolls of opaque black hair invented at an expensive stylist's one afternoon. Over all that shimmery architecture she would set one of her enormous and very expensive hats, held by elaborate, foot-long pins. She wore long leather gloves in colors matching her shoes and purse. She'd sashay forth after the Doctor left the house and walk, in those two-story high heels of hers, up and down the boulevards and stand for hours in front of store windows. This generally did get her the attention she both craved and feared so much. More than once the concierge of their building had to threaten some *sin vergüenza* who had followed her home to get the hell out of his lobby or he'd call the police. More than once Sra. Rosa would have to help her soak her swollen feet in warm water and baking soda, and then massage them for half an hour just to get the circulation going to the painted toenails. Srta. Guillermina had a pedicure twice a week, and a manicure whenever she felt the urge to adjust the color of her fingernails, which could occur daily.

As for her brother, he too left the house all day and sometimes most of the night. His practice had taken a leap after the war, patients appearing in droves in his private office, his clinic, and at the hospital. He smothered himself in his work as gladly as Guillermina smothered her face in garish makeup.

❧

Rogelio was overjoyed at the expansion of his household. The sound of his house full of women, young and old, the way they kept it clean and organized (so much so that he had to ask them to please not move stuff around so much, because the house was becoming one big obstacle course and every night he had to reestablish his bearings), and the smell of food cooking on the stove he now had were splendid bonuses to his life. He ate well and became pot-bellied, the ultimate symbol of prosperity. His legs began to ache these days, sometimes a glass of wine at the tavern went right to his head, and he noticed he craved sweets more and more. Often on the way home he'd stop at the kiosk at the southeast end of the plaza and buy a bag of hard candy, which he'd finish before dinner. He craved potatoes too, and liked the chicken soup with *fideos* and stale bread fried in oil and garlic that Sra. Rosa made. He didn't worry too much at the swelling in his legs, because truth was, all lottery ticket sellers suffered from varicose veins. You couldn't stand for hours in one place calling out, *"Iguales para hoy, tengo los iguales para hoy*, I got today's numbers," and not eventually end up with varicose veins.

Though he had many customers and they came all day long, he usually tried to be home by eight for early dinner, but one afternoon he stayed later, to sell his last ticket to a neighbor named Sr. Eusebio. Sr. Eusebio suffered from the trembles, a result of his having been beaten over and over at war's end when he was captured and then enduring the hardships of enforced labor as a prisoner of war building the Valley of the Fallen, a vast monument in the mountains outside Madrid to Franco's victory. It was a miracle he'd survived the ordeal, given that over half the prisoners working on this pharaonic structure died from starvation or dynamite accidents. Sr. Eusebio walked with a cane, and sometimes it was the only thing that kept him from falling down and twitching like an epileptic for five minutes. He'd walk along, get an attack, and stand there clutching his cane for dear life, while the sickness took over. Then he'd recuperate and walk off, unsteadily. The people in the neighborhood got used to standing alongside him, waiting for it to end, making sure he didn't fall or bite his tongue off or some other such inconvenience. If the attack seemed it was going to last longer or be more severe than usual, they'd send off for a member of his family to get him home.

Rogelio sold Sr. Eusebio what he considered to be his luckiest number and exchanged pleasantries with his customer, including settling a few of the grand affairs of the country not to mention those of God Himself. Sr. Eusebio then hobbled off, leaning heavily on his cane, and Rogelio listened carefully to make sure he continued walking and had no attack.

The sound of the stick and the steps had barely faded when Rogelio felt—
him. Close by.

"Who's there?" he said. It was the querulous question of a frightened
man, an old man, and he hated the sound of his voice.

Besides, he knew who it was.

"How's the neighborhood?" Bernardo said.

"Better without you," Rogelio said. The retort strengthened him a bit
and gave him back some self-respect.

"I've always been here, blind man. Always. You'd better get used to me
now, too, because I'm here on a case and I'm keeping an eye on all of you.
Your favorite criminal, that kid who murdered his mother three years ago,
remember him? He's back, somewhere around, and we mean to catch him.
You and that tart that visits you sometimes, you've seen him?"

"Anacleto? That poor boy? He hasn't been by, and you know that, you
just want to frighten me. I won't be frightened. If life and blindness can't
overwhelm me, you can't either. And as for that 'tart,' I'm pretty sure you
see her more often than we do."

Bernardo laughed at his bravado. "Rogelio, I can beat you into a pulp
just like that stupid cripple you sold your last ticket to. I could throw you
into the Manzanares from the Toledo Road Bridge, in full sight of every
pedestrian crossing at noon time, and no one would lift a finger to help
you. This neighborhood is full of communists and anarchists, and I'd get a
medal and a commendation if I killed everyone in it. Don't think we aren't
watching all of you."

Rogelio kept his courage. "You think we don't know that? We'd have
to be a lot blinder than I am not to know. There's no crime here. Read
your papers, your damned government newspapers just back from the
censors' office. I get them read to me every evening at the tavern, so if
you don't like to read, if that's too hard a task for that bullet brain in your
head, then go there and listen, like me. According to the papers there
hasn't been a rape or a theft or a murder in this neighborhood in years,
much less in all of Madrid. I guess the stories I hear about such things

now and then are just silly rumors."

"That's right. This neighborhood is crime-free and going to stay that way. I'm the *presence* here now, Rogelio. I'm the representative of this government and this system, and I like that responsibility very much. Things as they should be, let no one around here forget that. Not you, not that witch you live with, and not that pretty little piece with her proud ways that they say is your daughter."

Rogelio began to remove the tickets and numbers he had clipped to his vest, like a tinker closing up his wagon to go home. "We all know you are the presence, Señor. It's not news here. But when I'm here in this plaza doing my job, I don't shout bad tidings, so if you need a town crier, find someone else."

And with as much dignity as a blind man can muster, which is considerable, he turned and left Bernardo standing there. He was very glad he could not see what he knew to be the contemptuous smile on that depraved face.

No one ever brought Rosa-Laura roses. They were expensive of course, but you'd think, given her name, it might occur to some boy to give her one. She thought about that now and then because boys in the neighborhood and at the shop would bring her carnations, daisies, or even nard in spring-time. Nard, she had to allow, was a wonderful flower with a wonderful smell. Her Papa liked nard especially, and though she would never bring such a present home (flowers ended up in a jar where the sewers worked, on the top floor of her establishment), she'd take one thin-stemmed bloom to Papa to hold and stroke.

One day on the way home she stopped off at the flower stall in Emba-jadores to buy chrysanthemums to dress graves on the Day of the Dead, which was but two days away. On a whim, she asked the flower vendor how much roses cost. The answer caused her quite a bit of pain, but she bought half a dozen red ones anyway, along with three dozen white mums. As she crossed the street with the sweet smelling bundles, she noticed a shop on the other side with a small sign in the window. She stopped for a moment, shifted her pretty burden so that nothing was getting crushed, and walked over to read the sign. It stated the shop was "For Sale." She was familiar with the shop and the owner. He was a tailor who sometimes took overload from her own boss. The sign had just been put up, as she had not seen it before that afternoon and she passed by this place often. The man who owned the shop was old and wanted to retire. These days, business all over was suffering, but small businesses like this in poorer neighborhoods barely survived. If it hadn't been for her boss's sending over work now and then, the old man might have had no work at all for long periods during the year. This sign would be up for a long, long time. Rosa-Laura read the sign twice and then went on home, but the sign had planted an idea in her head, even if its harvest could be only a distant and very difficult thing.

"Who are those from, daughter?" Sra. Rosa said with much surprise when Rosa-Laura separated the roses from the other flowers.

"These are from me to me," Rosa-Laura said, and then had to giggle.

"Daughter, don't go strange in the head on me, all right? It's my turn to embrace decrepitude, not yours."

Rosa-Laura smiled broadly. The two of them had just learned "decrepitude" the other day, reading a story together. They collected these words and then Sra. Rosa would look them up in the *Dictionary of the Royal Academy of the Spanish Language* that Dr. Contreras kept at home. "OK, Mama. The mums are for the dead, but these roses are mine. I just saw them and I wanted some."

"Your fancy must have cost dear."

Rosa-Laura said nothing. She was not a spoiled girl, but she had wanted the roses more than dinner or a nice movie or a new scarf or anything else. Their smell filled up the whole apartment.

Papa came home late, with his lottery supplies, his cash, and an empty candy bag. He was very pale and looked ill.

"Papa, what is the matter?"

He grunted and sat down heavily. Sra. Rosa came over to look at him.

"Rosa, don't stare at me. I can feel your eyes boring right into me. I'm just tired, is all. I don't want dinner."

"I've made *cocido*," Sra. Rosa said.

"I can smell it," he replied, "and something else as well. Lots of mums. But can there be roses in this house?"

"Papa, you're amazing," Rosa-Laura said.

"Daughter, anyone with a quarter nostril can smell fresh roses. There's nothing like that smell, not even lilacs or nard."

Sra. Rosa kept on looking at him closely, refusing to desist. "I'm going out for a while," she said, finally.

"Mama, at this hour? Let me accompany you. Where are you going?"

"Stay with your father."

"Never mind both of you, for heaven's sake. I'm going to bed. My legs ache, and I'm tired, is all," Rogelio said. "I'm not going to the tavern tonight. Too beat."

The women shook their heads at this bad sign and left to go to an herbal shop in the neighborhood. On the way, Sra. Rosa told her daughter she didn't much like Rogelio's color, or the way his legs were swelling these days. She was going to buy herbs to wrap his legs with and some more to make him a tea that would purge him. And, she was going to talk to Dr. Contreras.

"He won't go to the clinic or see any doctor, Mama. He's more afraid of them than anyone I know."

Sra. Rosa grunted. *Too often the courage about dying is a cowardice about living*, but she knew that Rogelio was a brave man anyway. He just didn't like doctors and who did? A visit from the doctor in this neighborhood meant you were probably dying or dead, and a trip to the hospital meant it would be your last trip anywhere except heaven or hell.

The thing is, Rogelio was a good deal younger than she was. Sra. Rosa was nearly sixty, a very ripe old age, and lucky to have gotten that far, so Rogelio couldn't be much more than forty-two or forty-three by her figures.

"How old is your father?" she said.

"He was born in 1901. Ten years younger than you are and thirty years older than I am. He's fifty."

Rosa-Laura did the numbers, as always, as easily as taking a breath and without counting on her fingers. Sra. Rosa used her daughter's accounting abilities for every little thing, as if the child were one of those fancy cast-iron and gilt cash registers in the shops. In fact, the master tailor and his wife, doing the business accounts, used her ability the same way when they didn't have a minute to sit down at a hand-cranked adding machine to do columns of numbers.

The women bought the herbs, had a long consultation with the herbalist and then the pharmacist, and went home. Rogelio had fallen asleep, dressed. The women carefully unbuttoned his suspenders and pants, removed them, removed his socks and rubbed his feet with a bit of alcohol, which brought no more than a bit of a grunt and a moan of delight from the man. They covered him well, and retired to their corner of the room, to murmur and fuss between themselves.

"You were right Mama, we have to consult Dr. Contreras," Rosa-Laura said. "But he'll have to come here and visit Papa, otherwise it's no good."

"My God, daughter, he has done the unimaginable for us, put himself out no end. I have no idea what he suffered trying to help Mili that time, but it was surely grave. I was just going to ask him for advice, not a visit."

"I have money and you know that. Lots of savings, and I still have most of the money I won in the lottery years ago, in fact. We can pay Dr. Contreras."

"Daughter, that would insult him."

"I will speak to him. I want the two of them to be on a professional basis. I will not insult the doctor, but I expect Papa to be treated like a paying patient, not like some charity case."

Sra. Rosa sighed. She was worried about Rogelio but she was even more worried about Dr. Contreras.

On November 1, the women bundled up the white chrysanthemums Rosa-Laura had bought and took a tram to the Cemetery of the Almudena. They got off and walked past high, speared grills of iron fence to the entrance. Far and beyond the enormous iron gates, the colonnade, the cupolas and neo-gothic spires of the pantheons, the city of the dead spread out, white on white, forever. Cypresses bordered it, but the interior had few trees, just a chestnut or a flowering bush here and there, and was mostly stone walkways and main roads of tomb house after tomb house. Only the flowers and mourners presented much in the way of color, until you walked inside, heels tapping on the old blocks of the walkways, and the white on white suffused into the muted grays and blacks and dark greens of lichen, granite, cement, marble stained by centuries of rain, and iron fences and gates with a gritty skin of rust. Rosa-Laura felt the whole thing reeked of chaos as much as death. The "streets" ran every which way and often just thinned out into a cul-de-sac.

The sad thing was that they had no real graves to which they could kneel and offer their bouquets, only the *tumbas temporales*, the communal pile, and one of those miles away in Valencia. Sra. Rosa's mother's *tumba temporal* in Madrid had long ago been disinterred and the remains burned to make room for the certainty of more. Sra. Rosa and Emilia had had no money for a real burial, much less a grave site and headstone, at the time of their mother's death of course, and the family back in the village cared nothing about their errant daughter's remains. When she'd died, the sisters had washed their mother's body all by themselves, walked behind the horse-drawn cart that hauled it to the cemetery, and tipped the grave-digger and driver with the money left over after buying Mama ten years in the communal pile. They had hoped they would come into their inheritance by the end of that time and thus properly place the bones into a niche in a wall or even a real tomb, but it was not to be. Ten years later,

Emilia was sick and in childbed, and Sra. Rosa once again walked across town to the cemetery, this time all alone. She watched as the gravediggers disinterred and then burned a heap of bones, some of them her mother's.

"It was one of the blackest days of my life, almost as bad as the day I lost you," Sra. Rosa said to Rosa-Laura as they walked into the cemetery, their heels clattering on the cobblestones and sinking into holes and ruts well-worn on the endlessly turning paths. "It hurt to be so young and so alone. Let me tell you, daughter, it's the one thing I must ask of you. Don't wrap me in a shroud, and don't let them burn me at the end of my time. Give me a funeral, a burial, and a fiesta afterwards, food and singing. That's how I want it."

"Dear God, Mama," Rosa-Laura said. "Please let's not think of that. I promise to do it proper. You know that I will."

Mother and daughter finally found the communal site, a sort of potters' field right near the crematorium and the chapel, and laid their flowers before it, claiming all the poorest deceased of Madrid for the past ten years, all the dead of the war, all the ones dragged there in canvas-covered trucks at the end of the war to be shot against the cemetery walls and then buried in hastily-dug trenches beneath them. Kneeling to pray off to one side, their small bodies framed against a background of slabs of marble and granite, obelisks, angels, miniature gothic temples, grotesque nineteenth century cottages, and live people cleaning up gravestones, they begged God to let up on this dying business for a while and let them get used to living again.

⚘

When they arrived back home, Rogelio was sickly, and they made him a tea to purge him. They had been brewing him these horrible-tasting teas that gave him cramps and the runs for several days now. They also gave him warm leg and foot baths infused with more herbs that smelled up their home and didn't seem to help. Rogelio tried his best to tell them about Bernardo's visit, but he couldn't figure out a way to say the thing without upsetting them. He waited, miserable, unpurged of the one thing that would give him peace.

The next Saturday, after the siesta, Sra. Rosa brought Dr. Contreras. Saturday was a half day for Rosa-Laura, so she attended too.

"Do you urinate a great deal?" the Doctor asked.

Rogelio sighed with the awful truth of it. "All the time. The tavern keeper next to my corner in the plaza is going to start charging me one of these days for latrine use."

Sra. Rosa tightened her mouth at this. What questions doctors ask! It was such a wonderful and respectable profession, and yet they had to say such shameful things, sort of like a housekeeper who emptied chamber-pots, which of course, she hadn't done in years.

"I need to draw some blood from you, Señor. How much have eaten this morning?"

"Churros and chocolate," Rogelio said. "I wasn't very hungry and didn't finish the churros, but the chocolate went down well. Sra. Rosa makes it nice and thick."

"Anything else?"

Rogelio shook his head in the negative.

"You like sweets, eh?"

Rogelio smiled. "Yes, Doctor, always have. Always had a sweet tooth."

"That's because you have a tendency to diabetes," Dr. Contreras said, very quietly.

Rosa-Laura gasped. Sra. Rosa glanced at her. Rosa-Laura had a dry dish towel in her hands, but she was wringing it as if it were soaked. Sra. Rosa knew the word "diabetes," of course, and she knew it was bad, but she didn't know it was bad enough to make her usually imperturbable daughter gasp.

Dr. Contreras looked up mildly and smiled at the two ladies. His jowls sagged now, his face had a yellowish cast to it, and his head had but a few stands of light brown hair left but no silver. He was still tall, of course, but stooped slightly, and his weight had pretty much settled into his belly and buttocks. His eyes reminded Rosa-Laura of one of those brown bears at the zoological gardens in Retiro Park. A bit rheumy, yet glistening and still beautiful.

"Ladies, I am going to ask you two to take a walk in the plaza, get yourselves a cup of coffee or something for *merienda*, and allow me to talk with my patient comfortably here. Besides, I will be asking him to disrobe entirely, and even with this handsome screen, it's best you leave."

"First, please let me say something to you, Doctor, please," Rosa-Laura said.

Sra. Rosa frowned. *Now what?*

Off to one side, as Sra. Rosa gathered up her shawl and strove to eavesdrop without appearing to eavesdrop, Rosa-Laura said to the Doctor, very low, "Sir, I am terribly grateful at your kindness and generosity to my folks, but I must insist we pay for this visit. It is troubling to both my mother and me to keep asking you for favors. We must ask you to treat Papa like your other patients, for the sake of dignity."

Dr. Contreras smiled at this pretty, proud little speech. The girl was about eighteen, average stature, delicate, and exquisite in her loveliness. She didn't have the kind of plush, pillowy figure that called out to men these days, but she had a face made for sculpting in Carrara marble, and no man fond of women could escape its appeal. Her hair was thick, piled on top of her head and twisted into ropes along the sides, nearly red, a deep auburn that his poor sister had tried time and again to purchase from the hairdresser's. She had blue-gray eyes large and slightly myopic, with long fringed dark lashes. Her finely formed thick eyebrows must have embarrassed her and caused her to pluck (he could see a few red points where the weapon had missed and probably left its user frustrated and furious at the demands of style). She had a perfectly oval face and a slight overbite with a full upper lip pouting over the lower. A bow of fine gold freckles arched over the bridge of the chiseled, straight nose. A heart breaker, this one, or made to have her own heart shattered by falling in love with the one man who could not appreciate her. Right now, her lips were pursed fiercely, and she was facing him like an enraged kitten.

"Of course, I appreciate your punctilio, my dear," he said, "but my suggestion is that you wait a bit and let me see how much is needed here. After all, the National Health Ministry and its system will pay for much of my fee. But your father's laboratory work might prove an extra expense, and it is possible he may have to go to the hospital for a few days, so you could use your money to ask for a private room there."

Rosa-Laura's look of utter horror reminded him that people of her class feared the hospital unreasonably. They saw it as a place for dying, not getting better. He sighed.

"Señorita, calm yourself, we just have to get his blood sugars adjusted, figure out if he needs medicine, work out a diet—he will be on a strict diet from now on. Things like that. We will take care of him."

"You are so sure it's diabetes?"

He nodded and returned to his patient.

The women left, and he proceeded to examine the patient thoroughly. Rogelio's eyes were sunken and cloudy with atrophy. His skin was dusky now, yet his cheeks appeared flushed. His fingers showed early signs of circulatory problems, his legs were vined with purple broken blood vessels and spongy with edema. He was not fat, at least, which was for the best. Dr. Contreras had long fretted that Guillermina would become diabetic on him, and with her weight, it would have posed a considerable problem to regulate her blood sugars, not to mention her lack of control when it came to pastry and bread.

Finally, the Doctor asked Rogelio to put his clothes back on. Rogelio had endured the discomfort and embarrassment quietly, but as he was putting his night shirt back on, he said, "Dr. Contreras, I've been troubled these last few days with a problem, a thing in the neighborhood, you see. Don't you think all this fuss is nothing, just some worries on my part?"

"No, Sir, I am sure it is a physical manifestation of an illness, a disease, and it has been troubling you for more than a few days I suspect. At this point, my guarded diagnosis is diabetes, and I have told your family that."

Rogelio nodded at the west wall, where the light and some warmth pillowed in, and sat down on his bed.

"May I ask you, Sir, what problems do you speak of? Surely, your family can help you with them, and it's best you are not stressed now," Dr. Contreras said.

"Oh, soon I must tell them, Doctor, but it'll trouble them greatly. Just a thing that happened years ago in our neighborhood, a murder, you see, and a young friend of ours blamed, but we never believed it was him. Now, the copper who handled the original investigation, and frankly, a man whom we all think probably committed the crime himself, well we hadn't seen him for some time and now he's back, and searching for this friend of ours again."

The Doctor grunted noncommittally. Blind people had a different way of "seeing" things, and he didn't want to speak in case his voice revealed his bile and distress. *Lourdes and Bernardo.* He knew the names too well. Hadn't Sra. Rosa talked about them incessantly when she was trying to get over what had happened, never noticing how it affected him to even hear the man's name?

The next day, though it was Sunday, the Doctor came back and drew Rogelio's blood again. The Doctor had warned the women the night before not to let Rogelio eat or drink until he arrived. They didn't mention to the Doctor what a time they'd had with that ridiculous request. Papa had been as petulant as a spoiled housecat, and that was completely unlike him.

Rosa-Laura waited while the Doctor drew blood. He talked to her mother a minute, then deigned to speak to her, avoiding her questions, dispersing mostly pleasantries and admonitions not to worry so much, which made her worry all the more.

She left her mother with her father and went straight to church. Rituals had to be observed, on the off chance they might make a grand difference. She attended Mass, took communion (she had fasted with her father to help him undergo the trial, but it had only made him madder), and lit the usual candles. At this rate, the Church of San Lorenzo would have gone bankrupt if she stopped buying candles.

She prayed for half an hour, on her knees, after the Mass. For the sake of her petition for her father, she apologized profusely to Jesus and Mary for her stubbornness, her wicked thoughts, her sarcasm, her ruthless rebellions that made her so hard to work with and so suspicious of commands and directions. Most of all she apologized for her way of questioning everything, as if no one were telling her the truth just because she didn't like the sound of what they were saying. All the time she was praying, she was aware of the contradiction in promising to be good only because she wanted something in return.

She left the church and pushed her triangle of lace veil back off her face. She liked the lace, though most girls her age these days were wearing scarves or even hats. Lace was not in style. The wearing of heavy, inherited mantillas was for the very rich in fine cathedrals like Los Gerónimos or for the very traditional in small villages across the land. For her class, mantillas or even a lace veil said, "Spain," and that was not a country they were particularly happy with these days. Thousands of young workers flooded the frontier to France trying to get into that country or pass through it to Switzerland and Germany to search for the jobs they could not find in their own country. People were talking about something American called a Marshall Plan, and Europe was benefiting from it, but not Spain, which was actually still under blockade. Americans were very much the style. Girls wore scarves because they considered scarves American. It seemed to Rosa-Laura that it ill befit America to be snotty about Spain and refuse to deal with the Generalisimo or disperse some of that foreign aid. After all, they had recognized his government and rule within a month after he had finally smashed the resistance to his coup.

She hated politics. And she wore a lace veil because she liked it and everyone else's tastes could be dropped in hell.

She stepped onto the street and walked, eyes straight ahead, and turned down a small alley empty of traffic. It was a short cut to her home, pretty in its perspective (she loved a good perspective, the trick to the eye, the parallels that seemed so exquisite, so perfect in their deceptive meeting), yellow-brown and clay-brown like the rest of the neighborhood, the houses built atop high walls, windows about a story up, the usual wrought iron balconies and tile-bordered entranceways. Down the street, just at the corner, a young man leaned against a narrow entryway into a patio similar to the one in the building where she and her mother used to live. The worm-eaten, wooden doors to the patio were closed, but they were set back enough that he could stand inside the archway and hardly be seen.

She walked in the middle of the alley to avoid encounters with any cheeky boy walking toward her, though the flat, narrow sidewalks would have been more comfortable in the high-heeled suede shoes she was wearing. She walked carefully, not wanting to trip over a cobblestone or scuff her fine shoes. They gave her all of four inches more in height and lent a certain style to her posture. She was used to this kind of swaying walk by now and carried it off gracefully.

"I didn't think it possible you could get more beautiful," the young man said as she passed him and was about to take a right onto the next street.

Something in the voice made her do the unthinkable: she stopped and looked back at him.

"Mother of God, what are you doing here?" she said.

He was taller now, even taller than his mother had been. He was stocky, barrel-chested, square-headed as ever. His hair stood straight up, an indiscriminate brown in color, bleached reddish with sunshine as if he had been working in the countryside. His face was ruddy too, and his strong nose and bony cheeks dotted with freckles and blister stains. His eyes squinted and sat far apart. They bored into one with the intensity of someone who had poor vision and a penetrating consciousness. She had never thought Anacleto handsome. Other girls had said so, including Carmen-Victoria. Arresting, perhaps, in the way that quiet and withdrawn young men can be, but not handsome. Rosa-Laura could never forget Mili's casual comment—"You don't know what boys look like, do you?"

"I thought I'd see how things were," Anacleto said. "Are they still looking for me?"

"I don't know. I haven't heard anything, but it's risky anyway. Why come back? If someone who doesn't like you sees you, it'll just bring down the authorities."

"I thought I'd see how things were. You want to have a Sunday drink with me?"

"No."

"Ah, girl, you were always hard with me. Why? I adored you. Still do, I guess. Let me buy you a glass of soda, come on now."

"My father is sick. I have to get home. And anyway, I don't want to be seen with you, or with any boy for that matter. I think you're crazy to have come back."

She turned and took off, as fast as her elegant footgear would allow, then stopped and turned back, "Look," she said, "For God's sake, be careful."

It had begun with Bernardo's visit that day to Rogelio in the plaza. Had he just backed off then, stood to the side, done his job of watching, spying, as everyone would have expected and accepted, everything would have gone back to bitter normal. But he had set a buzz in Rogelio's head, either for a purpose or meanness or both. The buzz was transmitted to Dr. Contreras, and eventually to the others, so they were expecting fatalities right from the start and were already decided as to their reaction before his misdeeds began in earnest.

Sra. Rosa heard the bad news of Bernardo's presence back in the neighborhood not from Rogelio but from Dr. Contreras. She arrived early one morning at his house and found him up after a night with no sleep and three emergencies.

In the old days, this rude and regular regimen would not have even phased him. This day, he was sitting in the kitchen, pale, distracted, cold even as he suffered from the slow burn of the ulcers in his stomach and duodenum, and most of all sick from the memories of police stations and Bernardo's particular, personal brand of torture. As long as he was attending to his patients, he had managed to keep this hydra memory at bay, but once home, safe as it were, somehow the many-headed monster reared up, snarled, and corrupted the landscape. His heart was beating very fast as well, and he'd decided not to take his blood pressure. He knew what it was.

"Sir, let me make you some chamomile tea," Sra. Rosa said. She put down her bag and hung up her shawl. He said nothing for a while.

Then he said, "Make me some coffee. I've got to think for a while. I don't want to sleep."

"No, Sir," she said, as kindly as possible, "Really, you don't look well. You need to rest. I'm going to open the balcony doors and air this house out a bit. You need to go to bed and let me do my work."

He did not appear to hear her. Abruptly he looked at her, but his gaze was distracted. He could not keep himself from blurting out. "Do you know that that agent, Bernardo, is back in your neighborhood, looking for the boy that police say killed his mother, what did you call her?"

"Lourdes," Sra. Rosa said. Her chest suddenly began to hurt and her throat too. She did wonder if it were her heart, if this were the beginning of the *anginas*, but it was fear lodged there like a hard white eel, twisting and turning this way and that.

"He approached your brother-in-law, Sr. Rogelio, in the plaza. Threatened him, in fact, and mentioned you and your daughter as well, the fiend. He said he was looking for the boy, Lourdes's killer, but you know how that goes. There's always more to these things, and they're always happy to hint that there's more, thus leaving everyone nervous and guilty and ready to talk. Sr. Rogelio is an intelligent man and held his own from what I could gather. But there will be others in the neighborhood—the thing is, what is he really looking for? Or, am I just falling prey to that net of guilt they spread so efficiently, that feeling they disseminate that makes us all want to confess and confess and confess, even when we've done absolutely nothing?"

Sra. Rosa had some experience with this sort of upper class overthinking. She didn't answer his question, if that was what it really was, and went to the stove. She boiled milk for him instead of brewing coffee and brought him the pills he took for his ulcers and his high blood pressure. She searched for the tranquilizers he kept for Guillermina, but couldn't find any. He was careful about his narcotics, he was. He didn't argue coffee with her. He was too deep into his meditations upon evil, drank what she put before him, and took his pills docilely.

The Doctor was pondering a visit with Bernardo at the station, to bring him a bottle of the best cognac as a present, a peace offering or bribe as it were, but the whole plan presented huge difficulties. He didn't know what station the man would be at, for one thing. Clearly, he didn't have a particular post, though *uptown* was the best bet, at the Puerta del Sol center where the most secret of the secret police congregated and got their orders and hatched their plans in a serpents' nest deep in a dark building that dominated the square and sat over a labyrinthine dungeon rumored to be full of political prisoners. If he went there, even well dressed, proper, with a gift, he might not get out again alive and whole: would the monster even remember him, and if he did, would he consider such a visit just another example of the Doctor's meddling in his private affairs? The other weak part of that plan was, what if someone else drank from the bottle? This was not his own drawing room, his stepfather placidly seated in the big red leather chair, half drunk already, happy to receive libation from his respectful stepson. The Doctor had to rethink everything entirely. There had to be a way.

∽◦∾

He would have been very shocked had he known that Sra. Rosa began designing her own plans as soon as he told her Bernardo was back. She still had three ampoules of morphine left over from poor Constancia's last days. She could approach Bernardo in some side street, pretending to have information. He would suspect nothing from a being like her, she would ask him to lean down to hear her whisper, then she'd jab him hard. He'd fall, and half-insensate, she'd push a knife into his throat. Some problems in this plan occurred to her. What if a dose of three ampoules were not enough? What if a big man like Bernardo needed much more? How long would it take before it worked? (With poor Constancia one injection, half an ampoule, in her upper thigh and in seconds she was nearly coma-tose.) Would he yell? Should she dispose of the body (How?) or just leave it there? Would he even be alone? Perhaps she'd have Silvio to consider. Complicated. She had to think some more. She did not want Bernardo around, she didn't want him hurting Anacleto any more than he already had, she didn't want him threatening Rogelio any more, and she especially didn't want him talking to Rosa-Laura if it came to that. And, she did not want him beating Mili or killing her as she knew he'd killed Lourdes.

That evening she got home just as Rogelio arrived, and they sat togeth-er waiting for Rosa-Laura to arrive so they could all dine together. She was so nervous and unsettled, unable even to sit for a moment. Rogelio finally asked her what was up. She didn't answer him for a moment, considered lying to him, then reconsidered.

"Listen, Rogelio, I got to talk to you," she said. And she told him of her terrible notions and plotting. "OK, you tell me now, am I crazy? I don't care if I'm caught, believe me. It'd be worth the garrote. I guess."

He listened in that blind way of his, said nothing for a while so that she was sure she'd really shocked him, but then he said, very deliberately, very calmly, "Well, there's lots of problems with your plan, that's for sure. I may have a better plan."

So, it was his turn to shock her. His idea was less tricky and involved money. He knew a taxi driver, a rough beast, practically a Gypsy, capable of anything. Men like him always needed money, not to mention action. Would he blackmail them afterward? Sra. Rosa asked. Possibly. Well, what if he did? He'd be involved too, and anyway, you can't get blood out of turnips. Both of them were anxious for their family, for their friends and neighborhood, and there was no one to help them in this matter except themselves, so the taxi driver seemed like an excellent option.

⌒⋏⌒

A few days later, Rosa-Laura phoned her mother from work. It was terrifying, the final straw. Sra. Rosa was at the Doctor's house and when the phone rang, Guillermina answered it, expecting one of her cronies. She had a small circle of girlfriends, all of them as old, as overdressed, and loony as she was. They took *merienda* together, lately at a fashionable café on Serrano or Alcalá.

"It's for you, Sra. Rosa," Srta. Guillermina said to her housekeeper. "I believe it's your daughter."

Sra. Rosa was kneeling behind her in the corridor, getting ready to roll up a small Chinese carpet set over the hallway runner and protecting the entrance to the Doctor's study. It was time to bring it up to the roof and beat the dirt out of it, a very soothing if exhausting and dusty job. She had planned on pretending the carpet was Bernardo. She hesitated a moment, trying to understand Guillermina's words, then stood up quickly and felt her heart thudding so hard she almost threw up. She had spoken on the telephone all of three or four times in her whole life, in each case on behalf of the Contreras del Valle family. She'd never had a call from her daughter, and the first idea it pitched into her head was that someone had died, probably horribly.

Sra. Rosa took the phone from Srta. Guillermina gingerly and had to think a moment which end was which. "Yes," she croaked into the receiver, "*¿Digame?*"

"Mama? Listen, I'm sorry if I scared you, but—well, something strange has happened. I went home at lunchtime to get a magazine I forgot to bring to work this morning—wanted to show the tailor a suit—anyway, forget that. When I got there, that awful man, Mili's policeman, was outside our door. I had the feeling he'd been inside our house. Maybe I'm crazy, I'm just not sure, but he was standing there, and he scared me so much! He just looked at me, and then he asked me, well, how I was 'doing,' for heaven's sake. Nothing else. Well, there was one thing—he said I was prettier than he ever remembered—but that's just the usual garbage they all say, I mean, I could barely say anything, it was so creepy. I just went downstairs, and when I left a few minutes later, he was gone—I'm sorry if I scared you. This is ridiculous. I don't know why I phoned—it's just that, I searched for Papa to warn him, and I couldn't find him, and—"

"Calm down, daughter," Sra. Rosa said. She had fully regained her composure now that cold rage had overtaken her fear and demolished it. "He's a cop, a bully, it's his way. Um, anything in the house disturbed?"

"No. I'm surely wrong about his having entered. I don't know why I even said that. I'm sorry, Mama, this was thoughtless of me. I don't know what got into me. I shouldn't have called."

Good she didn't see Sra. Rosa's face at that moment because it might have frightened her more than Bernardo's. As it was, Srta. Guillermina, who had not moved from the hallway and listened to every word her housekeeper was saying, suddenly seemed to be flustered by something or other, pulled out a huge red and black fan, and began to beat up a wind enough to shake the peonies in the crystal vase on the console where the phone sat. Sra. Rosa glanced at her, smiled that metallic grin that she thought was her nicest, politest smile, and with it thoroughly scared Guillermina, who turned and ran to the sitting room.

"Um, daughter, I'm glad you called. That's what mothers are for, to help you get over bad dreams. You're a good girl, Rosa-Laura, don't worry about this. Um, maybe he was looking for Mili. But don't worry any more about it, understand?"

If she'd had any doubts or shame about what she and Rogelio had discussed, she didn't now.

◌◌

Mili too had some ideas about Bernardo's overlong stay on this earth.

After Lourdes's death so long ago and her three days in jail, Bernardo hadn't shown up for weeks. By the time he finally visited the pensión again, she owed a considerable amount of rent, she had begun to fatten from her pregnancy. He had laughed at her belly, her hips, and her swollen breasts. That had hurt her feelings. It didn't stop him from taking what he considered his, and it didn't stop him from paying the back rent, but she'd made a point of not responding nor doing anything that might make give him more pleasure. After that, she got fatter and fatter, and promised herself that this was the first and last time she'd endure this baby business, even though she felt healthy enough, without the sickness that other women complained about, and with a good appetite. The baby was born, with Aunt Rosa and her cousin attending, and soon after that, she got bored with the bed and the leaky breasts and the squalling kid—though it was true, he was a cute one, and thank God a boy—and she'd just gotten up one day, said, "So long, I'll see you all soon," and left. She got a message to Bernardo, who met her back at the pensión, glanced at the kid, told her he had enough bastards at home and his wife wasn't about to coddle any more, at which point, Mili said "What kind of balls does it take to follow orders from the damned wife, fellow?" and then added that he couldn't have Emilio even if he did want him. That bumpy back-talk got her some bruises that along with her ruined waistline, rump, and breasts, left her looking like an elephant for days and days. She had never forgiven him that.

Her room and board got paid. The landlady fed her and brought milk for the kid after the first two months. Mili wasn't about to be a wet nurse any longer than she had to. Stylish woman didn't do that stuff, and it was destroying the uplift of her tits. One day, disgusted with this mother's life she was leading, she went into her landlady's salon while the woman lay snoring on the sofa, dead drunk, and grabbed an envelope of cash left by Bernardo for a few months' rent. She went out, took a taxi uptown, found a good store, and ordered dresses and a skirt and two blouses to be made to her new size, bought a beautiful hat with a wide brim, the latest style, stockings at another nice shop on Mayor, brassieres and panties in silk and satin, and two pairs of expensive shoes on the Gran Vía. Then just to spite the universe, she took the drooling shoe salesman into the storage area and let him fuck her standing up, for which she got a third pair of shoes free. She came home feeling much better. Let the landlady explain to Bernardo where the money had disappeared to, let her ask him for more. The landlady was terrified of the man and wasn't going to kick Mili out for any reason, even a screaming baby, much less a little loan.

During the next three years, Bernardo visited her only infrequently, though every month the room and board was paid up. Other men came and went as well, and they were glad to help out with her necessities. She understood Bernardo didn't love her or else he'd get rid of that high-faluting homely wife of his and set her up properly, even marry her. She didn't mind that he didn't love her. What did bother her was that when he would show up, after some long hiatus, she always had this feeling about him, this intense desire that she couldn't control very well, this surrender to his strength and casual brutality, the way he called her "Baby," and the way he tilted his hat and lit her cigarette. This was the way things were in movies, and she liked that. She was as pretty as any of those movie stars, and he was Richard Widmark, only bigger, broader shouldered. Widmark was a *mariposa* compared to her man. But, understand it or not, every encounter showed her she was not the boss, and that was intolerable.

Now she hadn't seen him in months, but here he was, back in full force. He'd showed up at the pensión one night (a day before he talked with Rogelio, as it turned out) and having marched in as if he owned the whole house, found out that she was across the street at a tavern having a drink with a friend while little Emilio played with two other children. It wasn't as if Mili had left the boy alone or anything, because the other children's mother was sitting outside crocheting and keeping an eye on them all. Bernardo had walked into that tavern, pushed aside his overcoat and jacket just to let the man she was with see the gun in the shoulder holster, and then hauled her up like she was some common criminal and dragged her across the street. He picked up Emilio on the way and dragged them both upstairs, Emilio howling. In the salon Mili saw the landlady crouched in a corner, her eye blackened and her bottle of wine overturned and emptied on her carpet.

"*Joder*, Bernardo, you didn't have to hit her! It wasn't her fault! She's not my mother, she can't tell me where to go and where not," Mili had shouted.

"Shut up or I'll kill you," he said. Then to the landlady, "Get up, you slut and take care of the kid."

The landlady got up, shakily, and took Emilio. The boy didn't like her or her powerful breath any more than he liked being taken in from play, so he fought and wailed. She carried him kicking and scratching into her kitchen and gave him sugar cubes and rubbed his little privates until he finally quieted down.

In the room, Bernardo threw Mili down on the bed. She was used to this routine, and immediately began moaning and saying the words he wanted to hear, moving her hips and belly like an Egyptian dancer.

He rolled her over, knowing full well she hated that, it hurt, and finished quickly. Then just like that, buttoning his pants, the bastard told her he was going to take Emilio and put the child into a special school for officers' children, a school where he'd be disciplined and eventually trained to be an officer himself.

"He's only three!" Mili screamed. Had the man gone mad? "Say, you haven't been here in months, and now you show up, push the landlady around, fuck me in the ass, and tell me you want to take my baby! I thought your fancy high-class wife wouldn't have him!"

"You shut your mouth about my wife, you're not fit to talk about her at all. I've got plans, *zorra*, and a slut like you isn't part of them, that's for sure. You're out of the picture now, and don't think you can do anything about it, because whores are disposable, remember that. I'll give you some money to get along, more than you deserve, and you won't bother me again. As for the boy, you don't need him. He's just in your way. Take the money, hit the streets when it's finished, sell that fat *culo* of yours, and don't ever think of blackmailing me or causing me any problems or every cop from here to Chamartín will be on you, making your life hell. Do you understand?"

Mili understood. She walked over to her window, pushed aside the curtains and looked downstairs. She saw his car, a new one, much nicer than the old one, a Mercedes sedan, parked right in front of the butcher shop below, in a prohibited zone. Silvio sat in the driver's seat, smoking, or at least, she thought it was Silvio.

Silvio had always liked her.

༄

Downstairs, Bernardo got in the car and nodded at Silvio, who took off from the curb and moved into the light traffic easily.

"What'd she say?"

Bernardo said nothing to his sergeant's query. Either he hadn't heard him, or he didn't think the man was important enough to answer. Silvio knew it could be either one or both. He waited until they were nearly past the fountain at Atocha, hit the horn twice to move another car out of his way, and drove along the Castellana fast and smoothly.

"Well, what do you want me to do?"

"I'm giving her an envelope. I don't want to see her fat ass again.

When this promotion business gets settled, I'm moving my family into a new house, and I won't need any drain on my finances or any damned embarrassing ties to some slut. Fuck it, the *zorra* got so damned old and fat. Lourdes was twenty years older and so much more beautiful, so much finer a creature—the wrong whore died, that's for sure."

"That wasn't my fault," Silvio said. He had no expression on his face or in his voice.

"Did I say it was?"

"Get this straight, Captain, I'm no hick from the provinces. They assigned me to you to keep you in bounds, but I don't much like having to clean up after you. I'm the best officer you've ever had, and you know how well I follow orders, so don't go around insulting my honor."

Bernardo laughed. "Well, I'll give you an envelope for her in a couple of days, you can deliver it, and then, you can ask for reassignment. Or, you can follow my star, because I'm on my way up, and you're either with me or against me. And as for cleaning up after me, that bitch's kid needs to be in a military school. You haven't got any family, so you won't mind sponsoring him. It'll be the best school around, and there won't be any dishonor in that. I remember loyalty, and I remember betrayal. That and watching your tongue are all you have to remember."

Silvio listened and kept his silence.

⁂

Anacleto's plan involved little of the complicated algebraics of the other conspiracies being formulated by people who had necessity more than vengeance on their minds. Anacleto planned to find him, follow him, get him alone in an alley somewhere and rake a razor across his throat. He had a good straight razor, a bone-handled job he'd bought in the provinces, now sharpened and honed to hair splitting perfection. Augustín had given his big brother all the cash he'd had and wanted to come too, but Anacleto had forbidden the boy to accompany him.

"You got a life, you got a girlfriend, make something of yourself," he'd said to his brother. "If I get away with it, I'll be back, before this Christmas.

If they get me and I go to jail, forget about me—it's the garrote and there's nothing to be done about that. And, if I fuck up and don't get him, then it'll be up to you to avenge Mama. I'm sorry for that, but I'll do my best, so don't worry. I'll get the bastard."

His plan was so straightforward and he was so sure of the outcome that he had borrowed a car from a man he worked for, a sturdy, black, thirties' Plymouth he parked near the Puerta de Toledo and slept in. He did not drive it around the narrow back streets of the city at all, because Madrid had so few automobiles in those days that cars not Mercedes, police vehicles, or taxis, tended to stand out. Despite its conspicuousness, the bulky vehicle was the perfect headquarters during his vigil, guaranteeing mobility and the means for a quick getaway.

Late Sunday night a week after meeting Anacleto and a few days after Bernardo's visit, Rosa-Laura was helping Mama gather together their laundry into two cotton bags. Rogelio had already turned in hours ago, exhausted and ill. Sra. Rosa would take the washing to the Doctor's house and do it there in the nice modern machine he had, a beautiful sage-green and cream-colored round machine on stubby legs, with wringer and a hose attached to the kitchen sink. No tub and washboard for people like this family.

Rosa-Laura had recovered from the fright Bernardo had given her and apologized to her mother a dozen times. She was embarrassed she had lost her composure so easily, but police could do that to you. She had not an inkling of all the conspiracy flickering and sputtering throughout her world. She put the last towel on top of the second bag and said, "Mama, you'll never guess whom I saw right here in the neighborhood."

Sra. Rosa caught her breath. "Bernardo again, daughter?"

Rosa-Laura stopped cold, the towel halfway folded and cursed herself for being such a tactless, unthinking idiot. Quickly she said, "I saw Anacleto, Mama. A week ago, after Mass."

Sra. Rosa said nothing at all.

"I told him it wasn't smart for him to be here. I mean, are they still looking for him? I'd bet they are. They don't release their grasp, the police."

Sra. Rosa pulled the drawstrings of the second laundry bag tight.

"Mama?"

"You didn't tell me right away like you should have, but I didn't tell you something either. They are looking for the poor boy. Your father saw Bernardo too, before he came to our house. That monster said some things to him. That's what set off your Papa's spell of diabetes. If you see Anacleto again—best you walk away. Best you have nothing to say to the authorities if you have the bad luck to be questioned, do you hear me now?"

Rosa-Laura nodded. "So, that's it. Makes sense. I'll tell Anacleto about Bernardo if I see him again."

"Didn't I just tell you not to talk to him?! Just once in your life please do not be so hardheaded!"

Rosa-Laura smiled. "I'm my mother's daughter."

"You are and you aren't. Laura was a sweet thing, quiet, docile, though brave I'll admit, and your Papa is an angel. Can't say the same about you, child. True, you take after me, and I am your mother, but it's a mystery. I always thought Mili had her grandmother's soul, as well as the worst part of her own poor mother."

Rosa-Laura managed a smile. She put aside a small towel on the table because it needed mending. Over in the corner, her father turned in bed and sighed. She glanced at her mother and spoke in a lower voice.

"Mama, be fair. I go to Mass every Sunday. I may chafe at the rules and the traditions, but I submit. Eventually. And Mili, did she have a chance? Her Papa dead so young, her poor mother so sick and, the war, really, it's not her fault—"

"Excuses. Her situation was not so different from yours, and that two years you were taken away may have put the fear of God into you, yet you have a doubting nature. Is that your education or is it your inheritance?"

Rosa-Laura said nothing more. She would warn Anacleto if she saw him, and that was that. She owed him that much, human to human. As for her doubts and her beliefs, she remembered the story about Job that Sister Isabel told her one morning when they sat in the kitchen trying to warm up, busy with sewing.

Sister Isabel had loved that story. Rosa-Laura had to smile at the memory of it, the woman's delight in the unblinking ruthlessness of the tale. *God took everything away from Job, even his health, yet covered with sores, and suffering from great grief at the loss of his all, he still praised the glory of God and upheld Him. That's what it's about, child. Just because it's hard you don't turn from God. Whatever He gives you is whatever He gives you. Despise the poor of spirit who turn away the minute things get hard. This war for example. It's a test, a trial. We die or we endure. How dare we say to God, Why me, Lord? It's not a bargain in the marketplace, child, not some deal with a Gypsy over a horse. God gives us love and God gives us the Devil to pay. We make the choice how to deal with that.*

Rosa-Laura attended Mass regularly, prayed, and sought the peace of ritual even while gritting her teeth at the inconsistencies and injustices in the sermon. The more she knew, the worse her misgivings. When San Lorenzo's monsignor mentioned during some Sunday sermon or another that the serpent's fruit was not an apple at all but the "fruit of knowledge," Rosa-Laura let escape a big sigh and whispered, "Well, of course, that's *it*!", and got a sidelong glance from her mother.

But, come what may, when you entered a bargain you stuck to it, and that was what not only Sister Isabel had taught her, but her own mother.

"What are you grinning at now?" her mother said.

"Nothing, Mama. Just a sermon I remembered."

The two women piled the laundry bags near the door, turned off the last light, and went to their cots in the darkness after a goodnight kiss.

Bernardo was thoroughly enjoying himself prowling the neighborhood, threatening people, pushing them around, watching them powerless to do anything but curse him (and even that took some courage on their part). He visited the market place and took samples from the vendors, he got some do-not-disturb cash in unmarked envelopes from the Red Mill Night Club, the movie theater on Tribulete, and most of the tavernkeepers in the area, he emptied the plaza of Gypsies (not a bad thing as far as some of the neighbors were concerned), and everywhere he went, shopkeepers gave him presents and the local cops tipped their hats and saluted him.

One evening, he finally saw Anacleto, and if it weren't for the quick thinking of a family of Gypsies selling flowers down on Miguel Servet Street, he would have surely caught the boy.

Anacleto had just purchased two dozen carnations from the Gypsies, and looking up, saw Bernardo jump from his sedan with Silvio close behind, the motor still running. Bernardo headed toward him, coat flapping open, tie flipped behind him at the wind of his passage, and his hat flown off to parts unknown. The boy didn't wait for his change, he dropped the flowers and ran. The Gypsies suddenly exploded like fireworks, twenty where there had been but two or three a minute before, yelling and wailing and accidentally kicking over buckets full of flowers, raggedy children everywhere screaming and running back and forth, adding to the chaos. Bernardo hit the overturned wet flowers and skidded, then fell on his ass. Silvio stopped, evidently to ponder the situation, then he pulled out his gun and shouted, "Where'd he go?" at the Gypsies, who pointed in every which direction. Bernardo got to his feet, ran down Miguel Servet Street for a couple of blocks with Silvio behind him, people scattering right and left at the sight of the gun, but Anacleto was gone. When they got back to the corner, the Gypsies were gone too, a few battered carnations in the street the only testimony to their brilliantly disorderly prior presence.

Neighbors repeating the story later said this proved no goodness on the part of the Gypsies, because Anacleto had given them a hundred peseta note and got no change, quite a profit off a few buckets of carnations sold at one peseta the dozen. But then, someone like Rosa-Laura said, tartly and with such a temper that girl, "What exaggeration! Where did someone like Anacleto get a hundred peseta note? As if he carried them around with him all the time? And by the way, why was he buying carnations anyway? Funny thing to do for a guy supposed to be in hiding." Well, Rosa-Laura could defend the *desgraciados* of this earth and attribute kind intentions to them all she wanted, but who had ever seen a Gypsy do good for any good reason? And as for the flowers, to put on the grave of his poor mother, surely, like the dear loving son (and now, neighborhood hero) Anacleto was.

Stories like that helped the neighbors endure the cop's presence.

"Did you give enough?" the wife of the rent manager at the market place asked her husband after Bernardo left their office. "He'll send the garbage men to trash the back entrance, or have the cops overturn a few stands chasing some neighborhood boy through the main floor if you don't. Make sure all the vendors give him a basket, the best, the best."

"You want some of the girls to entertain you?" the manager of the Red Mill Night Club asked him when he came to collect. Bernardo smiled at him, his cold, tight-lipped, tilted grin that reminded the manager he knew all the secrets and could cash in any one of them at any time. Worse, Bernardo never took him up on his generous offer, though he told him to expect Silvio to show up and spend a free evening in the back room. It was a damned shame how that creature treated the girls and made it impossible for them to work until their bruises cleared up.

Bernardo took cigarettes—American blond, of course—from the kiosk in the plaza. The woman who ran it told the candy-seller by the metro bonnet, "I tell you, I gave him my only carton just so's he wouldn't accidentally tip my magazine stand over!"

Two months passed like this, and everyone was on edge.

Late one night, a Tuesday, or better said Wednesday, as it was three in the morning, Bernardo was waiting on a corner a block from the plaza, hidden back in a doorway, smoking a *Pall Mall*. He finished that one and used its glowering stub to light up another. He was wearing black kid gloves, hand-made for him, his camel-colored cashmere coat, which hung past his knees, and a doubled-breasted suit custom-made in one of the finest stores on the street now called José Antonio Primo de Rivera instead of La Gran Vía. At one point, he stepped out from the doorway into a shard of lamplight from down the street and checked his watch. Then he stepped back into the darkness and looked up at the sky. He could see some stars, for in a neighborhood this low-class there wasn't enough artificial light to dull them. A few ghostly scarves of cloud covered what was just a thin rib of moon.

He checked his watch again and said something under his breath. A scrawny cat wandered by and catching sight or scent or feeling of him, jumped in terror and took off, its mangy fur rising in a tense ridge from neck to tail. Again he glanced at his watch and took a long drag on the cigarette. He had smoked it only halfway, but he pulled out his pack, removed another, and lit it with the remainder of the one in his mouth.

He heard a car and looked up the street, but the car coming toward him had no lights on, and he squinted his eyes unconsciously, in an attempt to recognize it.

"Stupid fool, driving with no lights," Bernardo muttered. He stepped out from the doorway and walked into the light under the street lamp a building away. The driver flicked his fog lights on. The car stopped at the intersection, facing down the street toward the plaza, the motor running, the driver apparently hesitating. Bernardo snorted as if in disgust or perhaps impatience and took a step off the curb onto the cobblestones, his arm up to signal or halt the car, when it suddenly accelerated with a terrible voom and hurtled toward him. He opened his mouth wide in sudden astonishment and the cigarette dropped out. He jumped back, but the little sidewalk was very narrow, and there was no doorway close enough. The car struck him full on, barely three seconds having passed since it began its deadly trajectory, backed up over the body with a hard reverse, then accelerated forward over the body again. The driver flicked off the fog lights and took the dark corner of the tiny street so fast and with such carelessness, that he hit a hitching post and scrapped the corner of a building making a sharp turn into the plaza. The car then accelerated loudly across the plaza and down another street and was gone.

One of the neighbors threw open his window and shutters and shouted to the world, "I shit on your whore mothers, every one of you cuckold noisemakers and your fucking cars! Some of us are honest laborers and trying to sleep!"

No one joined in his protest or opened a window to commiserate or even lit a bedroom light, so he closed his shutters and window and went back to bed.

❧

The tobacco lady arrived that morning at six, to catch the commuters heading down the metro entrance to catch a train to work uptown or on the city outskirts. But to her intense surprise and no little fear, a crowd of policemen and a couple of official cars had blocked off the south-western corner of the plaza. She ambled over, ignoring the several commuters who were already lined up to buy their day's tobacco.

"Don't bother, Maria-Mártires, they ain't going to let you see it! We already tried!" her exasperated would-be customers called after her. She continued to ignore them. She saw the *sereno*; she knew he would exchange information for a pack of *Bisontes*.

"What we got?" She said, nudging him, her voice a whisper. There had to be at least twenty coppers there. They'd blocked off the street that emptied into the plaza at that point. It was a narrow street, last recobbled two centuries ago, with barely enough high-curbed sidewalk for one person, creaky old buildings bending over it, a strip of early morning light visible between the roofs. Some of the cops were standing to form a human barricade, facing the plaza and the tobacco lady, hands behind them, faces truly grim, furious even. Others just beyond them were walking around looking at things and talking to each other in low voices. Plain clothes cops and secret service agents were everywhere too, all in overcoats and well-shined black shoes. Everyone except the cops forming the barrier was smoking. She might make out well if they stayed long enough and needed more smokes—or, they might all, every one of the bastards, take a pack from her without paying.

"Careful, they already cleared everyone back. They're just as likely to arrest you as look at you," the *sereno* said. She saw how nervous, fidgety, he was. Who the hell in this neighborhood was important enough to warrant such a battalion?

"Come on," she said. "Who? What happened?"

He bent over to whisper in her ear. "Bernardo. I reported to him at midnight. Didn't see him again till the street cleaners came and got me this morning. *Four* a.m. Whore-shit, I suppose I'll be in questioning for a month over this. I might even have been the last one to see him—" He stopped because a break occurred in the police line as one cop was called back by another, and the tobacco vendor and the *sereno* both got a glimpse of what the street cleaners had found that morning:

Bernardo lay face up, spread eagled on the cobblestones, as gray and dead as a school lecture on good conduct. His cashmere overcoat fanned out wide, his hat and left shoe were nowhere to be seen, and the tobacco vendor saw in that quick glimpse of his head, twisted away from her at a very peculiar angle, that it was so mutilated it was unrecognizable.

"Mary, Mother of God," she said.

"Smashed to bits, flattened. Was a car, or a truck," the *sereno* whispered. "See how it stove in his head? I seen the body good, by the light of the garbage truck.

"No one got his wallet or the gun, or that coat. They just smashed into him, reversed over him, and ran it again. That's my reckoning. The other shoe is up the street, maybe where he was first hit. The Borsalino's over there in the doorway, but I didn't collect it. Didn't dare. You never know what the cops might pin on you."

The tobacco vendor nodded at his words. It occurred to her that though she might well have to give half her inventory that morning to the cops here, she would never have to worry about Bernardo's showing up again to ask her questions and take the only carton of her best blondes. The thought gave her a smile, despite the grisly scene, which now closed up behind the cops pulling together.

"Hey, you, woman, it's not a show, get the hell out of here," one called out to her. He glared at the *sereno*, who nodded and flapped his hand at her to back away.

⨳

Later on, the *sereno* stopped by her stand. She gave him another free pack of *Bisontes* and was all smiles. He lit up gratefully and told her, "What'd I tell you, Maria Mártires?—all evidence points to a car, a big one. It left some marks on the hitching poles taking a turn into the plaza too fast. Hit him, backed up, and hit him again, just like I said, then took off. Left plenty of skid marks. Just like I said! See, I could of been a copper if I'd wanted. Had good tires and was black."

The tobacco vendor nodded, storing all this information because she would be expected to reveal every word of it to her clients for the next couple of days until better news came along, though how it could get any better than this she didn't know. The last information the *sereno* had given her didn't surprise her any.

"Every car in Madrid is black, Don Faustino," she said to the *sereno*.

He was offended at this disrespect to his detective abilities and said haughtily, "Bits of paint stuck to the poles and the curbs and Bernardo. That's how we know."

⨳

Silvio showed up at his headquarters late that morning and was given the bad news. Where had he been, when he was supposed to be Bernardo's back-up? He told his superiors, behind closed doors, that he was over in the plaza in Embajadores waiting for his boss on order and had fallen asleep as the hours passed, though a colleague, an ordinary policeman who inadvertently shot his mouth off while trying to help, told the investigators that he'd seen Silvio with an attractive, well-endowed whore around midnight. He didn't see the need to add that often Bernardo was seen with the same girl; no need to speak ill of the dead. One story or the other, Silvio had an alibi. It was not unusual for Bernardo to roam the neighborhood without Silvio when it suited him, that's how brazen and unafraid of the neighborhood he was, and Silvio was a loyal, knowledgeable, and valuable agent for his government, a hero of Badajoz in fact, so that soon he was given Bernardo's job.

For a few horrible days the police questioned everyone and hauled a few people uptown. Rumors were flying like carrion birds. Then, just as suddenly as the investigation began, the police stopped it and let it be known—via *sereno*, tobacco vendor, market vendors, anyone who cared to listen to them and carry their version to the neighbors—that it was an accident, just something that had happened. The neighbors didn't much like that version at first, but then, "Ah, if it was really an accident, then it's God at work, see, it's divine justice—" and so forth. After all, it didn't really hurt the message of the story to transform a cold-blooded murderer into a drunk, confused driver. The bastard got his comeuppance one way or another. He deserved it, received it, harshly and justifiably, and not in the Devil's hell either but here on earth where all could enjoy it. Besides, it was by far the safest story for everyone concerned. After the tobacco vendor had repeated the part about the car backing up "to make sure" to several customers, the police visited her the next day, and she never again repeated that version of Bernardo's death.

༺༻

It worked out badly for Mili. Bernardo had given the envelope with her payoff to Silvio, and Silvio kept it. She didn't argue the point. The end result was that after missing a few rent payments, the landlady kicked Mili and her son out, and they had to bunk with Rosa-Laura, Sra. Rosa, and Rogelio.

Within a week, Emilio had broken every piece of crockery in the place, and emptied all the chamber pots on the tiled floors twice. The second time, Sra. Rosa grabbed him, spanked him hard, and then told him in terms even a three-year-old could understand that she'd kill him if he pulled a stunt like that again. She forgot her fine new elocution at the time, she was so mad, and sputtered out a great many *mierdas* and *bastardos*. Emilio hated her forever after that, but he feared her too and did stop distributing the contents of the chamber pots. When Mili got home and her baby told her that Auntie had hurt him and he hated her, Mili shouted at Aunt Rosa, but to her surprise, Aunt Rosa shouted back at her, and Rogelio moaned from his bed that they were all killing him. Rosa-Laura came home from work in the middle of this spectacular theatrical event and quickly hauled her cousin and baby cousin out for a long walk.

"Look, Mili, this is not working out. You have to leave, and soon. You know we love you and you know we can't have you here. It's impossible. Emilio is just too much for Mama to handle, and she has to get back to her job at the Contreras's, and my father is sick. Enough now, you can see this is not working out."

Mili said nothing, then began to cry. Rosa-Laura put one arm around her and hugged her as best she could while holding on to Emilio, who wanted to run into the street and destroy a car. He kicked Rosa-Laura as hard as he could, but she just kept her grip on him at arm's length.

"Oh, kid," Mili said, "It's such a mess! I should have let Bernardo take him, put him in a school, it would have been better for everyone. I just didn't think, you know, I wanted him with me, but it's too hard. I got to find a place for him, but he's mine, you know, he's my kid, and I'll miss him. But, I got to find work I guess. Or get married maybe. There's a couple of guys want to marry me. I just can't stand the idea, though, being tied down and all that."

Rosa-Laura sighed. She didn't blame Mili for not wanting to be married, but the woman had a child and needed help, not to mention some stability in that crazy life of hers. Maybe it was true that women needed husbands. Well, maybe not, look at her own mother—but Mili clearly was not doing well on her own.

It was late evening, a light mist was dropping over the buildings now gray and black instead of yellow and brown, and the taverns were fast filling. Lights and tinny music from a *verbena* in the Plaza Glorieta de Embajadores beckoned families, young lovers, gamblers, and men looking for company at the fair. Mili picked up her son with a sigh and kissed him three or four times. He stuck his thumb in his mouth and gripped her neck as if to never let her go or else, to strangle her. The two girls stood there in the penumbra, watching the lights, weeping, sentimental, until a couple of young dandies sauntered by and offered them a really good time, at which point Mili told them in no uncertain terms what they could do with their offer, their mother, their family, and their undersized penises.

Two long and miserable weeks later, Mili left and moved to a pensión at Chamberí, then entered Emilio in a nursery school there. It was an expensive proposition all in all, but Rosa-Laura and her mother knew better than to ask how she'd managed it.

Anacleto showed up one day on the steps of San Ginés Church, next door to her shop. She was sitting on a bench in the tiny patio of the church, resting before going to work from her long lunch-time, by herself, watching the street traffic on Arenal and ignoring the occasional man who passed by and asked her if she wanted company. Anacleto sat down next to her, without a word, and waited for her to speak.

Finally, she gave in and said, "All right, hello. What are you doing here, anyway?"

He cleared his throat and took a deep breath, as if summoning up his courage.

"Listen," he finally said. "I have to go. I shouldn't stay here in Madrid too long—"

"You've already stayed too long," she said. "After that business in the plaza last month—Mother of God, Anacleto, you've got to be tops on their suspect list. Can't you use your head and see that you're asking for trouble? If they get you, they'll keep you. No doubt. It's a mess, and I can't understand why you stick around!"

"I wanted to see you again," he said. "I followed you to work this morning."

"Phenomenal," she said. "Perfect. Silvio's been around the neighborhood. If he sees you..."

He tentatively touched her gloved hand next to him on the bench. She snatched it back and crossed her arms. She wouldn't look at him after that.

"Rosa-Laura, it's always been you. Always. I swear it. I know you're mad about Mili, but I never asked Mili to bother me."

"Right, and you didn't tell her not to, either, did you?" Rosa-Laura said. A couple of older women passed right by them on their way to the church and glanced at them. Both frowned.

"I came back to Madrid to take care of my mother's business with

Bernardo."

"I certainly do not want to hear about that. Watch what you say, for God's sake."

"I stayed because I saw you—I watched you, almost every day. I wonder—can't you give me some hope? I'm going back now, to see my brother and return something I borrowed from my boss, and then I'll leave the country. I'll go to Switzerland. There's jobs there. It's a beautiful, clean country, with lots of jobs for guys like me. I know other Spaniards who've gone, and I'm a hard worker. I'll save money, I'll buy you a house there, or here, or anywhere you want. I love you."

She finally turned at looked at him, but her voice was as hard as the seventeenth century stone church standing behind them. "Anacleto, are you asking me to marry you?"

"Yes. That's it exactly. Marry me. Now or later, just give me some hope."

"No. I don't love you. And that's that. And don't tell me I'm mean. Why should I get your hopes up for nothing? That would be truly mean. I know I'm supposed to marry someone, but I don't want to, and I don't want to marry you."

He had absolutely nothing in the way of a reply to this granite answer. Rosa-Laura stood up. "Look, I've got to go back to work. Get out of Madrid, don't be stupid. Don't give up your life because of a crush on a girl in the neighborhood who doesn't love you back. Leave the country. Marry some pretty Swiss girl, one of those nice blondes they have over there. Forget me. Forget Spain, for God's sake."

"Is it because you think I'm a murderer?"

"Oh my. I never believed you did it. Any of it."

He got up too and then turned to head in the opposite direction, but then he turned back for a moment and said, "I might've. I have it in me."

"We probably all do," she said. "Still, I don't believe it. Will you be with Augustín?"

Anacleto nodded. He was staring at her, as if to imprint the memory of her face forever in his mind.

She looked away from him at the street. She loved this street. It was always busy and had a kind of sheen to it, a stucco, tile, and cobblestone patina that made each shop and the signs they all affected in Art Deco squiggles or conservative block patterns so familiar and comforting. No trees hung over its narrow corridor, nor any plants draped the balconies, no bright colors dressed it up, and the people passing by all wore black. Yet, it was colorful in its way. Vivid in its age and dignity. She loved each street lamp, black iron, shiny and scroll-worked, nineteenth century in design, though most of them were quite new now that gas lamps were being replaced with more modern electric street lights in every neighborhood. It took money to live in this neighborhood, even though it was noisy and full of businesses, on this little street that led directly to Opera Plaza and then over to the royal palace. It wasn't overtly elegant and upper class like Princesa or Serrano, but it felt to her that history had walked its paving stones: knights and kings and ladies-in-waiting, crowds on their way to a fair or an execution in the Plaza Mayor, armies and tradesmen and delivery boys, ladies with Manila shawls wrapped all silky around beautiful shoulders.

"I found our father," Anacleto said.

This sudden turn in the conversation shocked her. "Where? He's alive? No one thought he was alive."

"He spent two years in a prisoner of war camp. Few survive that. He's living in the town where we're staying now. He never had any intention of returning to Mama. In fact, he married again."

"When?"

"When Mama was still alive. He told the priest she was dead, and well, what with the war and all, they didn't ask Papa for a death certificate, just took his word. She's a quiet woman, like Mama was, but not pretty at all. Papa said he'd had enough with pretty women. Told me to never marry a pretty woman. Said they live in their own world and never love you the way you love them. I guess it's true."

"Good-bye, Anacleto. God be with you."

"Rosa-Laura?"

"Now what?"

"Nothing. I'm not begging, don't you worry about that. I won't bother you anymore."

She walked away from him and entered her shop. He watched her and then stood and watched the shop.

"Girl," he said in a low voice to the air around him, "someday you're going to love someone like I love you, and it's going to be a disaster. I'm sorry it has to be that way and sorry for you."

But mostly, he was sorry for himself.

Finally, he walked away, and neither Rosa-Laura or anyone else in the neighborhood ever saw him again.

She hadn't planned to be so cruel, but she did care about Anacleto's welfare, and she wanted him out of the country. The best way to get him on his way, safe, was to demolish any hope of her ever loving him, and she was as good as demolishing hope in young men as she was at ripping out a badly sewn seam.

Two tailors at the shop had also asked her to marry them, young men with bright futures in the industry ahead of them. The first one was chinless, wore big glasses and was terribly shy, so she'd been much kinder to him when she said no than she had to her ex-neighbor and playmate. The second tailor looked like Raf Vallone, an Italian movie star she thought handsome but very much the rogue. (Most of his movies couldn't be shown in Spain, they were so scandalous. The censors would have had to cut ninety percent of them to ribbons.) That boy she treated even more coolly than she had treated Anacleto. He had other girls, she knew, and her vanity was stung by this.

After all that, she'd begun to loathe being in that shop, and could barely say *"Buenos"* to anyone when she entered or left. Her bad temper had vexed her so that one day, she skipped work and went to look at the shop for sale in Embajadores that she had seen some time ago. The sign was still up, yellowed now with the long siestas of full sunshine that had shone on it.

She knew that lots of women in Spain had their own businesses. Well, not "lots," but still—most market vendors were women. Women ran small shops all over the capital, grocery stores, sundries' shops, bakeries. Catalan women owned factories too. Admittedly, the latter were rich women. Dr. Contreras had once mentioned to her that he knew two women who owned a toy factory and a scissors factory. It was rumored Franco's wife owned *Gallerias Preciados*, an elegant department store in the center of town. Of course, she was hardly a role model for someone like Rosa-

Laura. But still, Rosa-Laura wasn't setting any sort of precedence. Spanish women had owned shops for centuries and still did, despite society's emphasis on home, children, and church as well as the prevailing laws that favored men in everything but especially in business, politics, and religion. Rosa-Laura considered all this, but she also considered the fact that most of the women in her own neighborhood were downright viragos, if not amazons. Why shouldn't she run her own business?

The shop boasted an inventory of three machines, a good supply of excellent cloth, and a small but very regular and solvent clientele. The owner was patient, as he had to be, but he wanted to retire. She made him an offer, based on every bit of her savings. He was suspicious, given her appearance and gender. She swore to him that she was over twenty-one, and more importantly, that her parents would co-sign any agreement made. This argument, his desire to be gone, and the money convinced him finally, though he kept looking her over as if she were a new kind of unsewable strange cloth the like of which he'd never seen before in his entire life.

She walked out of that shop owning it, then walked up Tribulete Street, passed her home, and visited her father in the plaza to make sure he was all right and doing well (he looked ill, but then, these days he often looked ill). Then she walked back home. Mama was still at work. Noon floated by like a boat in a cloudy winter lake. She plopped down on her cot for a siesta and suddenly burst into tears, an attack of nerves, frustration, joy, terror, all of it.

Soon after her business deal, she effected another transformation: she cut off her waist length hair for a cropped, boyish, highly fashionable style called a "piksi," a foreign word no one knew the meaning of. It was 1954, the American movie "Roman Holiday," dubbed in Spanish, had finally arrived at the best theaters, and every girl wanted to look like its young star, Audrey Hepburn. Rosa-Laura actually did look like her, especially with her new haircut. Carmen-Victoria even called her "*Owdray*" when she wanted to make her laugh.

The refusal to marry times three, the gamble of quitting her job, buying a shop at her young age, the cropping of her luxuriant hair—her mother had nearly collapsed with the shock, then recuperated as she always did, and seemed to resign herself to her daughter's craziness, after a while mentioning it only three or four times a week. The business proved hard with long hours but began to do well even under female ownership. She advertised for another seamstress and a tailor, with quite a few applications in job-hungry Madrid. The old owner did have a few clients, not many, but they had stayed with the shop, and she even attracted some clientele from the better side of town. Her old boss claimed she'd robbed them from his business, but she'd done nothing like that at all, they just showed up one day.

Yet, Rosa-Laura was not satisfied and she was not happy, and her mother told her it was because she needed a husband.

"You've turned down two good prospects," Sra. Rosa said to her. "The offers won't keep coming in forever."

"Your mother never married," Rosa-Laura said. It was a touchy topic, but she was not trying to bait her mother. It was just something she'd been thinking about lately.

They were in the *Chocolatería de San Ginés*, a café near her old workplace that oozed sugary, chocolate smells out into the alleyway of the Pasaje San Ginés and every day attracted Madrileños by the hundreds to its marble tables and long bar. It was late Sunday morning, and they'd walked uptown after Mass, then decided to treat themselves.

Sra. Rosa held her cup of chocolate and stared into it, looking for all the world as if she was reading something at the bottom of the velvety puddle. "Look, daughter, it's the same story as Mili, my mother was just a woman who wanted her own way, that's all. She knew the rules, she didn't like them, she broke them. It didn't take bravery or wisdom or thought, she just did it because she wanted to and had only herself to think of. She hated other women and considered them rivals or scores for her loan business. I don't think she was all that happy, because she got bested by a man above her station, and he left her just like that, without a thought. And,

Emilia and I were miserable. We were fatherless, and people looked down on us. You know we couldn't even get into a school. You know how we lost our inheritance. When the Republic came, there was big talk of schools for everyone, government-run, not church, and women could get divorces, and all the rest of it. But it was just talk, or at the least, they never got the chance to bring it all about." She dropped her voice and checked around to make sure no one was listening to all these conspiratorial confidences,

Rosa-Laura shook her head slightly, then signaled to the waiter she was ready to pay for their breakfast. When she finished, her mother was lost in thought and the look on her face was that old one, that pinched, tight, what-can-be-done-about-it-anyway look.

"Would you like to walk toward Atocha? Maybe visit El Retiro?" Rosa-Laura said.

"Oh, sure," said Sra. Rosa.

They both wrapped their scarves around their necks and went out. Rosa-Laura had on a hat, a simple black straw pillbox with a short veil. She had grown to love hats now that they sat so comfortably on her head.

They reached Atocha and strolled down the boulevard, enjoying the perfect day, neither hot nor cold, still and calm in that queenly way the air of Madrid had, nothing of a breeze to ruffle the royal mien. The acacias, locusts, London planes, and sycamores lining the street glimmered lime-green and silver with new leaves and the rich season.

"Stop banging that bald head of yours against walls," Sra. Rosa suddenly said to her daughter. Evidently, she had been stewing over Rosa-Laura's words. "There's rules to be followed, and quite a few you can't get out of, no matter how smart you are. You've done well, daughter, better than I could have hoped. Try to be happy."

Rosa-Laura didn't know what to say. Everyone thought that she was brilliant to have her own business, to be able to come and go as she pleased, with no boss (as if a demanding, fussy client weren't a boss). Yet, they felt sorry for her because she was unwed.

Nothing quite seemed right these days. Spring infuriated her. Saturday afternoon movies took away the bite but their illusion didn't last, and she was lonely, yet she didn't at all understand why she should be. She had her Mama, her Papa, friends, and her wonderful business. What could be lacking? Not a man, surely, because she felt nothing but fear and contempt when it came to men. Carmen-Victoria would talk about how she'd felt when she first saw Eduardo (who was getting a pot belly and a haggard look already, and barely twenty-five), and Rosa-Laura would listen politely and fail to understand. Worst of all, her own mother, who had suffered so terribly when she married, was now urging her to look for a husband and insisting she needed one. When she was able to escape the shop, Rosa-Laura went looking for new hats and the latest movie shows instead. She always took a friend with her on these excursions, Carmen-Victoria, if one of her sisters could baby-sit the kids. Rosa-Laura liked the company but more to the point, walking alone invited unwanted attention from every wild young bachelor and quite a few married men too. The scene frightened her and angered her too. She had no illusions about all the attention, because every woman between the ages of twelve and ninety-nine walking down a street in Spain these days got *piropos,* propositions and gestures from men hungry for women and drowning in the religious and political waters of the world they had created, inherited, or received as the outcome of losing the war.

"Let's go to the museum, Mama," she said. "Let's look at paintings all afternoon."

"You'd think you'd get enough of those in Church," her mother said. But she smiled at her daughter, and they turned at Castellana when they reached the bottom of Atocha, then headed toward the Prado.

Dr. Contreras was considering retiring but hadn't an idea what he would do with himself if he did. His sister, he was sure, would live forever and thoroughly enjoy her dementia, even when it manifested in nervous outbursts and nightmares. He hoped to outlive her so that she wouldn't have to be alone, and for that he needed some rest and some peace

He considered options. His patients, Quica and Isabel, had a large property in Guadalajara that they wanted to sell, and he was tempted. Guadalajara in the summer was hot, yet gorgeous with wild daisies, rock rose, tawny hillsides redolent of rosemary and pine. Maybe he could grow vines. Or at least, peppers and tomatoes. Would Guillermina be able to exist in the countryside? She was a child of the asphalt, and he really couldn't imagine her resettling outside the city.

Another option was the coast above Barcelona. Gorgeous. An extension of the French Riviera and just as beautiful if not more. He could learn to oil-paint and become one of those artists he admired and envied. He could drive back and forth to Barcelona. Guillermina might get used to Barcelona. They could study Catalán together. She liked languages and fancied she could speak French. Of course, Catalán was a forbidden language, but in the countryside so close to France, who would care about some retirees practicing new words?

"I'm thinking of driving up north to the coast in a few weeks," he said to Sra. Rosa. "I'm going to look at a property in Lloret de Mar."

"Driving?" Sra. Rosa said. This was the first she'd ever heard of driving. The Doctor always took taxis. They were cheap by his standards, fast, and easy to hire. One walked down to one's fine avenue, a taxi passed by very soon after, and one held up one's hand. Sra. Rosa had seen him do it a million times.

"You mean you'll hire a car and driver, Doctor, instead of going by train?"

He smiled at her benignly. "No, Sra. Rosa, I have a car of my own. I use it seldom, but now and then we go to La Granja because my sister likes the palace, and once we went to Segovia. Surely you remember that year we went to Segovia? We were gone an entire week."

"Sir, I'm very surprised. I thought you'd gone by train. When did you learn to drive?"

"To tell you the truth, I've known how since I was an adolescent. A friend of mine taught me. He had an Hispano-Suiza. Magnificent vehicle. We drove in the countryside. Of course, in those days there was less traffic than now, but I've never had problems. I keep a Mercedes coupe in the garage underneath the apartment building down the street, the one they built after the war. I never use it in the city of course. Madrid wasn't made for cars, really, except for the boulevards. Even now there are far too many taxis. They'll have to regulate them soon and keep them out of the center. I'm not sure Madrid, or any other city in Europe for that matter, will ever have much use for cars."

Sra. Rosa nodded. He was right of course. "It's hard to think of you driving, Sir. Why haven't you hired a chauffeur?"

"Actually, I like to drive. It gives me a nice feeling. Powerful, too. Our roads are awful, of course, but Mercedes have spectacular suspension systems. I'll drive to Lloret slowly and stop often, so I'll be gone at least a week. You must deal with Guillermina, of course."

Sra. Rosa nodded. Guillermina might fuss and complain at times, but she was amenable to Sra. Rosa's every suggestion ("Come now, Srta., it's time for a siesta. It's time for your bath. It's time to have tea. It's time to read. Let's rearrange all your dolls." And so forth) and never fought with her. Sra. Rosa played the role of beloved old auntie to her charge. Sometimes Guillermina would bring her friends, "the girls," over to the house for afternoon tea, and Sra. Rosa would spend the morning buying fine pastries, the best fruit, elegant foreign "sandwiches" from the *fiambre* stores. She liked doing that, and she liked the parties too. They created a good deal of clean-up and lasted for hours, but they made Guillermina so happy, and Sra. Rosa found herself enjoying listening to these crazy old women gossiping and gesticulating and devouring food and tea as if there were no tomorrow.

Every now and then, even Dr. Contreras attended them, which delighted the ladies, who adored him. Somehow, he fit in and didn't mind that he was entirely more educated and intelligent than the rest of the gathering, not to mention saner. They flirted with him and fussed over him, and he felt content.

He even felt happy these days. He had cut down his practice and devoted himself to his poorer patients. He had been given a huge party at the hospital in appreciation of his years of service, and it had touched him greatly. He talked to Sra. Rosa about it, and she'd noticed his eyes were slightly damp. They'd given him a crystal clock, a beautiful Swiss thing, that now sat in the dining room with all the other knick-knacks. He wound it up weekly and smiled in contentment when it rang on the hour. Sra. Rosa took to cleaning it with vinegar until both the Doctor and the Señorita complained about the smell, so she desisted and cleaned it with elbow grease only.

Sra. Rosa was very grateful that things had quieted down. True, Rogelio was ill and not getting better, and that would have to be faced, but her daughter was doing well and Mili seemed to be prospering and didn't visit more often than was necessary. She herself had settled in to the Contreras household like a hermit crab in a big golden conch; it may not have begun as her home, but it fit now, fit as much as the basement apartment.

What Sra. Rosa would always privately refer to as her daughter's downfall began innocently enough. The interior of Rosa-Laura's shop was small so sometimes in the warm weather she and her two assistants, Maria-Carolina and Maria-Mercedes would sit outside in the sunlit plaza and sew. Sunlight was better than shop light and certainly less expensive. On really warm days she didn't wear hosiery. After all, it was her own shop, and if she couldn't go bare-legged in her own shop, what was the use of owning it? She'd stretch out her legs in the sunlight and tan them, she'd sew, gossip with Lina and Merche, and feel very good. People would pass by, the women would look and comment to each other in low voices and keep on sewing. Sometimes instead of resting at siesta time (they all lived close by), they'd stroll the avenues together and look into store windows.

Once in a while, Carmen-Victoria would visit and stroll with them too. But that wasn't happening as much as Rosa-Laura would have liked any more, because her best friend had three children now, and it had become harder and harder to get a sister or her mother to baby-sit all of them at once. Eduardo and Vicky, as Carmen-Victoria called herself these days, had finally managed to move into an apartment with three extremely small yet marvelously separate rooms, well below Atocha and close to Vallecas. Rosa-Laura visited them at least twice a month and sewed clothing for the children or brought knitted goods her mother had made. Vicky seemed to think of her best friend as a sort of spinster auntie to her brood nowadays.

Ah well, maybe Rosa-Laura was jealous. But of what? The yearning persisted, that great empty stretch in her life that no amount of thinking or working or calculating numbers could fill. Next month she would be twenty-six. Older than her mother had been when she'd married. All her school friends were married now and had begun amplifying their families with a vengeance. Even Mili's family was growing, though she had not married. Mili would always have a man, and the primary man for some time now had been Silvio. She'd already had one child by him, and was pregnant with a second. Emilio attended a military academy "like his father wanted." How she'd managed that without proper papers for the kid was anybody's guess, though Silvio's influence could not be discounted.

Lina and Merche weren't married, but they were twenty and twenty-one respectively, and Merche was engaged. Rosa-Laura looked younger than either of them. The girls called her "The Boss" as if it were a big joke, but they were hard-working girls and awed at how well Rosa-Laura managed the business, so they all got along. Yet, Rosa-Laura felt much older. Maybe by about a hundred million years.

One day as the women sat outside in the sunlight finishing a wedding gown, Rosa-Laura happened to look up and over at the café two doors down. It wasn't noon yet, but all the *terraza* tables were full in the late morning at the start of a hot Madrid July. The denizens of the café were mostly men, though there were a few couples. She was glancing at each table without seeing, when suddenly she could not look any further.

He was tall and thin. Over six feet, an impossible height in this town of half-starved war children, stunted women, and crippled veterans. He had black hair combed straight back in a somewhat old-fashioned forties' style, a long face, hollow cheeks, large dark eyes under heavy eyebrows, a scornful mouth. Pale skin. He wore a nice felt hat, not a worker's cap, and a jacket carelessly slung over his shoulders. His white shirt had been ironed and starched by an expert, probably his mother, but an expert neverthe-less. He looked just like a famous bullfighter who had been killed several years ago, but younger and handsomer. The bullfighter had been an ugly man, yet very compelling, a romantic figure who plunged the whole coun-try into mourning when he last tempted fate in a bullring in Linares.

The man seated in the café presented an arresting figure. Amaz-ing posture, even seated, as if he'd trained for it. There was something familiar about that kind of posture, but it didn't occur to her just then, even though she'd already made the connection to the matador who had died so spectacularly in Linares. Rosa-Laura stared at him for a couple of seconds, her eyes widening in response to an urge she didn't even know she was capable of, when he suddenly looked directly at her. His gaze clearly told her he knew he was being looked at and was used to being looked at, indeed, *expected* to be looked at. She flushed hot pink and dropped her gaze immediately. Whatever words had been on her lips wilted and died like green damsel flies in the heat.

"What is it, Rosa-Laura?" Lina said.

"I—I'm feeling a little warm. Too much sun. Maybe I'd better get inside," Rosa-Laura said. She glanced at the café again, but he was still looking right at her, and now, curse it, he was smiling. She looked down at her sewing, took a deep breath to stabilize herself and regain some dignity, then got up and walked inside, slowly, her posture as erect as a spring lily. Her two assistants glanced at each other then looked at the café, but they saw nothing they hadn't seen before.

This miserable game went on for about a month. Just looking. Every time he'd catch her glance at him, she'd drop her head to her sewing, ashamed. Pretty soon, Lina and Merche caught on, and Merche said, "It's the big guy, isn't it? I don't blame you. He's some looker. He works at the turbine factory over at the Toledo gates. I know someone there. Sometimes he comes to the café too and sits with that guy. He told me the guy trained to be a matador but couldn't finish. I could ask my friend for an introduction."

"Don't be ridiculous. That's all I need now, a distraction just before autumn when the suit orders will be coming in," Rosa-Laura said.

Lina and Merche smiled. In this neighborhood they got maybe ten winter suit orders a year. It wasn't as if the shop were on Recoletos Street or the Alcalá. In this neighborhood they got wedding dresses, a hundred a year, and it was the end of July, way past June and weddings, but in August they often got the orders from girls who'd been seduced during the sweet springtime and needed wedding dresses, fast, with a very high waistline. Rosa-Laura would dart a few glances, then get up and go inside, then come out again a few seconds later. When the big guy was seated at his table, the boss couldn't sit still for a minute.

"Hey, Lina," Merche said a few days later, "I got an idea. It's the boss's birthday next week, and I told her mother I'd bring a cake to the shop. Sra. Rosa's going to make her late to work that day so it'll be a surprise. What if I asked my friend to come on over and bring the big guy?"

"Phenomenal," Lina said. "And bring one over for me too, or a couple of them."

The girls giggled and glanced over at the café. He wasn't watching the shop now that Rosa-Laura had gone inside. They looked at each other knowingly. "This is going to be fun," Lina said.

She felt like an idiot. It was June 13, Saint Anthony's day, and Carmen-Victoria had insisted she come. The day was warm, inclining toward hot. Thre was no shade, and the crowd was sizable. She stood off to one side of the patio of the Ermita San Antonio de la Florida, surrounded by both older and younger woman all dressed as *chulas*, the girls of Madrid, the colorful characters of a *zarzuela*, in fin de siécle polka-dotted and ruffled tight dresses, black silk shawls heavily embroidered with bright red, green, yellow, and blue flowers and trailing fringe two inches long, high button boots—the works. They knew how to use their fans, they all wore garish head scarves in the babushka style, they were all talking loudly in the deep guttural tones of the working class women of Madrid. Rosa-Laura wished she hadn't come to the church. She was embarrassed. She was ashamed. She wasn't in costume, but she did sport the *mantón de manila*, the colorful shawl, a nice one she had gotten fairly cheaply at the flea market last week. She was an idiot. If her mother could see her now!

"Have you tried for a pin yet?" Vicky said. She was giggly and excited. A sister was caring for her children, so she had the day off more or less, and outings like this were rare for her.

A marble bowl on a pedestal, like a fount for holy water, stood in the church patio, but it held straight pins, a pile of them. Rosa-Laura sighed, accepted the fact that she *had* come here after all and not just at Vicky's urging. Maybe afterward they could go inside and check out Goya's murals. She had heard they were phenomenal. She walked over to the fount, waited her turn behind a line of giggling women, old and young, and when it was her turn she closed her eyes and plunged her palm flat down on the pins, hard. Sure enough, when she lifted her moist palm from the pile of pins, several stuck to it. Well, will miracles never cease?

"Oh, a sign, a sign!" Vicky said. Rosa-Laura shook her head, exasperated, and pocketed the pins.

The pins told her she would get a husband. Since she and Luís had been seeing each other for almost a year now, it wasn't much of a stretch in the way of prophecies. The problem was, she loved him but was not all that sure he loved her. It was awful, loving someone. It had happened so suddenly, she hadn't been prepared at all, she had not expected this, she had no idea what had hit her and why she could not control it.

A San Antonio
Como es un santo casamentero
Le pide el matrimonio
Yamor sincero.

Vamos a la verbena de San Antonio
Que por ser la primera
No hay que faltar.

Since Saint Anthony
Is the saint of marriages
Ask him for matrimony
And true love.

Let's go to Saint Anthony's fair.
We shouldn't miss it,
As it's the first.

Somewhere around the back of this little church and up a hill was a grave-yard that few people ever saw. Only forty-three people were buried in it, the same forty-three shot by a French firing squad on May 3, 1808, and made famous by Goya's painting. The Ermita San Antonio de la Florida and its amazing murals served as the parish church of Príncipe Pío, the neighborhood where the executions had taken place over two days. Rosa-Laura had seen Goya's painting many times in the Prado. Her mother had told her about the graveyard one day after both of them had visited the museum on a Sunday and then sat in El Retiro Park by the pond and fed popcorn to the pigeons.

"No one knows it's there," Sra. Rosa had said to her daughter. "Seems sad, I guess, but that's your country for you. We don't want to learn anything from our history. I don't know why that is, but we're a hardheaded lot, we are." She tossed another puff of corn to the avian crowd cooing and fluttering around them. She had told Rosa-Laura once that somehow she associated the filthy birdies with the day Rosa-Laura was born, but she wasn't sure why.

࿐

Vicky nudged Rosa-Laura hard and said, "Mother Mary, girl, don't go all pensive on us now. It's not the time. Let's get inside and pray to St. Anthony for a husband."

Rosa-Laura sighed again. The pins in her pocket pricked at her thigh.

Arturo thought Lloret de Mar magnificent. It had a Roman fortification, like many towns on the Costa Brava, and the sea curved like liquid jade around a harbor full of fishing boats. Ancient, very ancient, and surely it would never change. No one in the world knew about the Costa Brava; it was the same as it had been a thousand years ago and would surely always remain so. Lloret was close enough to Barcelona so that if he hired a regular chauffeur, Guillermina could go shopping on the Ramblas every day if she wished. And best of all, he'd found a farmhouse a few kilometers from the sea that could be converted into a very nice country place for them. It was smaller than their home in Madrid, but then, the house in Madrid was too big for the two of them anyway.

The only thing that bothered him about all these big plans was the matter of Sra. Rosa. Now that her daughter was going to get married (and that had happened rather suddenly, hadn't it? He hoped the girl wasn't pregnant or anything. She didn't seem the type, but then that family did have a wild side to it, an embarrassing indication of their roots), Sra. Rosa probably wouldn't want to leave Madrid. Perhaps he should just accept the fact she was more than a servant but less than a relative and ask her to keep the house in Madrid clean and ready for their forays back to the city. She had told him once she hated to travel anyway.

They had family in Barcelona. The mother was his mother's second cousin, her paternal uncle's granddaughter. He didn't like that branch of the family very much, because they tended to look down their noses at his mother: Dolores del Valle, Sra. de Montero, had caused something of a family scandal with her three husbands. Yet, they had welcomed Arturo with open arms when he visited that afternoon and looked him up and down and pronounced him young and prosperous looking. A kindly familial lie. They'd made him a good dinner, with *romesçu*, of course, you couldn't get away from it here in what had been Catalonia before the war, but the fish had been superb and the vegetables exquisite. The sauce had given him heartburn and gas.

Their youngest son was not at home, and the mother had apologized. He had felt an air of unease or paranoia, but could not define it. Later, as he was about to leave, the boy returned home.

They were all in the salon, a large room with high ceilings, oriental carpets, and red velvet curtains. Its French windows overlooked the neighborhood square. The salon reflected a house that was clearly the prime property of a rich and important family. The family had asked the Doctor to stay with them, of course, but he had already booked a hotel room and besides, he knew they felt uncomfortable with him. Damn them. Did they know? Or was it something else? When the boy walked in around midnight, just as the Doctor was getting up to leave, the Doctor realized the unease was instinctive, not the result of any firm knowledge.

The boy was no more than sixteen, a bit wild or surly-looking as boys at that age can be. He was as beautiful as Orpheus, black-haired and black-eyed, of average height, fidgety, and pouting. If it weren't for all the restlessness, he would have been fit to be one of those statues brought up from the sea by fishermen in the area now and then, in this old Latin outpost.

There was something else about him too.

Well, the myth was that people like the Doctor could recognize others like himself; he'd believed that myth once long ago, but hated to test it, because to make a mistake and insult a man would have been lethal. Yet, men had spoken to him, indicated that they had recognized him. He had wondered over the years if he was too passive, too restricted, but at the same time, he felt ferocious, even now, at his age, determined to survive, determined to do his work and live his life and protect his family as a man should. He *mattered* in this very society that despised his kind. People cared about him and people respected him. No one could take that away.

The boy was presented to the Doctor as José-Maria Alejandro, his elaborate given name designed to capture and carry on the essence of both grandfathers.

The two older sisters, one nearly as pretty as Guillermina had been in her prime, rushed to coddle the boy. He scowled at them all, yet appeared to like his position as the spoiled youngest son. He kissed his mother's hand and stood, hands crossed in back, before his father, who expressed anger that the boy had not been at home at dinner.

"Your brother is upstairs studying. You may excuse yourself and join him," the father said.

Dismissed thus, the boy bowed slightly, formally, at the assemblage, and said, "IT was a pleasure to meet you, Doctor," in a rich young voice. He'd turned to climb the broad oak staircase that ended in penumbra one floor up.

"Alí, Alí, don't forget that tomorrow afternoon you're taking me to the cinema. You promised," the prettiest sister said to him.

The Doctor had almost fainted. He whitened, noticeably, and his mother's cousin said. "Arturo, are you all right?"

He nodded, smiled, recovered, and said, "I'm afraid I'm very tired. It's been a long day for me. I've been driving since quite early this morning and all, you know." He didn't add that the dinner was heavy, his stomach was rebelling furiously, nor did he add that he was terribly, embarrassingly, hotly infatuated with their beautiful young son.

The next day he asked around until he found the cinema where they would attend the matinee and sat in a café across the street. Of course, they'd seen him, as it was not that big a street or that big a café, and had come over to salute him. He was in agony.

He was too old. Much too old. Besides, the boy had a friend, an utterly charming creature who'd accompanied Alí and his sister to the cinema. The sister probably thought her brother's friend was interested in her, the way girls stupidly think these things without realizing.

Arturo wasn't even jealous. My God, he found himself thinking, this child must take care. He is rebellious, but he must contain himself. I must speak to him. But was his desire to speak just fatherly concern? Well, it had to be. He was far too old for this business, he was tired, he had established a routine that suited him and made him happy even. But he would establish contact with the boy, he would talk to him, he would let the boy know he was there for him. In cases like this, a father was unapproachable, a mother doting but consciously blind. The boy needed an older friend. Thinking over all that, he felt better.

When the film was over, the young people left the theater and found that their mother's cousin had left the café.

Sra. Rosa came down to the Plaza Glorieta de Embajadores one afternoon shortly after St. Anthony's Day to spy on her daughter's boyfriend.
Rosa-Laura had told her mother everything after going to the Ermita San
Antonio de la Florida on its saint's day and then wept childishly. Sra. Rosa
reacted like a boat overtaken by a sudden storm. She wanted her daughter
to marry, of course, because marry she must, but the whole thing nause-
ated her, especially since Rosa-Laura seemed so miserable and confused at
the time of her "confession."

Of course, Rosa-Laura would not bring a boyfriend home to meet
her parents until marriage was in the works and the engagement ready
for parental approval. Any other behavior would have been inappropriate,
even libertine, so, Sra. Rosa snuck off to the café to get a glimpse of him.

She sat down sat at a sidewalk table, the only woman there. When
the waiter, a typically lazy bastard with a big wen on his nose, probably
a sign from God of his unutterable worthlessness, finally realized she was
not going to leave, he sauntered over and asked her what she wanted to
order. She said, "*Gaseosa*, and don't bother with the *tapas*," as if the shiftless
beast were going to bring appetizers to a lone female customer who clearly
wasn't there to spend much money.

She saw her daughter's shopfront from her table and Lina and Merche
seated outside, chattering away. If stitches were words, those girls would
have sewn up the world a year ago. She also saw the particular table where
he sat facing the shop. And him, in profile. Quite a profile it was, too. His
hair was obscured by that fine hat. What kind of working man wore a hat
that nice? Or wore a tailored jacket, and cape-style at that? You dressed
your station in life, you did, but not this one.

As much as she feared men, as much as she thought she knew them
better than she deserved to, she had to admit she favored men too. They
had it easier because they were better, and they were better because that's

how life was. This man was the prize of the lot, handsome, tall to judge by the long legs in those nice slacks (again, why did he dress so well?), fine hands with long fingers, pale skin, a straight patrician nose, his lips curled in a sardonic half-smile, his mien entirely too self-satisfied. From the air of him, the elegance, fine clothes, calm disdain, she'd bet he was used to inspiring regard in others. Your typical Spanish attitude of entitlement, in its most extreme form. *¡Viva Yo!* She had seen the attitude in women as well, but she had always thought it suited a man more. What was the use of a woman being bold in a world that would slam you across the plaza for doing so?

"Please, God," she prayed silently, "please let him love her too. Please don't let him break her. Please. Please. Let him be good underneath all that damned arrogance."

She never asked herself why this had to happen, because she knew it just did. That was life for you. You got a little happy, a little rich, a little too pleased with your circumstances, and life slammed you against a wall, to face a firing squad. *Amor, amor, malo el principio y el fin peor.* Love, love, bad the beginning and worse the end.

Rogelio dressed himself slowly, fighting nausea and lightheadedness as well as the desire to just give up and lie down again. Rosa-Laura had sewn him a fine new suit, black, of course; he had been in mourning since Laura died twenty-seven and a half years ago and continued so as the deaths had mounted up through the years. That morning his daughter had left him a tiny spray of orange blossoms for his buttonhole, and he set it there now. The smell of the blossoms served to keep his nausea at bay. Sra. Rosa waited for him, patiently, on the other side of his screen. His daughter had early rushed off to Carmen-Victoria's house, where she would don the extravagant wedding dress Lina and Merche had sewn for her. Sra. Rosa had supervised the sewing and complained frequently to him about how incompetent her daughter's employees were and how useless.

"Well, why doesn't she sew her own dress?" he'd finally said, which was when he learned he was hopelessly ignorant of the rules of weddings. He hadn't known it was bad luck for a woman to sew her own wedding gown. "But my Laura sewed hers," he'd then said. Sra. Rosa's silence at this bit of information told him her belief had been corroborated, stunningly.

He felt around for his shoes and could not find them. He nearly got down on his knees to search under his bed before he realized that he might dirty his new pants doing so, despite Sra. Rosa's immaculate floor, cleaned daily. He squatted instead and swept his right hand under the bed while holding on to the bed with his left. No good.

"Sra. Rosa," he said. He grunted with the effort. "I can't find my shoes."

They walked to San Lorenzo about half an hour later. Sra. Rosa deposited him in a front pew and left to take a taxi to Carmen-Victoria's house, where everyone awaited her. Rosa-Laura would not leave the house until her mother had checked everything over and pronounced her fit for the ceremony. He took a deep breath and registered all the sounds and smells and feelings of the church. An altar boy scurried by, late perhaps. The sacristan, by contrast, was lighting candles and moving vases of flowers, his comings and goings measured, steady, quiet, as befitted a man with a duty tending the antechamber to the hereafter.

Beyond the front door of the smells of smoke, incense, and flowers, lay the deeper smells of musty brocade and old wood, stone—which latter had an almost earthy smell he always liked—and something animal, old sweat perhaps, or mice. The railing in front of him was smooth and mahogany-like or perhaps cherry, though it smelled only of polish and prayer. More likely it was oak, but then, he could not be sure. Everyone always assumed he had these magnificent powers of touch that were somehow supernatural, but he felt and smelled and heard and guessed like anyone else could. It was just that they never attempted to sense much beyond what their eyes could see. Really, eyesight must be amazing after all, because it so dominated the other senses and relegated them to secondary status.

Upstairs, he heard the violinist and the organist arrive and begin tuning their instruments. There would be a boys' choir too, but that bunch hadn't arrived. No one blind or sighted could mistake boys trouping into a church. He was surprised that his daughter had asked for a boys' choir rather than a tenor or a soprano.

"I like boys' voices, Papa," she'd told him when he asked. "They sound beautiful, but sad too. It's so ephemeral, a boy's voice, after all, not at all like a girl's or a woman's voice really, like something otherworldly."

Like happiness, she might have said. Or was he just being the typical father of the bride, miserable at losing his child, miserable at this passage from girl to grown woman? He took a deep breath, steadied himself against the back of the pew, and took one of the sugarless cookies from his left pocket that Sra. Rosa had given him to nibble. *Cookies*, he thought bitterly. Tasted like animal food. But, he stuck to his damned diet, did not smoke anymore, and had given up the afternoon beer and the evening wine, not to mention the bags of sourballs, the ice cream, and plates of pastries. He would forego heaven a while longer, if he could. He wondered if Laura waited impatiently for him in heaven as he so impatiently waited to see her again—see her? Would he see in heaven? That would be odd, to see for the first time his beloved.

Or, perhaps he was not a candidate for heaven.

He munched the dry pellet slowly, wishing he had a carafe of red wine to wash it down his gullet. He wanted to touch a grandchild and imprint his presence upon it more than he wanted to taste wine again, was all.

Well, she'd done it now. She'd succeeded in doing what every girl in her right mind wanted, and here she was, at the beginning of the happiest day of her life. The day that would confer meaning on her pitiful existence. Rosa-Laura glanced at the mirror on Carmen-Victoria's immense oaken bedroom dresser and saw a girl with an elfin face overframed by a voluminous gauze veil fluffing outward from a crown of orange blossoms. She squirmed in the corset. It was not there to keep her flesh in or up, it was there to support the padding filling out her bosom. Women had to have bosoms, one way or another. She hadn't realized till she was told by her dearest friends a few days ago that she lacked bosom and men required a plentiful bosom in a woman. It was a terrible revelation and undermined her courage. After all, later that night when all the satin and lace and corseting were removed, wouldn't he notice that her bosom had been removed too? Would he feel cheated? Would he spurn her or despise her or demand a refund?

Her shop, her talent at tailoring and dressmaking, her dry humor, her excellent school record, her honesty, even her pretty face—all meant nothing compared to that bosom.

And it wasn't as if they hadn't touched each other before. A year and a half of "courtship," a year and half of avoiding what they both wanted, in any way she could. Surely he'd noticed by now that the breasts he had kissed through her dress were not ample.

The ring dropped off her index finger to the tiled floor of Carmen-Victoria's dark, furniture-crowded bedroom. A bad sign? It was Mili's ring, borrowed for the day because a bride needed to wear something borrowed. The ring was a huge, old fashioned thing with a heavy coral stone.

"It's my good luck ring," Mili had said. Rosa-Laura picked up the ring and slipped it back on her index finger. No one could accuse Mili of lacking bosom. Mili was a handsome size fourteen and her breasts preceded her like the infantry precedes the cavalry. Today she was unaccompanied because her "fiancé" Silvio unnerved everyone in her family and was uninvited, but it was a given that by the end of Rosa-Laura's wedding, Mili would have found someone to light her cigarettes and dance with her and nudge her amplitude inappropriately. Emilio and her two sons by Silvio would be there, unfortunately, but what wedding didn't have its disruptive guests, someone able to overturn a punch bowl, say, or scream an epithet during the wedding anthem? Anyway, Emilio did look very handsome in his military outfit.

Carmen-Victoria's oldest girl would walk before the bride down the aisle and scatter white rose petals, while Mili and Mama would be her matrons of honor, her only attendants, both dressed in silk crepe dresses of dark aubergine. (It would be the first time Mama hadn't worn mourning since she was thirteen, and Rosa-Laura knew she would be itching to get out of her new dress and back into her rusty black skirt and sweater.) Rosa-Laura had sewn the two dresses herself, the pattern freely interpreted from a photograph she'd seen in a German magazine. Her mother and her cousin now looked like rich ladies seated at a café in Vienna, one very large, one very small, with mantillas of cream-colored, hand-made lace, and a string of pearls, Rosa-Laura's gift to each of them. The pearls were Mayorcan. She'd bought them at a little store on Alcalá Street just past Serrano.

She wiggled her right foot in the tight satin shoe. Its stiletto heel was four inches high, and its elegant ankle strap fastened with a pearl button. She would pay for her vanity by the end of the ceremony with aching feet from standing too long in one place.

Standing too long in one place. Sounded like marriage. Why did such ideas pop into her head? Didn't she have enough things to worry about, what with the bosom and all?

And besides, she loved him. How else could one describe this longing, this need, this anguish? His hand upon her throat, his kiss, his smile—she'd given up the shop for that, literally, because once married it would be his. She'd give up everything else if necessary too, she was so desperate to have him, she'd leave her country and abandon her folks. It was horrible and she didn't care, she was beyond shame at the indignity. She dreamed about him and had disgusting fantasies, some of which came from stories her girlfriends told her, some of which she'd read in forbidden books and magazines, and some of which just sprung up from seeds drifted into her garden of thoughts from who knows where.

One night recently she remembered with particular horror. She had gone dancing with him, pressing against his too tall body until she had felt his erection against her own belly, and she had not moved away from him. Indeed, she had pressed closer, keeping him interested, both of them knowing that she was going to deny him everything later on in the evening.

A few hours later, they had crossed the plaza in her neighborhood, walking to her home slowly, silently, barely able to look at each other they were both burning so. Just before the cement bonnet of the metro, he had turned and held her face in his hands, to kiss her. She tilted back her head, stretching her feet in the stiletto heels that were part of her daily uniform, and he bent down to her.

Just as their lips touched, a voice broke through: "Hey! You two! That's not done in public! Get along with you now!"

She jumped back electrified and saw the look on Luís's face and then the machine gun in the civil guard's hands. He was holding it on one side with his right arm, but at the ready, pointed at them. He was shorter than Luís by a head and looked rumpled and ridiculous in that shabby gray outfit and patent leather hat.

"What's a guard doing on police duty in the city?" Luís said. It wasn't much of a comeback, but they'd been caught unaware, netted by their own heated needs, and hadn't bothered to check around for cops or passersby just before the kiss. It was midnight, past curfew. They could both be arrested for violation of curfew, or for public indecency, or shot if the guard pleased, and they all knew it.

"Guards go where they want, and you don't talk back to me," the man said.

"Please, my love, please," Rosa-Laura said. Luís hesitated, and she was suddenly sick with fear that he might not heed her, that he was entirely capable of responding to the needs of some primitive male code that would get him killed.

"Get on home now. If she's respectable—" the guard started to say,

"Of course she's respectable!"

She started to say something then didn't. Neither man was listening to her. She let out a sob, then another, hysterical, disgracing herself thoroughly, but the torrent of sobs worked. Luís put his arm around her shoulder and walked off with her, the guard standing stock still behind them, gun at the ready.

It was then that she had decided once and for all, made up her mind. She didn't want an eternal boyfriend or any more of this longing. She wanted marriage. Respectability. Honorable tradition. There might be ways to cheat sex and keep convention at bay and even keep him interested and herself relatively satisfied, but the safest thing was marriage. Married, she had him for life. He couldn't get out of it. Thing was, she couldn't get out of it either.

⁂

Rosa-Laura attempted to sit down on Carmen-Victoria's bed, but she couldn't adjust the full skirts and short train properly. Her gloves were only halfway buttoned up her arms. The off-the-shoulder sleeves were much more uncomfortable than they should have been, and she didn't understand why. The front of her dress, her *décolletage*, wouldn't stay up, despite the splendid bosom. The whole getup weighed a ton. She was getting sick of the smell of orange blossoms.

Without knocking, Carmen-Victoria, Lina, Merche, and Mili marched in, all in a straight line along the huge high bed because the room was so small it was the only way they could fit. Mili was the last and stayed in the doorway, filling it up, leaning against the sides, smiling indulgently. If she was envious of the ceremony she would never have, she did not show it. Indeed, all morning long she had been making comments about how she could have any husband she wanted, including those of the women present. Rosa-Laura had had to soothe Carmen-Victoria twice already on Mili's account.

A husky, harsh little voice behind the line said, "Out of my way, God's sake, cramming up the place like this—I can't get in!"

They all backed out obediently, and Sra. Rosa entered. Rosa-Laura stood up, her cheeks flaming, her voice the wail of a lost child. "Oh, Mama, what took you so long? I needed you!"

"I know, my love, I know. Um, here, let me look at you."

⁂

Rose petals were scattered, boys sang with unearthly voices, father and mother wept, the priest intoned the Latin without thinking, the girlfriends sighed, the groom's friends smirked. Sra. Rosa was both sad and happy and cursed herself for being such an idiot. Rogelio wept but didn't know any better than to hold his head high, as if reaching toward the incense, the music, the distant delicate voice of his beautiful daughter agreeing to obey a stranger Rogelio had met but once. Mili pursed her mouth and day-dreamed, sad and sentimental, and watched her oldest son glowering in his uniform but saw only the ghost of his father. Dr. Contreras held his sister's gloved and perfumed hand, patting it now and then, and replenishing her finely embroidered batiste handkerchiefs. He had told Sra. Rosa to supply him with at least ten of the filmy things, because Guillermina adored weddings and always wept copiously. No one knew what the groom was thinking, but then, this had nothing to do with him anyway.

By late evening of that exhausting, silly day, Rosa-Laura barely had time for a second thought before the life force overtook her and fooled her into thinking passion was happiness, or might as well be. Second thoughts or not, though she might live to regret soldering her life to his, she would not regret love or passion or even foolishness, especially on that night. They took a train to Alicante the next day to spend a week walking on the undulating basalt and lime patterns of its seaside sidewalks and eating paella cooked over huge coal fires on the beach. They began the rest of their life together effortlessly and well. During that precious time, country and government, money and work, house and family, became lost to momentary pleasure, to life itself and the living of it.

EPILOGUE

Dr. Contreras woke up one morning in his lovely country home in Lloret de Mar and found that his sister's poor abused heart had stopped in her sleep. He buried her in Madrid at the Cemetery of the Almudena, because despite the city's having been the stage for her sorrow, it was also where she had been happiest. He made arrangements for her grave to be kept clean and well supplied with flowers and then returned to his new home. He was relieved that he had survived Guillermina and been allowed to bury her decently.

He did write to Sra. Rosa now and then, and often invited her and her family to Lloret de Mar, but they never found the time or the money or the energy to honor his invitation. Just two years after Guillermina died, his blood pressure finally punished him for the burden of secrets heaped upon it, and he suffered a stroke that left him in a coma. Mercifully, within a week, he died. He left his property to his cousin's children but did include in his will a small monthly stipend to Sra. Rosa as well as several boxes of beautiful books. He was buried in Lloret de Mar, not in Madrid, and for many years after his death, someone found the time to bring a little bundle of forget-me-nots and violets to the grave every Sunday.

Soon after his marriage, Luís applied to buy a house in a development of government-built, subsidized workers' housing on the south highway, in a barren place phenomenally hot in summertime. The half-built buildings were austere and shabby and the neighborhood a slum waiting to happen, but houses were impossible to find and even more impossible to own, and Luís considered himself lucky to have gotten on the list of prospective buyers.

When their name was called soon thereafter and a flat offered them, Luís managed to pull together the down payment by selling Rosa-Laura's business. He wanted her to work at home anyway. Rosa-Laura was cooking in the kitchen at her mother-in-law's house, where they had been living since they were married, when he came home and told her what he'd done. She turned without a word and flung a pot full of vegetable soup at him, missing his chest and hitting the wall with a horrendous splat, then grabbed a knife and attempted to kill him.

She went home to her mother after her mother-in-law, her uncle-in-law, and her sister-in-law managed to separate her from Luís. She stayed there three weeks, in bed, refusing to speak to anyone and crying herself to sleep every night. For the first time in her life, she missed the deadline on her customers' orders. Her mother and her father tried to talk her out of this insane behavior, but she turned her face to the wall and refused to budge. Finally, one day she got out of bed, cleaned herself, dressed, and went down to Glorieta de Embajadores to look at her shop. The sign had been changed, and Lina and Merche were sitting outside sewing. They jumped up when they saw her and hugged her, and she could see they were still happy-go-lucky. Lina was already planning to quit after her marriage next June, and Merche was talking about immigrating to America with her brothers.

That night, Luís came to his in-laws's house and told his wife he missed her. She knew it was his way of apologizing, and that he would never be the sort of person who openly admits he's wrong about anything. Divorce was illegal so she could not dissolve her marriage, and she knew she loved him so much she didn't really want to despite what he'd done. She missed him too, especially in bed, and besides, she was pregnant.

She did not return to her mother-in-law's house. As soon as the new flat was finished, she moved in, with Luís and their newborn, Rogelio.

Mili was little Rogelio's godmother, much to Luís's disgust. He wanted his own sister to be godmother, especially since his sister was good-hearted, intelligent, and responsible, none of which applied to Mili as far as he could see. Rosa-Laura announced her choice of godmother at the time of her son's birth, and Luís chose not to argue with her on this issue, knowing full well that other issues would come up that might require both strength and great maneuverability on his part. He was not about to let a woman best him in anything, but he was a strategist after all, and had his sights on the war, not any single battle.

After her appearance at the baptismal font in a dress so low-cut that all the pictures of the baptism had to be retired to a shoe box and seldom if ever shown to relatives, Mili lasted barely a year. One morning her neighbors in Chamberí found her on the sidewalk beneath her fourth story balcony. Rumors in the neighborhood had it the body was naked. She had fallen, jumped, or been pushed, and the police report opted for accident. There was no autopsy, of course, but they claimed she'd been drinking. It was true she had taken to drinking heavily the past years, and when she drank, she told bawdy jokes and also talked, incessantly. Often she had bragged to anyone who cared to listen that she was a woman who knew how to handle her problems and that anyone who messed with her had better watch out "...because I know stuff!"

Rosa-Laura had to identify the body at the police morgue; she cried for weeks afterward and let her house get filthy. Silvio took his sons, made some kind of arrangement for Emilio, and no one ever saw Mili's boys again. Rosa-Laura wanted to inquire, but her husband forbade her and her mother begged her to think of her own family, especially now that she had a child.

Arturo was Rosa-Laura's second son and Carmen-Victoria his godmother. Thus, Luís's sister would have to wait until the birth of her brother's third child, Rosa-Maria, to become a godmother.

Vicky and Rosa-Laura lived somewhat far apart, but they managed to get together to gossip over coffee at least twice a week and even arranged to spend vacations together, hauling their families and a ton of luggage up to a cool mountain village above Madrid where they rented a house and spent two to three weeks every summer for years, delighting in the escapades of their menageries. Eduardo and Luís became the best of friends.

Rogelio slipped away quietly one night and thus joined his Laura a month after the birth of his second grandson. Sra. Rosa found him in his bed the next morning. They buried him in a communal grave at the Cemetery of the South, and Sra. Rosa moved in to her daughter's household. Luís was appalled at the load of boxes she brought with her, especially since most of them were full of books, but he built a beautiful set of shelves in the salon for them and thereafter, found that he liked the leather-bound treasure his mother-in-law had inherited and even more, the regard it inspired in visitors.

Ten years after Rogelio's burial, his bones were reinterred in a wall niche, at a horrendous cost. Luís did not argue with Rosa-Laura over her having her father's bones interred rather than burned in the communal pile. His life was full, he was happy and free, and his household was secure, so he ceded that battle too. Besides, Rosa-Laura had always taken in sewing since her return to her husband's hearth, and she had enough money saved from that to pay for the niche herself.

Rosa-Laura's and Luís's fourth and last child, a ruddy daughter with huge blue eyes (the only one of the children not to have Luís's dark eyes), was born late in Rosa-Laura's life and proved to be the surprise of the bunch. They named her Laura-Rosa, and her godmother was Merche, back from America for a visit. Her godmother's new land proved prophetic. When the girl was only eight, a part-time teacher at the miserable warehouse for delinquents-to-be that served as a primary school in their neighborhood noticed the child had a startling ability with mathematics. Indeed, no one else knew it, but the child and her mother played math games all the time. It was fun for both of them as well as their little secret. Laura-Rosa was brought to the attention of a friend of her teacher, who taught at the University. He tested her for two weeks. The child found the testing delightful but rather easy. After that, it was recommended she be considered for a full scholarship to the University as soon as she was fifteen, and that she be tutored privately. But, instead of attending the Mathematics Faculty at the University of Madrid, she went to America when she was eighteen, to a university there that had offered a scholarship. Luís never quite got over the shock. Sra. Rosa disapproved. Rosa-Laura walked around the house for months afterwards with a dreadfully smug smile on her face and would discuss the issue with no one.

One morning soon after her ninetieth birthday, Sra. Rosa told her daughter, "I'm tired, daughter. I've lasted as long as I can, but my courage for living has run out. Um, damn it, I just can't go through another summer in Madrid."

"Mama, please," Rosa-Laura said. She scooped the last spoonful of oatmeal into her mother's mouth before the old woman could close it, wiped her face and punched up the pillow. No breeze filtered through the drawn Persian blinds, but the outside window was open to tempt one in. Rosa-Laura rubbed her mother's feet gently and commented about the price of fresh fish these days, but her mother was lost in the planning of her demise and would not be diverted. Rosa-Laura sighed, coughed, and went into the bathroom to fill a bowl with water for her mother's sponge bath.

Sra. Rosa never kept people waiting for her if she could help it. Just before the first heat wave of the long, gaseous, molten summer, she died. Rosa-Laura had gone to a doctor in the neighborhood clinic a week before and told him what her mother had said. He shrugged. "Leave her alone. Stop forcing her to eat when she doesn't want to. Who are we to interfere?"

It was decent of this doctor to admit that sometimes the wheel of the universe could roll on without the interference of modern medicine. Rosa-Laura didn't question the advice. In fact, she did not begrudge her mother the right to die, but the idea that she'd lose her again was hard to bear.

The morning Sra. Rosa chose to die, Rosa-Laura came upstairs to see if she could tempt her to taste a mash of fresh strawberries in sugar and red wine. Her mother's bed was still no wider than the cot they'd shared in Rosa-Laura's childhood, but the old woman was so small and shriveled that she lay planted in it as if it were one of those big dark beds with wall-sized headboards that people in the villages used. Señora Rosa lay on her left side with her head barely denting the pillow, her right arm supported by a second pillow, and her bony legs separated by a third. Her eyes were dull, heavy-lidded, and barely open, and her lips slightly apart.

Rosa-Laura knew that look, or that loss of look. She sat down on the stool next to the bed and put the bowl of strawberries on the floor.

"Mama," she said. It was not a question.

Rosa-Laura sat on the stool at least an hour, until Luís came upstairs to find out why she was taking so long. He saw her seated there, in the yeasty morning darkness, and saw the old woman curled over her pillows like a dry brown leaf that has blown onto the road.

"Come on, my dear, come downstairs with me now," he said.

But Rosa-Laura was thinking about all the complexities of the burial.

In the old days, like death itself a burial was *perpetuo*. A family buried its people in a deep plot in the cemetery, visited them with chrysanthemums on All Saints Day, or when the spirit called, and that was that. Husbands slept with the wives they'd beaten, wives with the husbands they'd nagged and screamed at, children, cousins, in-laws—entire clans resided together fertilizing the peace that had eluded them in life. Originally, they lay side by side, then, as the century began, they were buried in stacks of six like layers of pastry, yet forever, as it should be. Inevitably, space became scarce.

Nowadays in death urban Spaniards were not able to avoid residing in the everlasting city "piso." Just as their "houses" were flats in apartment buildings piled above the avenues and alleyways of the cities, their burial places were mostly niches in a high wall. The dead pretty much had to resign themselves (a task to which they were eminently suited) to sleeping a hundred to a wall, each niche holding not a body, but bones. A family could now buy as many as fourteen years in the communal trench, to put off paying for a permanent niche or consigning a family member to the fire.

Some people did prefer outright cremation, which used to be a mortal sin but was now permitted by the Church—after all there had been de facto cremation via the communal trenches for a hundred years now. Mama had told Rosa-Laura enough times, "For God's sake, don't burn me when I die, and don't wrap me in a winding sheet either, you must promise me that."

Rosa-Laura had rolled her eyes and promised, again and again.

Truth was, after a loved one has dissolved for ten to fourteen years in the communal pile, who could be sure a family member would be around to identify a mandible, a set of crooked teeth, or as in the case of Rogelio, a half-rotted wedding suit with recognizable stitching? If Rosa-Laura wasn't around when Mama's time was up, her bones would burn, no matter what Rosa-Laura had promised her.

Some people had money enough to buy real graves, and not just at a posh cemetery like the Almudena. In the Cemetery of the South over the grave of a Gypsy king there stood a life-size bronze Gypsy with tight pants, a cigarette in his mouth, and an Andalusian hat on his head, striking an attitude of death defying arrogance.

⌒◡⌒

The day of Mama's death Rosa-Laura called Laura-Rosa in America and asked the girl to call her back immediately (it was cheaper to call from the U.S. than from Spain). They talked for a long time, then Rosa-Laura hung up and created the mother of all lists. It began with calling a doctor, then calling the *tanatorio*. The neighborhood doctors worked only three streets away, in the Social Security Clinic that everyone in the neighborhood attended; the doctor who came was the same doctor who had counseled Rosa-Laura to allow her mother to die. He came quickly but exercised his right to complain loudly about how nobody in Rosa-Laura's family ever called him unless it was to declare a death. Rosa-Laura said nothing about her visit the week before and his advice, because all things considered, his grumbling was his way of applauding her family's toughness. Besides, he didn't have to be polite, his salary was paid by the state.

The two men from the *tanatorio* were quieter and more obsequious, because for all they knew, the corpse could be another member of the Gypsy nobility and not some poor old woman destined for the communal pile. Rosa-Laura had the insurance to pay for *las mortajas*, the preparations, and gave them her mother's best black dress.

"Look," she said, "No makeup. This isn't *La Marlena Dietrich* here." After they went upstairs, Rosa-Laura sent Luís to the bar for coffee, companionship, and *churros* and told him not to come back until lunch at three. He left gladly.

In the old days the family washed the body and displayed it in its own bed for a few days if its occupant had died in winter, or for a day or less if summer. Nowadays, the people at the *tanatorio* did that job. It was the eighties after all, the dictatorship had finally died with Franco in 1975, and a person tried to be modern. Besides, the city government was against home viewings and had declared them unsanitary. Gypsies were the only ones who still held home viewings, and as Mama might have said, what could you do with Gypsies anyway? Viewing of the body took place at modern, clean *tanatorios*, behind glass, with the body decently encased in a nice rented box. The next day the *tanatorio* held the funeral, and the employees there brought the body to the cemetery where the last prayers were said before burial. Rosa-Laura not only didn't have to clean and dress the body, neither did she have to rent a hearse and driver nor arrange for the funeral; the *tanatorio* people did all that. It was very convenient, it cost no more than years of monthly premiums at-a-rate-your-family-can-afford, and in all her life she had never begrudged a worker his job, but it left her feeling useless.

Past noon, she still hadn't done the shopping for lunch or dinner, she hadn't called anyone in the family yet, and she hadn't informed the neighbors. She sighed yet again and went over her list. The neighbors were the least of her problems. All Rosa-Laura had to do was tell one and the whole community would know in hours.

☙❧

That afternoon, after the body had been removed, Rosa-Laura sat in her bedroom staring out the window and planning what dress she would wear to the funeral.

She stood up and remembered that her oldest daughter might also need a dark colored dress for the funeral. Less than ten years ago, girls like her and her sister wore black most of their lives, as Sra. Rosa had. Sometimes with the overlapping deaths older women forgot whom they were mourning. Perhaps themselves. Rosa-Laura leaned her head forward onto the pane of glass. She was getting morbid, she was.

Sra. Rosa had been so offended by the dresses and the colors and the make-up her granddaughters wore. She wanted them to look elegant, but when they got dressed, she could not help herself, seeing them drinking from that fountain of beauty and presumption that she had never been allowed at, and said, "It's a scandal, it is. My own granddaughters. How can you let them, Rosa-Laura?" She never paid any attention to her grandsons' clothing, and Rosa-Laura never discussed it at all with her. Despite all that nagging, the girls had loved their grandma dearly.

Item by item, Rosa-Laura began building up another list, adding and subtracting, dividing and multiplying, sliding items from one point to another as if they were dominoes on the marble table of her contemplation. Tonight only the close family would come to the viewing, tomorrow everyone to the funeral. Their first son, Rogelio, his wife, their two children, Alejandro and Francisco. The second son, their bachelor, Arturo, whose name had proved ironically prophetic, though Luís still kept a blind eye to the matter (and Rosa-Laura had figured it out by the time the child was six). His best friend César, because wherever Arturo was, César came. Rosa-Maria, their oldest daughter, and Rosa-Maria's husband and their twins, Luísito and Laura.

Luís's brother and sister, the only siblings left to him, would come, as would his nieces, nephews, and maybe their children. His remaining three aunts and one uncle, and their children, the cousins—her husband had so many cousins it always took a very long time to list them all. The wives and husbands of the cousins. Maybe some of their children too, and if not, they'd all come tomorrow to the funeral. Isabel, Martita, Teresa, Edwardo, Marco Antonio, Amparo...whatever else her husband had given her, a big family had been the best and worst part.

Something suddenly occurred to her as she stood at the window, something very important. It was shocking she hadn't thought of it before. She rushed over to her closet and hauled out the chest where she kept her cloth.

Later, she went to the *tanatorio* early and checked everything over, then called out the manager to tell him that she wanted to change her mother's dress. "It's not her best dress," she said. "I just made her a much better one."

395

"Señora, this is not how things are done," the manager said.

"This is how I do things. I sewed this dress. My mother would have been proud. Look at this fine cloth, look how good my stiching is! I want you to get her out of that box and help me put it on her."

The manager called two assistants out, with little grace and a great deal of ill humor. Rosa-Laura didn't care what he thought, the important thing was that Mama got this dress, made of a black linen-silk mix, a beautiful dress with pearl buttons. In ten years, she'd recognize those buttons if she was around, God willing, and that dress wouldn't rot so easily nor those seams tear and disintegrate.

She waited in the anteroom while her mother's dress was changed, because for some reason they couldn't let her see the body undressed. Rosa-Laura couldn't help but wonder if Mama minded being in the *tanatorio*—a strange thought, and irrational, but she did wonder— because the old woman had hated morgues. Well, who wouldn't. Not death, morgues. Death was the rude and disagreeable neighbor who lived down the street, an unpleasant reality but a neighbor all the same. Once as Rosa-Laura and her mother were walking down the broad boulevard at the foot of Atocha Street, Rosa-Laura said, "Look, Mama, see all that construction? They're going to make that old hospital a big, fine museum. With modern pictures. It'll be named after the queen."

She expected her mother to sneer and snort, but the old woman said, very quietly, "It used to be a morgue."

"No, Mama, the hospital and the medical school were over there, remember? That wasn't the morgue."

"During the war," her mother mumbled. "Tables and tables. All violet and gray in the evening. No lights. I was looking—I was looking only at the small ones. Under the sheets." She shook her head, and said, as if to herself, "The sheets."

Her mother's words brought Rosa-Laura back to the day she got lost. It was not a memory she relished.

✺

The day of the funeral, the sky boiled to white. The air capping Madrid took on the consistency and color of powdered sulfur as the guests began to arrive for the funeral. Rosa-Laura once again had to marvel at how many people were in her husband's family.

Rosa-Laura had placed a small bunch of carnations on her mother's chest. A beautiful spray of mixed flowers—white gladioli, mums, carnations, and white roses—had arrived from a florist uptown who had received the order long distance from Laura-Rosa in America. Relative after relative came up to Rosa-Laura, kissed her, told her how sorry they were and how she could ask them for anything, anything at all. They had left off food at her house. They dabbed at their eyes, unfolded their fans, sat on too-small chairs taking fan-swipes at their faces to levitate a cool breeze, and caught up on the latest news. Aurora's oldest son was getting married, Paco would be visiting in the fall and someone had to provide him lodgings in their house, Uncle Juan wasn't long for this world and would be the next one to be viewed, his wife Perdita was as mean and tight as ever but her children adored her, can you understand that? Comfortable and safe in this gossipy embrace, Rosa-Laura settled softly into her sadness.

The drive to the Cemetery of the South from the *tanatorio* was short, but their car had Spanish air conditioning, that is, all the windows were wide open. She'd been glad to arrive. It was 2 p.m. but solar time was actually noon, and the sun's power was enough to percolate brains and boil bones. Rosa-Laura was wearing a dark blue dress; her leather shoes, her best pair, had heated to paste and stuck to her stockingless toes and bunions and heels with a promise of big blisters to come. She tried to concentrate on the ceremony.

Mama must be cooking in that horrible box. Still, the rented coffin was a very attractive one, blond in color, well carved, and as soon as the family was decently out of sight, the gravediggers would brush off the dirt, open it, and take Mama out and put her embalmed remains in the communal trench. Rosa-Laura gave a long sigh. Her husband glanced at her a bit worriedly, but she was hot, that's all.

Prayers were sprinkled over the temporary coffin, and finally, the men lined up to each toss a handful of dirt onto it, because serious traditions must be followed, even in the case of communal burials.

The women walked off together. They would meet at Rosa-Laura's house and help her with the huge, three-table lunch that would begin some time after four, slack off around six and begin again at nine. Maybe one of the family members would sing a sad folk song, maybe they would all sing together, a *faena* or something more classical, nothing wild or ribald like the *coplas* of Madrid, of course. Stories would be told about Mama. There were many of them.

Rosa-Laura took inventory of the cemetery as she waited for her husband to finish flinging his handful of dirt with his male relatives. She wandered off, somewhat distracted. Her feet hurt, but she hardly noticed. The flat slick sky smelled of butane, the cemetery was green only by dint of an obscene use of municipal water (and it was a very lemony green at that), the apartments of the dead were more gray than white due to pollution from the Toledo highway that ran next to the place. Over by the center of the community of the dead, she saw the Gypsy king and smiled. Mama always thought that statue was a disgrace and should have been taken away to rule over a garbage dump. Rosa-Laura liked it. The man was handsome, and handsome men were yet another thing you had to appreciate, one more fiesta of life.

Luís arrived. "Let's go now, *chatita*," he said.

"So much production for such a small person," Rosa-Laura said. "And that dress, it looked good, but she shrank since they got her in that place. It was too big. Can you imagine that?"

Luís said, "She was little, but she shook her fist at the sky, your mother." He looked above her head at the cemetery beyond—an easy proposition since he was so much taller than her.

"Did you know that when I was a baby, she stole milk for me from the houses she cleaned?"

He finally looked at her. She forced a smile so he would see she was OK.

"She isn't coming, *chata*. It's time you sat down and cried," he said.

"I waited 638 days, and that's forever when you're little. I never cried. I counted the things I'd do when she came to get me. I knew she'd come."

She saw Luís look up to check the bone-white sky, but not even a bird was written on it, much less some celestial answer, so she took his hand and turned away from the cemetery and toward home.

ACKNOWLEDGEMENTS

This is a work of fiction. It began germinating after I heard a series of stories, comments, and anecdotes about the Spanish Civil War from my sister-in-law, Gloria Sanchez de Bautista. For that grand inspiration, I thank her.

Andrea Young: I don't have words for what Andrea has given me. It's humbling to be a writer and yet have no words to express how I feel for her support, friendship, and inspiration.

Paul Rubin, Ed. *Texas Review*, for his past kindnesses and encouraging words and for allowing us to use the chapters printed originally as short stories in Fiestas.

Kit Duane for her excellent and incisive editing and commentary and for putting up with my numerous, frantic e-mails.

Denny Abrams, for his donation to the publishing costs, for believing in all of us.

Tom Farber for being the kind of publisher that trusts his writers and his friends.

My long-suffering husband for his support, his belief in me, and his enduring all my snarky comments about Spanish men.

My children and my Spanish family, for loving me and for being an endless wellspring for all my fictions.

The Road, and Nothing More is a first novel. Recipient of the 2005 George Garrett Prize in Fiction, and author of *Fiestas*, a short story collection, J. L. Bautista divides her time between northern California and Madrid, Spain.